TIME SNATCHERS

RICHARD UNGAR

TIME SNATCHERS

G. P. PUTNAM'S SONS
An Imprint of Penguin Group (USA) Inc.

G. P. PUTNAM'S SONS
A division of Penguin Young Readers Group.
Published by The Penguin Group.
Penguin Group (USA) Inc., 375 Hudson Street, New York, NY 10014, U.S.A.
Penguin Group (Canada), 90 Eglinton Avenue East, Suite 700, Toronto,
Ontario M4P 2Y3, Canada (a division of Pearson Penguin Canada Inc.).
Penguin Books Ltd, 80 Strand, London WC2R 0RL, England.
Penguin Ireland, 25 St. Stephen's Green, Dublin 2, Ireland (a division of Penguin Books Ltd).
Penguin Group (Australia), 250 Camberwell Road, Camberwell, Victoria 3124, Australia
(a division of Pearson Australia Group Pty Ltd).
Penguin Books India Pvt Ltd, 11 Community Centre,
Panchsheel Park, New Delhi—110 017, India.
Penguin Group (NZ), 67 Apollo Drive, Rosedale, Auckland 0632,
New Zealand (a division of Pearson New Zealand Ltd).
Penguin Books (South Africa) (Pty) Ltd, 24 Sturdee Avenue,
Rosebank, Johannesburg 2196, South Africa.
Penguin Books Ltd, Registered Offices: 80 Strand, London WC2R 0RL, England.

Design by Marikka Tamura and Annie Ericsson. Text set in Minion.
Library of Congress Cataloging-in-Publication Data
Ungar, Richard (Richard Glenn).
Time snatchers / Richard Ungar.
p.   cm.
Summary: Thirteen-year-old orphan Caleb is a "time snatcher" who travels through history
stealing valuable artifacts from the past for high-paying clients of his ruthless guardian.
[1. Time travel—Fiction.   2. Adventure and adventurers—Fiction.   3. Orphans—Fiction.
4. Crime—Fiction.   5. Science fiction.]   I. Title.
PZ7.U425Ti 2012
[Fic]—dc22
2011008017

ISBN 978-0-399-25485-7

1   3   5   7   9   10   8   6   4   2

In memory of Philip Azimov

I can't stop crying.

I'd like to say that it's the sight of the leaders of the two most powerful nations in the world shaking hands that's got my faucets going. But to be honest, which I'll admit is not a quality that most people connect with thieves, it's my allergies that are making me teary.

It's always like this for me in the spring. Especially when I'm around daffodils. And there must be ten thousand or more of the nasty yellow things, all prim and pretty for the special state visit of the president of the United States, here to ink the Great Friendship treaty with the president of China. I'm no expert on world politics, but I think the only reason the U.S. and China are becoming best friends is so they can buy each other's stuff at half price.

I move upwind of the flowers. You'd think that in a city square ten times the size of Yankee Stadium I could find a little elbow room. The only available spot is shoulder to shoulder with some Boy Scouts wearing gray uniforms with yellow neckerchiefs who are probably attending this historic event just to score merit badges. But who am I to talk? The reason for my visit to Beijing isn't any more noble. In fact, if those shiny-booted soldiers flanking the leaders knew the truth about why I'm here, they'd lead me away in handcuffs.

From my new spot, I've got a great view of one of the ten jumbo

1

screens set up in the square. But as far as seeing the actual, breathing leaders, they're not much bigger than specks. It might seem silly to travel all this way only to be watching the two great men on TV, but I don't really mind. After all, they're not why I came.

I'm much more interested in the building behind them: the Great Hall of the People. Personally, I would have named it the Great *Big* Hall of the People. The place is massive. Each of those tall gray marble pillars must weigh a ton. The odd thing is that it doesn't fit in with any of the nearby buildings. The Great Hall is boxy and severe, while all the other buildings have sloping roofs and lots of curves. Don't get me wrong. I like boxy and severe. Considering what I've come here to do, the flat roof is a definite bonus.

It's drizzling, but no one in the huge crowd seems to mind. They're all snapping pictures like crazy, and I don't blame them. After all, it's a truly historic occasion. The start of a golden era in U.S. and China relations isn't something that happens every day.

The leaders are making their way down the front steps of the Great Hall shaking hands with each other's second-in-command, third-in-command and fourth-in-command. I wonder what it must be like to be fourth-in-command of one of the strongest nations on earth. I suppose you have to be the patient sort. I mean, a lot of people ahead of you have to quit their jobs in order for you to rule the world.

I scan the crowd, looking for anyone who might cause trouble for me when it's time to carry out the mission. You can never be too careful in my business. People generally don't like to have their stuff stolen, so I like to do things under the radar. In this case, that means waiting a bit for the tourist count to go down and the honor guard with the cute but sharp bayonets at the ends of their rifles to go home for tea and dumplings.

Of course, I can't wait forever. If I've learned anything about traveling through time, it's that it's tough on the body. After about fifty continuous minutes in the past, time fog sets in: you start feeling dizzy, your thoughts become jumbled, your motor functions start slowing down, and even putting one step in front of the other requires a huge effort. After three hours, your lungs shut down and you literally die from lack of oxygen. The longest I've been in the past at one stretch is fifty-seven minutes, and it's a record I'm not keen on breaking. The only cure for time fog is to go back to the present, which for me means 2061, and stay there until it clears. That could take hours or, for a really bad case, a whole day.

That's why Uncle has set a thirty-minute time limit on all missions to the past. Trust me, it wasn't out of the goodness of his heart; it was more because if we all started dropping dead from time fog, he wouldn't have anyone left to steal for him.

So the rule is if a snatch isn't completed within a half hour, it's recorded as a failed mission. On your first failed mission, you only get hauled into Uncle's office and given a lecture. But if it happens twice in the same month, things can get a lot nastier; how much nastier depends on Uncle's mood at the time. And three strikes is the worst: that'll earn you a stint in the Barrens, a desolate and unforgiving wilderness where one month is the longest anyone has survived without going insane or dying.

A giggle catches my attention, and I turn to see a young boy wearing a red T-shirt that says BEIJING 2060, with a picture of a panda bear on it. He runs past me into the outstretched arms of his father. I watch, spellbound, as the father catches the boy and lifts him up high in the air before bringing him gently down to earth. The boy's mother is following him and, after he lands, they're all laughing and hugging each other.

My heart skips a beat. I wonder what that boy is feeling right now. Safe and secure, I bet. It must be amazing. To know you are loved. To know you are part of a real family.

I don't have any of that.

No mother. No father. No brothers or sisters. Given up for adoption at the ripe old age of three. Yup. That's me. Caleb the orphan, time-traveling thief. And seeing as I'm thirteen now, that means I've been family-less for ten years . . . but who's counting?

Sure, I've got a roof over my head and three square meals a day, thanks to Uncle. And there is some companionship, if you can call it that, with the other time thieves, who are all more or less my age. But it would be a real stretch to call us a family.

I can remember a time when things were different. Uncle acted like a real uncle and used to take me and the four others he adopted on field trips to the zoo to see the cloned snow leopards and the talking chimps that swore at you if you got too close. And there were other fun outings to museums, art galleries and concerts—not only in the U.S. but all over the world. Uncle liked to say that we were being "worldschooled," not homeschooled. He even had a name for us—his five orphantastics.

But a few years ago, everything changed. Uncle became moody and unpredictable. One minute he could be charming, and the next minute, he'd be getting out a pocket knife and reaching for your finger. My theory is that he's always been crazy but just hid it better when we were young. Abbie, my longtime snatch partner and closest friend ever since we were small—correction, *only* friend since we were small—thinks he had some kind of nervous breakdown. Whatever the cause, it's really stressful to be around him. So I try to keep my distance. Unfortunately that's next to impossible, seeing as I live

4

under his roof and he's the type of boss who likes to keep close tabs on all of his "time snatchers," as he calls us.

The crowd's thinning. I'd better start looking busy or someone might wonder what I'm doing here. I take one last glance up at the roof of the Great Hall. There, fluttering in the breeze, is the thing I've traveled a year back in time and seven thousand miles west for: the first flag of the Great Friendship. To be honest, it's nothing special: horizontal stripes of gold, red, blue and white—a combo of all of the colors in the Chinese and American flags. But I don't care what it looks like. All I really care about is stealing it.

I head for the park across the street from the square. It's sure taking a long time for that sun to go down. I could jump ahead in time a few minutes and get on with things, but who knows when I'll be in China again? I might as well try to relax and enjoy being here.

Going to the park is a bit chancy with my allergies, but it's either that or follow the noisy crowd to a place where the Chinese emperors used to hang out called the Forbidden City.

Entering the park through a gate flanked by two towering stone lions, I'm rewarded with quiet—exactly what I need before a mission. I stop for a moment on a wooden footbridge overlooking a small, still pond sprinkled with orchids. Not far away is a big grassy area where some adults in track suits are moving their arms and legs into graceful poses. Everything is so peaceful. Abbie would definitely love this place. But at the last second she got called in to be the third agent on a mission to 1671 England to steal the crown jewels from the Tower of London. So we're in different centuries right now. It goes like that sometimes.

The light is finally fading. It's time for me to do my thing. As I enter the square again, I become hyperaware of every little thing: the smell of those awful flowers, the laughter of a group of tourists. Even the feel of my footsteps on the concrete is magnified. Uncle says the Japanese have a word for this heightened sense of awareness: *zanshin*. But I just call it being sharp for the mission.

I hear a whirring sound and look up to see a helicopter. A big Russian job. It does a slow circle of the square and hovers for a moment right above the Great Hall before flying away.

There are only two tourist buses left in front of the Great Hall. I make sure no one's on board, take up a position between them and crouch down. It's possible someone could see me, but it's not likely. After all, I'm really not that interesting to look at. At least not until I go poof and vanish.

What I see next makes me frown. The guys with the shiny boots and pointy rifles are still in position right outside the bronze entrance doors of the Great Hall. Then I remember that a special dinner honoring the two presidents is taking place inside.

Well, I'll just have to work around them. Besides I don't intend to go in. Only up.

I yawn and rub my eyes. Anyone watching would think I'm just another tourist dead on his feet from a full day of sightseeing. I even look the part: Great Friendship T-shirt, blue jeans, sandals and a green knapsack that has seen better days. But when I rub my eyes, I'm really adjusting my ocular implant to night vision. The closest member of the honor guard is about twenty yards away. I switch to high zoom and can easily see the tiny spot on the left side of his chin that he missed shaving this morning.

Noise from above makes me look up. The helicopter is back. Exactly five minutes after making its last round. All right, that means I have a little less than five minutes to do the snatch.

It's showtime.

I tap my right wrist a few times. The tapping activates the time travel implant just under my skin. It'll just be a short hop. Twenty yards ahead, one hundred feet up and four seconds forward in time.

Closing my eyes, I feel the familiar rush of a timeleap: three parts dizzy, four parts excited and two parts weird sensation of not knowing where I am.

I land, lying flat on my stomach on the roof. I can't move. I'm still in time freeze mode: a state of total paralysis that happens after each leap through time. I'm not sure why it happens, but it has something to do with bodies adjusting to a new time/place. The good thing is that it doesn't last long—two or three seconds, max. Of course, it's all relative. Two or three seconds can go by awfully quickly when you land on a sandy beach in the summertime, but it can seem like forever when you turn up in the middle of a raging snowstorm wearing only your bathing suit.

The time freeze wears off but I stay still for a few seconds, listening. Just some faint traffic sounds coming from beyond the square. Rising to a low crouch, I glance around and get my bearings. I'm just about in the middle of the roof. Staying low, I crab walk my way toward the front of the building.

There, between the U.S. flag and the Chinese flag, is the flag of the Great Friendship. I lie back down on my belly and slither forward. Got to be extra careful now; I'm close to the front edge of the building, which means that the guards are right below. If I so much as sneeze, one of them is bound to hear me and say something . . . and odds are, it won't be "God bless you." Plus, even though I'd be surprised if the ancient Kalashnikovs they're carrying actually worked, it's not a chance I'm willing to take.

One more slither, and I'm there.

I hold up my left index finger. It's seven thirty-eight P.M. local

7

time, according to the readout under my fingernail. Oops. I had no idea it was that late.

I extend my right hand, place my fingertips on the flag and close my eyes, falling now into a deep meditative state. My fingers probe and compare the properties of the flag in my hand with the those of the original Great Friendship flag that were uploaded to my brain along with the rest of the mission data. The next moment, the answer comes back, and I breathe a little sigh of relief: it's the real thing, all right—not a fake.

You never really know what you're snatching until you do a scan. After all, the world's full of thieves—not all of them time travelers—and it's not beyond the realm of possibility that another thief could have gotten here ahead of me and switched the original for a cheap replica. The last thing I'd want to do is bring a replica back to Headquarters. That's a guaranteed failed mission.

No, the only thief I want switching the original for a cheap replica is me. Uncle's big on keeping what we do real low-key, and the best way to do that is to make it look like no theft was ever committed.

Speaking of replicas, I pull one from my knapsack. Uncle's assistant, Nassim, gave it to me for the mission. Personally, I think that it looks even better than the original, but no one's paying me for my views on the subject. In fact, no one's paying me for my snatches, either, unless you count the measly allowance Uncle gives out, which is hardly enough to buy afternoon snacks.

Money or no money, I have to admit that I love this part of my job. Nothing beats the rush of adrenaline right before a snatch. The more dangerous the mission, the greater the thrill. I'm not about to share this with Uncle, though. He'd probably find some way to take the fun out of it.

Laying the replica down, I feel around for the snaps holding the original to the pole. There are two of them. I try to unhook the snaps, but no go. I'll have to cut the rope.

I pull my knife from my jeans pocket. This is the delicate part. Uncle's clients are real picky types, and if I so much as nick the fabric, the customer will no doubt demand his money back. But that's nothing compared to what Uncle will do to me if I mess up.

Angling the blade, I begin cutting. It's going slower than I'd like, mostly on account of the rope being thick and my knife blade being dull. I should have sharpened it before I came. But you can't think of everything. I take a deep breath and carry on.

Just then, I see something that makes me freeze in place. A shimmering only five feet away. The shimmering is forming into the shape of a person. This isn't good. The only things that shimmer like that are other time travelers. But Abbie is in the seventeenth century, and nobody else was invited to this little party. I go back to cutting the rope, hoping that my eyes are playing tricks on me.

No such luck. Three seconds later, I'm not alone on the roof anymore. I groan when I see who it is.

Frank.

Like me, Frank is one of Uncle's time snatchers. He was a street kid when Uncle found him four years ago, living mostly off of leftovers thrown out each night by the restaurants on the Lower East Side. I remember going on the rounds with him once not long after he started and being amazed at his skill in picking garbage cans that had the cheesiest manicotti or the leanest pastrami. But it's been a while since I've hung out with Frank. Around the time that Uncle started acting weird, Frank changed too. He became obsessed with being the number one time snatcher and was, and still is, prepared to do anything to get there, including stealing from the one person who has more snatches than him—namely, yours truly.

I glance at my fingernail and frown. Only two minutes left to complete the snatch.

"Hello, Caleb," says Frank in a booming voice.

I nearly jump. For a second, I'm positive his greeting is going to alert the guards below and send them scurrying up here. But then I realize he hasn't spoken the words out loud—only over my mind-patch.

"Hello, Frank," I reply, using the same frequency. "Let me guess. You just happened to be in the neighborhood and thought you'd drop by and say hi."

"Something like that," he says, sauntering toward me as if he doesn't have a care in the world.

He might not be in a rush, but I most definitely am. I'm working away at the rope in a frenzy, silently cursing the amount of time it's taking.

"Well, it was great seeing you. Now, if you don't mind, I'm kind of busy here," I say.

"I can help with that, Caleb," says Frank. "You see, there was a little mix-up at Headquarters. You're supposed to be in London with Abbie and the others. This is my snatch."

"You're lying," I say. There's no way I'm falling for Frank's story. He knows he's three snatches behind me this month. He came to stall me until my thirty minutes are up, then claim the snatch for himself and tell Uncle that he had to do it because I failed. It's not a bad plan, but I don't think he's thought it all the way through. Uncle might not view Frank's hanging around my snatches waiting for me to fail as a good use of his time.

"Move away from the flag and hold your hands out to either side where I can see them," he says.

"Sorry," I say. "Go find your own flag."

I'm through the rope now. My fingernail tells me I've got forty-five seconds to get out of here.

I reach for my wrist to initiate the return timeleap. But just as I do, Frank grabs my arm.

Instinctively, I unleash a kick to his shin, and he releases his grip. We spin and face each other across the roof.

Ten seconds to complete the snatch.

I reach again for my wrist, but at the same moment, he lunges at me and I'm forced to block his punch. We square off again. Frank's smiling now. He knows my time is running out.

A whirring sound catches my attention. The helicopter is on its way back.

He pulls a black-handled knife with a wicked-looking blade out from under his shirt. I recognize it immediately as the same one I always use for chopping onions back at Headquarters.

"You stole that from the kitchen!" I say in disbelief.

He smirks at me and says nothing.

I'm seething. But what choice do I really have? My own knife is puny compared to his. I might be able to disarm him, but we're both black belts in karate, and at best I'm looking at a stalemate. Besides, he's already won. My thirty minutes for completing the snatch ended about five seconds ago.

For a moment, I consider leaping twenty minutes back in time and doing the snatch over, so that I'm long gone before Frank even shows up on the roof. But apart from having to deal with time fog, I doubt it will work anyway. Frank's not stupid. If l go back to try to outwit him, he'll counter by leaping even further.

And how did he get the data for my mission anyway? That's secret information and the only people who know are myself, Uncle and Nassim. I doubt Uncle or Nassim would have told Frank, if for no other reason than they would want him busy completing his own snatches, not poaching mine. No, something doesn't smell right.

Sighing, I pick up the replica flag and am about to hand it to him when he stops me.

"Nice try, Caleb but I'll take the other one."

"If you insist," I say. "But you'd be making the wrong decision. I already had the copy up on the flagpole when you landed. I was only pretending to cut it down to make you think it was the original." I'm lying of course, but I figure it's for a good cause: if Frank's going to succeed in spoiling my day, then at least I want him to work for it.

Frank smiles, steps even closer and says, "All right. In that case, I'll take both."

Hmmm. I wasn't counting on that. Well, at least he'll have the embarrassment of trying to figure out which one is the original when he gets back to Headquarters.

I fork them over and watch glumly as he stuffs them under his shirt. The sound of the helicopter is nearing. I calculate the odds of making a quick getaway. Not very good. Frank is holding the blade inches from my chest. If he sees me go for my wrist, he could easily slash me before I make it halfway there.

He looks up at me and smiles one of his big jerk smiles. "You think you're better than me, don't you, Caleb?"

I'm tempted to agree with him. After all, it's the first sensible thing he's said since he arrived. But instead I say, "If you think poaching my snatches will get you in Uncle's good books, you're wrong."

"To be honest, I don't know why Uncle doesn't get rid of you," Frank continues. "You're more of a dreamer than a time snatcher. I don't get distracted with dreams. That's the difference between you and me. Dreamers dream. But snatchers snatch."

"That's a brilliant observation, Frank," I say, "coming from some-one who has only fourteen snatches this month to my seventeen."

Frank glares at me for a moment, but the next instant, his fea-tures soften into his usual smug expression.

"Don't be late for supper tonight," he says. "I'm cooking Peking duck. My girl's favorite."

It takes all of my concentration to keep my expression neutral, but inside I'm fuming. I know he means Abbie, and the way he said that, it sounded as if he wanted me to think there was something going on between them.

Just then there's a deafening noise. The helicopter blades are slic-ing the night air right overhead. A powerful search beam shoots out, sweeping the roof only feet away from where Frank and I are standing.

Frank glances up, but at the same time he's tapping away at his wrist. No point holding back now. I tap furiously at my own wrist. As soon as Frank has both hands free, he waves them in the air like crazy, and screams at the top of his lungs. It sounds like he's shout-ing "stop thief," but then again it might be "roast beef"—it's impos-sible to tell with all the racket of the helicopter. Anyway, I can't very well ask him because the next moment he disappears.

Which is what I should be doing. But for some reason I'm not. I'm still here.

Just then, I'm caught in the search beam.

"*Bú yaò dòng*—do not move!" says a voice over a loudspeaker. Nice of him to translate for me, but I could have managed it on my own. I've got an implant that instantaneously translates all words I hear into English.

I try tapping again at my wrist. Pounding footsteps and shouts are getting closer.

I look up to see three guards running toward me. One of them has his gun drawn.

Nowhere to run—I'm already backed up to the edge of the roof.

I step behind the U.S. flag and hold it up in front of me, as a kind of shield.

They wouldn't shoot the U.S. flag on the first day of the Great Friendship, would they?

I close my eyes tight and brace myself.

The guards are only feet away now. The one in the lead reaches for me.

But all he grabs is air.

I land between two parked cars on the north side of Franklin Street, right across from Headquarters.

It's now eight minutes past four, local time, which means I was away for thirty-two minutes: exactly the same amount of time that I spent in the past. All of our time patches are preprogrammed that way for missions. It makes sense when you think about it. With time travel, you can spend a half hour in the past but choose to return to the present with only two minutes having gone by. Do that often enough, though, and you'll soon be falling asleep in your soup.

A yellow rickshaw speeds by, missing me by about six inches. Since the city went China-crazy, most of the cabbies have traded in their Fords for these oversized tricycles with seating for two in the back. They're not much to look at, but they sure get great mileage.

One thing that hasn't changed, though: it's still impossible to find a cab in New York. Correction: New Beijing. That's what the mayor says we have to call New York City for the next year. It's not so bad, I suppose. The people of Beijing have it worse. They've got to call their place *Dà Píng Guǒ*, which in Mandarin means "the Big Apple."

I'm drowning in a symphony of horns and curses. The second I stumble onto the sidewalk, someone's yelling at me to move and someone else is trying to sell me a fake Rolex watch. Normally I'd happily agree with at least one of those suggestions, but there's nothing I can do. My time freeze hasn't thawed all the way.

Finally, my body starts listening to my brain and I take a few more steps, scattering some pigeons clustered around a guy who's flicking wontons at them.

Something crunches under my feet. It's the partial remains of an Indian dinner. But that's just the appetizer. There's trash strewn everywhere. You have to wonder at some of the things people throw away. For instance, not more than three feet from me, there's a perfectly good coffeemaker, an only slightly used Chinese/braille keyboard and a burgundy love seat that might be a bit faded but otherwise looks in great shape.

The stench is awful. If the garbage strike doesn't end soon, I'm going to have to spring for one of those pine-scented face masks that are fast becoming a fashion accessory in New Beijing. I really shouldn't complain, though. If it's a choice between walking down a stinky sidewalk in New York and a close encounter on a rooftop with gun-wielding Chinese soldiers, I'll pick stinky every time.

A huge advertisement for EastWest Jeans purrs, "Hello there, handsome. Come on. Try a pair close to your skin," while another shouts, "Hey, guy, need a caffeine fix?" Call me antisocial, but I'm not crazy about having a conversation with billboards.

I'm not eager to arrive at Headquarters. Any way I look at it, it's going to go badly for me. So why hurry back?

Instead of crossing, I make a beeline for the Chi Break booth up the street. These booths started springing up all over Manhattan minutes after the U.S. and China inked the Great Friendship. I don't know many words in Chinese, but *chi* means "life energy." The point of the booths is to provide pleasant, calming experiences that will

16

restore your chi so that you can get on with the rest of your day feeling all fresh and relaxed. Of course, like everything else in New Beijing, restoring your life energy doesn't come cheap—a half-hour session will set you back a hundred bucks. Luckily, in addition to being a thief, I'm also an expert at bypassing security systems and tinkering with payment records.

I step into the telephone booth–sized unit and shut the door behind me. With a few choice voice commands, I disarm the security system and convince the automated administrator that I'm all paid up.

Within seconds, a vanilla smooth voice comes on and says, "Welcome to Chi Break, Robert. May the breath of the winds speak softly in your ears. What is your selection today?"

Robert is the name I use when I'm out in public or doing something slightly illegal. Abbie chose it for me. She says I look like a Robert, whatever that means. I have to admit it's growing on me. I just hope no one takes liberties with it and starts calling me Roberto or, even worse, Robbie.

For a second, I consider trying something different this time. After all, how much Mountain Meadow can one person stand?

"Mountain Meadow, please," I say.

"An excellent selection. Enjoy your Chi Break, Robert," the machine responds. The lights blink out, and suddenly I'm inhaling fresh air and the fragrance of wildflowers. It's all an illusion, of course, but everything looks, sounds and feels so real, right down to the drops of early morning dew on the tips of the long grass sweeping the meadow. Give me another hour of this, and I'll be totally relaxed.

Except that I don't have an hour. I've only booked ten minutes, which is just enough to take the edge off. I'd stay longer, but I should be getting back to Headquarters and reporting in. If I'm really late,

Uncle will kill me. Well, maybe not actually kill me. He might only torture me. Yes, that's it. A good old-fashioned Chinese water torture in honor of the Great Friendship.

I will my shoulders to relax.

A memory takes hold. I'm a toddler walking with my mother, a carpet of soft grass beneath our feet. "Smell this one, Caleb," she says and holds a purple flower under my nose. I scrunch my nose and sneeze. She laughs. My mother's laughter is the sweetest part of the memory. I try desperately to hold on to it.

"Your Chi Break is over, Robert," announces the machine's simulated voice. My mother's laughter slips away like smoke.

I sigh, exit the booth and head home. Soon, 179 Franklin Street comes into view. It's a nice-looking building: six stories, red brickwork and wood trim over a funky entranceway. Most of the tenants are what you'd expect to see in Tribeca: a decent Greek restaurant on the ground floor, an artists' co-op on the first, a canine dental surgeon on the second and a law firm specializing in entertainment law on the third floor. Nothing out of the ordinary.

You'd never guess that the fourth and fifth floors are the headquarters of Timeless Treasures, a company that provides unique goods for the ultrarich: special-ordered hard-to-get items from the past.

The way I heard it, the army had secretly tried for years to develop a prototype for time travel but could never quite make it work. So they shelved Project Chronos, as it was called, and destroyed all the records. Or at least they thought they had destroyed everything. The truth was that a certain truck driver for the waste disposal firm got it into his head to deliver the documents to a warehouse that he had secretly leased. After two years of late nights picking through a hundred boxes of documents, the truck driver (who, by the way, also happened to have a degree in quantum physics) pieced together enough information to build his own time travel system—and unlike the army's versions, his worked.

"Truck Driver Builds Greatest Invention of Twenty-First Century" is what the newspaper headlines would have said if they had ever found out. But they never did. The truck driver never told anyone, including the army. He quit his job, became "Uncle" to a handful of adopted children and, when he decided they were old enough, sent them out into the world to steal stuff for wealthy clients who didn't ask too many questions. The rest, as they say, is history.

For a company that doesn't advertise, business sure is booming. As a team, Abbie and I are averaging four snatches a week, and so are the other teams. Throw in a few solo snatches, and that translates to about fifty a month. Abbie, who along with her other skills has a natural talent for intelligence gathering, found out that Uncle's clients pay on average a hundred thousand bucks for each little memento from the past. So we're talking a cool five million dollars every month . . . tax free. That's a nice piece of change.

It doesn't take me long to get to work. I live in a dorm on the fourth floor with the other male time snatchers, Frank and Raoul. Lydia, who is Frank's snatch partner, shares the other dorm room with Abbie. The kitchen, lounge and Nassim's office are also on four. Uncle's office and our workstations are on five.

I mostly use my workstation to research local customs and other things that might come in handy when I'm on a mission. It's amazing what you can find online—stuff like what the cave dwellers in the Pecos River Valley of Texas ate for breakfast in 9,500 B.C.

One of the things Uncle taught us early on was that the more you know about the way people lived in the time/place you're going to, the less you'll stick out like a sore thumb. And when your job is to steal things from under people's noses, blending in is a must. I have to admit though, unlike Abbie, who can sit at her workstation for hours on end, after twenty minutes my legs start doing drum solos, and I have to get up and do a few karate kicks. So I don't spend as much time on research as I probably should.

I glance up to the dorm window. There's no sign of activity. Good. I don't think I could deal with Frank right now.

Climbing the stairs to the front entrance, I'm fully aware that my every move is being recorded. Uncle likes to know who's coming and going.

On entering the lobby, I notice that the artists' co-op has a new exhibit: a hologram of pink bowling balls orbiting what looks like a teapot with spouts at both ends. Each time a ball passes by one of the spouts, an image of the Arctic flashes on an overhead screen and the temperature in the lobby drops by two degrees. Nice.

As I press the Up button for the elevator, I don't feel anything other than a slight chill due to the bowling ball exhibit. But a dozen different sensors are checking me out, confirming my identity. It's all part of Uncle's elaborate security system to keep out certain undesirable types, like the police or Internal Revenue Service. Of course they wouldn't have any problems visiting Cohen and Chen, Attorneys-at-Law, on the third floor or bringing their dogs in for a teeth whitening on two, but as soon as they ask for four or five, they'll get an "out of service to those floors" message.

The inside of the elevator is pretty much like any other old-fashioned elevator in New York, oops—New Beijing: a steel cage that feels like a prison once the door clanks shut.

"Four," I say.

"For what?" a voice squawks, and Phoebe's elevator attendant persona appears on the wall screen: smart royal blue pantsuit with red piping on the arms and legs and a double row of silver buttons up the front. A matching pillbox cap completes the picture. I have to admit, she looks fairly sharp for a computer.

Of course, if you called Phoebe a computer to her face, she'd be highly insulted. She likes to think of herself as a regular person. It's true that Phoebe's operating system is sprinkled with human DNA (which allows her to do a trillion calculations a second without breaking a sweat), but it's a real stretch to talk about her as a real person. On the other hand, she's gotten quite good at mimicking certain human personality traits and can do "annoying" better than any real person I know.

"Not that kind of *for*, Phoebe," I say and take a deep breath. But it's too late. The feeling of calm from my Chi Break is quickly evaporating.

"Well, then, what kind of *for* do you mean?" she asks.

"You know," I say. "One, two, three, four."

"Five, six, seven, eight," says Phoebe agreeably.

Except that she's not being agreeable. She's being difficult. Which would be fine if she were keeping intruders from nosing around Timeless Treasures Headquarters. But right now it's just plain annoying.

"Phoebe, I've just come back from China, and I'm hot, tired and thirsty, and I've got to report in. So can you please take me up to the fourth floor?"

A long moment of silence passes. I know what she's doing. In baseball it's called icing the hitter. She's trying to throw my balance off, to remind me how big and important she is and how small and insignificant I am. I suppose it's possible I'm reading too much into her little act. Maybe a human quality like nastiness is really beyond her. I mean, when you get right down to it, all she is is a bunch of

DNA-saturated synthetic neuro-dendrites with a few microchips—and not even top-of-the-line, either.

"Well . . . okay," says Phoebe, finally. "Since you said please."

When the doors whoosh open, I step out into a dingy reception area. Cracks run through the walls, and the paint has peeled away in places to show swatches of green-striped wallpaper. A water pipe pokes through near the ceiling, although it looks like someone has made a halfhearted attempt to hide it by painting it the same mustard yellow as the walls. A threadbare sofa that might once have been white sits forlornly under a slightly crooked sign that says NEW BEIJING EXPORT COMPANY.

The sign, like the crummy reception area, is all just a front.

I flop down on the couch and reach a hand underneath. Every time I do this, I cringe, thinking my fingers are going to encounter a lumpy mass of used Great Friendship Extra Chew Bubble Gum. Luckily, the only thing I feel is the Access button. I press it, and the south wall slides back, revealing the real reception area for Timeless Treasures.

Except today there's not a lot of revealing going on. In fact, it's pitch-black. Not even the dim light from the fake reception area has managed to penetrate the gloom beyond the wall. If I could, I'd switch to night vision, but my ocular implant doesn't work inside Headquarters. I stand and take two blind steps forward. The wall slides closed behind me.

All of my senses kick into high alert as I brace myself for the inevitable attack.

Ten seconds go by.

Could I be wrong? Maybe the attack isn't coming.

Twenty seconds pass. Still nothing.

Maybe . . . and then something like iron grips my neck and throat. The assault is so swift I don't have time to even breathe.

"Four letters," a husky voice whispers. "Chinese sailing vessel dating from ancient times or food containing zero nutritional value."

I'd like to help Nassim out with his crossword puzzle, but the mechanics of the situation make it impossible for me to grunt, let alone utter a four-letter word.

He must realize it too, because he eases his grip slightly.

"H-hello, Nassim," I splutter. "I'm reporting in."

The large man releases me. He snaps his fingers and the reception area swims into focus. The first thing I see, floating in front of me, is a three-foot-high hologram of the company logo, a snake wrapped around an hourglass. Just above the logo in floating orange neon letters is Uncle's inspirational message of the week: *A failed snatch is like half a sneeze.*

Uncle may have some faults, but I've got to admit he's got a certain way with words.

I rub my neck while Nassim flips open his handheld. He's the latest in Uncle's string of personal assistants/bodyguards. He also tutors us time snatchers on karate, including at no extra charge, surprise attacks that are virtually impossible to defend against.

The word around Timeless Treasures is that Nassim knows twenty-seven different ways to immobilize an opponent using only his left thumb. According to Abbie, he made some bad bets at the racetrack, and Uncle bailed him out. Now he owes Uncle a pile of money, which he'll never be able to repay on his paltry salary. But I'd be surprised if he and his deadly thumb manage to last even another month. Next week, Nassim will have been with Uncle six months, which is usually when Uncle dumps his assistants.

"Ah, yes, the Beijing mission. Kindly hand it over," says Nassim.

So polite. It's hard to believe this is the same guy who was throttling me just a moment ago.

"I . . . I don't have anything for you," I say.

"How can that be?" says Nassim, his eyes narrowing. "Did you not complete the snatch?"

"Well, when I got to the snatch zone, the Great Friendship flag wasn't there."

Nassim's crossword-puzzle-solving fingers are twitching. He doesn't like surprises. They mess up his paperwork. For a long moment, he just looks at me, saying nothing.

"Someone else must have snatched it," I say finally to break the silence.

I don't like lying to Nassim. He's a decent guy. But if I tell him that Frank and I were going at it again, he'll have no choice but to go straight to Uncle with the news. And Uncle isn't the sympathetic type.

"I'll have to record it as a failed snatch," says Nassim.

I nod. It's not so bad—yet. Thankfully, I've got no other failed snatches this month.

"Please wait in the lounge while I complete my report," he says.

I nod again, and just before I turn to go, I whisper, "Junk," in answer to Nassim's crossword puzzle clue. He rewards me with a toothy grin and a clap on the back that sends a fresh jolt of pain up to my poor neck.

I walk down the hall to the lounge. It's a combination of living room, dining room and mission briefing room. It also has a large walk-in closet with a full wardrobe of clothing for different centuries and places and cubbyholes for each time snatcher where Nassim puts our clothes for upcoming missions. But since he doesn't know much about women's clothes, Abbie and Lydia are allowed to pick their own.

Immediately I notice that the old water cooler has been replaced with one of those new rock water fountain ones. According to Uncle, waterfalls, even small ones, are supposed to be calming and improve the chi of the room. I'm surprised to see something so fancy in the lounge. It's not that Uncle can't afford it. But when it comes to spending on us time snatchers, he's usually on the cheap side.

I grab a drink from the new fountain and gaze out the small window. One thing that hasn't changed is the view: solid brick everywhere you look. When I was eight, I managed to open the window, reach across and scratch my name in the brick with a pair of scissors. Uncle found out and I spent the next three days cleaning the kitchen, lounge and bathrooms. Which, when I think of it now, seems a light punishment compared to what would happen if I pulled the same stunt today.

"Long time no see, Caleb. Try to steal from any other agents lately?" says a voice.

It's Frank, standing just outside the doorway.

I take a long drink of water before I speak. Winning an argument with Frank is a bit like trying to catch a fish with your bare hands. Even so, there's no way I'm going to let him walk all over me.

"You've got it backwards," I say. "You stole from me, remember?"

Frank laughs his annoying, superior laugh, and then says, "You're right. I stole from you. But only because you were taking way too long to do a simple snatch, so Uncle sent me to get the job done."

I don't believe him for one second. Apart from the fact that he's changing his tune—when we were on the roof together he claimed that it was supposed to be his snatch—there's no way Uncle would send him to finish my snatch. Would he?

I throw a mask over my emotions and gaze past him. What's taking Nassim so long? I wish he would hurry up and finish his report so I can get out of here.

"Aren't you curious about where everyone is?" he asks, ending my peace and quiet.

"No," I say.

"They're lugging bags of garbage to 2059," Frank says. "I would have joined them, but Uncle's asked me to do a special job for him."

I look back out the window. Did he say "everyone"? That can't be. I'm supposed to meet up with Abbie for our mission to 1826 France. Of course, Uncle could have reassigned her to garbage duty. Either that, or Frank's lying.

"Don't you want to know what the special job is?" he says.

"Not really," I say, knowing that he'll tell me anyway.

"Sure you do," he says. "It's a collection. I get to take the Time Pod. Want to come along?"

Frank's pressing my buttons. He knows I can't stand hearing about collections, which is just a fancy word for kidnappings. It's Uncle's latest project: snatching young homeless kids from the streets and training them to be time thieves. Since a wrist patch can only transport the person wearing it, Frank has to take the Time Pod—a time travel machine that looks like a big steel drum from the outside but on the inside has seating for up to four people.

Uncle's got this grand vision of a hundred kids working for him, snatching stuff from across the centuries so that he can satisfy the growing demand for memorabilia from the past. He says he's doing these kids a favor, that without him, they'll just die on the streets. But I don't buy it. Just because they're street kids doesn't mean their lives are free for the picking.

According to Abbie, he's already got seventeen new recruits. Most of them are four or five years old. You'd think that there would be a lot of escape attempts. But that's actually pretty rare. If Uncle's anything like he was with us at that age, they probably all adore him.

As for us senior time snatchers, the fear of what Uncle would do to us once he found us is enough to keep us from bolting.

This isn't just paranoia; this is fear based on the real facts. And the facts can be boiled down to two words: *memory wipe.*

All you remember wiped away in minutes. It's a brutal and unforgiving weapon, and I have no doubt that Uncle would use it like he did with Vlad, who tried to make a break for it in thirteenth-century Morocco.

The way I heard it, Uncle sent Nassim after him. Nassim found Vlad, crushed up a couple of memory-wipe pills and poured them into a drink. Soon after Vlad drained the glass, all his memories also drained away. But it didn't end there. Nassim brought him back to Timeless Treasures and planted new, false memories where the old ones used to be. I guess that's why Uncle didn't kill him right off. No point wasting a fully trained time snatcher if you can reprogram him. Poor old Vlad. Two weeks later, he was killed on mission to 1983 Pamplona, Spain—gored at the running of the bulls.

"I hope he isn't a biter like the one last week," says Frank, with as much emotion as if he's talking about the weather. "That was a bit awkward. I really wanted to teach the kid some manners, but Uncle doesn't like it when they show up at the Compound without any teeth. What do you say, Caleb? Care to join me for a little fun?"

I shake my head. Inside I feel like I'm going to explode. I'm done waiting for Nassim. I stand up and head toward the door.

Frank takes a quick step to block me. Although we're both

thirteen, he's got four inches of height on me, and right now he's making a point of using each one of them.

Just then Nassim appears by the doorway. "Caleb, I've finished the report. You can go now. Please pick up your clothes for your next mission on your way out. Oh, and by the way, Abbie's back from London. Frank, kindly move so that Caleb can pass."

So she *is* here. I glare at Frank but he doesn't meet my eyes. He's too busy trying to stare down Nassim. After about five seconds, he gives up and steps to the side.

Personally, I like Nassim, but Frank can't get over the fact that Nassim has better access to Uncle than he does. The only thing that stops him from trying to order Nassim around is that Uncle might not like it. That and the thirty pounds more muscle that Nassim has over him.

On my way out of the lounge, I reach into my cubbyhole and grab the clothes Nassim has chosen for my next mission—a fine white linen shirt, burgundy waistcoat, a pair of black breeches and sturdy Wellington boots. As I change in the boys' washroom, I stand in front of the mirror and practice facial expressions. Apart from the thrill of the snatch itself, one of the things I like about a lot of snatches is the chance to be an actor—someone totally different than my day-to-day self. Snatches can be like performances. Any common thief can steal something, but I like to think that, through creativity, I've raised my snatches to a whole new level.

Or rather, Abbie and I have raised *our* snatches to a whole new level. Uncle adopted Abbie a few months after me, and we did everything together growing up. So when it came time for Uncle to put together teams of time snatchers, it was natural for us to be paired up. Which is a good thing, because I wouldn't want to be with anyone else. Not only is Abbie the best natural thief I've ever seen, but she can also size up a situation in an instant; that can sometimes mean the difference between life and death in this business. She's saved my hide more than once over the years. Also, we know each other so well that sometimes I only have to think about asking her something before the answer's already halfway out of her mouth.

I spend a few minutes on surprise and disgust and then switch to anger. Now, there's one I can do with my eyes closed. All I have to do is think of Frank, and my face immediately morphs into a believable expression of rage.

As I head down the hall, I see the door to the fire escape partly open. Abbie and I hang out there a lot, before and after missions. The view of the city isn't the best, since all we can really see is the brick wall of the building next door, but if you look straight up through the struts of the iron stairs, you can see a fair-sized patch of New Beijing sky.

Abbie is lying on her back on the landing, knees bent, a cushion propped under her head. Her long auburn hair spills over the sides of the cushion. Not surprisingly, she's already dressed for our mission in a long-sleeved blue dress with a bit of lace at the bottom and velvet slippers. A frilly white bonnet is perched on one knee.

Abbie's facing away from me, but as soon as I step out onto the landing, her left arm rises and two fingers waggle in my direction. Her other hand pats the floor beside her.

"Hi, Cale," she says.

"How'd you know it was me?"

"Your knee clicked."

"Traitor," I say to my knee and sprawl down beside her.

"How was Beijing?" she asks.

"Interesting. I didn't have much time to explore, but there's a great park with huge stone lions and a footbridge over a lily pond. People were hanging out and doing Tai Chi and stuff."

I leave out the part about my rooftop encounter because I can use a mental break from all things Frank right now.

"How was the Tower of London?" I ask.

"Hot and stuffy," she says. "We should get danger pay when we travel to time/places before the invention of air-conditioning."

I laugh and feel some of the tension of the day's events melt away.

"Well, I'm ready for France when you are," I say, referring to our next mission.

"Yes, I can see that you are," she says, eyeing me up and down. "Nice boots."

"Thanks."

"Let's play a game before we go," she says, looking up at the sky.

I follow Abbie's glance. There aren't enough clouds to play our favorite game: Name That Presidential Cloud.

"Why don't we play Heels of Fortune?" she says.

A good second choice.

"Okay. Do you want to go first?" I say.

"No, you go," she says. "I went first last time."

We lie quietly, neither of us saying a word. I tune my ears to the sounds around me. There's no shortage of noises—car horns, the drone of an airplane, the wind whistling through the metal stairs. I ignore all of these and concentrate on the sounds coming from just beyond the entrance to the alley. I can't see the sidewalk from where I'm sitting, but I'll be able to hear anyone approaching.

I don't have to wait long before I hear a set of footsteps.

The smacking of heels on sidewalk is fairly pronounced, and I detect a slight drag on the left foot. But this game isn't about guessing correctly. In fact, it's the opposite—the more outrageous you are with your predictions of who the person is and what they do for a living, the better.

"Two hundred and fifty-five pounds, male," I begin, "with a wad of chewing tobacco that he keeps permanently tucked inside his right cheek, as a reminder of his failed dream to play second base for the Yankees. He's wearing a crisp white shirt, plaid pants and tortoiseshell glasses and is carrying a brown fake leather briefcase with samples of a new line of scented nose warmers. Your turn."

"His shirt *was* white," she begins, "until about an hour ago when the ketchup from his Beijingburger got away from him a little, so now there's a red stain the shape of Florida on his right sleeve just below the elbow. Plus, although you'll probably never get to see it, on his lower back there's a tattoo of a ski-jump-shaped nose inside a heart and below it the words 'Mom Nose Best' . . . you go now."

The sound of heels striking sidewalk stops suddenly, two seconds of silence follows and then I hear a gargantuan sneeze.

Excellent. When you're playing Heels of Fortune, any kind of bodily eruption is like found treasure in the hands of a skilled player.

"The glasses, plaid pants and briefcase are all part of an elaborate disguise," I say. "In fact he's no nose warmer salesman. His name is Victor Sanayovitch, and his real job is duster for FIST—Fingerprinting and Investigative Society of Toledo. He is currently on a mission of utmost secrecy . . . and his sneeze is no ordinary sneeze—something very special flies out of his nose. Your turn, Abbie."

She laughs. The footsteps are at their peak now. In a few seconds, Victor will be out of earshot.

"When Victor sneezes," she says, "what he's really doing is spraying fingerprint dust on the pretzel handed to him by Lorenzo, proprietor of the Piping Hot Pretzel vending cart stationed at this very moment directly in front of Headquarters. The pretzel is still warm when Victor runs the prints through his FIST mobile database and finds a match. Lorenzo is no innocent pretzel seller. When he was in kindergarten, little Lorenzo regularly traded his macaroni and cheese for Claudio Fazio's meatball sandwich. Then he'd throw away the bread and use the meatballs as poker chips in his regular lunchtime game behind the monkey bars."

I snort my approval.

"C'mon, let's see what he really looks like." Abbie takes off down the fire escape.

"Or she," I say, clambering down the steps after her.

We race out of the alleyway and glance right. Immediately, I see two people who are the correct distance away to be our guy—one is a large woman dressed in a black spandex workout suit, and the other a short bald man carrying a poodle under one arm.

"Who do you think?" says Abbie.

"Hmmm. It must be her," I say. "She looks like she can throw a pretzel a great distance."

"I think it's him," she says.

As we watch, the man stops in his tracks and lets go with a monstrous sneeze. It's too much. Abbie and I run back to the fire escape and collapse on the bottom step, roaring with laughter.

We recover at about the same time, but then I look at her as if I'm about to sneeze and this sends us both into another laughing frenzy. Finally we stop for good.

"That was fun. Ready for Operation Shutterbox?" she says.

Abbie likes to code-name all of our missions. She says it makes our job more glamorous.

"Ready," I say.

Our mission is to snatch the first photograph ever taken. We'll be leaping to 1826 and landing just outside the village of Saint-Loup-de-Varennes in France. The snatch will take place at the home of the inventor of photography, Nicéphore Niépce. Nicéphore's wife and son are supposed to be away visiting relatives. The only possible complication is Nicéphore's brother Claude, who may be at the home at the time of the snatch. The file says that he's a mad-scientist type, with the emphasis on mad.

I give a contented sigh. Apart from the tingle of excitement I always feel before a mission, there's also the thrill of going to a time in history where no one else from the twenty-first century has ever been before. To say nothing of the pleasure of getting away from Frank and spending some time with Abbie.

From the mission data, it looks like a straightforward snatch. Who knows? Maybe we'll even have time for some of that wonderful crusty French bread.

"I've got the replica," Abbie says. "Want to see it?"

"Sure."

She slips one hand under her long dress and pulls out a pewter plate about five inches wide by eight inches high.

The black-and-white image shows a barn, a pigeon house and a bit of the horizon.

"Kind of boring looking," I say. Still, I can understand how owning the first photograph ever taken in the history of the world would be a thrill for one of Uncle's customers. After all, there's only one first photograph, and whoever ordered it probably couldn't care less what it was a photo of or even if Niépce got his thumb in the shot.

"Have you been practicing your French?" Abbie asks, twisting her hair into a bun.

She's big on mission preparation, which in her mind includes learning at least some of the local language spoken wherever we go.

"La plume de ma tante est sur la table," I say straight-faced, repeating a sentence I remember hearing from a Speak French Like a Parisian holo.

She laughs. "Do you know what you just said?"

"Yes. I said that you are my sister and that we are the children of Nicéphore Niépce's brother Bernard's wife's youngest sister, and we have come for a short visit," I say, repeating the cover story for Operation Shutterbox.

"Very funny, mister. Actually, you said that your aunt's pen is on the table."

"Did I really?" I say, eyes wide in mock surprise.

In truth, I don't know much French, but with my translator implant, it doesn't matter. As soon as someone speaks to me in a different language, not only will I understand what they are saying, but also the next words that come out of my mouth will automatically be in that language.

"Yes, really," she says, adjusting her bonnet. *"On y va."*

"Eva? Who's she?"

"It means 'let's go' in French."

"Oh."

"On three," she says. *"Un, deux, trois!"*

"Quatre!" I add, just to show off. But it's too late. Abbie's already gone. I touch my wrist and follow her back in time.

III

August 14, 1826, 11:19 A.M.
Saint-Loup-de-Varennes, France
Operation Shutterbox

When I open my eyes, my first thought is that they sure know how to make clouds in this century. They're big and fluffy, with lots of character.

"Time to get up, Mr. Daydreamer," says Abbie, standing over me.

I'm leaning back, elbows propped on a bed of soft grass. It's so comfortable. The air smells sweet, and I make a point of taking several lungfuls.

"Uh. I can't just yet," I say. "Still time frozen. Hey, I think I see a new president. Well, maybe not a *new* one. I mean one I've never noticed before . . ."

"Really? Who?"

"John Quincy Adams. Look, there are his lamb-chop sideburns and his nose and bald head. It's him. I can see him so clearly."

"I'm happy for you," she says, deadpan. "C'mon."

I stand up and brush myself off. The field we've landed in borders a dirt road leading to a cluster of houses. That must be the village of Saint-Loup-de-Varennes. I understand now why our landing spot is away from the action. It would be hard to find an inconspicuous place to land in such a small village.

As we walk toward the snatch zone, the back of my hand brushes against Abbie's and a warm shiver passes through me. I sneak a glance at her, but she's looking straight ahead and has got on her Mona Lisa smile. If she has noticed that we touched, she's not letting on.

We continue walking, kicking up clouds of dust as we go. I can see the houses clearly now: sturdy-looking stone structures with thick wooden shutters painted in bright greens and reds. Flowerpots with yellow flowers sit on some of the window ledges. I make a mental note to stay away from them in case they turn out to be daffodils.

We stop at the last house on the left. The place is large: two stories with a tower at the rear. My eyes linger for a moment on the second story. That's where the inventor Nicéphore Niépce has his laboratory, and that's where the snatch object should be right now.

I knock on the door.

There's a scraping sound, and the door swings open. Standing opposite us is a handsome man in a formal white shirt with a high collar. I judge him to be about fifty years old, which is just about the right age to be the inventor. Except that he can't be because the holo of Nicéphore in the file shows a bald man and this guy has wild black hair sticking out in every direction. He must be Nicéphore's brother Claude.

I'm about to mindspeak this to Abbie when she says, "Good day, sir. Our mother—"

"Hurry, the three of you get inside!" Claude orders.

I only count two of us, but who knows, maybe he's counting himself.

The inside doesn't disappoint. There's a large sitting room with several comfortable-looking divans and armchairs arranged around a fireplace. Hanging above the fireplace is an oil painting of a man who bears more than a passing resemblance to Claude. I can also see part of the staircase that leads to the second floor.

"They are coming!" Claude bellows.

"Who is coming?" Abbie asks.

"Them," he answers, staring at the door as if someone is about to come barging through. "The tricolored beings."

The *tricolored beings?*

"Orange, blue and red," Claude continues. "But they cannot fool me. I have something that can turn them all white," he says in a hushed voice. With that, he takes one final look at the sky, slams the door and bars it with a stout wooden staff.

"Under the divan! And you, there," he shouts at an empty patch of air, "get down before they see you!"

Then he jumps up onto one of the armchairs and yells, "Let them come! I will thrash the cake eaters!"

"Cale, we need to take control of this situation," Abbie says.

She's right. Even though we still have plenty of time to complete the snatch—twenty-four minutes by my fingernail—we might never get it done if we keep letting Claude call all the shots.

"Agreed. Remember Montevideo, 1963?" I say.

"Perfect," agrees Abbie. "You choose."

"Why don't you be the tree this time?" I say.

"Done," she answers.

Abbie crawls out from under the divan and stands up straight. She brings her palms together in a prayer position, raises her left foot and places it in the crook of her right knee so that she's only standing on one leg. She begins in a low voice,

> *"By the dismal tarns and pools,*
> *Where dwell the Ghouls,—*
> *By each spot the most unholy—*
> *In each nook most melancholy,—*

37

There the traveler meets aghast
Sheeted memories of the past—"

Wow. The Gothic poetry is a totally unexpected and nice touch. I'm pretty sure she picked it up from Uncle. When he was going through his Dark Lord phase, he used to spew out that kind of stuff all the time.

More important, she has Claude's attention now. He stares at her for a moment, turns to me and whispers, "There is something seriously wrong with your sister."

"This has happened once before," I say without skipping a beat. "We must get her to higher ground immediately. That is the only way she will snap out of it."

Then I step behind Abbie and grab her underneath her arms. "Is there a second floor, monsieur?"

He nods.

"Quickly, help me get her up the stairs." As I say this, I'm mentally crossing my fingers, praying that Claude will play ball.

He hesitates for a moment, then bends over and bridges his arms underneath her legs. Despite all this, Abbie impressively manages to hold her pine tree pose.

Together, we drag her to the foot of the stairs.

"Good work, Cale. Just don't drop me, okay?" she mindspeaks.

"Your safety is assured, madame," I mindspeak back, although I can really only vouch for my end. If Claude spots one of those three-colored beings, all bets are off.

Slowly, we carry Abbie's rigid body up the stairs. As soon as we stop on the second floor landing, Claude abruptly lets go of his end.

"Open Hades' gates," Abbie cries out as her legs land with a thump. But she recovers quickly, resumes her pine tree pose and starts reciting more Gothic poetry.

There's a scent of rotten eggs in the air. Four worktables are covered with strange-looking pieces of equipment. I spot some flasks and beakers filled with green and gold liquids. Maybe the smell is coming from one of them.

We're in a large room about the same size as the entire first floor of the house. The light is dim, and all of the windows except for one are covered with plywood. At the center of each boarded-up window is a small wooden box. I know from the briefing materials that the box is called a camera obscura and that when light passes into it from outside and hits the metal plate inside the box, this triggers some kind of chemical reaction, causing an image of whatever the camera is pointing at to form on the plate.

In the dim light, I almost miss seeing him. But there he is, bent over a contraption resting on a table in a far corner of the room— Nicéphore Niépce. He looks exactly like his file holo—aquiline nose and bald as a bowling ball. Like his brother, he's elegantly dressed in a waistcoat and high-collar white shirt.

Without looking up, he shouts, "Come quickly, Claude, the image is beginning to form!"

But Claude seems more interested in looking out the only window that hasn't been boarded up.

"My God, the clouds are about to burst open! They will be here soon!" he says.

I ignore Claude and stride over to where Nicéphore is bent over a metal plate fixed in a vertical position over a silver basin. He has a glass in one hand and is slowly pouring its green liquid contents over the plate. As he does this, a dark rectangle emerges on the plate's silver surface.

"Do you see how clear the image is?" says Nicéphore without glancing up. "Half a glass of bitumen of Judea with a few drops of lavender oil, that's the key! Such a mixture is much superior to silver chloride. And do you know what is best of all, Claude? The weather does not matter!"

Well, it may not matter to you, but it sure has your brother worried. I don't especially want to be here when Claude announces that the three-colored ones are seeping into the house through cracks in the walls.

I gaze at the image as it continues to form on the plate and compare it against the one in my mission file. This is definitely it—the side of the barn is taking shape and a bit of the pigeon house too.

You can't beat a moment like this. Here I am watching the world's first photograph develop. Too bad Abbie is missing it.

"Two hooks hold the plate in place," I relay over my mindpatch. "You won't need a tool, but you'll have to make sure you hook the replica in exactly the same way. Also, the plate has to be wet. You'll see two glasses on the table. I'm pretty sure the one on the left has water in it. Once you have the replica hooked in, pour some water over it."

"Got it," she mindspeaks.

I glance back at her in admiration. Of all the classic yoga poses, I like pine tree the best, but there's no way I can hold it as long as Abbie. I'm about to suggest that she try some other kind of tree to give her muscles a break, when Claude yells, "Nicéphore!"

Nicéphore looks up and sees me standing next to him.

"Who are you?" he asks.

"My name is Robert," I say. "I am your brother Bernard's wife's sister's son."

"Oh," says Nicéphore, sounding about as excited as someone who has just watched a button fall off of his pantaloons.

40

"Nicéphore, it is starting! We must take action!" Claude shouts.

Nicéphore sighs and walks over to where Claude is by the window.

"There is nothing there," says Nicéphore, in a weary tone that suggests this is not the first time he has uttered these words to his brother.

"Snatch time," I mindspeak, and see Abbie already moving quickly toward the worktable.

"Look carefully, my brother. The tricolored beings are clever. They hide in the rain."

"I am looking carefully. The only things out there are trees," says Nicéphore.

Abbie is standing over the worktable and pulling out the replica. This is the critical moment. If either brother glances back right now, she'll be caught red-handed.

I run up to where the men are standing and point to the sky. "There!" I say. "One of the tricolored beings. I see him!"

Claude and Nicéphore crane their necks in the direction I'm pointing.

"What color is he?" asks Claude, his voice shaking.

"Orange and blue," I whisper, recalling how Claude had described them earlier, "with a touch of red."

Claude has a smug smile on his face. Nicéphore's eyes are narrowed to slits as they search the sky.

I glance back quickly at Abbie. She is arranging her dress over the snatch object. She takes two steps to the right and resumes her pine tree pose.

"This is sheer lunacy," says Nicéphore finally, turning away from the window.

As he turns, he spots Abbie and says, "Who is this girl?"

She ignores him and chants:

"The spirits of the dead who stood
In life before thee, are again
In death around thee, and their will
Shall then overshadow thee—be still."

"She's my sister," I pipe up. "Please excuse her. She is not well. I must get her even higher. Is there access to the roof through the house, monsieur?"

Nicéphore looks from me to Abbie to Claude. I can almost see the gears working in his brain. Poor guy. He must be wondering if it's just his imagination or if everyone around him is losing their marbles.

"That way," he says, pointing to a set of rough wooden stairs near the last window.

I consider asking Claude for a hand, but he looks occupied.

"Come along, sister," I say. Abbie keeps her palms together and walks stiffly with me up the narrow staircase.

The attic only has one tiny window. I stoop to avoid hitting my head on the overhead beams. The room is completely bare except for a simple table and chair. Set into the slanted ceiling directly above the table is a hatch that I almost miss seeing.

I'm about to touch my wrist when Abbie stops me. "Wait, we're not on the roof yet."

"No need to," I say. "We can timeleap from here."

"True," she says. "But who knows when we'll be back in France? C'mon, let's see what the view is like from up there."

Checking my fingernail, I see we've still got eight minutes left. "All right."

I climb on the table and tug at the hatch. On my third try, it opens and light spills into the attic along with some fat raindrops.

42

Abbie scampers onto the table, and I boost her out to the roof.

"Climb up and join me, Cale. It's glorious out here!"

I grab hold of both sides of the hatch, hoist myself up and then crawl on all fours to a spot beside her.

She's right. It's a great view. The road winds past the village into a forest, emerges on the other side and then finally disappears between some distant hills.

It's raining hard now. If we don't timeleap soon, we'll both be completely drenched. But since it's a warm rain, I don't mind it so much. Besides, it feels good to be up here, just the two of us, the snatch under our belts.

Just then Abbie stands up and thrusts her hands to the heavens.

"The spire shudders under the cries of travelers gone mad," she chants, "while the demon's ill-gotten rubies lie undisturbed beneath still, deep waters."

I smile at the sight of her.

I can't help noticing how wet she is and, more to the point, how her wet dress is clinging to her body. While we're on the topic, I also can't help noticing how different her body looks from the way I remember it to be. There are definite curves there. Female curves.

New feelings swirl through me. I look away, embarrassed. But it doesn't seem like Abbie noticed anything. Or, if she has, she's not letting on.

After a moment she sighs. "I'm ready to head back now. You?"

"Sure," I say.

I catch a last glimpse of Abbie as she touches her wrist and is gone.

Just before I timeleap, I gaze out at the horizon. The rain is letting up and the sky is definitely brightening. I wonder if there'll be a rainbow. But I don't stick around to find out. Tap, tap at my wrist and I leave 1826 far behind.

I land in the same place we left from—the alleyway beside Headquarters. Abbie is already there, just coming out of her time freeze.

"I'm going to go ahead and hand in the snatch object, okay, Cale?" she says. "I need to get out of these wet clothes as soon as possible."

I grunt in the affirmative, which is about all I can do until I'm out of my time freeze. As she turns to go, I try not to look at her. That is, I try not to look at her in the same way that I was looking at her on the rooftop in France. Why is that so hard to do? After all, this is Abbie we're talking about. She could be my sister, for all the time we spent together growing up.

As soon as my time freeze thaws, I follow Abbie's trail of drips to the sidewalk and then up the front walk to Headquarters.

"Don't young people these days have any respect?" says Phoebe as soon as I step onto the elevator. Her persona is a little gray-haired woman who looks like she's being swallowed up by a huge armchair. She's knitting something, but I can't tell what it is just yet.

"How do you mean?" I say.

"Just look at your feet," she says, stabbing a knitting needle in the direction of the floor.

I look down. A small puddle, a souvenir from France, is forming near my boots.

"Er . . . sorry. I'll clean it up."

"When?"

"I don't know . . . in a few minutes. As soon as you let me off on four, I'll look around for a rag or something and then come right back."

"And what am I supposed to do in the meantime?" she says.

"You're not the only one who uses this elevator. I get a lot of traffic, you know. They're all going to think I had a little accident on the floor. How can you do this to your grandmother?"

"You're not my grandmother, Phoebe. In fact, you're nobody's grandmother."

She falls silent, and I grind my teeth. True or not, did I really need to add the second bit about her not being anyone's grandmother?

"You hurt my feelings," she says predictably.

I've got to stay calm and work this out. Otherwise, I'll never get to the fourth floor. I wonder what Abbie did about her drips? She was even wetter than me.

"All right, what would you like me to do? Wipe it up with my sleeve?" I say.

"Is your sleeve dry?"

I run my fingers along my sleeve. The outside is still pretty wet, but the part closest to my body is bone dry. "Half and half," I say.

Phoebe's persona looks up from her knitting and gives me a grandmotherly smile. "Well, then, you may use the dry half."

I drop to the floor and wipe the puddle away.

Finally, the elevator starts to move.

"What are you knitting, Phoebe?" I ask to lighten the mood.

"A noose," she says, and we ride the rest of the way in silence.

IV

The couch squeaks in protest as I sit and press the Access button.

The opposite wall retracts, revealing the reception area for Timeless Treasures. It's totally lit up, but even so, before I move, I ready myself. Although Nassim prefers to strike under cover of darkness, he has also been known to launch surprise attacks with all the lights on.

All is quiet, though, when I step through. He must still be with Abbie, completing the paperwork for Operation Shutterbox.

No one is in the hall or in the lounge. Then I remember Frank saying something about going on a collection for Uncle and that the others had traveled back to 2059 on garbage duty.

I enter the boys' dorm, kick off my boots, strip off my wet clothes and flop down on my bed. The room has two double bunk beds. Mine is the lower bunk nearest the door. Raoul, a junior time snatcher, has the bunk above me. Frank sleeps in the other lower. The top bunk above Frank has been empty for about two weeks. Johan, its most recent occupant, went missing during a mission to Renaissance Italy. The word around Timeless Treasures is that he tried to escape but Uncle found him working as a street musician in 1553 Florence and shipped him off to the Barrens as a punishment, leaving Raoul without a partner. Before Johan, there was Vlad, and before Vlad, there was Rudy, who used to sneak out of the dorm late at night and wander the streets of New Beijing aimlessly, carrying a lock of hair that he said belonged to his dog. There were also a couple of others whose names I forget.

In any event, Frank uses the top bunk now as extra storage space for all of his junk. From the look of things, he's brought back souvenirs from every mission he and Lydia have been on plus all of his solo missions. If Lydia did the same, I'm betting the two of them could make a killing holding a garage sale. Some of Frank's stuff, like the coins and pocket watches, doesn't take up that much space, but throw in the upper half of a seventeenth-century suit of armor, a twentieth-century wet suit and a fifteenth-century crossbow, and that bed fills up in no time.

I'm tired. Two snatches is a lot for one day. Of course, Uncle wouldn't call it two because I came back empty-handed from China. Well, I don't want to think about that right now.

I let my thoughts wander, and an image from Beijing pops into my head—of the father swinging his young son through the air. I wish I had known my own father. The way Uncle tells it, just before she died, my mother signed the papers giving me up for adoption. "Your father was never in the picture, Caleb. He abandoned you and your mother right after you were born," was all he said.

For a long time I used to think Uncle made up the whole story of me being adopted so that I'd see him as a hero, saving me from a life on the streets. And if it was a lie, I figured, then Uncle must have kidnapped me—grabbed me away from my parents just like Frank is going to do to that kid. Which, quite frankly, is what I wanted to believe. I just couldn't stand to think of my parents as being dead or as having abandoned me. But now I don't know what I think. A few times, I came close to traveling to my own past to find out the truth. But I stopped myself each time, afraid that if I did go back and found out the real truth, it would be too much for me to handle.

I reach under my bunk and search until I feel the driftwood. It's in its usual spot snug between the bed frame and the mattress.

I found the hand-sized piece of driftwood three years ago on a mission to Tofino, Canada. I read once that real artists don't start with a fixed idea of what their sculpture's going to be. Instead, they try to uncover the sculpture from the piece of stone or wood. I don't consider myself an artist, but I like that idea: taking layers off of something to discover what's really underneath. It took me a whole year to figure out what my wood carving was going to be. I'm fairly sure that I'm uncovering a face, but the jury's still out on whose.

My progress is slow, but I've got it to the point where you can see a bit of the nose and the eyes.

I flip the wood around and look at it from different angles. I wonder if it will have a happy or sad expression.

Running my fingers along the surface, I allow my mind and body to relax. With any luck, I can make some good progress before it's time for supper. But after about a minute, I find it hard to keep my eyes open.

Nassim's voice over the intercom wakes me.

"Good evening, people. Dinner will be in five minutes. The word for this evening is *piào liàng,* translation: 'beautiful.' Everyone must use this word in a sentence at dinner this evening."

I groan. Uncle has been on this Mandarin kick for about a month now. He's convinced that, with the Great Friendship, it's just a matter of time before Mandarin becomes the language of choice for conducting business in the West. Don't get me wrong. I like learning new languages as much as the next guy. But does it have to happen at mealtime?

With some effort, I trudge to the bathroom and wash my face. No matter how tightly I close the tap, water still drips from the faucet. "The only place where a leaky faucet is *piào liàng* is in the desert," I think. Not bad, but I doubt the others will appreciate it.

When I get to the lounge, everyone is already there except for Uncle. I take my usual seat next to Abbie.

Abbie runs a hand through her hair and flashes me a smile.

Lydia is seated on the other side of Abbie. She likes that spot because she can see her reflection in the window. As far as she is concerned, there are not nearly enough mirrors in the world. Apart from loving herself, Lydia's a bit of a mystery. She laughs hard at all Frank's inane jokes, however, which puts her on his team as far as I'm concerned.

Across from Lydia is Raoul. Now, there's a guy who gets my sympathy. He wants to do well but just hasn't got the talent. He can't seem to size up a situation and take appropriate action, which is almost second nature for the rest of us. And he tends to drop stuff. Again, not a great quality for a thief. None of this was obvious while Johan was his partner because I think he used to cover for Raoul. But now with Johan gone his flaws are more noticeable. It's anyone's guess why Uncle still keeps him around.

"Uncle has asked that we start without him," says Nassim, and immediately I can feel the tension in the room go down.

"He will join us as soon as he finishes up with a client," he continues, and the tension ratchets back up a notch.

"Caleb, will you say the prayer, please?"

I look down at my plate. Saying the blessing is still fairly new. Uncle introduced the idea a couple of weeks ago, saying that studies show that saying a prayer before eating has spiritual and physical health benefits. Healthy or not, I hate it. We're not allowed to say the same one twice, and all the variations of the easy ones are already long used up. Then I remember something I saw on a Domino's pizza billboard on West Broadway.

"A slice is twice as nice as rice. Amen."

Nassim opens his mouth as if he's about to say something but then closes it.

Frank gets up. "Abbie, would you like to help me serve the Peking duck?"

She jumps out of her seat, as if her pants are on fire. "You made Peking duck, Frank? You're amazing."

And there it is. She thinks he's amazing just because he can cook a dead bird. But this isn't the first time I've heard Abbie say the words *amazing* and *Frank* in the same sentence. Why anyone would be impressed with Frank easily makes my top ten list of life's greatest mysteries (I have it as number four, right between Stonehenge and the Pyramids). Maybe it's his looks: I suppose he could be considered handsome by some members of the opposite sex, what with all those muscles and teeth. Not that he has more teeth than average—they're just so blindingly white. Or maybe it's his take-charge attitude. Whatever. In my book, Frank is totally false: he cares only about himself. Plus, if he sees you as a threat, he'll do everything in his power to take you down.

I slouch in my chair. Much as I can't stand Frank, I have to admit he's good at everything he does, including cooking. And with the Great Friendship, he's expanded his repertoire to Chinese dishes.

A minute later, he returns, toting a huge platter with a shiny brown roast duck on it. Abbie is right behind him with a plate of cucumbers and a bowl of sauce.

He starts carving up the bird with expert strokes. Frankly, I'm surprised that Uncle okayed this meal. That duck must have been *très* expensive.

Just then, Nassim sits up ramrod straight. Next, I hear crisp, military-like footfalls coming down the hall. Only one person walks that way.

"Good evening, all," says Uncle as he sweeps into the room. He's wearing a bright yellow silk robe with red dragons up and down the sleeves, which, as he likes to point out, is a *hanfu,* the same kind of robe the emperors of ancient China wore. But it doesn't end there. He's got a funny-looking black hat on that looks like the ones university students wear when they graduate. Except that his has strands of pearls dangling from the front and back. And to top it all off, tucked into his belt is the most amazing sword I've ever seen: polished dark wood handle encrusted with rubies and emeralds and a wicked-looking blade.

"Good evening, Uncle," we all say at once.

He tilts his head up and breathes in. "Glorious!" he says. "Who is responsible for this wonderful aroma?"

"Frank cooked tonight, boss," says Nassim.

"Excellent," says Uncle, taking his seat at the head of the table and digging in.

We eat in silence. The key to eating when Uncle's around is to finish before him because he doesn't like people eating when he's talking. The problem is he's a speedy eater, and sometimes it's really tough to keep up.

While I chow down, I sneak glances to see how far along he is. On my third glance, Uncle's already dabbing his mouth with his napkin.

"A wonderful meal," he proclaims. "My compliments to the chef." He tips his head toward Frank.

"Thank you, Uncle," says Frank, beaming.

"No. Thank *you*, Frank!" Uncle repeats. "Did you know, people," he continues, "that in addition to his fine abilities as chef, Frank completed fifteen snatches so far this month?"

While everyone else oohs and ahhs, I'm doing some quick calculations in my head. By my count, including the Great Friendship flag, Frank actually has sixteen snatches to my eighteen. But Uncle said fifteen. He must not have counted the Great Friendship flag as one of Frank's completed snatches. But why not?

"Before we begin with the sentences you have been asked to prepare," says Uncle, "I'd like to tell a short story."

I fidget in my seat. It's going to be a long night. Despite what he said, Uncle doesn't tell short stories.

"This particular story is true," Uncle says. "Some of you may have heard it before. It is the story of the beginning of Timeless Treasures."

We all smile. Each of us has heard the story at least a million times. But it's one of his all-time favorites, and it would be unwise for any of us to point that out.

"At the time, I was a young man, not much older than each of you," begins Uncle. "One of my favorite activities was to wander through Central Park late at night and see what I could see."

What he really means is "steal what I could steal."

"One night, while prowling the park," he continues, "I came upon an old woman seated on a bench. She looked no different than any of the other deranged people I had often encountered on my nocturnal wanderings—her hair was a frazzle of gray, and she wore layers and layers of mismatched clothes. A shopping cart next to the bench contained all of her earthly possessions. I approached her very

52

carefully with my hands in full view. One had to be that way with the old ones, you know, because some of them grew their fingernails quite long and weren't shy to use them if they felt threatened.

"In fact, the old woman was not particularly pleased to see me. I distinctly remember her baring her yellowed teeth, much like a cornered animal, and growling at me to leave."

"So what did you do, Uncle?" asks Lydia. Leave it to her to encourage him. Why is she even asking the question? We all know exactly what he did.

"Well, Lydia," says Uncle, "I actually would have left the park at that point, had I not noticed that one of the old woman's hands was clenched tight around something and that, even as she was warning me away, she kept sneaking glances at her fist. I sensed that whatever she held in her hand was very important. At that moment, I made up my mind not to leave until I found out what it was."

"How did you get her to show you, Uncle?" she asks.

If I wasn't afraid that Uncle might intercept it, I would have mindlinked Lydia to tell her what I thought about her inane questions.

But Uncle doesn't appear to mind. He smiles at her and continues.

"I reached into my pocket, withdrew a silver dollar and offered to give her the coin if she would show me what was in her hand. I know what you are all thinking. Why should I give something for nothing? But in fact I was about to gain something very valuable from the old woman, my friends. Something that made my little trade of the coin worthwhile.

"I could tell that she did not entirely trust me, so I laid the coin on the bench next to her. Quick as a wink, one of her hands reached out, snatched up the coin and buried it deep inside her clothes."

"Did she show you what she had in her hand then?" asks Lydia.

"Not right away," continues Uncle. "In fact, she just growled again at me to leave. But a bargain is a bargain, and I was not about to depart until the old woman had held up her end. Since she was not forthcoming, I had to convince her to open up her hand. One can do that, you know, with fingers. Particularly old, brittle fingers."

I cringe. That part always gives me a queasy feeling.

"At last," he continues, "I could see what those old arthritic fingers held. It was a yellowed and creased slip of paper folded in four. I unfolded it and discovered that it was a playbill from Radio City Music Hall. The playbill advertised the 1965 Christmas Spectacular starring the world-famous Rockettes.

"Although it was old, the image on the playbill was clearly visible: a line of a dozen or so long-legged and scantily dressed dancers, standing storklike on one leg, smiling faces tilted up toward the bright lights of Radio City Music Hall. There was a crude circle drawn in black ink around one of the dancers.

"'Is that you?' I asked the woman, pointing to the circled dancer. But of course I didn't need to ask. I already knew that it was. And do you know what I did then?" asks Uncle.

"No, we don't, Uncle," Lydia lies.

"I placed the playbill back in her hand and went on my way." He pauses for a second before continuing, for dramatic effect. "Ever since that chance meeting in the park, the image of the old woman's gnarled fingers clinging to that ancient playbill, grasping, one might say, at a piece of the past, has been etched in my mind.

"And several years later, when I came upon an opportunity to develop a way to travel through time, it occurred to me that I could do a great service to humanity by providing people with access to precious pieces of the past, much like that old woman's playbill.

"The rest is history, as they say. I recruited each of you, my very first time snatchers, to assist in the retrieval of special treasures from the past."

Uncle pauses again, and I wonder if he's waiting for us to clap or something. It's a great story, all right. The thing I've always wondered about is what happened to his silver dollar. My guess is he didn't go home without it.

He looks wistful for a moment, then clears his throat and says, "Now, are all of you ready with your sentences? As a reminder, the word for this evening is *piào liàng,* which means 'beautiful.'"

I nod along with the others, even though I'll have to make something up on the fly. Luckily, Uncle usually starts at one end of that table and never at the middle.

"Caleb, you're first," he says.

So much for that theory.

"The, uh, sunset in Beijing is *piào liàng,*" I say.

"Nice," says Uncle. "Lydia, you're next."

"There's nothing more *piào liàng* than a well-performed snatch," she says.

"Marvelous!" Uncle pounds the tabletop. "Raoul?"

"This meal is *piào liàng,*" he says.

"Yes, it is, Raoul," Uncle says, smiling. "Frank?"

"The person who helped me serve tonight is *piào liàng,*" he says with a sly smile in Abbie's direction.

I shoot a glance at Abbie. I can't believe it. She's eating it up. Actually blushing. And now she's gazing at Frank with a faraway look in her eyes.

"And finally, Abbie," Uncle says.

She glances at him for a second and then looks right back at Frank, all dreamy-like. For his part, Frank's beaming his thousand-watt smile right at her.

This is too much. I feel like crawling into a hole.

Abbie clears her throat and says, "Black, curly hair is *piào liàng*."

Make that a really dark hole.

They're still making eyes at each other when I finally decide I've had enough.

"May I be excused, Uncle?" I say, standing up. "I'm not feeling well."

"In a moment, Caleb," he says. "First, I'd like to announce the winner of time snatcher of the month."

Even though there's more than a week left in June, Uncle's already made his decision.

I sit back down again and glance over at Frank. He's got a smug smile on his face. I'm sure he thinks he has this month all locked up. Difficult as it is now to live with Frank, if he wins, that will be the third month in a row, and he'll be unbearable to be around.

I don't hold out much hope of winning myself. I would, I suppose, if Uncle based it purely on the number of completed snatches, but he obviously doesn't. In fact, I have no clue how he goes about making his decision.

"This month's winner is . . . Lydia!" announces Uncle.

Lydia is barely able to contain herself. She leaps up from her place at the table, claps her hands and shouts, "Yay!"

"Congratulations, Lydia," he says, "on a job well done. Have you chosen your reward?"

Is he kidding? Lydia lives for moments like these. I'm sure she's known for at least a month where she wants to go. The prize for winning is an all-expenses-paid weekend at one of Uncle's vacation properties. He's got about a dozen different holiday homes tucked away in some pretty cool locations.

"Yes, Uncle, I know exactly where I'd like to go—to your castle in Scotland," she says.

That's a surprise. I would have figured her for a beach holiday. But then again I hear Uncle's castle has a lot of mirrors, which would be a big drawing card for Lydia.

"Excellent. Nassim will help with the arrangements. Caleb, if you are still feeling unwell, you may leave the table."

"Thank you, Uncle," I say getting up.

"*Bú yòng xiè*, Caleb. You are welcome," he replies. "Frank will put some dessert aside for you so that you can have it when you're feeling better."

Frank, ever-obedient as far as Uncle is concerned, leaps out of his chair and heads for the kitchen. My eyes meet Abbie's for a second, and I see surprise and confusion in them. Doesn't she get why I'm leaving the table?

As I pass the kitchen, Frank pokes his *piào liàng* head out.

"I hope it wasn't anything I said," he says, smirking.

He'd love for me to react. To yell at him or push him or do anything that he can use against me. But I refuse to give him the pleasure. I keep my eyes straight ahead and brush by him. I can feel his eyes on my back all the way to the dorm.

I flop down on my bunk and take out my carving. Looking at it now, I decide it's not good at all. I'm tempted to throw it against the wall and see what smashes first: the carving or the wall. Instead I put it back in its place and bury my head in the pillow.

I must have slept, because I wake up to rays of sunlight poking through the blinds. Snoring from above tells me Raoul is still asleep. Frank's bunk is empty. I swing my legs over the side of the bed and trudge to the bathroom. Gazing at myself in the mirror, I run my fingers through my scraggly hair. It's definitely getting too long. I could use a haircut. Maybe after my mission.

Mission! I almost forgot. I've got the London mission today or, as Abbie calls it, Operation Bumbershoot. And I'm supposed to meet her there. What time, though? I draw a complete blank. I brush my teeth, head over to the wardrobe closet in the lounge and find the clothes that have been placed in my cubbyhole. A floor-length kaftan? That seems fine for a desert mission but a strange choice for twenty-first century London. For a moment I think of asking Nassim about it but then I decide not to—he's a careful type, so I'm sure he must have a good reason for wanting me to dress this way.

I duck back into the dorm and slip the kaftan on over my sandals.

Next, a pit stop in the kitchen for a glass of orange juice and some toast. While I munch, I check the cooking schedule stuck to the fridge door. It's my turn to cook tonight. Cooking is not my first love . . . or even my second, third or fourth. In fact, on the likeability scale, I'd put it right near the bottom, just above saying the dinner prayers. Unfortunately, hating to cook is no excuse in Uncle's world.

I swing the fridge door open, expecting the worst. But it's not so bad. There are three or four kinds of vegetables and lots of pasta sauce: it won't be a gourmet meal like last night, but at least it'll be something.

"You've got something on your face," says a voice.

"Good morning, Phoebe," I say, reaching for a napkin.

Wiping my mouth, I glance at the wall screen. Phoebe's persona is wearing a black evening gown encrusted with tiny crystals and is carrying a matching purse.

"Have you seen Abbie?" I ask.

"First, what do you think of my outfit?" she says.

I don't usually have an opinion about clothes for computer personas, but the only way I'll ever get an answer to my question is to have this conversation first.

"Very nice," I say.

"Go on," she says. "What else?"

"Very nice and . . . very sparkly."

Phoebe's persona frowns. "And . . ."

"And very . . . slimming," I add.

There's a long silence as she no doubt analyzes the compliment quotient in my words.

"All right, I suppose that will do," she says. "Now I will answer your question: Abbie just left for London."

"Okay, thanks," I say, heading out of the kitchen.

"But if I were you, I wouldn't go just yet," Phoebe continues.

"Why not?" I say.

"Well, just look at the way you're dressed."

I think for a moment before continuing the conversation. The thing with Phoebe is she loves to argue. Give her an opening, and she'll go for your throat. I'm already regretting having said good morning to her.

"Thanks. I'll consider your advice," I say finally.

"You'll 'consider my advice'?" she says. "If I were you, I'd be doing more than considering my advice. I'd at least be changing out of those pajamas."

I just smile and head for the fire escape. It's much easier to time-leap from outside than inside. Uncle says it has to do with the fact that this building, like a lot of others in Tribeca and SoHo, has a cast-iron frame behind its brick walls. Apparently, the cast iron interferes with the frequencies needed for time travel. I'm no scientist, but it seems to me that if you're going to run a time-travel thievery business, wouldn't it make more sense to find a place that's time-travel friendly?

I'm about to tap my wrist when I realize that I forgot to do something. I hurry back inside.

"Back so soon?" Phoebe snickers.

"Phoebe, can you please upload the briefing notes for the London mission to my patch?"

There's a moment of silence, before she says, "I can. But it'll cost you."

I snort involuntarily. "Cost me? But isn't it your job?" I regret the words almost as soon as I say them.

"I'll consider your advice," mimics Phoebe.

Must stay calm. Counting quietly to ten usually works. I'm at nine and seven-eighths when a short beep from my wrist tells me that the mission information has been uploaded.

"Thanks, Phoebe." As I step out onto the fire escape, I think I hear Phoebe say something, but I can't make out the words. It could be "you're welcome" or maybe just an insult that sounds like that.

I slowly open my eyes and see brick walls, cobblestones and a bit of sky. I've landed in an alley.

It feels good to be on a mission again. I take a deep breath and step out onto a sidewalk. Mid-morning, and it's already sweltering. Dozens of shoppers are out and about. The street is crammed with small shops and pubs. The one closest to me, the Lazy Lizard Pub, has a sign showing a lizard lounging in a hammock. Right next door to it is Ye Stinky Cheese Shoppe, and it's sure living up to its name.

Then I remember. The cheese shop. That's where I'm supposed to meet up with Abbie. I'm almost there when I feel a tap on my shoulder.

"Good morning, Cale," says Abbie, smiling. "What do you think?"

Why is everyone asking me for my opinion on what they are wearing? First Phoebe and now Abbie. It's not like I'm any kind of fashion guru. Far from it.

Abbie does a slow spin. Her costume for the snatch is a navy blue pinstriped power pantsuit with horn-rimmed sunglasses. To complete the picture, her auburn hair is tied back neatly in a bun. If you didn't know she was a thirteen-year-old time-traveling orphan, you would think she was eighteen and probably someone's executive assistant. Still, it wouldn't be my first choice of disguise for a snatch at an umbrella factory.

One thing I'll admit, though. Abbie's outfit makes her look . . . well, female. If her idea was to distract me, it's definitely working.

"Uhh. It's chic," I say, hoping I got the pronunciation right.

She waves me over to a bench, and we watch the steady stream of shoppers. I'm very aware of her sitting next to me. In fact, I'm more aware of her body next to me than I am of anything else in the world right now. She shifts position, and I can feel her leg touching mine. What's going on? There's room for about four people on this bench, so why is she crowding me? Except it doesn't feel like crowding at all. It feels like something else. A new and strange feeling that, ever since France, my brain has been working overtime to figure out. I'm not sure I like this. But then again, I don't want her to move her leg away, either.

"Don't you just love the hustle and bustle of this place?" she asks and moves even closer to me.

"Yes, excellent hustle and bustle," I agree, squirming.

An elderly woman in a paisley dress toddles by and gives me a disapproving look.

"Don't mind her," Abbie says. "I think you look cute in pajamas."

"These aren't pajamas," I say. "Nassim picked out—"

"No need to say anything, Cale. I'm touched that you were in such a hurry to meet up with me that you forgot to get dressed. By the way, how are you feeling? You cut out early last night. Do you think it was something you ate?"

"I'm fine," I lie. There goes my good mood. Now all I'm feeling is annoyed and confused. Annoyed that someone who supposedly knows me so well can't figure out that the real reason I left the table early was because she was totally ignoring me and making goo-goo eyes at Frank. And confused because I don't know what to do with these new feelings I have about Abbie. Should I tell her? Not tell her? I'm dying to know how she feels about me, but there's no way I'm asking. What if she doesn't get it? Or what if she says she thinks of me like a brother? I'll be totally crushed. Maybe I should write to Ask Natasha. I could sign the letter "Baffled in New Beijing." Or better yet, I can mail it from here and sign it "Loveless in London."

"Good. I'm glad you're feeling better," she says, standing up. I feel a small wave of disappointment as the contact between our legs is broken. "Time to get going. The Brolly Shoppe awaits."

"Did you say 'shop'? I thought we were going to an umbrella *factory*."

"Didn't you read your briefing notes for Operation Bumbershoot, Mr. Pajama Top?" she says, pointing across the street. "The umbrella we're after is in that shop right over there."

"I don't see why we have to come all the way here just to pick up a stupid umbrella. There are plenty of umbrella shops in 2061." I can hear the negative tone in my voice, but I can't help it. I'm in a foul mood.

"Maybe, but none of them carry the umbrella that Winston Churchill, Britain's Prime Minister during World War II, brought with him to Harrow School in 1941 when he made one of the most famous speeches in history," says Abbie. "You know . . . 'never give in . . . '"

"I don't see why he even bothered with an umbrella," I say. "I mean, it's not like he had to walk far to get there. He had his own chauffeur. Besides, what is Churchill's umbrella doing here, in an umbrella shop in Kensington, sixty-five years later?"

Children pour out of the cheese shop, poking at each other. Their laughter stabs my ears.

Abbie squints at me. Her expression is halfway between concerned and annoyed. "I don't know how it got here. What's the difference? Why are you in such a bad mood?"

Glad you finally noticed, I feel like saying but instead just sit there, the perfect picture of gloom.

"Is this about Frank?" she says.

"Maybe," I answer.

She sighs. "I don't see what your problem is with him. Did you taste that duck he cooked last night? It was awesome."

"That's nothing," I say. "Wait till you see what I'm cooking tonight."

"Oh, really?" she says, moving closer. "What is it?"

"I . . . uh . . . can't tell you just yet," I say, immediately regretting my words. After all, when it comes to cooking, there's no way I can compete with Frank.

"Cale," says Abbie, taking half a step back, "you should really try to get along better with Frank. He's not so bad."

"Not so bad? He's been poaching my snatches! What could possibly be 'not so bad' about that?"

"I think you're overreacting. Frank told me all about it. He said you were walking around Beijing sightseeing instead of doing the snatch. So Uncle sent him to do it."

"And you buy that?" I blurt out. I can't believe what I'm hearing. From my own snatch partner, no less. "Frank told me all about it." What else is Frank telling her? I can feel my face getting hot.

"Let's talk about something else," she says, "like how you're going to do the snatch in your long underwear."

"This isn't long underwear!" I say a little too loudly.

"Whatever. Pajamas. Wait, I've got it!" Abbie's eyes are shining.

She does a pirouette on the spot. "Nineteen sixty-two. Paris. The Hope Diamond heist. Remember?"

"Sure, I remember," I say. How could I forget? It was a perfectly executed snatch. For a month after, no one had a clue the world's largest diamond had been stolen. But the best thing about Paris was the bowl of French onion soup. Easily the best I've ever tasted in my life. Just thinking about that bowl of soup is easing the tension in my shoulders.

"Well, same thing," she says. "Only this time, we switch roles. You'll be the VIP, and I'll be your aide-de-camp. Also, I'll do all the talking."

"Hold on. Didn't I give you a two-word allowance in Paris?" I ask.

Abbie flicks a piece of fluff off her suit jacket. "Well, maybe," she says slowly. "All right. You get two words, Cale. But that's all."

"Plus variations," I say.

She raises her eyebrows. "You drive a hard bargain, mister. Okay, plus variations. But you'd better pick them fast. We've only got sixteen minutes left."

I think for a moment and then say, "*Cincinnati* and *Ohio*." Technically, they're place names and not real words, but Abbie doesn't seem to object.

"Fine. Now, you see the Brolly Shoppe's picture window?" she says, pointing. "We're going to cross and stand right in front of it. As soon as we get there, start swooning."

"Swooning?"

"You know: fainting, falling down, collapsing, hitting the deck. Whatever you want to call it. Just make it look real, okay? And here," she adds, handing me her sunglasses. "Take these, Your Excellency."

"Your Excellency?"

"Uh-uh." Abbie shakes her head. "Remember? No talking from here on in except for your two words . . . and variations."

I nod and we cross the street. A strong smell wafts from the Ye Stinky Cheese Shoppe.

As soon as we arrive in front of the umbrella shop, Abbie turns to me and says in a loud voice, "You're looking pale, Your Excellency. In fact, if we don't find some relief for you from this bright sun, I'm afraid you may not be able to carry on. But look, Your Excellency, good fortune is smiling on us. An umbrella shop!"

"Cincina!" I shout.

The carved woodcut sign above the door says JOHN WESTERBROOKE AND SON, ESTABLISHED 1835. And below that, in mirrored glass, UMBRELLAS, TROPICAL SUNSHADES, FOLDING UMBRELLAS, WALKING STICKS.

I gaze at the display. Someone has gone to a lot of effort to build a wheel made entirely of umbrellas. I continue to stare until I see Abbie's face reflected in the window. She's giving me the look of death.

"Swoon!" she commands over my mindpatch.

I swoon. To my credit, it's a brilliant bit of acting: I go down heavy, banging my elbow and scraping my knee on the sidewalk.

A chubby man appears at my side and helps me up. Another man, this one wearing suspenders and a narrow brown necktie, comes rushing out of the umbrella shop to help. Out of the corner of my "royal" eye, I can see Abbie's frown turn into a tight smile.

"Your Excellency, are you all right?" she asks.

"Nati. Nati," I say, stumbling a bit.

"We must get you inside and sitting down, Excellency." Abbie takes my arm. I feel a tingle at her touch, which surprises and embarrasses me at the same time. But I don't think she notices. She's too caught up in her performance.

"Sir, would you be so good as to assist?" she asks the man wearing suspenders.

"Certainly, miss." He takes my other arm and they lead me into the Brolly Shoppe. I play up my dizzy monarch role, swaying slightly before they plop me down onto a chair.

There are umbrellas everywhere: hanging from the walls and the ceilings, standing tall in bins scattered throughout the shop. Big. Small. In every color of the rainbow. There's even an umbrella with a map of London on it.

"I'm so sorry about this," Abbie says to the shopkeeper. "His Excellency has a very delicate constitution. He simply cannot tolerate being out in the sun for long periods of time."

"Ohi. Cinci," I concur.

The shopkeeper looks at me with wide eyes and then says to Abbie under his breath, but loud enough for me to hear, "He don't speak the Queen's English, then? Tell me, in his own country . . . is the boy somebody important . . . y'know . . . high up?"

She looks him right in the eye and whispers, "He wasn't until two weeks ago. High up, that is. But then his older brother, the king of Lower Slobovia, died."

"The king—you don't say," the shopkeeper whispers back, his eyes even wider than before. He skips to the front of the store and flips the sign on the door to Closed.

"It was sad, really. He died of . . . too much sunshine," Abbie says.

"No! You don't say," says the shopkeeper.

"I'm afraid so. But not to worry. Except for his sunlight allergy, His Excellency is in perfect physical condition."

Abbie glances around the shop, looking impatient. I have to admit it—she's smooth. Still, I wouldn't mind if she got to the snatch part a bit quicker.

The shopkeeper breaks the silence first. "Well, we do have umbrellas here, miss. Perhaps Your—I mean, His Excellency would like one."

"That's very generous," says Abbie, smiling. "But you mustn't feel obliged to *give* His Excellency an umbrella."

"Cin, cinnat, nati," I agree wholeheartedly.

"Well, I wasn't exactly thinking 'bout giving it to him for fr—" begins the shopkeeper.

But by then, Abbie is already halfway across the floor of the shop. She plucks a green umbrella with an intricately carved handle from a glass display case and examines it.

"This is the one, Cale," she mindspeaks to me. Out loud to the shopkeeper she says, "This umbrella will be acceptable."

The shopkeeper's face goes white. "Oh, not that one, please, miss. It's a one of a kind, you see. A Frederick Blackman. You can see his initials carved right there in the handle. There are only a handful of Frederick Blackmans left in the world and only one in this color. Picked it up at Randolph Churchill's estate sale for a song. It might even have been used by Winnie himself at one time. I'm terribly sorry, but it's not for sale. How 'bout a very nice—"

"Sir, quickly"—Abbie cuts him off—"what level of security are you cleared for?"

"What d'you mean, miss?" asks the shopkeeper.

There he goes with the wide eyes again. Only this time, he leaves his jaw hanging open, too.

"I mean, sir," says Abbie, still clutching the Frederick Blackman, "your telephone is about to ring, and I must know this instant if your security clearance is high enough for you to answer it!"

"Well I—" begins the shopkeeper.

The next second the phone rings.

"Never mind." Abbie rushes toward the counter. "I'll get it."

"Hello? Yes, Your Majesty," she says. "Thank you, ma'am. His Excellency's trip was very comfortable. Buckingham Palace? Of course we can. As soon as His Excellency recovers."

Abbie nods into the phone. "Yes, I'm afraid so. His Excellency's had one of his spells. . . . Oh, that's very kind, ma'am. Thank you, but really there's no need for your personal physician. . . . We are here at . . ."

She pulls the phone away from her ear for a moment and looks inquiringly at the shopkeeper, who has taken up a position behind the counter.

"The Brolly Shoppe, miss," he pipes up. "Tell 'er Majesty yer at the Brolly Shoppe on Kensington High Street. And that Nick Wester-brooke is taking personal care o' you. That's Westerbrooke with an *e*," he says, straightening his tie.

She nods quickly and turns her attention back to the phone. "The Brolly Shoppe, ma'am. And we're being attended to by the owner himself . . . a Mr. Westinghouse. . . . Yes . . . I'm certain we'll be able to depart shortly. Mr. Washinghook has offered to sell us one of his umbrellas so that His Excellency can carry on without a relapse. . . ."

Abbie continues. "Yes, I did say 'sell,' ma'am. . . . No, I wouldn't dream of asking Mr. Westernwind to simply gift it to His Excellency. . . . Well, that's true, I suppose. . . . I don't think he realizes how important it is for Britain and Lower Slobovia to maintain good relations. . . . But, truly, ma'am, I would not want to embarrass him—"

"Wait!" yells the shopkeeper, hopping over the counter. "Tell the Queen that I'll give it to His Excellency for free. And tell her that Nick Westerbrooke is a friend to all nations o' the world."

Abbie smiles. "Thank you . . . uh, Nick."

"Atti O." I give him a nod.

"Yes, ma'am, he has," she says. "He is a most delightful fellow. All right. I will happily do so." Then she hangs up.

"Mr. . . . Westermess?" Abbie says, looking at Nick. "Her Majesty thanks you immensely and says that she will commend you personally when she comes and visits your shop."

"Thank you. Oh, thank you." The shopkeeper kisses Abbie's hand.

After a moment, he holds his hands out and says, "May I?"

She gives a little nod and hands him the Frederick Blackman. He turns and heads my way, cradling the umbrella in his hands. When he reaches me, he kneels and presents it to me sideways like a knight tendering his sword. "Please, Your Majes . . . I mean Your Most Excellency. I would be honored if you would take this umbrella as a gift of friendship from the British people."

"Cincina. Ohi. Ocinci," I say, which is my longest speech of the day.

"His Excellency says thank you," Abbie translates as she helps me to my feet and hustles me to the door. "Farewell and thank you, sir. You have done a great service to your country."

"An honor, miss," says the shopkeeper, giving a little bow.

"Hio!" I waggle three of my royal fingers his way.

We begin walking away but don't get more than five steps before the shopkeeper comes running up to us, out of breath. "Miss, did the queen say when she was coming by?"

"No, but don't let that worry you," she says. "She's really not allowed to say those sorts of things over the telephone. Security concerns, you know."

"Oh, yes, of course," says Nick. "Well, I'll be here. I always am."

"Good," says Abbie, nodding. She turns back my way. "Come along now, Your Excellency. We're expected at the palace."

She slips her arm under mine and continues walking. There it is again. The same squirmy but exciting feeling I felt before. Abbie, on the other hand, doesn't look the least bit uncomfortable. Did she take my arm as part of the act? You know—the loyal aide-de-camp leading the monarch of Lower Slobovia to his next social engagement? Or is she doing this because she likes me? I mean, as in she *really* likes me.

A peek at my fingernail tells me we've completed the snatch with three and a half minutes to spare. That's plenty of time to find a quiet spot for the timeleap back to Headquarters.

The sun hits my eyes and I hoist the umbrella over my head, wrong end up.

"Nati?" I inquire, and this sends us both into gales of laughter.

It feels good to be here with Abbie, walking together and laughing. Just the two of us. I want to hold on to this moment forever.

"How'd you do that thing with the phone?" I ask.

She gives my arm a little squeeze and fishes something from her pants pocket. It's a blue sphere about the same size as a Ping-Pong ball. "It's fairly new. Uncle only got them in this week. It can set off anything you want within fifty feet."

"Impressive," I say.

She replaces the device in her pocket, slips her hand inside her suit jacket and pulls out a folded yellow umbrella. She's smooth. I hadn't even seen her steal it.

"Why two umbrellas?" I ask. "We only needed to snatch one."

"Two is always better than one, Caleb of Cincinnati," she says. "Besides, who knows? It may rain on our next mission."

"Where is our next mission, anyway?" I say. It's easier to ask Abbie than to check the mission schedule myself.

"I don't know," she says. "It's listed as TBA."

To be announced. So Uncle hasn't yet provided details of the snatch to Nassim or to Phoebe. That could be because he hasn't gotten around to doing it. But more likely it means that there's something special about the snatch—something that Uncle wants to tell us himself.

I'm about to say something, and that's when I see them. A family of five walking our way. The parents are holding hands and smiling. Right behind are three children, two girls and a boy. The older girl looks to be about my age. I peg her sister at twelve years old and her brother around five. He has the same mousy brown hair as me. The girls have grabbed hold of his arms and are swinging him along as they walk. The expression on the boy's face is one of total happiness.

I stop and watch them pass. Feelings begin to stir deep inside me. Strong feelings that I don't completely understand. I push them away. Out of sight, out of mind.

"What's the matter, Cale? Is everything okay?" Abbie says.

"Sure," I say. "Everything's fine." But even as I say it, I know it's not true.

"Why don't I handle the check-in with Nassim," she says, grabbing the Frederick Blackman from me. "You take a break. And maybe a shower too."

Abbie ducks into a narrow lane. I'm not more than a couple of steps in before she vanishes. I raise my arm and sniff. Eww! She's right. I give my wrist a tap, and the only thing I leave behind in London is my body odor.

VI

June 23, 2061, 9:33 A.M.
Tribeca, New Beijing (formerly New York City)

I land near the side entrance door of the brownstone across the street from Headquarters. My sudden arrival six inches from where she's standing startles a tall, spiky-haired woman and her Chihuahua. The combination of the woman's scream and the yappy dog's bark feels like someone's driving a spike into my ears. I generally like to land in quiet, out-of-the-way places where my arrival won't attract attention, but what can I do? This is New York. Correction: New Beijing.

As soon as the time freeze wears off, I backpedal and mutter my apologies. But the little dog isn't the forgiving kind. She lunges for my ankle, which I suspect is as high as the wretched thing can jump, and I spend the next minute and a half trying to shake her off.

Finally, I manage to rid myself of the ankle biter and cross the street. The mega-sized screen at the top of 181 Franklin is flashing the results from last night's game. Boston Red Sox 8, Beijing Blue Dragons 1. I don't see why they even bother announcing the score: no one around here gives two hoots about the Blue Dragons. If you ask a hundred New Yorkers what they like least about the Great Friendship, they'll all say the same thing: swapping the Yankees with Beijing's pro baseball team. No one would have objected if it had been the horrible Knicks, but the Yankees? It's like a stab through the heart.

I pause for a moment in front of Headquarters. It's one of those

73

perfect New York days: light breeze, warm but not too warm and a brilliant blue sky. I take a deep breath and fill my lungs. It amazes me sometimes how much my moods are influenced by the weather.

Then the front door opens and Frank steps out. Good-bye, perfect day.

"Hey, Caleb, what's up?" he says.

As he walks down the steps toward me, I study his grin. When you live with someone, you get to know their facial expressions. Even at ten paces away, I can tell that this isn't his usual "I'm better than you" smile. There's something else to it. A slight raising of one eyebrow. A subtle flaring of the nostrils. Yes, this look says "I know something you don't know."

"Nice dress," says Frank. "Been out shopping for a matching purse?"

There's more than just the usual snicker in his little jab. He's definitely holding back. Then it clicks in my brain.

"It was you, wasn't it?" I say. "You changed my clothes for the London mission."

"Are you accusing me?" he says and I immediately know from his tone of voice that my guess is right on the money.

"Accusing you?" I say. "Me? Never. You were right. I was out purse shopping. You won't believe the choices they had. In fact I saw one that I almost got for you. It was made from porcupine skin. You just have to be a bit careful when you use the shoulder strap."

"Very funny," he says.

I begin to walk past him.

"Hey, not so fast." Frank steps in front of me and puts a hand on my shoulder. I lift it off.

"If you don't mind," I say, "I'm in kind of a hurry."

"Really?" he asks.

"Yeah, really," I answer.

"So unfriendly. That's hardly the way to speak to your roommate. Especially when he's about to do you a favor."

That's precious. I can't remember the last time Frank did me a favor. But instead I say, "You're right. I should be friendlier. Let me see . . . oh, yes. Your duck last night was . . . ducky."

"Thank you, Caleb. I got quite a few compliments. Abbie's was the best, though. I'm actually going to see her now. She likes to hang with me, you know."

It's a good thing he can't see past my closed mouth, because I'm grinding my teeth big-time. If I was being honest with myself, which is something I usually try to avoid, I'd have to admit that Frank's not stretching the truth about Abbie liking to hang with him. I've seen it myself.

"And," continues Frank, "here's my favor—a heads-up that Uncle is looking for you. He wants to see you right away."

This is rotten news. But I can't let Frank know that he's succeeded in making me feel miserable. I mentally flip through all my available options. I choose cagey.

"Yeah, I know," I say, as casually as I can manage. "I'm on my way to see him right now. He needs my opinion on something."

Bull's-eye! There's an immediate change in Frank's face. Mostly around the area of his eyes. Only a moment ago they were gleaming with sheer delight at my suffering. Now they're narrowed to slits.

"Really. What does he need your opinion on?" he asks.

"Oops," I say. "I'm not supposed to talk about it. See you later."

I step around him and bound up the steps. Who knows? Maybe what I said is true. Maybe Uncle really does want to pick my brain; to consult with me on a matter of national importance like what color to paint the bookshelf in the lounge. But I doubt it. It's not his style.

There's only one reason Uncle ever wants to meet with me one-on-one: to chew me out for something I did wrong.

"Four, please, Phoebe," I say, as the elevator door closes.

"Hold your horses," she answers. "First, did you notice what I'm wearing?"

I sigh and turn to the wall screen. Phoebe's persona is dressed in a skin-tight lime green bodysuit and her head is covered by a helmet with the Timeless Treasures logo on it. The racing bib she's wearing over her suit says 99.

"Bobsled?" I guess.

"Close," she says. "Luge. I'm in training for the next Olympics."

In my wildest dreams, I don't see how a computer can compete in the luge event at the Olympic Games, but I keep the thought to myself.

"Well, good luck with that," I say. "Can you please bring me to four?"

"Sure thing," says Phoebe. "Regular speed or express?"

If I don't answer, she'll tell me anyway, so I say, "How fast is express?"

"Eighty-six miles an hour—the same as the top speed of the luge," she says.

"And regular speed?" I ask.

"Slow as a tortoise," she answers.

"Well, then," I say, "I'll take tortoise."

"Wimp," snaps Phoebe, and finally we begin to move.

As I step beyond the fake reception area, Nassim looks up from his crossword puzzle and says, "Uncle wants—"

"To see me. Yeah, I know," I say. "Frank already told me. Any idea what it's about?"

"No," says Nassim, "he didn't say."

"What's the temperature like?" I ask.

"Sunny, with a chance of late-afternoon violence," Nassim answers.

"Great." I'm definitely not looking forward to this. Nassim's forecasts are usually reliable. My only hope is to get in and out before Uncle starts thundering.

"Caleb's here, boss. Shall I bring him up?" Nassim says over his handheld. He nods once, says, "Okay," and hangs up. "He's ready for you."

That makes one of us.

I follow Nassim past the lounge and the dorms. He holds the stairwell door open and the sound of my feet climbing the metal stairs echoes loudly. My heart is thudding, my palms are sweating and my stomach's tied in a sailor's knot. I wonder if this is how a prisoner on death row feels when he does that final walk.

It might not be so bad if Abbie was with me. At least I'd have someone to share my misery.

When Nassim waves me into Uncle's office, I get a strong whiff of something that smells a bit like cedar, only sweeter.

My nose isn't the only thing that's surprised. I can't believe my eyes. The place looks nothing like it used to. Gone are Uncle's big walnut desk and the gold-trimmed Louis XVI visitor chairs. Also gone is the picnic painting that Frank lifted right out of Monet's studio in 1867 France, which is a shame because I truly liked that painting. Instead, there's a huge ink on silk showing a misted-over mountain with a pagoda perched halfway up.

There's also a long, low table of polished mahogany and a huge wooden screen that goes almost all the way up to the ceiling. The screen is red with images of silver dragons and pink flowers. The two miniature stone lions near the doorway look a lot like the ones I saw in Beijing. A two-foot-long bronze sculpture of a three-legged toad rounds out the décor.

The only holdover from Uncle's old office is a small display of framed photographs on the back wall: pictures from the old days. One shows me sitting on Uncle's lap, one pudgy hand wrapped around his neck and the other gripping a toy soldier. I must have been four or five at the time that picture was taken. Whatever happened to that toy soldier? I wonder. And whatever happened to the old Uncle?

A scraping sound brings me back to the present. Nassim is moving the wooden screen to one side, revealing a huge aquarium. My eyes detect a flash of movement. Something is definitely swimming around in there. Something big.

Uncle is turned away from me. He's wearing a green silk *hanfu* tied with a red sash. There's a huge silver dragon embroidered across the back of the robe, and his jeweled sword is tucked under the sash.

Since there aren't any visitors' chairs, I take a spot on the floor.

If all of this is meant to lull me into a relaxed state, it's not working. In fact, my shaking legs are a dead giveaway. I press my hands down on my knees to keep them still.

Uncle finally turns to face me. As he does, his face breaks out into a huge smile.

"Ahh, Caleb. *Zǎo shàng hǎo!*" he says.

I have to admit there's something special about hearing Chinese spoken with a Brooklyn accent. At least I'm guessing it's Chinese. My translator doesn't work inside Headquarters, so I have no idea what he just said.

"Good morning, Uncle," I say.

"Not just a good morning. A *great* morning!" He leaps up onto the low table between us, points his sword toward a ceiling mural of swirling stars and planets and proclaims,

"The cool of bamboo invades my room;
moonlight from the fields fills the corner of the court;
dew gathers till it falls in drops;
a scattering of stars, now there, now gone.
A firefly threading the darkness makes his own light;
Birds at rest on the water call to each other;
All these lie within the shadow of the sword—
Powerless I grieve as the clear night passes."

It seems for a moment as if he's going to keep going, but instead he hops off the table and looks over at me with a sad smile.

"Isn't it beautiful?" he says, dabbing at his moist eyes with his sleeve. "Doesn't it stir the very depths of your soul?"

"It certainly does stir things up," I say truthfully, though it's more my stomach than my soul.

"Caleb, do you know who wrote those words?" he asks, sword slicing the air.

I feel a sweat breaking out on my forehead. I haven't got a clue.

"You, Uncle?" I say.

He lets go with a huge belly laugh and the thing in the aquarium noses up to the glass. "No, not me . . . but *xiè xiè*—thank you for the compliment." He hops off the table. "The name of the person who wrote those words is Tu Fu. Some say he was the greatest Chinese poet ever."

"Very impressive," I say.

"Yes. Greatness does impress, doesn't it?"

"It certainly does," I answer.

"Do you see this sword, Caleb?" he says.

How could I not? "Yes, Uncle."

"It is an enhanced replica of the sword that belonged to Zhu Yuanzhang, the first emperor of the Ming Dynasty. Zhu rose from the ranks of peasants to become one of China's greatest military leaders."

Enhanced is Uncle's way of saying "souped up." The word around Timeless Treasures is that Uncle's sword can do more than just slice and dice.

"Care to join me for some tea?" he asks, tucking the sword back under his belt and sitting down across from me.

He claps his hands twice, and Nassim appears with two teacups, pots, utensils and what looks like a wooden box with slats on top. He gently places the box down on the table, carefully arranges all the tea things on top of the box and then pours water into the cups, each of his movements slow and graceful.

My eyes flick to the aquarium. The big thing is a black turtle. No, not one. Two turtles. Swimming lazily near each other.

I glance back in time to see Nassim snag one of the cups with a pair of tongs and pour the water from it into a large ceramic container. He does the same with the other cup and then scoops tea leaves into yet another container. After that, he lifts the first container up high, tilting it until the water cascades into the container holding the tea leaves.

If this is what it takes to make a cup of tea, next time I'm ordering coffee.

As Nassim hands Uncle his cup, I sneak another look at the aquarium. The turtles are snapping at each other. And not little love bites, either. They're really going at it.

"Did you know, Caleb, that the Chinese have been enjoying making tea in this way for thousands of years?" says Uncle.

"That's a long time," I say.

"We can learn a lot from the Chinese, you know," he continues. "Wouldn't you agree that the Great Friendship is the single greatest historical event of this century?"

I nod and sip my tea. Personally, I'd rank the Great Friendship in second place behind McDonald's first hamburger sale on the moon, but I'm not about to openly disagree with Uncle. I glance behind me. Nassim has left the office. It's just me and Uncle now. He's leading up to something, I'm sure of it. I try hard not to stare at a particularly long vein in his forehead that twitches slightly every time he speaks.

"Do you know how it is that the Great Friendship came about?" Uncle asks, and there goes that vein again.

"Umm. Not really," I say. It's true. World politics is not my strong suit. I don't listen to the news much, and the only news I ever read online is the sports section.

"I will tell you, then," he says. "It came about as a result of the two greatest powers in the world realizing they had a need that only the other could satisfy."

"I see, Uncle," I say, but the only thing I really see is the smackdown going on in the aquarium.

"Think about this," he says. "There is one universal need, one common longing of all people, that neither of the two greatest powers can satisfy. It is society's endless appetite for nostalgia. The need for a small piece of the past to claim as one's own.

"That is where Timeless Treasures comes in," Uncle continues. "We alone can satisfy that need. But that is not all. With the success of the Great Friendship, the potential market for our services has expanded exponentially. There are five billion people living in China, Caleb. If only one percent of one percent of all of those people decided to avail themselves of our services, that would translate into half a million new customers!"

Half a million. That's a big number. Even if Abbie and I and the other time snatchers quadrupled the number of missions we're doing each week, there's still no way we'd be able to keep up with that kind of demand.

"We must seize the moment. With change comes great opportunity! The time is ripe for the growth and expansion of Timeless Treasures! The time is ripe to increase the number of time snatchers from five to one hundred!"

Uncle's eyes are gleaming. He really believes what he's saying. My mouth goes dry. I don't like the sound of this. More time snatchers means more collections like the one Frank invited me to go on, more innocent children being kidnapped.

"A project this large cannot be accomplished by one man alone, Caleb," he says, his forehead vein twitching like crazy. "Generals will be needed to make the dream a reality."

My hands begin to shake. I feel a strong urge to get up and leave. But I can't go anywhere until the meeting is over.

"Very soon," Uncle says, "I will be assembling the team that will lead Timeless Treasures into the next phase of its development. And, Caleb . . ."

"Yes, Uncle?" I say, my voice trembling.

"I'll be monitoring you and Frank very closely over the next little while," he says, smiling. "So far, this month you are leading him in completed snatches by a score of nineteen to sixteen. But if you look at the relative complexity of your snatches versus his, I would say that he is in the lead."

I grind my teeth. I should have guessed he'd be hauling out the numbers and comparing my totals with Frank's. But it's not just that. Uncle's expert at twisting the results to whatever he wants them to show.

"Do you know why Frank is doing so well?" he asks.

Yes—because he's been poaching my snatches, I want to say. But if I mention that, Uncle will either not believe me or twist things around so that it's my fault somehow. So instead I say, "No, Uncle."

"I'll tell you why," answers Uncle. "It's because he has an extra quality about him that none of my other time snatchers seem to have, including, I'm afraid, you, Caleb."

I feel myself getting very warm. Please let this meeting be over soon.

"Frank has what I call, a 'zeal for the steal,'" Uncle continues. "He is enthusiastic about every single mission. He is singularly focused on the snatch and doesn't let the clutter of everyday life interfere."

"I'm not Frank, Uncle," I say, and as soon as the words are out, I regret saying them. Not because they aren't true, but because I didn't try to hide my dislike of Frank when I said them.

"That is exactly my point," continues Uncle. "You are not Frank. But to succeed, Caleb, to meet the high expectations that I have of you, you must become more like Frank."

I'd rather die than be more like Frank . . . which, come to think of it, Uncle could easily arrange.

"Think about what I am saying to you," continues Uncle. "I am telling you these things so that you can improve yourself. So that you can be the time snatcher that I have always thought, and still think, you can be. Am I making myself understood?"

"Yes, Uncle."

"Wonderful," he says and stands up. "Now, before you go, I'd like to show you my most recent acquisition."

He strolls across the room and runs his fingers lovingly over the aquarium's glass wall. Then he opens a small hatch on top, saunters back and sits down cross-legged behind the low table. My stomach clenches. Uncle's not the forgetful type. If he leaves a door or in this case a hatch open, you can bet there's a good reason for it.

"Very impressive," I say.

"In China, the turtle is a symbol of long life and happiness," says Uncle. "It is said that when a turtle reaches the age of one thousand years, it is able to speak just like you and I."

Maybe, but judging by the way those two in the aquarium are going at it, I'd be surprised if either of them make it past the next ten minutes, let alone the next thousand years.

"Let me share a little secret with you," Uncle continues. "I didn't purchase Shu Fang and Ting Ting for good luck. I bought them because I find them very entertaining. Especially when they've been denied nourishment. In that regard, I would venture to say that they're not unlike humans. Do you know what happens when the human soul is denied nourishment?"

"Uh . . . no, Uncle. I don't know," I say.

"When one's soul is deprived of nourishment, it withers," he says. "Withers and crumbles into nothingness."

I watch as Uncle's fingers tiptoe across the table and scuttle up the side of a glass jar. They linger at the top for a second and then dip down inside.

"Jelly bean?" he asks.

It seems like an innocent question, but there are no innocent questions in Uncle's universe. Everything is said or done for a reason.

I have a sudden urge to bolt. To get out of here before . . . before what? I run a hand through my hair and try to get ahold of myself. Got to stay calm. My eyes search out the photo of Uncle and me from the time before, when things were good. I'm out of luck: Uncle's blocking my view.

Just as I say "Yes," Uncle moves his hand as if to flip the jelly bean to me. But instead, he tosses it toward the tank. Before he can say anything, I'm up and lunging for the aquarium.

"Get it!" he shrieks and jumps up.

The bean makes the tiniest of splashes as it enters the water.

I plunge my left hand and arm into the tank. Shu Fang and Ting Ting immediately stop their snapping and make a beeline for my body parts.

My fingers thrash through the frigid water. On my second sweep, they brush against something small and hard. The jelly bean! Just a bit farther. I reach out some more and . . . it squirts away!

I lurch forward again ignoring my aching shoulder. There! Got it!

A searing pain rips into my wrist. Turtle jaws have found me. I want to scream, but not in front of Uncle. I bite down hard on my bottom lip to stifle the yell.

I try to yank my arm out, but Uncle has an iron grip on my forearm, holding it down. Tears stream from my eyes.

"Please . . . let go." I want to sound strong, but it comes out as a whimper.

"You have let me down, Caleb," says Uncle. "I am deeply disappointed. Of all my time thieves, you have a special place in my heart. You were the very first one I adopted. My firstborn, you might say."

Firstborn, but not first-loved. Frank's got that spot all locked up.

"Frank mentioned to me that you have been short-tempered with him lately. That trivial things seem to upset you and that you are taking it out on him and the other time snatchers," Uncle continues,

85

keeping his grip firm. "This simply will not do. I need all of you to be getting along. Especially when we are on the cusp of the next great chapter in the history of Timeless Treasures. Don't you agree?"

The turtles' jaws continue to tear at my exposed flesh. The pain is excruciating. I feel as if I'm about to pass out.

"Y-y-yes, Uncle," I manage.

"Good, I'm glad you see it my way," he says.

He pulls my arm from the tank and releases his grip. I cradle my ravaged wrist in my other hand.

"Well?" Uncle asks. But it's more a command than a question. It's clear what he wants me to do.

Slowly, I bring my hand up and slip the jellybean between my lips. I bite down hard and grimace as a strong licorice taste fills my mouth.

When I look up, he's smiling.

"You may go now, Caleb," he says.

My entire body is shaking, and I make no attempt to hide it. As I leave, out of the corner of my eye I see Shu Fang and Ting Ting circling the aquarium, searching for a way out. But there is no way out. Not for them. And certainly not for me.

VII

Come with me," says Nassim, when he sees me exit Uncle's office.

I follow him down to the fourth floor.

It's obvious the redecorating demon didn't make it as far as Nassim's office. The place is really drab: no water cooler waterfalls, no stone lions, not even a single three-legged toad sculpture. The only personal touch is a small photograph in a simple wooden frame on the desk. It's a picture of a man sitting astride a chestnut brown horse. If not for the fact that the man looks much older than Nassim, he could be his twin. Same strong jaw, high cheekbones and flat nose. I've seen the photo before. My guess is it's Nassim's father, but I've never asked him. He's such a private guy that it wouldn't feel right.

I sit quietly in the visitor's chair as he starts rummaging through a first aid kit.

"I believe this will work," he says, fishing out a large gauze pad and squeezing some antiseptic onto it. I grimace as he gently swabs my wound.

"Looks like Shu Fang's work," he says removing a fresh bandage from the kit.

"How can you tell the difference?" I say. Call me racist, but in my book, one turtle looks just like another.

"Here is how," he says, pulling up his left sleeve, revealing some nasty red marks. "This is Shu Fang."

Then he rolls up his right sleeve. The marks on this arm are deeper and uglier. "And this is Ting Ting."

Why is he showing me this? Is this some kind of trick to gain my trust so that I'll open up to him and then he can go straight to Uncle with everything I say? No, Nassim isn't that type of person. Maybe he's trying to tell me that I'm not alone, that he's also had the pleasure of experiencing Uncle's anger in exactly the same way.

He finishes bandaging me. "There. That should do it," he says, replacing the first aid kit in his drawer.

"Thanks," I say. "I really appreciate it." I turn to leave.

"You're welcome, Caleb," says Nassim. "I'll see you at supper. By the way, what are you making?"

Making? Why is . . . Oh. I almost forgot. It's my turn to cook tonight.

"I call it Peking pasta," I say quickly.

"Sounds mysterious."

"Believe me, it is." I've got the name of the dish. Now all I've got to do is figure out how to make it.

"Uncle sends his regrets. He will not be able to join us tonight," says Nassim once we're all seated at the table that evening. "But at his request, we will continue with our Chinese language lessons. The word of the evening is *zuò mèng*. Which means 'to dream.' Everyone must either use *zuò mèng* or its noun form, *mèng*, in the sentence of their choosing or describe a recent *mèng* that they had."

The only advantage of pulling cooking duty is not having to go first in these ridiculous word games.

"Caleb, you're first," says Nassim.

Wrong again. I make busy ladling out the Peking pasta. So far, I haven't received nearly the number of compliments that Frank got for yesterday's supper, but I figure the night is still young.

"I pass," I say.

"You can't pass," says Frank. "You've got to play just like the rest of us." He's eyeing the bandage on my wrist but, surprisingly, doesn't ask me about it.

"He's right," Lydia chimes in. "No dropouts."

"I'm not dropping out," I say. "I just want to go last for a change." I wonder what Frank's going to come up with for his sentence. Probably something about how he sees Abbie in all his *mèng*s.

Nassim looks at me for a moment before saying, "Very well. Raoul, you're first."

Raoul clears his throat. Along with being an excellent snorer, he's a first-class throat clearer. He does it every chance he gets: before talking, after talking and even while talking. More than once, I've offered to go with Raoul to visit Dr. Margolies on the second floor to see if anything can be done about the various sounds coming out of his mouth. You know, maybe a little canine dental surgery to clear the old nasal passages. So far, though, he hasn't taken me up on my offer.

"The new Monsoon from Forbidden City Ford drives like a *mèng*," says Raoul.

I stifle a laugh. I've seen the same slogan on not less than a dozen billboards in SoHo.

But Nassim must not have seen the ads, because he says, "Very good. Lydia?"

"*Zuò mèng* the impossible *mèng*," she croons and blessedly stops there.

"Uhhh, okay. Abbie?" says Nassim.

I turn to look at Abbie. I haven't had a chance to talk to her since I came back from London.

Then I glance at Frank. His usual smug look is gone. Good. That means Mr. I Am the Center of the Universe has no idea what she's going to say, either.

"I had a *mèng* last night," Abbie begins, her voice breaking slightly. She has a very serious look on her face. I can feel the tension in the room as she takes a breath.

Then she looks straight at me and says, "You were in it, Cale."

My stomach twists in a knot.

"We were on a mission. Somewhere in Asia. I don't know exactly where or when. But we had to climb a mountain to get to the snatch zone. A very steep mountain."

The room is completely quiet. Even Raoul has stopped his throat clearing.

"Somehow we got separated, and I got stuck on a high mountain ridge, surrounded by cliffs too steep to climb down," she continues. "I couldn't stay there, because there was no shelter at all from the cold wind. And night was coming. The only direction I could go was up. So I climbed higher, hoping desperately that I would find shelter."

Abbie pauses, and I let out a breath that I didn't know I was holding.

"I finally arrived at the narrow ridge at the top of the mountain. The wind was really strong, and it was snowing hard. So hard that I couldn't see more than a foot in front of me. But somehow I sensed that the snatch object was close by. And that if I reached for it, I would be able to grab it.

"So I did. I stretched my arm out as far as I could. But all my fingers snatched was snow. And as I lunged forward to try again, I lost my balance and began to fall . . ."

My mouth is dry. I drop my fork onto my plate.

"What happened then?" asks Lydia, her eyes wide.

"Then Caleb caught me," says Abbie, looking over at me, smiling brightly.

Relief floods through me. I shoot a glance at Frank. He doesn't look too happy.

"What about the snatch object?" asks Lydia.

"That's the weird dream part, I guess," says Abbie. "It had fallen also and landed not far from us. But even though we could hear it, Caleb and I couldn't find it."

"You could hear it?" says Lydia.

"Yes. It was"—Abbie pauses as if searching for the right word—"crying."

Lydia is on the edge of her seat, and when I look down, I realize that I am too.

"You mean the snatch object was a child?" Lydia says.

Abbie shrugs her shoulders. "I don't know what it was. I never actually saw it."

"But didn't you know what object you and Caleb were going to snatch?"

"It was a *dream*, Lydia. They're not always logical, you know."

"Well, what happened after that?"

"After that . . . I woke up," she says.

Frank's the first to speak. "It's clear what that dream means, isn't it? It means that Abbie can't count on her snatch partner." His smug smile is back again.

Abbie glares at him and says, "I don't see how you get that, Frank. Caleb's the one who caught me."

"He's also the one who left you stranded high on a mountain. And on top of all of that, the snatch failed. So it's obvious you can't count on him."

I'm on my feet. I want to hurt him. To wipe that smug smile right off his face.

"That was uncalled for, Frank. You may leave the dinner table," says Nassim.

Frank stands and gives me one of his trademark smirks. He knows he's rattled me. Which is exactly what he wanted to do. As he leaves the room, I have another disturbing thought. What if he's right? What if Abbie can't count on me? What if something happens to her because of me?

That's ridiculous. It's just a stupid dream. And why did she even tell it? I guess it never occurred to her that Frank would twist its meaning like he did.

After all the dinner dishes have been cleared away, Nassim asks Abbie and me to stay behind. We slump down on the couch.

He presses a button on his handheld and the wall screen lights up. The three-dimensional hologram appearing directly in front of the screen is fuzzy at first and then sharpens. It's a silver door with a design etched into it of a snake intertwined around an hourglass. There's only one door like that: the one to Uncle's office. I watch as it slides open.

"Hello, Abbie and Caleb," says Uncle.

He's seated cross-legged on the floor in a red silk *hanfu* with a crouching dragon design and a yellow sash. I swear, Uncle must have a larger collection of ancient Chinese emperor robes than anyone else in Tribeca, or maybe even New Beijing.

"I'm so glad you could join me," he says. "You must think this is a bit silly, me talking to you like this when it would appear I could easily walk down one flight and have this conversation in person."

No comment. *Silly* is not a word that comes to mind when I think of Uncle. *Calculating,* yes, *ruthless,* definitely, and sometimes even *charming.* But never *silly.*

"A face-to-face meeting would have been my preference as well," he says. "But alas, work has called me away yet again. As you watch this, I am in Shanghai."

That was fast. He must have caught the supersonic express from La Guardia. I suppose he could also have timeleaped there, but Uncle prefers to travel the conventional way.

"Big things are afoot with Timeless Treasures," continues Uncle, "but I won't speak about that just yet. Suffice it to say that you will both find out soon enough."

I take a deep breath and let it out slowly. Even though he isn't physically in the same room as us, I'm still getting the jitters.

"The reason I have brought you into my office, so to speak," he says, "is to show you something."

The camera pans his office. First the wall mural, then the wooden screen and the aquarium. I catch a glimpse of Shu Fang—or is it Ting Ting?—and I wonder if they've been dining on any other wrists lately.

Uncle's hologram floats across the office and stops beside a small table I've never seen before. "I procured this table from a craftsman in Hunan Province, China. It was built during the Tang dynasty and is made entirely of bamboo. Exquisite, isn't it?"

"Yes, Uncle," I say. It feels ridiculous to talk to a holo-movie, but who knows—Uncle could be listening in and watching us at this very moment.

"But a table, even a table from the Tang dynasty, is just that, isn't it?" he continues. "Merely a surface for something to rest upon."

We both nod.

"I have in mind something special to rest upon this table," Uncle says. "Allow me to show you."

He snaps his fingers and the wall screen in his office lights up. A second later, an image flashes on the screen: a 3-D drawing of a vase.

"It looks quite ordinary, doesn't it?" says Uncle.

If it was anyone else asking, I'd say yes in a heartbeat. The vase has a long neck and two loop handles. It's base color is cream, but the flying dragon and phoenix designs are both painted blue. It's the kind of thing you'd find in any of the high-end antique stores on Second Avenue. But this is Uncle we're talking about.

"This drawing is not from the artist's imagination. It is an accurate depiction of a real vase," he says. "If you look closely, you will see a mark painted on the bottom. This particular vase bears the reign mark Da Ming Xuan De Nian Zhi, which means it was made during the Ming dynasty and the reign of the Xuande emperor. We also know that the artist was Wu Yingxing, that the piece was crafted on April 23, 1423, near Jǐngdézhèn, China, and that it was presented as a birthday present to the emperor on September 28, 1425. It left China on board a ship piloted by the famous admiral Zheng on May 10, 1431. The voyage was perilous, and the ship came close to sinking when it came under fire from pirates. In the end, however, both the ship and the Xuande vase survived the voyage.

"Upon arrival in the Ottoman Empire, the vase was regifted to Sultan Murad II. After that, the trail goes dead until 1967, when the Xuande Ming vase was exhibited for the first time in the West at the world's fair Expo 67 in Montreal, Canada. That is the last reference in the public record to the Xuande vase. Following Expo 67, it simply disappeared from sight."

Talk about information overload. I hope Uncle's not going to quiz us on this afterward, because if he does, I'm going to fail miserably. Especially if he asks us to spell some of those names.

There's a long silence. Uncle does a slow half turn away from the camera. Then he turns back again, and the camera zooms in on his face. His eyes look moist. His forehead vein isn't twitching at all, which is a rare sight.

"Excuse me for my momentary display of emotion," says Uncle, wiping away a tear, "but the thought of something so precious disappearing from the world is almost too much to bear.

"What makes the Xuande vase so precious, you may well ask. After all, it was far from the only vase crafted during the Ming dynasty. There were scores like it and some perhaps even more beautiful. Well, I will show you what makes it unique."

He pauses and the camera does a slow pan of his office, lingering for a moment on the small bamboo table before returning to the screen and zooming in for a tight shot of the bottom of the vase.

"Look closely. Do you see the small star next to the reign mark?"

I nod, and Abbie says, "Yes."

"That star is the symbol of the house of Confucius. It tells us that Wu Yingxing was a descendant of one of the greatest Chinese philosophers, perhaps the greatest thinker in all of history.

"During his lifetime, Wu produced more than two thousand works of art, including perhaps three hundred vases and other works of pottery. But only on the Xuande vase does the Confucian symbol appear above the reign mark. The scholars I have consulted are divided as to why the symbol appears on this piece of work and not on his others. Some say it is because this piece was commissioned by the Xuande emperor, who was also a descendant of Confucius, and Wu wanted to endear himself to the emperor. Others say that it was only near the end of his life that Wu found out he was a descendant of Confucius, and so he painted the symbol on the Xuande vase, his last great piece of art. But my own research has lead me to a third theory. A theory that I prefer to keep to myself until I am holding the vase in my hands."

It's a fascinating story. I glance at Abbie. Her jaw is clearly in the down position.

The camera zooms in on Uncle's face. "Your mission is to snatch the Xuande vase from Expo 67 before it vanishes," he continues, and now his tone is all business. "You will depart tomorrow and timeleap to six fifty-five P.M. local time on July 8, 1967, landing one hundred yards from one another."

A staggered landing. Standard operating procedure on important missions. The theory is that one person suddenly appearing out of thin air attracts less attention than two people.

"You must complete the snatch by seven-thirty P.M. local time," he continues. "If you are unable to snatch the Xuande vase by then, I will allow you a one-time grace period of fifteen minutes for this mission. But for the sake of your physical health, I wouldn't recommend relying on the grace period."

I raise my eyebrows. It must be an important mission for Uncle to allow us to go over the usual limit and risk time fog. I like the way he puts it too: "for the sake of your physical health." Very caring.

The camera stays zoomed in on Uncle's face. His thin lips are set in a tight line, and his ice blue eyes are gazing right into mine. Which is quite a trick, since he's just a hologram, after all, and until now I've never known a hologram to look me in the eye.

"Don't fail me, Caleb," he says.

"I won't, Uncle," I answer. My injured wrist throbs in agreement. It isn't lost on me that he didn't say anything to Abbie about *her* not failing him. My personal theory is that he expects more of me than he does of Abbie. Again, it goes back to Uncle thinking of me as his first adopted. But there's more to his remarks than just that. He believes Frank's lies.

"That is all," says Uncle. "Nassim will answer any other questions you have."

The screen goes dark. My palms are sweaty, and I wipe them on my pants.

Nassim turns to us. "Any questions, guys?"

We shake our heads.

"Good," he says. "Then I will see you in the morning." He heads to his office, probably to work on his crossword puzzles.

"What happened to your wrist, Cale?" Abbie asks once we're alone.

"I had a little run-in with Shu Fang," I say.

"Who?"

"One of Uncle's snapping turtles. He's very territorial," I say. "Don't worry. It looks much worse than it feels," Now, why did I just say that? To make Abbie feel better? I don't want her to feel better. I want her to feel worse. Or at least sorry for me. No, not that either. What I really want is for her to pay me a little more attention and pay Frank a little less.

"Hey, you never told me about how your meeting with Uncle went," she says.

I shift to face her. "Okay, I guess. He showed me his new aquarium and talked about withering souls. Then he mentioned some great new vision he's got, treated me to a jelly bean and I left. Oh, yeah, and he wants me to be more like Frank."

"Wait, back up . . . what great new vision?" asks Abbie, switching to mindpatch, which is probably a good idea, since it's a safe bet Uncle has listening devices in here.

"Well, he didn't get into details," I answer over her mindpatch. "Just some talk about expanding Timeless Treasures, that he can't do it all himself and that he needs generals."

"Okay. So what'd you say?" she asks.

"About what?"

Abbie rolls her eyes and says, "About what? About what we're talking about, Mr. Space Zombie. Didn't you tell Uncle that you thought it was a great idea?"

"Well, no," I answer. "I mean he didn't exactly ask me for my opinion. Just told me what was coming."

"I can't believe you!" Abbie says. "Don't you see? He wasn't telling you all that just to make pleasant conversation. He wanted to know what you think. And you know what else? If you'd shown the least bit of interest, I'm pretty sure he would have offered you a new job—a promotion—helping him with the expansion."

"How do you know for sure?" I say.

Abbie stands up from the couch and glares down at me. "I don't!" she says, this time out loud. "Nothing is for sure! You know what your problem is? You *think* way too much. If you want something in life, you've got to go for it!"

Like you going for Frank, I want to say. But I bite the words back just in time.

"Maybe you're right," I say instead. Truth is, I don't know what I want. But there's one thing I'm sure I don't want, and that's moving up the corporate ladder and becoming Uncle's second-in-command.

"Good night, Cale. I'm going to bed," she says. "I suggest you do the same. We've got a big day tomorrow."

"Okay, I will. Good night." I watch her leave the lounge. I'm tired, but there's no way I'm going to bed yet. Something's bothering me about our conversation. Abbie got really angry when I said I didn't go gaga over Uncle's expansion plans, like I didn't get what he was talking about. Oh, I got it, all right. Got it and want nothing to do with it. But she thinks I was just being thick. Maybe she's worried that she can't count on me anymore, that if I can't even follow a simple conversation with Uncle, then for sure my brain won't be able to function properly when we're out on missions. If that's what she really thinks, then she and Frank deserve each other.

But no. I refuse to believe that. Maybe she truly thinks that I want to be number one with Uncle and now I messed it up. Which means she really doesn't know me at all. So why should that surprise me? I hardly know myself these days.

I've got to stop all these negative thoughts about Abbie. But my brain isn't listening. The nasty thoughts keep bubbling to the surface.

Another reason I'm in no rush to go to bed is that as soon as I enter the dorm, Frank will no doubt grill me about my big meeting with Uncle. And Raoul will want to get his two cents in by way of snores, throat clearings and other assorted noises.

No, it'll be much better to wait until later. With any luck, they'll both be asleep, and I can just sneak in.

I stretch out on the couch and, after a few moments, close my eyes. And fall fast asleep.

VIII

June 24, 2061, 7:08 A.M.
Timeless Treasures Headquarters
Tribeca, New Beijing (formerly New York City)

Rise and shine, Cale," Abbie chirps.

"Already up," I mutter, which is partly true, because I'm half slouching on the couch.

"Hey, did you sleep here?" she asks.

I grunt in the affirmative. It's still too early in the morning to put together complete sentences.

Abbie's already dressed for the mission. She's wearing oval, pink-tinted sunglasses, floppy hat, tie-dyed T-shirt and faded blue jeans. She looks pretty, in a 1960s hippie sort of way.

She hands me a blue denim knapsack with a large white peace symbol painted on. I don't have to ask her what's in it because I already know: an exact replica of the Xuande vase that we'll leave at the snatch zone when we steal the real one.

I push myself up to a sitting position and take stock of my various body parts. My neck is sore, and my left arm is tingling. I dreamt that Shu Fang leapt out of the tank, crept down the hall and bit me while I was sleeping, infecting me with slow-acting venom that started in my arm and was making its way to my heart. Right before I was about to die, I gave all my worldly possessions, consisting of my knife and my carving, to Nassim, who placed them inside a manila envelope neatly labeled "The Last Earthly Possessions of Caleb the Time Snatcher."

"C'mon," says Abbie. "Time to get going, sleepyhead. We've got Operation Blue Bird!"

"Operation what?"

"Blue Bird. Don't you remember that beautiful phoenix on the Xuande vase? It was painted in cobalt blue. Hence, Operation Blue Bird!"

"Hence?"

"Are you making fun of the way I speak?" she says.

I shake my head because it takes less effort than talking.

"Get up. We're going to Montreal," she says.

"Really?"

"You know very well we're going to Montreal, Mr. Stalling for Time. But I bet you didn't know that it's my favorite city in the world."

"Why?"

"Why? Because it's beautiful, and it's the city of romance!" She winks at me, and for the hundredth time, I wonder what she's really thinking when she says stuff like that. Better not to analyze.

I'm standing now, which I consider quite an accomplishment. I definitely deserve a reward. How about another hour of sleep?

"Let's go, Cale. I'll be waiting for you at the fire escape."

"All right," I say, still groggy.

"*À bientôt!*" she says.

"A . . . what?" I ask.

"That's French for 'see you soon,'" says Abbie.

I try to dredge up something clever to say, but before I can, Abbie's already on her way out of the lounge.

I trudge to the bathroom and look at myself in the mirror. There are circles under my eyes, and I've got a serious case of sofa hair. I step out of my clothes and clap on the shower. Water shoots from the jets, already preadjusted to my personal preferences for temperature and pressure.

I hold my bandaged wrist out of the way so that it stays dry. The shower feels good. For a blissful moment, I close my eyes and let the water wash away the stress of my meeting with Uncle, my run-ins with Frank and my less than smooth conversations with Abbie. Lately I've been feeling like my life is spinning out of control. And the most frustrating thing is that I don't really know why it's happening or what I can do to stop it.

I make the water as hot as I can take and stand under it for another minute before finally clapping it off. With the towel draped around my waist, I jog back to the lounge. There's a Rolling Stones T-shirt, blue jeans and a pair of Adidas sneakers laid out for me. Perfect for a trip to the 1960s.

On my way to the fire escape, I chug the last bit of orange juice straight from the container.

If I stopped to think about things, I'd probably be nervous about this mission. After all, it's not every day that we get a personal briefing from Uncle about a snatch. And even more rare is having Uncle as the customer. Not to mention his little warning to me about not screwing up.

Well, then, it's a good thing that I'm not thinking about any of those things.

"All set," I say as I step outside.

"Groovy, man," says Abbie, flashing me a peace sign.

Still smiling, she taps her wrist and disappears. Just before I do the same I see a bird, a sparrow I think, soaring high above me, heading west. Following it with my eyes, a feeling of exhilaration passes through me. I tap my wrist and am still thinking of the bird when I leave 2061.

IX

I land in a narrow lane bounded by a building on one side and a row of tall shrubs on the other. There's a nice fragrance in the air—jasmine, I think. As soon as the time freeze passes I walk around to the front of the building. It's much more impressive from the front: big and white, with huge, rounded red doors and a green tiled roof. From my briefing data, I know it's the Republic of China Pavilion. Either it's a very popular pavilion or they're serving free food inside, because the line to get in looks impossibly long.

Just then I feel a prickling sensation on the back of my neck—as if someone's watching me. I do a slow turn, pretending to take in the sights but really trying to spot my silent watcher.

Nothing. Just the usual crowd of camera-toting tourists.

Maybe I just imagined the whole thing. That wouldn't surprise me, given how jumpy I've been lately.

I walk briskly along the line, on the lookout for Abbie. There must be three hundred people here. Standard operating procedure says that we should mindlink each other if we don't establish visual contact within thirty seconds of landing, but where's the fun in that? Instead, I continue along, keeping my eyes peeled for Abbie's big floppy hat.

"You're getting warmer, Daddio," she hippiespeaks over my mindpatch.

I glance up and spot her about ten feet away, close to the front of the line. I have no idea how she managed to land that far up the line without anyone noticing, but Abbie is an expert at melding into crowds.

"Hey man," she drawls as I walk up. "Ready to rock out?"

"Uhh . . . yeah. I can . . . dig it," I say.

Abbie laughs and says, "Groovy. You're one hip cat!"

"Thank you," I say. I don't know if they actually said thank you in the 1960s, but my well of sixties slang has suddenly run dry.

"What's that odor?" I ask, sniffing. There's a strong scent of mango in the air.

"Ain't it the most?" she says. "All the mademoiselles are wearing it."

It seems kind of silly to me to walk around smelling like a piece of fruit, but I don't say anything.

Three men wearing red suspenders, shorts and green kneesocks walk by. One of them is whistling a tune I don't recognize. The breeze carries the sounds of children laughing, snatches of a dozen different conversations and the rumble of the minirail overhead.

"Let's get on with things," says Abbie. "We've only got twenty-seven minutes, and I want to fit in some time for souvenir shopping."

But I hardly hear her. The feeling of being watched is back. Stronger than ever. I bend down, pretending to tie my shoelaces and then spin around quickly. There! Right next to the Information kiosk. I only see him for a split second before he ducks behind a group of tourists. It wasn't much more than a glimpse, but it was long enough for me to see that he was tall and had dark hair. I try to tell myself not to jump to conclusions about the identity of my stalker. After all, there must be hundreds of tall people with dark hair walking around Expo today.

Maybe, but there's only one person I can think of who would choose watching me over enjoying Expo.

Frank.

"Abbie, do you get the feeling someone's watching us?"

"Yeah. I noticed it right after you arrived," she says without turning her head. "Every time I try to ID him, he slips back into the crowd."

I nod. "He's fast. What do you think we should do?"

She turns and looks at me. As in stares at me. Then she says, "I think you should keep your hair long, Cale. You look good that way. And whatever you do, don't ever cut this cute little thing here."

She reaches out and tugs on a curl I never paid much attention to. As she does, her finger lightly touches my forehead and a warm shiver goes through me.

"Seriously, Abbie. What do you think we should do?"

"Seriously? I say ignore him. Whoever he is, it's better if he doesn't know we're onto him."

I feel a headache coming on. I don't trust Frank. If it really is him, the fact that he's here right when I'm about to perform what is quite possibly the most important snatch of my career has got to mean trouble.

We inch past a Chinese garden with sculpted bushes and low tables where women in bright red silk robes are serving food. The sign on the wrought iron gate says JADE CAFÉ.

There's another surge forward, and along with a hundred others, we spill through massive red doors into the Republic of China Pavilion. For a moment, I'm dizzy. The hall is enormous. Twelve columns of red marble reach up to the high, ornamental ceiling. Floating near the ceiling are a dozen multicolored kites, including a dazzling one that looks like two birds joined together. A large mural depicts a six-masted sailing ship tossing in a green sea, the waves made even more turbulent by the presence of a huge blue sea serpent. On the far wall is a floor-to-ceiling smiling portrait of the president of the Chinese republic, Chiang Kai-shek. Display cases house objects from ancient China, including a golden Buddha, musical instruments that I don't recognize and beautiful jade carvings of an ox and a tiger. Soothing music fills the hall. Pretty, silky-haired Chinese women wearing red dresses with green sashes are performing a dance on an elevated stage at the center of the hall.

Beyond the stage, an escalator goes to the second level. But my feet are in no hurry to go anywhere. There's so much here to see, and I want to take it all in.

"C'mon, Cale," says Abbie. "We'd better get started."

I check my fingernail. I can't believe it. It's already twelve minutes past seven. Not counting overtime, there's only eighteen minutes left to do the snatch.

"Right," I say. "Switching to mindpatch. First stop: the fuse box."

She throws her shoulders back, gives me a salute and says, *"Oui, mon capitaine!"*

We make our way to the far end of the pavilion and find the fuse box just where the briefing data said it would be, on the back wall of an exhibit called "The Emperor's New Clothes." It is at eye level, two feet behind a life-sized replica of a Sung dynasty emperor wearing a bright yellow *hanfu*. I slip between the wall and the emperor. The position of the emperor is a stroke of good luck. It will partially block the view of anyone curious enough to see what I'm up to. Abbie, with her back to me now, completes my cover.

I hold my hand out and nudge her gently. She fishes in her pocket, withdraws a thin wire and places it in my hand. *"Merci,"* I whisper and insert the wire in the fuse box's keyhole. After a few jiggles, the small door opens. At a glance I can see that it's a standard setup, or at least standard for the 1960s: a control panel with sixteen switches that regulate the heating, cooling and electricity for the building. But it's the lights that I'm really interested in. They're on a timer, set to go off one hour after closing time.

I nudge Abbie again, and this time she hands me what look like two peanuts, one red and one green. But they're not for munching. I slip the green one, a remote control, into my pocket. The red one has microcircuits that will override the timing mechanism for the pavilion's electricity. As soon as I place its magnetized surface next to the right fuse, the lights in the pavilion will be completely under my control.

Just then she whispers, "Trouble at six o'clock."

Palming the device, I close the fuse box and turn around just in time to see a pudgy man with a Rolleiflex camera hanging from a strap around his neck park himself in front of the emperor.

"Geez, will you look at that," he says. "I almost thought he was alive."

"I know," says Abbie, breezily. "When I first saw him, I was sure he was going to sneeze all over me."

Smooth.

The man laughs and his camera bounces up and down against his jiggling belly.

"Come on, Robert," Abbie says to me. "Let's go see the rest of the exhibit."

We smile and move on. But after a few feet, she stops to admire a fuchsia *hanfu* with a phoenix pattern inside a glass display case.

"Now, that would look great on me."

I'm only listening with one ear. Most of my attention is directed back toward the emperor.

The man has been joined by a tiny woman with big hair and a frown etched on her face. Judging from their matching blue and white little travel bags, I'm guessing it's his wife.

"Don't stare," Abbie mindspeaks. "You're making it too obvious."

I turn my head so that now I'm only seeing them out of the corner of my eye.

"Hon," says the man, taking a couple of steps back, "stand next to the emperor guy. Put your arm around him or something. Pretend you're helping him rule the world."

She shuffles over to stand beside the emperor. Neither of them is smiling.

Drops of sweat dot my forehead.

"It's seven twenty-five," I mindspeak. "If they don't leave soon, we'll have to do something."

"I know," Abbie says. "Let's give them one more minute."

"Move in a bit closer, Louise. Good. Now tilt your head this way . . . perfect. All right, say, cheeeeese . . . got it! Now, one more."

I concentrate on my breathing. Have to stay calm.

"Sidney Halpern!" Louise roars. "I'm not going to risk missing the People's Flying Acrobatic Troupe because of you." She grabs his arm and leads him away from the exhibit.

Bless you, Louise, I mouth silently, and Abbie and I move quickly toward the fuse box.

I finish attaching the device and program the override. At my command, all of the lights in the pavilion will go off. We will then have thirty seconds to do the snatch before the backup generator kicks in. There's no going back now.

We hurry to the escalator. Abbie gets there ahead of me and scoots right up. I get stuck behind a man and a young, red-haired boy. I'd like to pass them, but they're standing side by side and there's no room to go around.

"Look, Daddy!" the boy shouts. "Those people are as tiny as my soldier!" He reaches into his pocket and pulls out a plastic figurine.

The sight of the toy soldier triggers something inside of me; strong feelings and memories. For a moment, the escalator is gone and the mission forgotten. I am a young boy perched on Uncle's lap, proudly showing him my toy soldier. I'm filled with forgotten feelings of warmth, of belonging, even of love.

I try to hold on to the moment, but it vanishes in an instant, and I'm plunged back into reality.

"They're small because they're far away," his father says.

"How do they do that?" the boy asks.

The father laughs and says, "It's not *them* doing it, Zach. It's the laws of perspective."

I glance down. Twenty-eight minutes past seven. I'm cutting it really close.

Finally, the escalator reaches the third level and I'm off, sprinting past an exhibit of stuff made from bamboo, including a wicked-looking crossbow.

Then I see it—encased in glass. The thing that Abbie and I have traveled ninety-four years back in time to snatch: the Xuande vase.

It looks more impressive in real life than on the holo-video that Uncle showed us. The dragon is beautifully detailed, and every scale on its body is exquisitely rendered. Right beside the vase is an old wooden crate with a miniature copy of the flying dragon etched on one side. The inscription beneath the two items reads:

Ming vase from the reign of the Xuande emperor. Brought to Edirne, the capital of the Ottoman empire, inside this crate in 1431 and presented as a gift to Sultan Murad II

"There'll be plenty of time to admire it later," Abbie mindspeaks. She's right.

My body is shaking. I can't afford another failed mission.

I slip a hand inside my pocket and press the remote control. Immediately the lights around me start winking out. As I switch to night vision, the polite tourist chatter of a moment ago morphs into grumbling, yelling and swearing in a dozen different languages and people start running in every direction. All of this confusion is good.

But out of the corner of my eye, I see something that isn't so good.

The boy from the escalator has invented a new game. It's called "climb up onto the railing and see if you can reach the pretty kite that looks like two birds."

His parents are looking the wrong way, toward the escalator.

In my mind's eye, I picture what'll happen if the boy falls. It's not pretty. I figure it's at least a forty-foot drop to the first level.

The boy is standing on the railing now, reaching for the kite. His left leg begins to wobble. He's losing his balance!

The boy or the snatch? I only have a split second to decide.

In that second, I see my future flash before my eyes: if I'm good and do everything expected of me, I can look forward to years of nabbing innocent children and training them to steal things just to keep Uncle's rich, greedy clients happy.

I race for the railing, bumping into screaming, panicking people running the other way in the dark. Where is he? There! I reach up and grab the boy by the back of his pants.

We collide and tumble down onto the floor together.

Abbie's angry voice blasts across my mindpatch. "Caleb, what are you doing? Get over here and help me get this case off!"

It's a fair request. After all, taking the glass case off the vase is definitely a two-person job.

But fair or not, all I can do right now is lie on the floor, knapsack beside me, and try to get my breath back.

The lights come back on, and there's the boy's father, rushing our way. He picks his son up and hugs him. I stand up just as the mother arrives. She joins in, making it a three-way squeeze session.

Abbie's voice comes back. "Get out of there!"

"I . . . I can't," I say.

I know it sounds ridiculous, but I can't think of anything else to say. Anything that makes sense, that is. It's the logical time to go. The boy is safe, and everyone (except probably me) is about to live happily ever after. But logical or not, my legs won't move. So I just stand there, watching the hug.

At the edges of my mind, I feel storm clouds gathering. I've just done something very bad. Broken one of the biggies. "While on a mission, thou shalt not interact in any way with members of the local population except as necessary to perform the snatch," is the rule in the Timeless Treasures Field Agents Handbook.

I swallow hard. Uncle doesn't take kindly to anyone breaking a "thou shalt not." If he finds out, the best I can hope for is a stint in the Barrens. Just thinking the word *Barrens* gives me the shivers. The place is an unforgiving wasteland. If the torturous heat doesn't get you, then the scorpions and snakes will. Wiping a bead of sweat from my forehead, I stand up just as the long hug ends.

A small crowd has gathered now. A woman steps forward and says something to the father. She gestures to the rail and then points at me. He turns, sees me and begins to walk in my direction.

I should run now. Last chance, my brain is screaming at me. Or is it Abbie shouting over my mindpatch? Either way, I ignore the voice and just stand there. The father holds out his hand, and I take it in my own. His grip is warm and strong.

"Thank you for saving our son," he says, eyes brimming with tears. "I'm Jim. Jim Rushton. This is my wife, Diane, and this is Zach."

Diane also looks like she's about to lose it. The only one with dry eyes is the boy, Zach. He's staring at me like I jumped right off the cover of one of those old Superman comic books.

"I'm Ro . . . Caleb." I'm surprised to hear myself say my real name.

We all stand around awkwardly for a moment, until Zach tugs at his mother's hand and asks, "Mom, can Caylid eat ice cream with us at the café for my birthday?"

"I don't know, Zach," Diane says. "He probably has to get back to his own family . . . but I suppose you could ask and see if he's available."

Zach lets go of his mother's hand, takes a step toward me, glances at his Mickey Mouse wristwatch and says in a serious voice, "Caylid, are you 'vailable to eat birthday ice cream with me and my mom and my dad? I'm four years old, but I'm gonna be five in . . . how many minutes, Daddy?"

Jim takes Zach's wrist and says, "Three minutes, Zach."

"In three minutes," Zach repeats.

"No, you're not 'vailable, Mr. Hero," comes the once-sweet voice of my snatch partner over my mindpatch. "Now, make like a banana and split! We're already into our fifteen minutes of overtime. If we don't do the snatch pronto, we're both going to be in deep trouble with *you know who*."

My mind is racing. Fifteen minutes of overtime. Three of those minutes already used up. Subtract a couple of minutes to get to the Jade Café. Take off another five minutes for having a quick ice cream and then another two for the walk back. That leaves only three minutes to spare. But what if the ice cream doesn't come in five minutes? Well, I can always give some excuse and hurry back here.

And what about the lights? I slip a hand into my pocket. The remote is still there, but it's useless against the backup generator. I'd have to wait until the system is reset, and who knows how long that will take? Well, maybe I can just forget about the lights and do a quick smash and grab.

This is crazy. How can I even be thinking of going for ice cream? This is the most important mission of my career. Abbie is counting on me. And Uncle has already made it crystal clear that I'd better not fail.

Zach tilts his chin up toward me, waiting for my decision. I don't even know him. He's just another small boy at Expo 67 with his family, isn't he? If I say no, he'll be disappointed for maybe a minute, but at his age, he'll probably forget all about me by tomorrow. So then why am I making such a big deal of this. Why can't I just say no?

Jim and Diane are looking away, waiting for me to say something.

Zach sticks a hand in his pocket and pulls out his toy soldier. Then he lifts the hand holding the soldier as high as his almost-five-year-old arms will allow him, and with his eyes locked on mine, says in a grave voice, "My soldier is ordering you to come."

Emotions swirl through me. I want to laugh and cry at the same time. Images flash into my head: of the father in Beijing lifting his young son high in the air, of the smiling boy in London being pulled along the sidewalk and swung by his two sisters. Looking at Zach, I see more than just a four-year-old boy holding a toy soldier. I see myself and all my hopes and dreams for a normal life as part of a normal family. I can't say good-bye to him. Because if I do, I'm afraid—no, more than that, I'm terrified—that I'll lose an important part of myself.

But what about Abbie and Uncle and . . .

What about me?

I raise my hand slowly, palms out and listen to myself say, "All right, soldier. I surrender."

Then I switch to mindpatch and say to Abbie, "I'll be back in a few minutes."

She doesn't answer, which means she's either turned off her patch or is very angry with me. Or both.

July 8, 1967, 7:36 P.M.
Expo 67, Montreal, Canada
Operation Blue Bird

The Jade Café looks even more impressive from the inside. While I was waiting to get into the Republic of China Pavilion, I'd noticed the fancy shrubs, but now I can see that they're actually carved in different animal shapes: tortoises, birds and even a bear.

"My most fav'rite flavor in the whole wide world is chocolate ice cream," Zach announces as we sit down at our table. "And my other most fav'rite flavor in the whole wide world is strawberry ice cream."

"You can only have one most favorite flavor, Zach," says Jim.

"Daddy's right," says Diane, pulling a pack of crayons and some paper from her bag and setting them down in front of Zach. "Only one most favorite per customer. You've got to decide, sweetheart."

"And butterscotch ice cream," Zach adds, reaching for the crayons. Everyone laughs, including me.

It feels good to laugh. And there's another feeling too. One that's making me feel all warm and tingly inside. This one's a bit harder to nail down. A kind of "rightness" is the best way I can describe it. Like I'm meant to be here at this moment. With Zach, Jim and Diane.

The place is packed. Lots of families with children. I wonder, do they think that I, Caleb, time thief slash orphan, am Zach's older brother, maybe? Just a normal person who is part of a normal family?

"Where's *your* mom and daddy?" Zach says, bursting the bubble of my fantasy.

"They are . . . not here," I say, realizing as soon as I've said it how dumb that must sound. I half expect to hear Abbie chime in with "Good one, *O Master of the Obvious.*" But my neural receptor stays silent. There's only seven minutes of overtime left. I should really get going. But the thing is, I don't want to go yet.

"Why not?" Zach says, reaching for a blue crayon and drawing a large circle. "Don't they like it here?"

I glance across at Jim and Diane. They're both rolling their eyes apologetically, but I can tell they're also waiting for my answer.

Just then, the waiter arrives with our ice cream. I swirl a big spoonful of vanilla around in my mouth. By the time I swallow, I've already thought up a great story of how it is that I'm here without my parents. It goes something like this: my dad is a top heart surgeon and couldn't come because the Belgian ambassador had a sudden heart attack while on a state visit to Washington, and my dad was flown in Air Force One to attend to him. And my mother, well, she couldn't come because she's in the High Arctic teaching children to read, and she couldn't get a flight because the airport's closed due to bad weather. But they both thought it was a good idea if I came to Expo 67 anyway, so here I am.

But amazingly, when I open my mouth, the lie doesn't come out.

Instead I say, "I don't live with my parents, Zach. I live with . . . my uncle."

"Uncle who?" Zach looks up at me, modeling his new chocolate ice cream mustache. "I have Uncle John and Uncle Tim. And I also have Auntie Mary and Aunt Lois, but they're not uncles, they're aunties."

I laugh and say, "He's just Uncle. He doesn't have another name."

Zach scrunches his eyebrows and draws two figures with a brown crayon. "Is he nice?"

I don't say anything.

"I'm sure he's nice," Jim answers for me. "C'mon, Zach. Finish up. It's almost time to go."

Zach looks right at me and says, "My uncles are nice. Uh-oh. There's no green." He spills all of the crayons onto the table. "What color should I make the grass?"

I look over the color choices. "How about purple?"

Abbie's voice breaks in over my patch. "If you're not here in one minute, I'm gone." Her flat tone tells me that she's beyond angry. I stand up quickly.

"Uh . . . thanks for the ice cream," I say. "I've got to go now."

Zach springs up from his chair, wraps his arms around me and squeezes hard. "Mom, can Caylid come with us tonight to that La Road place where they have all the rides? I'm gonna go on the pyramid ride and then on the big water coaster for my birthday."

"It's La Ronde, Zach. Not La Road," Diane corrects him. "I'm sure Caleb would love to come, sweetie, but he probably has other plans."

Zach releases me from the hug and says, "C'mon, Caylid. I'm five now. I can go with you on the water coaster. Right, Daddy?"

"I . . . uh . . . well, I don't think I've got other plans," I say. "I mean, I'll try to see if I can come, but Uncle, he might want me back . . ."

Jim smiles at me and shrugs. "If you can make it, we'd all love to see you. Do you know La Ronde? There's a ride there called the Gyrotron. You can't miss it. Just look for two pyramids. We'll be there in about an hour."

"Okay," I say.

I hurry toward the café's exit. At the same time, I try reaching Abbie over my mindpatch. No answer.

Where is she? Maybe she already left 1967. But would she really have left when there are still . . . I glance at my fingernail again—only two minutes of overtime left! I feel a cold sweat break out on my forehead. There's no way I can do the snatch in two minutes. But I've got to try.

I sprint to the front of the pavilion, pushing people out of my way as I run. Taking the escalator steps two at a time, I arrive at the snatch zone, breathless.

Thirty seconds to go.

There's a small crowd gathered around the exhibit. But Abbie isn't one of them.

If I had more time, I'd create the perfect distraction. Maybe a little fire with some nice, thick smoke.

Too bad I don't have more time.

I push through the crowd until I'm standing right in front of the glass case. Next, I grab my knife, cut a strip off my shirt, curl my fingers in a fist around it so that a quarter inch of handle is sticking out, and wrap the strip of cloth around my fist.

"Kiaaaaaah!" I cry as I smash the glass case.

I'm guessing that the reason why none of the thirty or so people watching have tackled me yet is because they're too stunned to act. That's fine by me. In fact, it's exactly the reaction I was hoping for. Of course, you can't expect stunned to last forever. I figure I have about five seconds max before it gives way to angry.

Still, you can do a lot in five seconds.

I pull the Xuande vase from the shattered case. For a split second, I think of putting the replica inside the case, but what's the point of that? Everyone here has already seen me snatching the original.

At least, I'm hoping it's the original. With everything going on lately between me and Frank, I can't be sure of anything. I glance around. The crowd is still mostly passive, but there are a few guys who look like they're ready to take me on. I've got to do this quickly.

I run my fingertips lightly over the vase, comparing it against the specs in my mission briefing notes. Two seconds later, I've got the results of the scan.

It's a fake!

I can't believe it! No, I can believe it. Frank has done it to me again. But I'm not going to let him get away with it. Not this time.

Uncle's words echo through my brain: "It left China onboard a ship piloted by the famous admiral Zheng on May 10, 1431 . . . upon arrival in the Ottoman Empire, the vase was regifted to Sultan Murad II. After that, the trail goes dead until 1967 . . ." The ship voyage! That's where Frank must have done the switch!

A hand grabs my arm, and as I shake free, the vase falls to the ground, shattering. I've got to get out of here right now!

I tap away at my wrist. I really shouldn't leap from here. There are easily over fifty people who will see me. But I'm in survival mode.

Just then, I hear a familiar voice.

"Move in a bit closer and crouch down, hon, so that I can get you and the smashed vase in the same shot," says Sidney Halpern, aiming his Rolleiflex. "Now, hold still . . ."

He takes the shot, and as the flash goes off I can feel my body begin to fade.

The last words I hear before I leave the twentieth century are Louise's: "If you say 'hold still' one more time, Sidney Halpern, I'm going to smash *you*."

XI

I'm gasping for air. The wind's been knocked out of me. My knapsack lies half open a foot away, the top of the replica Xuande vase poking out. I turn over onto my back. Patches of blue and white. Clouds? I blink and look again. No, not clouds. Sails. Six glorious, massive sails, billowing in the wind.

I've got to hand it to Uncle. He sure knows how to make a time travel device. I mean it's no small feat to land hundreds of years in the past on the deck of a sailing ship at sea. One small slip in either time or space, and I'd be floundering around in some very cold water.

Too bad Abbie isn't here with me. On second thought, she probably wouldn't be all that impressed with anything I do. After all, I'm not Frank.

Well, you can have your precious Frank! I want to say. No, I don't want to just say it. I want to shout it. And this might just be the most perfect place in the whole world for shouting; what with the wind howling and twenty-foot-high waves crashing against the side of the ship.

There'll be plenty of time for feeling miserable later, I tell myself. Right now I've got to stay focused.

I take a deep breath. The air is sharp and tangy. A spray of water catches me on the sleeve.

Heavy footsteps boom behind me, and I turn to see a giant of a man.

He looks a bit like Nassim on a bad hair day. But minus a few teeth.

He shouts something at me, and I don't have a clue what it is. My translator must not be working. From his tone, it's clear he isn't saying "good to see you."

As I scramble to my feet, a huge blast rocks the ship. I crash against the netting near the bow. Another blast, and this time I fall down onto the deck. Immediately, I wrap my shaking hands protectively over the back of my head.

For the next two seconds, everything's eerily quiet. It's as if the world has stopped.

Then the screaming starts. Horrendous, soul-ripping screams. And, in between, shouting from somewhere in front of me. Someone's barking out orders. Plumes of gray-black smoke everywhere. The smell of gunpowder. Flames licking up from a dozen points along the deck carried to new locations by the gusting, swirling wind.

I whip my head around toward the source of the shouting. The giant is there, clinging to the rail. Except he's not all there. A big chunk of his left arm just below the shoulder is missing.

There are others too: men in tattered clothes, some crawling, some pulling themselves along the deck using only their hands. And yet others who aren't moving much at all.

Get out of here, Caleb. This isn't what you signed up for. But I refuse to listen to the voice in my head. The Xuande vase is somewhere on this ship. And I'm not leaving without it.

Lurching forward now. Moving is difficult. It feels as if I'm climbing a hill instead of walking along a flat deck. Out of the corner of my eye, I see small furry things scurrying past me. Rats.

Another blast. I'm thrown sideways into some rigging. There's a hand ensnared in the net—not attached to an arm.

You will die unless you get out of here now. I rack my brain, hoping to recall even one sighting of my future self over the age of thirteen as proof that I'll live through the next few minutes. But I come up empty.

Yet another blast shudders through the ship, and now I'm hugging the deck, bracing myself for the final one that will end my pitiful existence on this planet.

My funeral will be short but memorable. Uncle will deliver the eulogy, and Abbie will be there looking stunning in a black leather pantsuit. Will she cry? I hope so, but I kind of doubt it. Frank will be standing close to her, a little too close. Nassim will be itching to get back to his crossword puzzles but will have to endure Phoebe's reconstruction of the last moments of my life complete with alternate endings for everyone to vote on.

Crawling forward. There's a doorway, but it's so far away. Inch by inch is the best I can do.

Finally, after what seems like an eternity, I reach it. The curtain to the lower decks.

As I push it to one side, smoke pours out, thick and black, searing my eyes and sending me into a coughing fit.

I pull my shirt up over my mouth and nose and gingerly place my foot on the first step.

On the third step, my foot brushes something and I almost stumble and fall. I kick whatever it is to the side and keep moving.

Men are coming up the steps. Coughing. Their eyes wild. I wait for them to pass and then carry on.

For a moment, I forget where I'm going and what I'm doing on this ship. It must be time fog making my thoughts all muddled. I've been in the past for probably close to fifty minutes now. My brain is screaming at me to get out of here. But I can't.

Finally, I reach the hold. The smoke is so dense I can't see more than two feet in front of me. I cough into my shirt and grope around with my hands. They touch barrels, coils of rope, crates . . .

The vase must be in one of them. Squinting through the smoke at the letters on the crates. But I can't make them out.

"Where are you?" I shout out loud. The fear in my own voice scares me.

Feeling around in the semidarkness. It has to be here somewhere. My hand brushes against something hard. Got it. An iron bar.

Levering the bar between the wood staves, I pry the lid of the first crate open.

Silk.

Push it aside and on to the next. A hacking cough escapes me, and I'm afraid I won't be able to stop. Water is entering the hold now. Dark, dirty water. Rising fast.

Wood splinters all around as I break open the next crate.

Tea.

And then the next.

More tea.

Panic is setting in. What if I'm on the wrong ship? Or on the right ship but the wrong voyage?

Only one crate left. This one has no letters on it. But there's an image: a flying dragon. Could it be?

I picture the crate from the Xuande vase exhibit at Expo 67—yes, it had a flying dragon design on it, same as this one!

The water's up to my chest now, and I thrash around. Bits of things float past me: part of a chair, a wheel, two or three small casks. Must be gentle.

I lever the iron bar again. There's a cracking sound as the wood begins to give. I push a bit harder, but instead of the lid bursting open, two of the wood staves snap.

I plunge my hand in and waggle my fingers, hungry for the feel of the Xuande vase.

Can hardly breathe through the smoke.

My fingers connect with wood chips. I dig through them, deeper into the crate, ignoring the needle-sharp slivers piercing the flesh of my arm. There! The edge of something hard. The vase!

Quickly, carefully, so as not to damage it, I pull the vase from the crate.

My heart beats faster as I hold it up in front of my eyes. For a moment I'm seeing double. I could swear there are two vases in front of me. Dizzy, I shut my eyes tight and wait for the feeling to pass.

I open my eyes. Better. Only one vase now. And it looks like the real thing. But I have to know for sure.

I close my eyes again and brush my fingertips against the smooth surface of the vase. Why is the scan taking so long? It must be the time fog interfering.

I repeat the entire process again. This time, success. In seconds, the comparison is completed and the truth becomes known.

The truth is ugly.

I'm holding a twenty-first-century machine-made vase.

Frank!

Raw white anger is whirling inside me, gathering itself into a fist of emotion. I raise the fake Xuande vase high over my head.

In my mind's eye, I can see myself hurling it against a wall. It would feel good to watch it break into a million pieces. So good.

I stop myself at the last second. Frank would want me to react this way, wouldn't he? To lose control. No, I refuse to let him win. Gently, I place the replica back inside the crate.

A plan starts to form in my mind. The first stop is Headquarters and a few words with Phoebe.

Tap, tap, tap on my right wrist.

Come on. Come on. Why haven't I left yet?

I start to shake and place a hand on the wall to steady myself. But the wall is gone. And so am I.

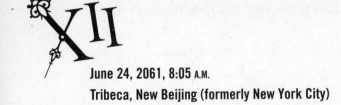

XII

June 24, 2061, 8:05 A.M.
Tribeca, New Beijing (formerly New York City)

I land in the alley of the apartment building two over from Headquarters. I'm still fuming from Frank's latest interference in one of
my snatches. Correction . . . in one of Abbie's and my snatches. Which
leads me to my next question: doesn't he get it that by making me
look bad, he also makes Abbie look bad? Or maybe somehow he spins
things with Uncle so that whatever goes wrong is only my fault.

I've got plenty of time to think about all of this because between
the time freeze and the time fog, I'm not going anywhere soon. A
parade of New Beijingers hurries past the entrance to the alley. I find
it amazing that there are entire lives being lived out there that have
nothing to do with my own. I know it sounds weird, but every once
in a while, I get the urge to follow some of these people just to see
what a normal life is like. And do they wonder about me in the same
way? I bet they have no idea that the skinny teenager sitting alone in
the alley with his back against the brick wall spends his days (and
nights) stealing stuff from the past.

As soon as the time freeze wears off, I hurry to Headquarters. I'm
still a bit time fogged, but not enough to keep me from moving.

"Four please, Phoebe," I say, out of breath.

"My, oh, my, we are in a rush today, aren't we?" says Phoebe. Her
persona isn't immediately obvious to me, although it involves a pair

126

of binoculars, a stepladder and a T-shirt that says OSTRICHES ARE PEOPLE TOO.

"Phoebe, I need to know how he did it," I say as the elevator door closes.

"Shhh," she says. "You'll scare them away."

"Scare who away?" I hate getting sucked into Phoebe's little games, but I'm going to need her in the right frame of mind to have any chance at getting her cooperation.

"The orange-crowned warblers," she says in a whisper. "They're very nervous types. If they feel pressured, they'll fly away."

"I'm not going to pressure them," I say.

"It has nothing to do with whether you are going to pressure them or not. It's whether they *think* you are pressuring them."

Why do I find every conversation with Phoebe so difficult?

"Well, then, what should I do?"

"Just speak normally," she says. "No, cancel that thought. Your normal would make any bird feel pressured. Pretend that I'm the Wizard of Oz and you've traveled all the way from Munchkinland to ask me for a favor."

"That's ridiculous," I say before I'm able to bite my tongue.

"Fine. This conversation is over."

"No, wait. I'll do it," I say. "O Great Oz—"

"Good start," she says.

I glance at the wall screen. Phoebe has traded her T-shirt for a royal robe and her ladder for a throne. She is seated and flipping through a magazine article titled "10 Things to Do in the Emerald City at Night."

"Can you please tell me where and when Frank was when he snatched the Xuande vase?"

"I know. But I can't tell you," Phoebe answers.

"Why not?" I ask.

"I was threatened with death," she says.

"You're a computer. You can't die," I remind her.

"There's death and there's *death*," she says. "I can die, believe me, but it'll be awfully hard for him to kill me. You see, I've hidden my critical components in different places."

"Please, Phoebe—er, Great Oz," I say. "Frank's been poaching my snatches."

"The Great Oz knows all," she says, sighing. "But like I said, the last time they were here, he threatened me. So I can't say any more. What is it with you guys? I don't see why you can't just get along and all work together."

"Did you say *they*? Who was with Frank?" I ask.

She clips a coupon from the magazine and says, "I love two for ones. With this one, if you order the roast beef dinner at Emerald City Steak and Frites, your companion gets a second entrée of equal value for free. How good is that?"

"C'mon, Phoebe. I've got to know," I say.

"My lips are sealed," she says, making a noise that resembles a zipper being pulled. "But I'll give you a clue. She's got long reddish hair that's in need of a good wash."

I feel like I've been stabbed in the back. Abbie! A storm is brewing inside of me.

Got to think. Well, if Phoebe won't answer questions about where and when Frank was, maybe she'll answer ones about where and when the Xuande vase was.

"All right," I say. "No more questions about Frank. I'm going to mention a few time/places where the original Xuande vase might have been right before Frank snatched it. All I need you to do is say if I'm hot or cold."

"Fire away," says Phoebe. "This could be fun."

"May 9, 1431, Shaolin Pier, China, near the loading dock for the *Tian Fei*," I say. I might as well start with the obvious.

"Chilly," answers Phoebe.

"September 23, 1425, the road from Xanxi to the Forbidden City," I say, thinking that Frank could have switched the vase en route to the emperor's birthday party.

"Cool as a cucumber," says Phoebe.

This isn't working. "What's colder," I ask, "cool as a cucumber or chilly?"

"It depends on what you're wearing," she answers.

Exasperating.

"April 23, 1423, Wu Yingxing's home," I say.

"Lukewarm," she says. "But that's only because of the way you said it."

"Well, then, what is the right way to say it?"

"I can't answer that," says Phoebe. "I can only say hot or cold."

"But you haven't been saying only hot or cold," I say, my voice rising, "you've been saying chilly, cool as a cucumber and lukewarm, and telling me I said stuff wrong."

"I don't have to play, you know. I've got other things to do with my time." Her lower lip is thrust out. I count to ten slowly to calm myself.

Better.

I think about what she said a second ago about Wu Yingxing's home being a lukewarm guess. Maybe she said that because he didn't make the vase in his house—maybe he made it somewhere else.

"I'm sorry. Just one more, okay?"

"Well . . . all right. If you promise to be nicer."

"I do. Now how about this: April 23, 1423, the place where Wu Yingxing made the vase."

"Hotter than Hades," she says.

Bingo. "Thanks, Phoebe. I owe you one," I say.

"Yes, you do, Caleb, and the Great Oz will be collecting very soon," she says.

"Well, then, I guess we're done here. If you'll just let me off on the fourth floor, I can handle the rest myself," I say.

"Is that it?" says Phoebe. "As soon as you have what you need from me, you cast me aside, like an empty carton of Thai takeout?"

"I wouldn't put it quite that way," I say.

"What way would you put it, then?" she asks.

She's trying to guilt me into staying longer. No way. I've got to get going and put my plan into action. It's simple, really: get to the time/place where and when Wu Yingxing made the Xuande vase, snatch it right after he makes it and replace it with the replica that I've got in my knapsack. Then, when Frank appears later, he'll be snatching a replica and replacing it with another replica. There's a chance he might scan my replica to see if it's the original, but I'm betting against it; after all, when you've got an ego the size of Frank's, the idea of someone outsnatching you wouldn't occur to you.

"Sorry, Phoebe," I say. "I suppose I might have been a bit insensitive."

"Hmmmph. More than a bit," she says.

But as she speaks, the elevator whirs into motion. I'm starting to have doubts about this whole business; that is, going to 1423 to outsnatch Frank. He can be dangerous. What if he knows I'm coming?

What if he's already set up some traps for me to get me in even further trouble?

The elevator door opens, and I step out. The hall is quiet. No one is around, which suits me just fine.

"Phoebe, does Frank know that I'm taking this trip?" I ask.

"Not yet," she says cryptically.

"What do you mean, 'not yet'?"

"It means exactly that," answers Phoebe. "He won't know until he comes in for his usual update of your recent activities."

My throat tightens. "You give him regular reports of everyplace I've been?"

"Well, not about your trips to the bathroom," she says. "Unless it involves traveling to the past to do it."

So Frank's been getting all my snatch information from Phoebe! I wonder what Uncle would do if he found out? And then it occurs to me: what if Uncle already knows? What if he's the one who told Frank to follow me?

"Phoebe, you can't tell him about me going to 1423," I say. "If you do, he'll try to outsnatch me again."

"Not my problem."

"Please?"

"Well . . . maybe I could be persuaded not to tell him about one little planned trip of yours," Phoebe says.

"Thank you, Phoe—"

"But it will cost you," she continues.

"All right, how much?" I ask.

"A thousand dollars."

"What?"

"The Great Oz has spoken. I'll take it in unmarked twenties."

"You know I don't have a thousand dollars," I say. "Besides, even if I did, what would a computer do with money?"

"That's my business," says Phoebe. "Now, pay up or I'll tell him you're going to Jǐngdézhèn."

"This is blackmail!" I shout.

"A girl's got to make a living," she says. I can hear the smile in her voice.

"Look, if you don't tell, I promise I'll bring you back something from China," I offer.

"Now you're on the right track," she says. "Make it something nice. No T-shirts, okay?"

"Fine. No T-shirts."

"And it's got to be something Uncle doesn't already have," she adds. "If you can manage that, and I like it, I'll waive my usual thousand-dollar fee."

This is a ridiculous conversation. And I have no idea what Uncle has and what he doesn't have. But the only way to end this is to agree.

"Deal," I say.

I step out of the elevator and head to the lounge. In the wardrobe closet, I find a long hooded Buddhist monk's robe and a pair of sandals. I also spot a cloth bag that's perfect for carrying the replica of the Xuande vase.

"Take an umbrella with you," says Phoebe. "They're calling for rain."

"How does he get away with it, Phoebe?" I ask.

"Beg your pardon?" says Phoebe.

It strikes me as strange that a computer is asking me to repeat what I've just said. After all, it's not like she's hard of hearing. She's probably just playing with me. "I said, 'How does he get away with it?' What I mean is, how can Frank shadow me while I'm on missions and interfere with my snatches without ever getting into any trouble with Uncle?"

"That's easy," she answers. "He's more devious and ruthless than you, and an expert manipulator."

She's right. Frank is all those things. But I can't be like him. I don't want to be like him. And if life was fair, Frank wouldn't get away with half the stuff he does. But life isn't fair, is it?

"And while we're on the subject of manipulation," she says, "since you're not a bad kid, I'm going to share another little tidbit with you."

"Okay."

"Your snatch partner might not be going all the way to the dark side."

I swear I can feel Phoebe's eyes on me studying me for a reaction, which is of course ridiculous because she doesn't have any eyes, unless you count all the hidden cameras sprinkled throughout Headquarters.

"What do you mean?" I ask.

"Well, she's spending an awful lot of time in the company of a certain person with curly black hair. And she seems to be liking it," says Phoebe.

"How can she possibly like him?" The words burst from my mouth before I can stop them. It's not like I even want or need Phoebe's advice on the subject.

"I didn't say she likes him," she says. "I said she *seems* to. There's a difference. And it's a big one. Personally, I don't think Frank gets the difference. He just thinks his hormones are irresistible to all members of the opposite sex, including Abbie. But what he doesn't get, what he hasn't figured out," she continues, switching to a whisper, "is that Abbie has an endgame."

"An endgame?" I whisper back.

"Yes, indeedy," says Phoebe with a trace of satisfaction in her voice. "She's playing him like a violin."

"What's she after?" I ask.

"How should I know?" Phoebe hisses. "I'm not a mind reader."

Her tone tells me she's finished sharing. "Right," I say heading for the fire escape. She's certainly given me a lot to think about.

"And one other piece of free advice," she says just as I'm about to step out onto the fire escape. "If you like someone, they'll never know it unless you show it."

I feel my ears getting warm. How does Phoebe know?

"I . . . I have to go," I say.

"So go, then," she says. "I'm not stopping you. And don't forget my present!"

As I program my wrist for 1423, I think about Phoebe's words. "She's playing him like a violin." If Phoebe's right, then Abbie is only faking liking Frank. Which makes me feel a lot better. Maybe she really is on my side.

Even so, my problems are far from over. I'm playing a dangerous game, trying to outsnatch Frank. If I go back earlier in time to beat him, he'll just counter by going back even earlier.

But if I do nothing, that's the same as inviting Frank to ruin my next mission and the one after that. No way. This time I'm going to take a stand. This time I'm not going to let him win.

XIII

April 23, 1423, 9:09 A.M.
Hills near Jĭngdézhèn, China

I'm rolling down a hillside.

There's no way to stop myself until the time freeze is over, so I just go with the roll. For the next three seconds, my mind conjures up images of all sorts of nasty obstacles that I'm about to crash into, including sharp-edged boulders and thick tree trunks.

Luckily, the slope eases off around the same time that my time freeze thaws. It's a good thing too, because only a few feet from where I finally come to a stop, the slope changes from gentle and soft to steep and rocky.

As I stand up and brush myself off, I make a mental note never again to program my patch when I'm time fogged. Luckily, I wasn't far off. I'd actually planned to land on the hill—but on the crest, not the side.

Even though I'm not at the top, I still have an excellent view. A few hundred feet below is a village partly shrouded in fog. I see about thirty thatched huts, but there might be more hiding under the mist. That must be the village of Jĭngdézhèn.

But what really gets my attention are a dozen or so egg-shaped structures scattered on the surrounding hillsides. Dark smoke rises out of some of them, and clustered around each is a sprinkling of smaller, square huts.

A narrow trail skirts the hillside about fifty feet away, and I start moving toward it, picking my way over boulders and through thickets. Some of the bushes have sharp nettles, and a couple of times I have to backtrack to avoid them.

By the time I reach the trail, my shirt is drenched in sweat. Just as I turn onto the path, a young boy appears on the trail ahead of me. He's barefoot and wearing only a tattered shirt that comes down to just below his knees.

"Hello," I say, giving him a friendly wave.

The boy just stares at me.

I'm not expecting him to say hello back. At least not in English. But I'm hoping that he'll say something, anything, so that my translator can kick in.

He continues to stare at me. It's starting to get on my nerves. I know it's juvenile of me, but I stare right back at him, hoping that if he won't say anything, at least he'll blink first and look away.

No such luck. In fact, the boy is soon joined by some of his friends, also barefoot and barely dressed, who join in the staring contest.

I try again, this time with the older ones. "Hi, there," I say.

Nothing.

Somehow, word must be getting out about me, because more people keep showing up. I'm soon surrounded by about twenty kids and adults.

I pick one of the adults for my next attempt at communication. "Excuse me, but I have come from very far to find the artist Wu Yingxing. Can you please direct me to his studio?"

No one's answering me, but there is some progress. A few of the adults have taken their eyes off me and are talking among themselves.

An old man finally steps forward. His brown face is weathered and heavily wrinkled.

Before I can say anything, he reaches out with a knobby finger, touches my face and traces a line down my cheek. Then he turns to the others and says, "So white. And the white is soft."

The good thing is my translator is working. The bad thing is he's just announced to everybody that I'm a pillow, and now they all swarm me, wanting to touch my face.

Then it dawns on me. I should have looked before I leapt. That is, I should have figured out that I would likely be the first white person these people have ever seen. And I should have disguised myself better before coming here. Should have but didn't. It's this business with Frank. It's got me making mistakes.

So much for flying under the radar.

"Wu Yingxing is an artisan with the Imperial Guild," says the old man, and I breathe a sigh of relief. It's my first real breakthrough since I arrived.

"Thank you," I say. "Can you please show me where his studio is?"

I must have said something very funny, because I can hear tittering and chuckling in the crowd.

The old man finally replies. "He does not have his own studio. He works with many others."

"I see," I say. And I really do. Artists in every century have always had a tough time getting by. It makes perfect sense to me that he'd want to split the rent.

"I would be grateful if you can lead me to where he works," I say.

The old man looks at me for a moment and then turns and says something to the others in a voice too soft for me to pick up. Whatever he says, though, sparks a heated debate. I only catch snippets of it because everyone is talking and there are too many voices for my translator to handle at once.

The lively discussion goes on for about five minutes, and then, just as suddenly as it began, everyone falls silent. The old man turns to me and says, "We were not able to agree on who shall have the honor of accompanying you to the workplace of Wu Yingxing. So it has been decided that we shall all go."

"Thank you," I say. "But that's really not necessary."

Necessary or not, I'm outvoted. We start out along the trail, adults in front, children at the back and me sandwiched in between. The footing is tricky in spots, so I walk mostly with my head down, focusing on where to place my next step. When I finally look up, I'm surprised to see that our little delegation isn't headed toward Jǐngdézhèn at all. Rather, we're headed away from it, toward one of those egg-shaped huts on the next hillside.

This is great. I've got my own honor guard. And what will I do when I find the real Xuande vase? Tell them all to close their eyes for a moment so that I can exchange it for the replica and then vanish?

Our procession continues along the trail and up the hillside. The old man is setting a blistering pace, and I'm huffing to keep up.

A wave of dizziness comes over me, and I stumble forward and almost fall. I was afraid of this. I knew I should have spent more time in 2061 before coming back to the past. The short visit to New Beijing obviously wasn't long enough to clear my time fog.

After about twenty minutes of walking, we arrive at the top of the hill. The air is filled with smoke and some smells that I can't identify. I crane my neck to see around the nine or ten adults from my procession who are standing in front of me.

The hilltop is a hive of activity. People are hurrying around and shouting back and forth to each other. Still, when I look closer, I can see that there seems to be an order to the madness. Everyone, and by that I mean the men since there aren't any women in sight, has his own job to do. Some carry firewood. Others are seated on the ground kneading or pounding what looks to be white clay. Yet others are forming the clay into shapes, pouring it into molds or trimming the edges with knives. There are five guys sketching outlines of animals directly onto the clay vases.

My gaze shifts to the egg-shaped hut. It's easily the size of three of the square huts and is made entirely of sunbaked bricks. I'm guessing this is a kiln, where the clay vases and other objects are fired at high temperatures to harden them into porcelain. Two men are peering into it through small holes. They are wrapped mummy-like from head to toe in strips of clothing. Even their faces and hands are covered.

Someone says something, and my honor guard parts like the Red Sea, giving me a clear view of the workers. And them of me. Then, as if on some hidden signal, all the workers drop to their knees and kowtow deeply in my direction.

Another wave of dizziness hits me. This one's stronger than the last one, and it takes all my willpower to stay upright.

"What's going on?" I ask the old man, once I've gathered myself.

"The workers believe you are T'ung," he says.

"Who?"

"T'ung," he repeats.

He must see the blank look on my face because he says, "T'ung is the god of the potters. He had a human life before he became a god. It is said that when he was a young man, he leapt into the blazing heat of the kiln to attempt to save some workers."

"Did he get them all out?" I ask.

The old man smiles. "The men were not in the kiln, only the dragon fish bowls they had made. But until T'ung appeared, each time the men tried to fire the dragon fish bowls, the bowls emerged from the kiln scorched and ruined. And each time this happened, the eunuch masters who ruled over the workmen beat them badly with sticks. When T'ung heard of the men's plight, the next time they tried to fire the dragon fish bowls, he leapt into the blazing heat of the kiln."

"And then what happened?" I ask.

"The dragon fish bowls emerged from the kiln perfectly fired. But T'ung had vanished. From that day forward, the workers worshipped T'ung as god of the potters, and on the very same spot where the miracle occurred, the workers built a temple in his honor."

What a nice story. Too bad they have the wrong guy. I'm just about to break the news to the workers when I stop myself. The story's got me thinking. Maybe I could be T'ung, at least for a little while . . .

"Please tell them to rise and get on with their work," I say to the old man.

He says something and everyone begins to get up slowly.

"Can you also please find Wu Yingxing? I would like to speak with him." My words come out slurred. It must be the time fog.

The old man turns to one of the workers, who hurries away. In a moment, he's back with a skinny man who looks better dressed than most of the others.

On seeing me, the thin man immediately drops to his knees and kowtows.

"Is this him?" I ask the old man.

He nods.

I reach my hand forward and signal for Wu to stand.

"I am an admirer of your work," I say, "and am honored to meet you."

"Next to your great works, Heavenly Master, the work of my hands is awkward and childlike," says Wu.

What a flatterer. I'd like to stand around and trade compliments with him but I've got to get this done quickly. The time fog is really beginning to do a number on me.

So I cut to the chase and say, "There is one piece in particular that I admire."

"May it please the Great T'ung," he says, "any piece of my work that finds favor in your eyes, I will bestow upon you as a gift from your humble servant . . ."

It's an offer I can't refuse.

But just as I open my mouth to put my order in, he continues, "Except for one piece that I have already promised to the emperor."

Rats. Nothing's ever easy.

"Would that piece by chance be a vase with a dragon and phoenix design on it and the symbol of the House of Confucius painted next to the Mark of the Reign?" I ask.

"My Lord sees all," says Wu.

"Not all. Just some," I say. "Before I leave this place, it would please me to gaze upon this work that you have promised to the emperor." Wow, I'm even starting to talk like a god.

"Certainly, Master of All Artisans," says Wu.

He gives a little bow, does a half turn and shouts in the general direction of the kiln, "Shen, have you fired the special order for the emperor yet?"

One of the mummy men, presumably Shen, shouts back, "It's in the kiln and I can go get it soon."

Soon. Now, there's a great word. It can mean anything from two seconds to two years, depending on what you're talking about and who's doing the talking.

I'm about to open my mouth to cross-examine Wu on how soon is "soon" when I hear a commotion coming from the next hillside. I

141

turn and see a large procession, about fifty yards up the trail, headed our way.

My stomach clenches when I see a white face framed by curly black hair among the group.

Immediately I duck behind Wu. There's still a chance Frank hasn't seen me yet. I've got to act fast. But you can't hurry up a kiln. Those things are hot—well over a thousand degrees.

My eyes ping-pong between Frank's procession and Shen stationed outside the kiln. They're closer now—only about thirty yards away.

Just then, Shen springs into action, opening the kiln doors and stepping inside.

I sprint toward the kiln. Except that it's really more trot than sprint. My legs feel so heavy that running is simply out of the question.

After what seems like forever, I finally reach the kiln and hurry inside, closing the doors behind me. A wave of intense heat washes over me, and it's hard to breathe.

It's dark inside, but the small holes let in enough daylight for me to see. I remove my cloak and say, "Where is it, Shen?" trying to hide the very ungodlike desperation in my voice.

"Here, O Great One," he says, pointing to a small ledge on the kiln's second level.

And there it is. The Xuande vase. Even in the dim light, it's magnificent. The dragon and the phoenix have been exquisitely rendered in cobalt blue, and the overall effect is breathtaking. Funny I should feel that way about it. After all, I've seen the vase on a holo and also in replica form. I guess nothing beats the real thing.

A wave of dizziness rocks me, and I reach out a hand for support.

But there's nothing to hold on to, so I sink to my knees. My head is still spinning, and for a moment I forget where I am. I try moving my arms, but they feel disconnected, like they belong to someone else.

Shen drops down beside me, looking bewildered. Ordinarily I'd say something reassuring but I've got my own problems to deal with right now.

I close my eyes for a moment and then open them. There is something important that I must do. If only I could remember what.

A vase. Yes, something about a vase.

Crawling on all fours now toward a beautiful vase depicting a flying dragon and phoenix.

There are markings on the vase: a reign mark and, right above that, a small star symbolizing the House of Confucius.

I take a deep breath of the hot air. My thoughts begin to clear and then in a flash I remember what I have come here to do.

Still, I hesitate. A cold sweat breaks out on my forehead as panic seizes me. What if it doesn't work?

No. Positive thoughts only. It must work. It will work.

With Shen watching, I remove the replica from my bag and set it down next to the real Xuande vase. I use my cloak as a pot holder to pick up the original and place it inside my bag. I can feel the heat of the vase clear through to my hands, and I almost drop it.

Shouts. Coming from nearby.

Shen doesn't move or say anything. He looks stunned by my actions. I can guess what's going through his mind. He's probably asking himself if I'm a god or a thief. Whatever he picks as his answer, I don't envy him. He's got to explain all of this to the others.

Because I'm not sticking around.

The doors to the kiln burst open. Angry shouts cut through the gloom. Just before I touch my wrist, something catches my eye. It's a small cream-colored porcelain tortoise. There's writing on the tortoise's shell. Without a second thought, I use my cloak again to grab the tortoise and place it inside my bag alongside the Xuande vase.

The last thing I see before I touch my wrist and leave 1423 is Shen's wide, questioning eyes.

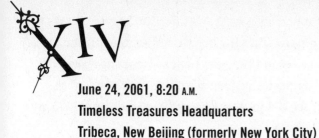

XIV

June 24, 2061, 8:20 A.M.
Timeless Treasures Headquarters
Tribeca, New Beijing (formerly New York City)

I land on my belly beside the bottom rung of the fire escape in back of Headquarters. It's hot and humid, and it's a good thing I'm lying down, because in my time-frozen, time-fogged state, there's not much else I can do. My shoulder feels warm and then I realize that's because it's rubbing up against my knapsack that has the Xuande vase inside it. All around me is quiet.

I take lungfuls of the humid New Beijing air and feel the time freeze lifting.

My fingernail tells me that it's only twenty minutes past eight in the morning, but it feels a lot later than that. When I take an unauthorized side trip during a mission, I always program my return to the present as if I didn't take the side trip at all. That way my little excursions aren't obvious to anyone checking my file.

After a few more minutes, I stand up and make my way to the front of Headquarters.

I start up the steps. Everything looks quiet. I have a sudden urge to turn back and start running. Or, in my present condition, shambling. It might be the cowardly thing to do, but I have no problem with that. What's really stopping me is knowing that if I did make a break for it, it would be only a matter of time before Nassim found me and brought me back. No, whatever is waiting for me, I'm going to face it head-on. I step onto the elevator.

"Fourth floor, please, Phoebe."

The wall screen comes on. Phoebe's persona is dressed in army fatigues and is slithering on her belly across a muddy battlefield.

"You're in big trouble," she says.

"What do you mean?" I say, but already my stomach's twisting into a knot.

"Frank's been asking everyone if they've seen you. He's furious with you about something, although he won't say what. I haven't seen him this angry in months."

"Good," I say. But my shaking voice is giving me away.

"Good?" repeats Phoebe. "Ice cream is good. Holo-flicks of space aliens getting zapped are good. But Frank being mad at you is Not Good. Trust me, I've been there."

Not for the first time, I wish I had taken the stairs.

"The fourth floor, please," I repeat.

"Show me what you brought me first," she says. The screen changes, and Phoebe is decked out in a four-star general's uniform. She's standing in front of a large map of Europe and is moving some pins around.

I sigh, reach into my bag and pull out the porcelain tortoise.

"You got me a turtle? Are you saying that I'm slow?"

"Not at all," I say. "Uncle says that the tortoise is a symbol of long life and happiness. And, besides, it's not just a turtle. It has some writing on it, too. How rare is that?"

"Hmmm. Hold it up so I can read it," she says.

I hold up the tortoise. Its off-white shell is covered in Chinese letters painted cobalt blue. Then I hear Phoebe recite:

"*Sitting alone in the dark bamboo,*
I play my lute and whistle song.

Deep in the wood no one knows
The bright moon shines on me."

For a blissful moment, it's quiet on the elevator. Then I hear a long sigh.

"Now, that's what makes getting up in the morning worthwhile," says Phoebe. "You know, I've been thinking of trying my hand at this. That is, writing some verse for a special occasion. Hey, I've got it. I can compose something for your funeral."

"My funeral?"

There's a scratchy sound coming from Phoebe that might be her laughing.

"Frank's really pissed at you, Caleb," she says. "His word not mine. I wouldn't rule out a little holiday time for you in the Barrens for this one."

"What are you talking about?" I say. "It was my snatch. He had no business being there at all."

"True," says Phoebe. "But it's all about spin, isn't it? And, don't take this personally, but when it comes to spinning things to Uncle in his favor, Frank's got you beat six ways from Sunday. If something bad happens to you, can I have that neat little driftwood carving you've been working on?"

"What can a computer do with a wood carving?" I ask.

"I was thinking of hanging it in the elevator as a kind of conversation piece. When my riders ask me about it, I'll say it was carved by a dear friend who tragically passed away before his time. Wait, maybe I won't hang it. Maybe I'll just sell it. They say art is worth a lot more after the artist kicks the bucket."

"Very funny," I say.

But I'm not laughing. I figure it's going to be a long time before I laugh again.

Time to hand the vase in to Nassim.

As I enter the lounge, my eyes immediately zero in on Abbie, cozied up next to Frank on the sofa. From what I can tell, she's enjoying his company, nodding at every gem that comes out of his mouth. He's wearing a blue, gold, red and white Great Friendship T-shirt, with the sleeves cut off to show his muscles. I watch as Frank flashes one of his megawatt smiles at her. She throws her head back and laughs. Lovely.

He looks my way. First his eyes flick to the cloth bag under my arm and then lock on to me. There's pure hatred in his stare. Lucky for me he knows as well as I do that Uncle has cameras all over this place and that if he tries to smash me or the vase, he'll be in big trouble.

I glance away. So much for a quick hand-in. It looks like it's been a busy morning and no one's turned in any snatch objects yet. Which means I'll have to wait my turn. Or I should say Abbie and I will have to wait our turn, since it was a team snatch.

Frank holds up his hands and announces, "Show and tell time, folks. Rat face, you're on."

He's looking straight at Raoul when he says this. Raoul opens his mouth, no doubt to protest his new nickname, but wisely says nothing.

As Raoul unslings a bag from his shoulder, we all gather around.

Raoul is smiling, but I can see his hands shaking.

There's a hush as he withdraws a large U-shaped object from the bag. But it's quickly replaced by laughter from Frank and a smirk from Lydia.

"A toilet seat?" says Frank in between guffaws.

Raoul's turning a shade of twentieth-century fire-truck red. "It belonged to the crown prince of Moravia," he says with great dignity.

It has the opposite effect of course. Lydia snorts, and Frank doubles over with glee.

I glance over at Abbie. She's still sitting next to Frank. It looks like their knees are touching.

Frank recovers just long enough to ask Raoul, "Hey, is the throne still warm?"

This draws gales of laughter from both girls.

Then Frank does something unbelievable. He reaches over and puts his arm around Abbie's shoulder. But what's even more unbelievable is that she doesn't even flinch. She actually lets the thing stay there.

Just then the door to Nassim's office slides open. The laughter stops.

"Caleb and Abbie, you're first," says Nassim's voice from beyond the doorway.

I head toward the open door. Without looking, I sense Abbie making her way from across the room.

It's pitch-black beyond the threshold. I gently place the cloth bag containing the Xuande vase down on the floor, assume a fighting stance and wait for the attack. A coordinated defense would be better, but for that, Abbie and I would need to be on speaking terms.

I'm two steps in now, concentrating on keeping my breathing regular.

Fifteen seconds pass. Thirty. Still nothing.

At the forty-second mark, I relax slightly. Big mistake. The whirlwind attack leaves me gasping for air and my right arm in an arm bar. The slightest shift, and it will snap like a twig.

"Eighteenth-century poison of choice. Seven letters."

Normally, I'd hold out a bit longer, but the pressure on my arm is unbearable.

"Hemlock," I cry out.

"Excellent!" cries Nassim, releasing me. He snaps his fingers and light fills the room, revealing a miniature stone bridge over a floor painting of a jade-green pond. A sculpture of a Mongol warrior in full battle gear toting a curved blade stands on a pedestal just inside the entrance.

You can definitely see Uncle's touch in the redecorating.

Floating above everything is a red neon hologram of Uncle's saying of the week: "Don't dwell in the past. Steal from it."

I massage my sore arm and watch as he whirls to face Abbie at the center of the small stone bridge.

Abbie's opening move, a flying side kick, is flawlessly executed. Nassim blocks the kick and counters with an elbow strike, which Abbie blocks just in the nick of time.

"Goliath was one. Ten letters," shouts Nassim.

"Philistine," she yells without hesitation, unleashing a torrent of punches, all of which Nassim deflects, but not without some effort.

They move gracefully, trading kicks and jabs for a while but without any serious scoring on either side.

"Enough," says Nassim finally, signaling a stop. "So what do you have for me today?"

Abbie looks at me for the first time. It's clear from her eyes what she's asking. She wants me to do the talking.

"Here it is, Nassim," I say reaching into the cloth bag, "The Xuande vase."

I can feel Abbie's eyes still on me as I remove the vase. But I don't look her way.

Nassim squints at it and says, "Are you certain this is the original?"

"What do you mean? Of course I'm certain." But sweat is already starting to break out on my forehead.

"The reason I ask," he says, "is that this is the second Xuande vase that's been turned in today. Frank turned one in earlier."

"Well, why don't you just scan it?" asks Abbie. "You'll know in a minute."

Nassim looks at us for a moment and then says, "I have special instructions on this one. If there is any doubt, Uncle wants to handle any testing personally."

I try to keep my expression neutral, but it's so hard. What if this one isn't the original either? What if I snatched my own replica or if Frank managed to get back there again? Impossible. This must be the original. But did I scan it? My mouth goes dry. All I can remember is that I was in a big rush to get out of there . . . so maybe I didn't. But it shouldn't matter. I snatched it the moment they opened the doors to the kiln after it had been fired. There's no way Frank could have gotten there before me. Not this time.

"Fine," I say. "Uncle will see that I'm right."

I let out a long breath and turn to leave, but Nassim says, "Before you guys go, I have a few questions."

Panic stabs me. I've got to stay calm. He's just doing his job, that's all. He's not out to nail me.

He turns to Abbie and says, "How did the snatch go? Any complications?"

"Nassim, I gave—" I begin.

"I didn't ask you, Caleb," says Nassim, cutting me off. "Please allow Abbie to answer."

"There was one complication," she says.

"What was that?" Nassim asks.

I'm holding my breath and sweating big-time. A thousand thoughts roll around in my head. What if she tells Nassim that instead of focusing on the snatch I was spending time with Zach and his family? Or what if she says that she suspects that I messed around with history and tells him to check my file for any side trips to the past? Either of those what-ifs will force Nassim to go straight to Uncle. And then . . . well, best not to think about that part.

Abbie turns and faces me. I meet her glance, careful not to show any emotion.

"Well," she begins. I hold my breath again. "Expo 67 was just so amazing that we didn't want to leave!"

I exhale slowly and feel the relief flooding through me. She backed me up!

"Very well," Nassim says. "We're done here. You can go."

We nod and leave Nassim's office. As we pass through the lounge, I can feel Frank shooting daggers at me with his eyes, but I keep my glance straight ahead until we're out of there.

"Thanks for backing me up in there," I say.

"You're welcome," Abbie says. Her tone is polite and cautious, as if to say she's just doing her job as my snatch partner, nothing more and nothing less.

"How did you manage it? The snatch, I mean," she asks as we walk down the hall.

"It wasn't easy," is all I say. I want to tell her everything, but one thing is bothering me. It's what Phoebe said about Abbie and Frank coming to see her.

She frowns at me. She knows I'm holding back. Thankfully, we reach the door to the boys' dorm before there's time for any more awkward silence.

"Look, I'm really tired, so I think I'll go rest for a while," I say without looking at her.

"Okay. See you later, then," she says. Her tone is flat.

"Yeah. See you." I slip inside the dorm.

I have the dorm to myself. As soon as I flop down on my bunk, I realize I wasn't lying when I said I was tired. Maybe I should take a nap. All I've got to do is close my eyes and—

A slamming door wakes me.

"I'm going to get you back, Caleb." Frank's voice cuts through the air like a blade.

"What?" I ask, groggily.

"You know exactly what I'm talking about. The Xuande vase mission. You planted a replica, hoping that I would steal it. And I almost fell for it. Don't think I'm going to let this one go easily. I never forget when someone crosses me."

"And I never forget when someone poaches my snatches," I say, fully awake now. It was probably the wrong thing to say, but with Frank there is no right thing to say. And what did he mean when he said that he "almost fell for it"? He did fall for it. He's messing with my mind. I've got to stay calm and not let him get to me. He can say whatever he wants, but as soon as Uncle scans the vase, he'll know that the original is the one I turned in.

"Is that so? Do you know what Abbie thinks about all of this?" he says, and the words burn me.

Frank doesn't wait for my answer. "She says you've been distracted lately. That you messed up the snatch this morning."

I can feel my cheeks burning.

"You don't know anything!" I shout. So much for being calm. How much does he really know?

Frank laughs and heads out of the dorm. There's really no reason for him to stay. After all, he's accomplished what he came here for—making me very angry.

I have a sick feeling in the pit of my stomach. Frank is bent on revenge. That's never a good thing.

I reach for my carving and knife. It's a long time before I'm able to calm down again.

XV

June 24, 2061, 11:00 A.M.
Timeless Treasures Headquarters
Tribeca, New Beijing (formerly New York City)

Get up, Caleb," says Raoul, bursting into the dorm. "Nassim mind-patched me. He says you have an appointment with Uncle. Frank is already there, and Abbie is on her way. You've got five minutes to get to the fifth floor."

"Are you serious?" I ask, but I know the answer just by looking at Raoul's paler-than-usual face.

I stash my carving and scramble off the bed. Why does Uncle want to meet? And then I remember. The Xuande vase. Nassim said that Uncle wants to do the scanning himself. He must have done it, and now he wants to meet with us to announce the results. Why not just tell Nassim and have him tell us? My stomach clenches. None of this can be good.

I take a pit stop in the bathroom. After I wash my hands, I let the faucet run for a minute. Watching the water spiral down into the drain usually relaxes me. But not this morning.

I head upstairs. When I arrive at reception, Nassim is hunched over a crossword puzzle.

"Hello, Caleb," he says.

He sounds cheery, but you never really know with Nassim. The guy keeps a pretty tight rein on his emotions.

"Hi," I say. "I'm here for the meeting with Uncle."

"Right, let's go."

The big man turns, and I follow him down the hall.

I've got nothing to worry about, I try to reassure myself. The more I think about it, the more I'm convinced that there's no way Frank could have outsnatched me on this one. I got the Xuande vase at the earliest possible instant. If he'd gone back any earlier in time, it would still have been baking in the kiln or it wouldn't exist at all. So why does it feel like I'm marching to my own execution?

The door to Uncle's office slides open. Nassim and I enter.

Frank and Abbie are seated cross-legged on the floor, their backs to me. Uncle is standing by the aquarium, hands at his hips. He looks sharp in a forest green *hanfu* with matching red dragons down the arms and a red sash. His jeweled sword is in its usual position tucked under the sash.

Two vases rest on simple small tables in the middle of the room. I wonder idly what happened to that special bamboo table Uncle showed us on the holo. Maybe he's saving it for after the scan.

From here I can't tell the vases apart. In front of the vase on the left, a simple white placard says FRANK. A second one, with my and Abbie's names, stands before the second vase.

No one moves a muscle when I enter. Uncle appears to be totally engrossed in the aquarium. Which is strange because nothing is going on unless you count Shu Fang and Ting Ting swimming lazily through the water. I've never been jealous of a turtle before, but if someone offered me the chance to switch lives with either one of them for however long this meeting took, I'd say yes in a heartbeat.

"Caleb, *zǎo shàng hǎo!*" says Uncle, turning.

"Good morning, Uncle."

"Please." He gestures toward a spot on the floor between Abbie and Frank.

Nassim stays put by the doorway, arms folded over his chest.

As I sit down, Frank shoots me a glance, but I ignore him.

"Now that everyone is present, let us begin," says Uncle. "You may be wondering why I have called you here this morning. But I think not. I think that you know the reason. After all, the three of you are very intelligent."

I glance at Abbie out of the corner of my eye. She's sitting ramrod straight and looks as tense as I feel.

"And being the intelligent time snatchers that you are, you would have very quickly deduced that something in this room is not quite right. What do you think that might be, Caleb?"

My mouth is dry, and my words come out raspy. "There are two vases when there should only be one."

"Precisely. But why should I complain? I send my time snatchers out to steal one Xuande vase and instead they come back with two. I should be overjoyed, should I not?"

He leaves the question hanging out there. None of us dare touch it.

"But in this case there can only be one original, isn't that right, Abbie? The other must be a replica."

"That's right, Uncle," says Abbie. To her credit, I don't detect even a slight hitch in her voice.

Uncle turns back to the aquarium and presses a button on the control panel. Scores of tiny goldfish stream into the aquarium. In a flash, one of the turtles—Ting Ting, I think—is upon them, devouring several with each snap of his jaws. Shu Fang appears content to wait for leftovers.

"Well, then, we have a dilemma. Frank, I will start with you. This was not your snatch. How was it that you became involved?"

"It's true, Uncle," Frank says. "This wasn't my snatch. But I happened to see Caleb and Abbie at Expo 67 when I was there on . . .

other business. So, I decided to keep an eye on them just to make sure they didn't mess up."

"Whatever would make you think that two of my top time snatchers needed a babysitter?" says Uncle. His voice is so cold. I've never heard him speak to Frank this way.

I can sense Frank squirming beside me. There's no good answer to that question. Even for Frank.

"I . . . I don't know, Uncle. It was just a feeling I had."

Uncle paces slowly back and forth in front of the aquarium, hands clasped behind his back. It looks like he is deep in thought, weighing Frank's words. But it's all a show. I'll bet my carving that he planned exactly how this meeting would go long before any of us stepped into his office.

"I see. You had a 'feeling.' Tell me, then, at what point did you decide that it was incumbent on you to perform their snatch?"

"At about the twenty-eight-minute mark from when they arrived, I checked up on them and noticed that neither of them was at the snatch zone. So I thought I'd better do the snatch myself."

A sound escapes from Uncle's mouth that I've never heard before. I can't be sure, but I think it's a kind of mocking laugh.

"You seem to have known quite a bit about their snatch," he says. "What time they arrived, where the snatch zone was and, apparently, what the snatch object was. How was it that you knew all of this when mission information is strictly confidential between me, Nassim and the assigned time snatchers?"

"Caleb was bragging about it in the dorm," says Frank without skipping a beat. "He said it was a very important snatch to you, Uncle, and rubbed it in my face that he and Abbie were picked to do it and not me and Lydia."

"That's a lie," I shout.

Uncle raises his hand toward me. "Do not interrupt, please. Now, Frank, before you performed the snatch, did you scan the snatch object to determine whether it was a replica?"

"I couldn't do a proper scan because I didn't have the mission file," Frank answers. "But I didn't need to. Before they abandoned the snatch, I overheard Caleb tell Abbie that he had scanned the snatch object and that it was the original."

He's lying through his teeth. But I can see why. He's trying to pin the blame on me.

"Hmmm," says Uncle, "if the one you snatched was the original, how is it, then, that there are two vases here?"

"Theirs must be a replica," says Frank.

"I see," says Uncle, turning toward me.

"And what do you say, Caleb? Is your vase a replica?"

"No, Uncle, it is not," I say.

"Well, then, we are no closer to discovering the truth, are we? Abbie, is there anything you care to add to the discussion at this point?"

"No, Uncle," she says.

Is that all? Isn't she going to say something like "the one we snatched is definitely the original"? Or "it's obvious that Frank is lying"? Or even just "I agree with Caleb"?

Uncle lets out a long sigh. "I suppose we should put an end to this mystery. Nassim, the hammer please."

Hammer? I can't believe it. He's going to smash one of the vases! I don't understand . . . destroying it won't tell him if it's a replica. And what if he destroys the original by mistake?

Nassim strides over to where Uncle is standing and hands him a silver hammer.

"Now, let us see. Which one will we start with first. How about yours, Frank?"

I can see that Frank is trying to hold it together but his right knee is shaking like a leaf. Here's his chance. Maybe if he says it's a replica now, he'll get off a bit easier. But he says nothing.

In a single motion, Uncle raises the hand with the hammer well over his head and brings it smashing down on Frank's vase.

With a loud crash, the vase shatters into about twenty pieces.

Nassim, broom and dustpan in hand, moves forward, but Uncle holds up his hand, "Not just yet," he says. Then he bends down, picks up one of the shards and examines it.

I exchange glances with Abbie. It's clear from her wide eyes that, like me, she has no idea what's going on.

After a moment, Uncle drops the shard to the floor and moves to his left. Now he's standing over the vase that I snatched from the kiln near Jǐngdézhèn. The hammer is still in his hand. I have a sick feeling in my stomach. Surely he won't.

Uncle lifts the hammer high over his head, pauses and then brings the hammer smashing down on the Xuande vase.

I gasp.

Somewhere in my brain, it registers that the sound made by the hammer's contact this time is different. But that thought is overruled by another that screams, *He has just destroyed the original Xuande vase!*

The broken remains of the Xuande vase lie on the table. Without a trace of emotion, Uncle lays the hammer down, picks up two of the fragments, studies them and places them back on the table. Then he picks up the largest fragment and turns it this way and that.

As he does this, I notice what looks like a thin dark line on one side of the fragment. At first I think the line is painted on, but then, as Uncle continues to rotate the piece in his hands, I realize that it is not a line at all. It's an opening. The piece is hollow.

Uncle reaches beneath his *hanfu* and withdraws a pair of twee-zers. Next he inserts them into the narrow opening in the shard.

My mouth goes dry. On either side of me, Abbie and Frank are craning their necks forward.

When he withdraws the tweezers, they are gripping something. A strip of paper? No. Not paper. But something that is paper thin.

A smile plays across Uncle's lips as he holds the brittle thing up to the light.

"Exquisite. Do you know what I'm holding?" he says.

I'm glad Uncle didn't put my name at the end of his question, because I have no idea.

"This is a fragment of one of the earliest versions of the *Analects* of Confucius. Have you heard about the *Analects*, Caleb?"

"No, Uncle, I haven't," I say.

"The *Analects* are the teachings of Confucius, first committed to writing by his students. One of his most passionate students was his grandson, Zisi, who recorded his grandfather's teachings on strips of bamboo.

"The strips were passed from generation to generation among the descendants of Confucius. Certain of them were acquired by an artisan by the name of Wu Yingxing."

Uncle is in his element. I'm trying to focus on his story, but all I can do is stare at the pieces of the broken Xuande vase.

"Wu did not have any children to bequeath his treasure to. So, when he became old and sensed his own death was near, he decided to do something special. He made a vase with hollow walls and slipped the precious bamboo strips inside. And to mark the vase as the special one, he engraved upon it the symbol of Confucius."

Uncle shifts his gaze from me to Frank. I let out a long breath.

"Well, Frank," says Uncle, "it appears that your vase was the replica and that Caleb and Abbie's was the original."

Frank says nothing.

Uncle steps to the right, bends down and picks a shard off the floor. It's a large, crescent-shaped piece of Frank's replica. He touches its jagged edge with his middle finger and smiles.

"Have you had trouble with your hearing lately, Frank?" he asks.

"No, Uncle," says Frank, his voice shaking slightly.

"That's odd," says Uncle, "because I distinctly recall telling you that I do not want you interfering with Caleb and Abbie's snatches."

Uncle presses the shard's sharp edge against his own palm. For an instant, I think he's going to draw blood, but he pulls the shard back at the last second.

Frank stays silent, his eyes riveted to Uncle's little hand play.

"But since you assure me that your hearing is sound, I must conclude that perhaps you were distracted when I told you this. That perhaps you were only listening with one ear. Do you think that is possible?"

Frank nods. My heart is pounding. Uncle is going somewhere with all of this.

"I'm glad you agree," says Uncle. "That is what I thought too."

Quick as a flash, Uncle bridges the distance between him and Frank. Reaching out with the speed of a viper, he grabs Frank by the hair and swings the shard in a fast, downward motion, slicing off the top part of Frank's right ear.

"My ear!" Frank cries in pain and disbelief, bringing a hand up to the side of his head.

"Why are you acting so surprised?" says Uncle. "By your own admission, you have only been using one of your ears. It's clear that you had no use for the other one."

I'm too stunned to move or to say anything.

"Nassim, please escort Frank from my office," says Uncle. "And do take care. I would prefer that he not bleed on the carpet."

"Yes, boss."

Frank, clutching his ravaged ear and sobbing, allows Nassim to lead him away.

I place my elbows on my knees to stop my legs from shaking. But it's no use.

Uncle picks some fluff off his *hanfu*, looks at Abbie and me and smiles as if nothing has happened. Then he says, "The two of you have performed admirably. As your reward for bringing me the Xuande vase, I will allow you to pick your next assignment from among the upcoming missions."

Reward? I can't believe it. He's going to let us go.

"Th-thank you, Uncle," Abbie stammers. I hope he's not expecting me to say something, because I don't think I can manage it right now.

"No, Abbie. It is I who must thank you and Caleb. Nassim will handle the mission selection process with you. Please allow him a few minutes to finish attending to Frank."

We nod and turn to go. I'm about to follow Abbie out the door when Uncle calls me back in.

Oh, no. This is it. I knew it. Here comes my punishment.

"Yes, Uncle?"

"Did you know, Caleb, that in his *Analects,* Confucius said something that you would do well to bear in mind?"

"What is that, Uncle?"

"He said, 'If a man takes no thought about what is distant, he will find sorrow near at hand.'"

"I see. Thank you, Uncle," I say.

"You are most welcome, Caleb. Again, my congratulations on a snatch well done."

I nod and quickly leave his office.

I catch up to Abbie by the stairwell.

"What did he say?" she asks.

"He said I'd better spend some time thinking about my future. Or bad things are going to happen to me."

"Why would he say that?"

"Oh, I don't know," I say. "To scare me maybe? Intimidate me? Or threaten me? Take your pick."

Abbie is quiet for a moment. "Let's try to forget about all this," she says, finally, "and focus on something pleasant. I found out what our mission choices are. Do you want to hear them?"

"Sure," I say. But it's not going to be easy to forget what just went on in Uncle's office.

"We've got two," she says. "The first is Bridgeport, Connecticut, on October 14, 1871 to snatch the first Frisbee that was ever flown. The other mission is to snatch silver coins from a Viking hoard near the village of Harrogate, England, on November 27, 954. Personally, I prefer Bridgeport. The weather in the northeast of England in November can be so unpredictable. Besides, I already know what I want to wear to Connecticut, and I've got the perfect name for the mission."

"Which is?"

"An ankle-length plum-colored dress with a bustle and some lace and frills on the—"

"I meant the mission name," I say.

"Oh," she says. "Operation Fling."

I have to admit, it's a pretty good name. "Fine. Bridgeport it is."

"Great. I'll go and let Nassim know," she says.

"Thanks."

I expect Abbie to go off in search of Nassim, but she just stands there, shifting her weight from foot to foot and finger-brushing a loose strand of hair—signs that there's something on her mind.

"Is there anything else you want to talk about?" I ask.

"Well . . . I know I didn't say too much during our meeting with Uncle . . . ," she begins.

"You were kind of quiet," I agree.

"Frank is going to be very angry, Cale. I just didn't want to make things worse by saying something that would make him even angrier at us."

"Angrier at me, you mean," I say. "For some reason, he doesn't seem to hold things against you."

The words are out of my mouth before I even know it. And there was a bit of a snarl in my voice that I'm not especially proud of. But why shouldn't I be upset? It seems like Abbie is saying that if she had to choose, she'd prefer making me angry over making Frank angry.

"Look, let's forget I said anything and just start getting ready for Bridgeport," she says.

"Okay," I say. But I'm not really okay. The meeting with Uncle has left me feeling totally drained, and I don't have the energy right now to try to figure out whether or not I'm right to be upset with Abbie.

Without a word, she turns and goes off in search of Nassim. But even after she leaves, I can still feel the tension in the air.

XVI

October 14, 1871, 11:17 A.M.
Bridgeport, Connecticut
Operation Fling

I land on a roof. If this is someone's idea of a joke, I'm not finding it very funny. I know mission landings are purposely programmed not to attract attention, but this is a bit much. I've got half a mind to complain to management.

But since I've already had more than my share of interactions with management lately, I'll let this little incident go by.

It feels good to be away from Headquarters and the suffocating atmosphere of Uncle's office. My thoughts go back to his parting words about sorrow being "near at hand." Abbie said not to think about it. To think about something pleasant instead.

Okay. So how's this: it's a good fifteen-foot drop to the hard ground, and I'm betting there aren't any pillows lying around to break my fall.

As soon as the time freeze wears off, I slither backward on my belly until my legs dangle over the edge. A stone gargoyle crouches nearby. From the expression on its face, I'd say it's hoping for an unhappy result. Without giving myself a chance to back out, I let go and fall the rest of the way.

I hit the ground rolling, which turns out to be a good thing, because when I finally stop and sit up I hardly feel sore at all. The first thing I notice is the wood-frame buildings. Nice and solid-looking. They line a street that is not much more than a mud track. You'd think that a mud street wouldn't have a lot of foot traffic, but all sorts of people are out and about in Bridgeport today: men in smart-looking jackets and bowler hats, ladies in long, frilly dresses and little boys and girls dressed not much differently than the adults.

I spot Abbie lounging outside a storefront under a sign that says MALLEK & SONS, BLACKSMITHS.

"Good morning, Master Caleb. It is always delightful to see you, even though I can't say the same for how you are dressed."

She stretches the words so that they sound vaguely foreign. Abbie seems to be in a good mood. I'm glad. I don't like it when there's tension between us.

Still, there's no way I'm taking responsibility for the mud-brown, pleated jacket, stiff shirt and dark green pants I'm wearing. After all, except for socks and underwear, I don't have any choice in my mission clothing, and she knows it. Besides, Abbie shouldn't complain— my outfit is hurting me way more than it's hurting her. The one thing that's not too tight is the bowler hat.

She, on the other hand, looks comfortable in a purply-blue dress that sticks out at the back and is tied in front with a large red bow. Her long auburn hair is partly hidden by a white bonnet tied with a pink ribbon under her chin, and she's holding a small yellow umbrella that looks a lot like the one she lifted from the shop in London. I actually have to stop myself from staring. She looks . . . well, beautiful.

"Great day for a snatch," I say to cover up my awkwardness.

She smiles demurely and then begins to stroll along the mud track. I fall into step beside her. We walk in silence for a while, past a post office and a stable. A barefoot young girl wearing a pale yellow dress and sucking on a candy races by us. I don't need to ask Abbie if this is the right way to the snatch zone. Her sense of direction is flawless.

"So?" Abbie says.

"So what?" I ask.

"Spill it, Cale," she says. "I want to know the whole thing. How you outsnatched Frank for the Xuande vase."

I clear my throat, but I'm really just stalling for time. Be calm, I tell myself. There's no reason to be upset at all. Abbie is perfectly entitled to know. She's my snatch partner, after all.

"Why do you even care?" I blurt out. So much for being calm.

Abbie stops and turns toward me. "What kind of a question is that? We're partners . . . and friends. Of course I care."

I can't look at her, so instead I gaze at the mud puddle by my feet.

"What's bothering you?" she asks.

There is a bit of sky reflected in the mud puddle, but the next moment it's chased away by dark rain clouds.

"Do you really want to know?" I say, glancing up. "Fine, I'll tell you. I know that you and Frank went to see Phoebe."

I watch her eyes carefully. I'm taking a risk with all this. If she's on Frank's side, then she'll go straight to him with this conversation. But I need to know.

"I had to," she says, her words coming out slowly.

"Had to do what?" I say. "Had to spy on me?"

"I wasn't spying on you," Abbie says. "I only went with him because I need to know how he's doing it."

A black buggy drawn by a skinny white horse passes us going the other way.

"You know how he's doing it," I say. "I've already told you. He's showing up at my snatches—*our* snatches—and sabotaging them."

"That's not what I mean," Abbie says. "Don't you find it strange that, with all the sabotaging he's doing, he's not getting in trouble with Uncle?"

"You call getting part of his ear lopped off not getting in trouble?" I say.

"Well, you're right about that," she says, resuming walking along the track. "But that's the only time I've heard of Uncle punishing him."

"So what are you saying?"

"I'm saying that Uncle doesn't know about half the things he does," she says. "Frank handed in the Xuande vase, or at least what he thought was the Xuande vase, but he hasn't always handed in the snatch items he steals from you. Do you remember the flag of the Great Friendship? He never gave it in."

Why am I not surprised? When I think about it, I can see Frank's twisted logic; by interfering in my snatches but not turning in the objects, he can get me in trouble without bringing attention to himself. Now I understand why at dinner the other night, Uncle came up with fifteen completed snatches for Frank while I counted sixteen.

"Why are you helping him?" I ask, cutting to the chase.

"Is that what you think I'm doing?" She starts laughing.

"This isn't funny, Abbie," I say. "Like I said—I know you were with him when he went to see Phoebe."

She glances around as if to make sure no one's listening. "Cale, Frank has found a way to get around Phoebe."

"What do you mean?" I ask.

"I mean," she continues, "he's getting Phoebe to share information on stuff that he shouldn't be getting, like our mission data. But that's not all. What would you say if I told you that except for his regular missions with Lydia, there's no record of any of Frank's other trips to the past?"

"I don't believe it," I say. I can buy the fact that Frank is getting Phoebe to share data on Abbie's and my missions. He's probably using bribery on her, same as I am. But getting Phoebe to regularly cover his tracks on all his nonmission trips to the past? That's huge. I don't think even Phoebe would agree to do that. It could put her in big trouble with Uncle.

"Well, it's true," says Abbie. "Do you want to know how he's doing it?"

I nod.

"He's hypnotizing her," she says.

It's my turn to laugh. "That's ridiculous. You can't hypnotize a computer."

"You can with one that has human DNA inside it."

She's right about Phoebe's infrastructure containing DNA. Still, Phoebe under hypnosis? What, does he wave a pocket watch back and forth in front of a screen? I find the whole thing hard to swallow.

"Abbie, how are you involved in all of this?" I ask again. "Why didn't you tell me anything before? And why is Frank letting you in on all his little secrets?" My questions come out rapid-fire.

She looks at me for a moment. It's impossible to read her expression, but I can tell that she's weighing her words carefully before saying them.

"Cale, Frank and I . . ."

My heart sinks. I already don't like the sound of this. I can't meet Abbie's eyes, so I look over her shoulder at a building with a wood sign in gold-lettering that says EPHRAM P. ABERNATHY, NOTARY PUBLIC.

"We . . . he thinks I really like him," she finishes.

"And do you?" I ask. "I mean, you're always looking at him like he's the last piece of chocolate cake."

"It's not what you think," she says.

"Well, what is it, then?" I say.

"It's not anything," Abbie says. "It's just that I need to know what he knows."

"Why?" I ask.

"Isn't it obvious? The only way to survive around here is to keep your eyes and ears open. Something that you don't seem to be very good at doing."

"Well, there's a difference between keeping your eyes open and keeping your eyes on Frank," I blurt out.

Abbie stares at me for a moment. "Will you get it into your thick head that I'm not with him?"

I look down at the ground. I want to believe her, I really do. But if I buy into what Abbie is saying, that means all the attention she's paying Frank is just one big act. And if she's acting with Frank, what's to say she's not also acting with me?

"Listen," she says. "In case you haven't noticed, things aren't like they used to be. We're not little anymore. Uncle's not going to watch out for us. In fact, he's getting harder on us all the time. And if you think things will get any better if and when Uncle retires, you'd better think twice. Because Frank is going to take over, and from the looks of things, he'll be even worse than Uncle." She pauses. "It's each time snatcher for himself, Cale. That's the only way to survive."

I let her words sink in.

"I guess that means you're for you and I'm for me," I say, my stomach clenching.

She stops by a red building with a hitching post in front and turns to me. "What's wrong with you? It's like you're a different person . . . I don't even know you anymore."

Abbie's right. I am a different person. Ever since Frank started messing with me, and even more, ever since I saw Zach on the escalator at Expo 67. But how do I explain it to her? How do I even explain it to myself? I run my hand over the rough grain of the hitching post.

"I want . . ." The words come slowly. "I want something more," I say.

"What more do you need?" Abbie asks. "You've got an interesting job, opportunity to travel, and a snatch partner who's hotter than a pocket nuke." She raises up the hem of her dress a fraction of an inch and flashes some ankle.

"And a boss who holds my wrist under the water so that his snapping turtles can finish their lunch and a roommate who stays up late at night thinking up new ways to get me in trouble," I add.

After a moment, she says, "You don't have a choice. This isn't exactly a job you can quit, you know."

"I want to . . . I *need* to change my life," I say, thinking of Zach, Jim and Diane.

She doesn't say anything for a moment. A tall man clutching a walking stick with a horse head knob ambles by, tipping his hat to her in passing.

"Don't do it," she says finally. "If you run and Uncle finds you, which you know he will . . ."

Instead of saying the rest, she traces a circle in the air right in front of my forehead. I feel a shiver race up my spine.

"Besides, if you leave, I could get paired with 'I love myself' Lydia," Abbie continues, scrunching her nose. "I'd rather spend a week in the Barrens than have Lydia as my snatch partner for even one second."

I laugh and feel the knot inside my stomach relaxing. The truth is that if I ever did leave, the hardest part of all would be leaving Abbie.

We pass another storefront. The sign says NORMAN'S GENERAL STORE in four-foot-high curling letters. I stop and stare. Displayed in the big picture window is a miniature battlefield, complete with towering cliffs and two armies taking aim at each other with rifles and bayonets. I'm guessing there are at least a hundred miniature soldiers. All of them are beautifully carved and detailed.

I have a sudden inspiration. "Hey, can you wait here for a minute? I've got to check something out."

"Okay, but don't take too long, O Easily Distracted One," says Abbie. "We've got some business at the Frisbie Baking Company to take care of, remember?"

How can I forget? We're here to steal a very special pie tin. Special because it's about to be the first Frisbee ever flown. Where's the Chinese angle, I wonder? Ever since the start of the Great Friendship, most of our snatches have had something to do with China. Well, maybe, like our mission to France, there is isn't any Chinese connection to this one. Although you never know. It could be that one of Uncle's rich clients wants to give the world's first Frisbee as a gift to the Chinese ambassador to the U.S. Whatever, it's not really any of my business.

What is my business, however, is being on time for the snatch. If I time things right, I can make my purchase at Norman's, take a short side trip to 1967, spend a few minutes there and still get back here with only a minute or two of 1871 time having elapsed. There's one problem, though. Since Phoebe keeps track all of our time in the past, Uncle will know about my side trip if he looks at my file. Frank too, for that matter.

Maybe I can hypnotize Phoebe into erasing the record of the trip, like Frank does. Except I don't know how to do that yet. Why am I even worrying about that? If anyone looks into everywhere I've been going, I'll be in trouble anyway.

"Be right back," I say.

A bell tinkles as I enter the shop. It's dim and quiet, and the air smells musty and stale. A man in a green waistcoat is standing at a polished oak counter. Behind him, shelves are stacked with maybe a hundred colored bottles of all different shapes and sizes. I hear shuffling from the back of the store. Well, at least I'm not the only customer.

"Excuse me . . . but are those soldiers for sale?" I ask, pointing to the window display.

The man looks up, removes an unlit pipe from his mouth and squints at me from behind wire-rimmed eyeglasses.

"Norman, I says to meself, the lad's a *Grosvenor*. But now I ain't so sure. Yer clothes are a huckleberry above most Grosvenors' persimmons. A *Cunningham,* more likely. Aye. But then again, yer face is a bit too peaked fer a Cunningham. Good thing too. They're all a bunch of scalawags. And ugly as sin, to boot. So, you've got me perplexed, lad. Who in Sam Hill are ye?"

I straighten up and say, "My name is Robert. Robert . . . Franklin," I add hastily.

He lights the pipe, sticks it in his mouth and looks me up and down now, frowning.

"Franklin, Franklin," he begins. "Can't says I heard uv no Bridgeport Franklins. Yer not tryin' to hornswoggle me, are ye, lad?"

"Uhh, no," I said, guessing that it was a bad thing to hornswoggle someone. "I . . . I'm from . . . Canada," I lie.

"By the horn spoons! I'da never of suspicioned it." He removes his pipe, smiles and I get a glimpse of crooked, yellow teeth. Still smiling, he lets fly a big ball of spit that sails past me and lands somewhere on the other side of the store.

Ordinarily I'm okay with small talk. But Abbie's waiting. Plus there's still a lot I have to do. I walk over to the window display and pick up one of the wooden soldiers from the battlefield.

He can't be more than three inches tall, but he's magnificent: dressed in a navy blue greatcoat with white piping down the arms and gripping a field rifle with a long bayonet.

"How much for this one?" I ask.

Norman chuckles and blows out a ring of bluish-gray smoke, "You've got a good eye, lad. Picked the biggest toad in the puddle, y'did. 'Tis a shame 'e's not for sale."

In a single gesture, he snatches the soldier from me and returns him to the battle scene.

"If the Rebels are to have any chance at whuppin' those Loyalist ruffians," says Norman, "it'll be in no small part due to the grit and unflinchin' leadership of that man, Captain Randolph Percival."

I root around in my pocket. I could have sworn I'd been allotted four half-dollar coins for the mission, but my fingers only find three.

I pull out a coin and place it in Norman's hand.

"It's unthinkable," he continues. "The men all look up to him. They'd be left like nomads in the desert, like sailors adrift at sea. In a word, rudderless." The hand stays open.

I fish out a second coin and place it with the first.

"Their spirit will be crushed beyon' repair, udderly exfluncti-cated," says Norman. His hand is still open, but he's really working that pipe stem with his teeth now.

I'm starting to sweat. Only one coin left. What if I need it for later? I could easily have pocketed the soldier when he wasn't look-ing. Except that would have been stealing. And, if I can avoid it, I don't like to steal outside of missions.

So I pull out my last coin, place it with the others and his fingers curl up like the tentacles of a sea creature. Norman raises his other hand in a salute.

"*Adieu,* Captain Percival! Happy trails." He plucks the soldier from the edge of the cliff, hastily wraps him in brown paper and tosses him to me.

"What's taking you so long, Caleb?" Abbie says over my mind-patch.

"Just finishing up," I answer.

Norman turns away from me for a moment, bends down and places another soldier in the empty space where Captain Percival used to be.

But a moment is all I need to tap out a sequence for 1967.

A bell jingles. I glance up and my breath catches in my throat as I recognize the person coming in through the back door: it's my future self.

Running into one of my other selves always feels strange. The first time it happened, Abbie and I were in Paris in 1920, snatching a cat drawing by Van Gogh from the exhibition at the Grand Palais. As we were heading out, this guy who could have been my identical twin said I'd left something in there. It turned out he was right—I'd forgotten a piece of bubble wrap that I'd brought along to pack up some of the stuff. Weird, huh?

Right now, though, I'm wondering what my future self is doing here. Hopefully, it's me returning from 1967, which is actually my plan. But what wasn't part of my plan is seeing my future self burst into the same room as me. Couldn't he have waited a few more seconds until I had gone? I've got enough to worry about without having to explain to Norman why he's seeing double. So I give my future self my best sour look. Then the captain and I leave 1871 in a hurry.

XVII

July 8, 1967, 8:32 P.M.
Expo 67
La Ronde, Montreal, Canada

When I open my eyes, I see a boy riding a green striped zebra, a young girl on a polka-dot rhinoceros and a paunchy older guy riding a lemon yellow ostrich.

Just to be sure I'm not dreaming all this, I close my eyes and open them again. Everyone is still present and accounted for, including me alone inside a Cinderella carriage. We're all going around and around. Staticky waltz music blares from overhead speakers.

The carousel slows and stops. I step out and breathe in the night air.

All the rides are lit up. People are everywhere; large men in white shirts with skinny ties, skinny women in pastel dresses, ticket takers wearing pillbox hats. I hear a jumble of sounds: laughter, shouts, the rush of a train. Glancing up, I see a blue and white flag with the Expo 67 symbol, sixteen stick figures arranged in a circle, fluttering in the evening breeze.

The tension in my shoulders eases a bit. I made it back.

I have a sudden vision of Abbie, still waiting for me outside Norman's General Store. I hate leaving her like that. Maybe I should have taken my chances and told her the real reason why I went into the store. But I'm not ready.

Anyway, I've got a more immediate problem: how, among all the thousands of tourists here, am I ever going to find the three I'm looking for? And then I remember Jim mentioning that they were going to go on a ride that had two pyramids.

I begin walking, keeping my eyes peeled for pyramids. People stream by me going the other way. Some scrunch their noses when they pass by, and one, a priest, actually crosses himself. I long for a pair of those jumping shoes that I saw last week in the display window of FAO Schwarz on Fifth Avenue. You slip them on and you can hop about twenty feet in the air without breaking a sweat. I could use a pair of them right now to escape this suffocating crowd. I glance down at my well-worn shoes. There's a brown smudge on the outside of the left one. Horse dung, vintage 1871. No wonder I've been getting the evil eye.

Cutting through a family of five, I find a small patch of grass and bend down to wipe it off. I'm about to stand when I see something that makes me freeze in a half crouch.

Frank.

He's loafing near the Lost Children booth, one foot up on a bench, casual as can be. There's a bandage over what's left of his right ear. My heart is beating double-time, and alarms are going off in my brain. What's he doing here? I don't think it's because he likes Ferris wheels. Is his plan to snatch Zach? Then I remember his words to me in the dorm: "I never forget when someone crosses me." And here I am about to lead him straight to Zach. I can't let him see me. Maybe I should just leave right now. No. First I've got to make sure Zach is all right and that Frank isn't watching him.

I jump into the crowd and let it pull me along until I'm well away from the spot where I saw Frank. And then just to be sure, I keep walking for another ten minutes. Which seemed like a good idea at the time, but doesn't seem so hot now. What if in my rush to put distance between me and Frank I've also been walking in the opposite direction from the pyramids?

I am about to head back when I hear a hundred people screaming.

It's coming from a white, pyramid-shaped building that's easily five stories high. Bingo!

The place looks nothing like an amusement park ride. The entire structure is covered in a web of steel triangles. Just to the left is its twin, except smaller—maybe only two stories high. There's something otherworldly about the two buildings, as if an alien race brought them to Earth and plunked them down right here. A high open track connects the buildings and little cars shuttle riders from the larger pyramid to the smaller one. The screaming is definitely coming from the smaller pyramid. There's a sign in front of the ride that says LE GYROTRON.

I walk briskly to a spot with a good view of the end of the ride and settle in to wait.

A hand grabs my shoulder. I whirl and break the grip with an upper block. I'm about to follow with a jab to the solar plexus, but when I see who it is, I hold my punch at the last second.

"Jim?"

"Caleb?" says Jim.

I unclench my fist. "Uhh, sorry. I guess I'm a bit jumpy."

"No, it's my fault. I shouldn't have surprised you like that," he says. "Anyway, glad you could make it." He's staring at my old-fashioned clothes.

"I wouldn't miss it," I say. I arrange the bowler on my head at a jaunty angle, grin and add, "I got these clothes just in case I ever need to time travel to 1871."

He smiles and glances past me. "Hey, look. Here they come."

Zach's running down the exit ramp toward us, face flushed. Diane is ten paces behind, walking with a noticeable wobble.

"Daddy, I did the Gyrotron! I wasn't afraid at all. First we were flying in outer space and then a monster in a volcano ate us! Now I want to do La Spitoon!"

Jim laughs. "It's La *Pitoune*, not La *Spitoon*. Look who's here, Zach."

In the instant before we make eye contact, a thousand different thoughts and feelings churn inside me. What am I really doing here? Does my showing up matter? I mean, here he is with both his parents in roller-coaster heaven. What more does a kid need?

"Caylid!" He jumps up and wraps his arms around my waist.

"Happy Birthday, Zach." I fish the brown paper package from my pocket and hand it to him. He peels back the wrapper, and his eyes light up. He turns Captain Percival over in his hands and touches the point of the bayonet.

"He's perfect!" Zach shouts.

"Glad you like him," I say. But just then, I feel the skin on the back of my neck prickle.

I whip my head around, expecting to see Frank standing nearby, a smug expression on his face.

Nothing.

I scan the crowd. Where is he? A father snapping pictures of his family. A hot dog vendor wiping mustard off his serving counter. A mother bending over a stroller, coaxing her kid to have a drink. I don't see him. But that doesn't mean he's not here, watching us right now.

"Zach, I've got to go," I say. "I'll see you later, okay?"

He tears his eyes away from the captain just long enough to look up at me and say, "Don't go, Caylid. We have to play soldiers."

"He will next time, sweetie," says Diane. "I'm going to give him our address so that he can come visit us, okay?"

She rummages around in her purse and finds a scrap of paper and a pencil.

"If you find yourself anywhere near Boston, Caleb," she says, scribbling away, "we'd be delighted to see you."

"Yes, Caylid, find yourself and come to my house," Zach chimes in. "Five five Derne Street, Bostonmass."

Diane is about to hand me the paper when I hold up my hands. "That's okay. I can remember it."

She looks at me oddly for a moment and then puts the note back in her purse.

"Promise you'll come?" Zach says.

"Sure. I promise," I say.

"We gotta shake on it." Zach reaches out his small hand.

His grip is firm like Jim's and warm like Diane's.

A thousand thoughts swirl around in my brain. But the one that keeps hammering at me is, How could I have been so stupid? By my coming here, I've put Zach's life at risk!

The thing is, I don't know what to do next. It's getting harder and harder to think straight. Is it time fog? I've got to warn Jim and Diane. What will I say? That they should keep an extra eye on Zach because he's about to be kidnapped by my roommate from the future?

My head is bursting. Got to get out of here. Got to go somewhere where I can think properly.

"I've got to go," I say again without looking at Zach. I turn quickly and begin walking away.

There it is. The tingling sensation again.

I whirl around.

Nothing.

Off to my right, I spot the men's room and duck inside. The place is empty. I lock myself in the last stall.

Got to calm down. Focus on my breathing.

But I can't. My nerves are shot.

Just then the washroom door opens. The sound of music and laughter drifts in.

The stall door next to mine creaks open. I glance quickly under the green metal divider and see Frank's white running shoes.

My heart is beating like crazy. I've got to get a grip on myself.

I try to tap a sequence on my wrist, but my fingers are shaking too much.

"What a great idea! A game of hide-and-go-seek. And by the looks of things, you want to hide first. That's fine with me. See how accommodating I can be, Caleb?" Frank's voice stabs into me.

I chance a glance under the divider. The feet are gone. Where is he?

I stay silent. He's only guessing it's me. He can't know for sure.

Just then, the door to my stall rattles. He's pushing on it. I scramble forward and throw my back against it.

"This is . . . what is that 1960s expression for having fun? A gas? Yes, that's it. This is a gas, Caleb! We really should play games more often. Abbie and I like to play games together too, did you know that?"

Frantically, I reenter the sequence. As I do, I ease up on the door for a second. But that's all it takes. The next moment, the flimsy lock gives way, and I'm hurled forward as the stall door crashes open.

XVIII

October 14, 1871, 11:26 A.M.
Bridgeport, Connecticut
Operation Fling

Complete and utter blackness. And cold. So cold. I must be dead. Frank must have finished me off right after he demolished the stall door.

Or has he? Maybe I'm still in the bathroom stall and he's turned the lights off and is still coming after me. Panic rips through me. I rub my eyes and activate my ocular implant. I'm in a room the size of a closet with walls made of rough wood. The bench on which I'm sitting is also made from wood and has a big hole carved into it. That's good, isn't it? There was no wood in the bathroom stall at Expo 67, only metal dividers. So my timeleap must have worked. But where am I?

Getting hard to think straight. How long have I been in the past now? For sure it's been over a half hour counting the time at Expo 67. But how much over?

Bridgeport, Connecticut. That's where I must be. Unless I made a sequencing error and landed in some other place in some other year. Which is entirely possible, given that I had to deal with Frank trying to bash down the stall door while I was entering the sequence.

Got to think calmly. All right, what else do I know about this place? Well, for one thing, it stinks. I don't need my ocular implant to tell me where the awful smell is coming from—the hole in the bench.

I've landed in an outhouse.

I stand, reach for the door, open it a crack and peek through.

Daylight. But just barely. The sky is dark and filled with clouds. There's a row of buildings maybe fifty feet away. Trees between me and them. I hear horses whinnying.

Opening the door wider, I notice that the nearest building has a flat roof. My pulse begins to race. Could it be the same roof that I landed on the first time I came here? Sure enough, there's the gargoyle.

Abbie! Is she still waiting? How long has it been? Five minutes? Ten? Or even longer? If my sequencing was halfway decent I should have arrived back here in 1871 with only a few minutes gone.

I run along a path skirting the back of the buildings until I reach Norman's. Luckily, the back door is unlocked. As I step inside, a bell jingles and a wave of sweet-smelling pipe smoke washes over me. Through the dimness I can make out shelves stacked with colored bottles. Norman is by the front with his back to me, arranging something in the display window. And he's not alone. There's a boy standing near him, wearing a jacket that's way too tight.

I should know. After all, the boy is me. Or rather, was me a couple of 1871 minutes ago.

I smile at my past self, but he's clearly not amused. He scowls at me like I've just put ketchup on his breakfast cereal or something. Then, before I have a chance to scowl back, he vanishes.

Norman turns, sees me and says, "No need to go out that way, lad. Unless of course you have to use the privy."

"Right. I'll go out the front," I say, stepping past him. "See you."

"Wait just a moment, lad!" he says.

Great. What now? Have I forgotten something? I feel the blood drain from my face as I suddenly remember. The captain! He's expecting to see Captain Percival in my hand. I quickly shove a hand in my pocket and make a bulge so that he thinks something's in there.

"Yes?" I ask, cool as I can manage.

"You weren't honeyfugglin' me 'bout bein' from Canada, were ye?" he asks.

"No, sir," I say, reaching for the front door with my free hand.

"Good," he says, smiling.

I scoot out the door and down the steps and jog across the lawn. Except it's a time-fogged jog, which means it's closer to a wobbly walk than a run. Abbie's got her hands on her hips—never a good sign.

"What were you doing in there so long?" she says. "I was just about to come drag you out."

"Sorry," is all I say.

She doesn't say anything, and we continue walking. I can feel the tension in the air and try distracting myself by admiring the hand-carved wooden signs on the buildings we pass. But it's not working. I trip on a stone and lose my balance. Abbie shoots me a look.

I check my fingernail. Fifteen minutes left to do the snatch.

"Abbie . . . ," I begin.

"Don't say it, Caleb," she says. "I don't want to know. If you're doing stuff on the side, the less I know the better."

So that's why she's angry. She thinks I'm moonlighting. Going off and stealing stuff for myself.

"It's not like that . . . I mean . . . ," I begin, but time fog is making me slur my words.

"Listen," she says, stopping in front of a narrow building with a brass sign above the door that reads CONNECTICUT STEERAGE COMPANY. "I'm your snatch partner, remember? Not your girlfriend. You don't have to explain everything to me. All I need to know is that I can count on you for the mission. Okay?"

Not your girlfriend. The words echo in my brain. Tears are gathering in the back of my eyes. I push the feelings down. Deep down.

We don't say anything or look at each other the rest of the way. The street, the buildings and even the people suddenly seem drab to me. It's as if someone came with a giant vacuum and sucked the color out of everything.

The front lawn of the Frisbie Baking Company is decked out for a party. A big blue and red banner strung up between two sturdy oaks announces OFFICIAL OPENING DAY—ALL WELCOME. Twelve tables adorned with white lace tablecloths are arranged on the lawn in a semicircle around a makeshift stage.

I can't help thinking about what would happen if it rained. I guess they'd move the whole party inside. But since all the tables and chairs are already outside, where would everyone sit? I don't know why I'm even worrying about this. After all, I'm not organizing the event, only stealing from it.

A young boy plops down on the grass and manages to crawl halfway across the lawn before his mother chases him down and scoops him up. Four men in white suits belt out a tune about the prettiest girl in Abilene, wherever that is.

Without even a glance at me, Abbie goes off and sits at a table near the stage. Well, if that's the way she wants to be, good riddance, I say. I find a seat at the furthest table from her.

The singing stops. A woman in a long ivory dress steps onto the stage. She raises two pale hands and clasps them together as if she's about to pray. A breeze comes up and carries with it the scent of freshly cut grass.

"Ladies and gentlemen," she begins. "Today is a great day for our beloved town of Bridgeport." Then she glances up at the gathering storm clouds and back at the crowd.

Most of the tables are filled. It's a mixed group—a few older men and women, some families with young children, a few teenagers and some college types. Without exception, everyone's fidgeting. My guess is that they've all skipped breakfast for this. I hope we're not in for a long speech. My fingernail tells me that Abbie and I have eleven minutes left to complete the snatch, and Uncle didn't give us any overtime on this one. Also, my legs are beginning to feel like jelly, and I've got a massive headache.

"Today is the grand opening of the Frisbie Baking Company," she continues.

Applause all around except for two guys at my table wearing brown trousers and stiff white shirts who are talking to each other in low voices. I figure them to be about my age, maybe a little older. Every once in a while, the larger boy stares at me.

I'm positive they're talking about me. I glance back at them. The bigger one reminds me of Frank. Same dark, oily hair. Same smirk.

"And in honor of this momentous occasion," she says, "the proprietor of this venerable establishment, Mr. William Russell Frisbie, has a treat for us all: blackberry pie! Baked fresh this morning. Mr. Frisbie, please take a bow."

As one, all heads turn toward a bearded man with fierce eyebrows in a white apron and baker's cap standing to the left of the stage. He waves at the crowd and the quartet bursts into a chorus of, "We love you dearly, oh, yes we do . . ."

The sky is growing darker by the second. If they don't get on with things, we'll all be eating soggy blackberry pie in the rain.

The husky boy stares at me. I do my best to ignore him.

A troop of waitresses appears as if from nowhere, carrying trays laden with dozens of pies. As soon as they're set down, the hungry diners descend on them.

I dig into my piece. It's pleasantly warm and tastes divine. If only I had a glass of milk.

"Enjoyin' your pie, pisspot?" a voice next to me whispers, startling me.

I feel a kick of adrenaline as the boy who had been staring puts his arm across my shoulders and leans in real close. So close that I can smell the blackberries on his breath. My body tenses.

Abbie's voice comes over my mindpatch. "Don't pay him any attention, Caleb. Just focus on the mission, okay?"

As usual, what she's saying makes perfect sense. "Focus on the mission." "You don't have to explain everything to me." And my new personal favorite, "not your girlfriend." Yes, thank you, Abbie, for your pearls of wisdom.

"Let go, please," I say.

"Not yet. We've only jus' begun gettin' acquainted," Blackberry Breath says.

"Heads up," Abbie mindlinks me. "The first one to fly is ours."

The mission. I've almost forgotten. But right now, it seems to me that snatching the world's first Frisbee in mid-flight isn't all that important.

"Let go, now," I say. I'm aiming for strong and confident, but in my time-fogged state, the words come out soft and fluffy. I've got to stay alert. But it's getting harder and harder to form any real thoughts.

Blackberry Breath doesn't let go. If anything, he tightens his grip on me.

With all the strength I can muster, I lift my right hand and place it on top of his.

For a split second, my hand rests there, not quite sure of what to do. But then my years of karate training kick in, and with a single pistonlike motion, I bring my left arm forward and then back, my elbow connecting with his solar plexus. He doubles over, gasping for air.

I stand up slowly, swaying like a drunkard. His friend is glaring at me, but doesn't step any closer.

A flash of movement catches my attention. Instinctively I raise my hand in an upper block. But it isn't a fist that's flying my way. It's a spinning pie tin. It glances off my arm and lands on top of Blackberry Breath.

I bend down and pluck the tin off his back.

Abbie appears beside me. She takes one look at the boy crumpled on the ground, frowns and says, "Let's get out of here. Now."

I follow her into a narrow alley between the Frisbie Baking Company building and the post office. Just then the clouds finally burst open and rain comes pelting down. But I hardly feel the rain. In fact I hardly feel anything. The time fog has wrapped me in some sort of cocoon, where almost all my thoughts have turned to mush and my body is disobeying the few coherent commands my mind is able to give it.

In a deep corner of my brain, a small voice is telling me to fight it. Telling me that there is something urgent I must do.

But for the life of me, I can't figure out what that thing is.

I'll ask Abbie. She'll know. But when I turn to ask her, she is gone.

The raindrops beat a steady drum on the ground. A tiny stream forms near my boots. I gaze at the pie tin in my hand and wonder why I'm carrying it and what I should do with it.

I spot a small pile of garbage off to one side. I take slow, plodding steps toward it. "Good work, Caleb," my brain is telling me. Since there's no more pie left in the tin, then it can be only one thing:

garbage. Proud of my logic, I set the pie tin on top of the garbage. The perfect solution to my problem.

Something is niggling at me: the beginnings of a thought. Trying to push aside my perfect solution. I mustn't let it.

There's no stopping it, though; the thought keeps buzzing around in my brain like a moth near a flame. There is something else I must do. What is it?

Think! But I can't. It's so hard.

I must leave this place.

But if that's the thought, it makes no sense at all. Why should I leave? Instead, I sit down in the rain. Yes, it's much better to sit here and watch the raindrops fall.

Something is going *plink, plink*. The sound is like music. I must find out what's making such beautiful music.

Again. *Plink. Plink.*

Looking to my left I see a pie tin atop a small pile of garbage. That's where the wonderful music is coming from. *Plink, plink* go the raindrops into the tin. Filling it up.

Another thought breaks through, telling me to touch my wrist.

Such silliness.

I would much rather continue listening to the rain music.

But the thought keeps coming back, pestering me.

All right, I will do what the thought says. But only so that I can go back to watching the pretty raindrops and listening to the rain music. My fingers reach up and tap lightly at my wrist in time with the raindrops.

There. Done. Now I can go back to my rain music. But what happened to it? I listen hard, but the music is only faint now. Maybe if I bring the pie tin closer to me. Yes, that's the answer.

I reach out my hand to the pie tin and, as I do, I feel something happening to me. Disturbing my perfect peace. It feels as if my entire body is vibrating.

Just before I slip away, just before I leave 1871, I curl my fingers around the pie tin and slip it under my jacket. Good. Wherever I'm going, at least I'll have my music with me.

XIX

June 24, 2061, 12:02 P.M.

Tribeca, New Beijing (formerly New York City)

I land in the alley beside Headquarters. My body aches all over, I have a horrible headache and I can't move. Otherwise I feel great. The only thing I can do is wait for the time freeze to melt away and for the time fog to begin to dissolve.

I close my eyes in an effort to ease the throbbing pain in my head, and after a moment, I'm able to move my hands enough to cover my ears against the traffic sounds that feel like arrows piercing my brain.

This must be what a hangover feels like.

Slowly, my thoughts start to make sense. That was close. It was stupid of me to stay in the past that long. And it was stupid of me to hit Blackberry Breath. But he started it.

I stand up slowly. It's a good thing my patch is preprogrammed to land at home. In my time-fogged state, there's no way I could have even hit the right century.

Leaving the alley, instead of turning right, toward Headquarters, I turn left. Better to walk off some of the time fog before I face Nassim. As I cross under West Street and head for the Greenway, it begins to rain; not quite the steady downpour that I just left behind in Bridgeport, but I'll take it anyway.

Some people can't stand the rain. I'm not one of them. In fact, there are some times, like right now, when rain definitely suits my mood. The fact that I almost botched Operation Fling has left me a jangle of nerves. But it's not only that. It feels like everything is spinning out of control.

As I continue to walk, some of the power comes back to my legs. Two bicycles pass me, and their tires kick up water, spraying my pants. I've got a good view of the Hudson now and, across it, the skyline of Hoboken. The buildings on the New Jersey side look dark and dreary, crowned by a thick canopy of rain clouds.

I think about Zach. Maybe I should just forget about him. His life is none of my business. They say if you save a life, that makes you responsible for it. I don't believe that. Zach has two parents. He doesn't need me. But what if Frank tries to snatch him? I can't let that happen.

I'm still holding the pie tin under my jacket. I take it out and point it toward the Hudson. A good toss would probably make the river. It would be so easy—just bring my arm back and let it fly. I know it would be stupid and that Uncle would seriously punish me for it once he found out. But strangely enough, even knowing all of that, it's still hard to resist. I remember reading once that people who are afraid of heights can sometimes find themselves drawn like magnets to stand at the edge of a steep cliff. That's kind of how I'm feeling right now . . . being pulled to do something totally crazy.

With effort, I slip the tin back under my jacket and keep walking. The rain has let up, but the sky is still blanketed by clouds. As I turn onto Franklin, a gray cat rockets across the street in front of me and scoots underneath a parked rickshaw.

Arriving at Headquarters, I take a deep breath to steady myself. "Four, please, Phoebe." I can hear the fatigue in my voice.

"Certainly, Your Wetness," replies Phoebe. "But first take your shoes off and carry them. I just vacuumed."

Phoebe's persona is dressed in a low-cut leopard skin leotard.

The dark smudges around her eyes match her jet-black Mohawk. A tattoo proclaiming DEATH LIVES is etched on her right biceps.

"There. Can I go up now?" I ask, after I've removed my shoes.

"Certainly. But when you get off, I suggest you hold your nose," she says.

"Why?"

"Because Raoul is cooking tonight . . . if you can call it that."

"What's he—"

"Broccoli," she says.

"And what else?" I ask.

"There is no what else," says Phoebe. "Just broccoli."

I nod. Let the others complain about the meal, or lack of it. I'm not hungry anyway.

I head straight for the dorm. What I really should be doing is turning the pie tin in to Nassim. If I don't, I'm sure I'll hear about it. But I'm just not up for it right now.

Thankfully, the room is empty. I flop down on my bunk, pull out my carving and get to work on the area around the eyes. The weight of the knife in my hand feels good and the repeating motion of the blade digging into the driftwood is comforting, almost hypnotic.

"Good evening, people," says Nassim's voice over the intercom. "Dinner will be in five minutes. The word for this evening is *xiao*, translation: 'the respect that children give to their parents.' Everyone must use the word in a sentence of their choosing at dinner."

This is no language lesson. It's a new form of torture. Since none of us have parents, my guess is that Uncle wants to hear all about how much we respect him. There's no way I'm going. Abbie probably won't even notice I'm not there. She'll be too busy gazing into Frank's broccoli-colored eyes.

I strike hard with my knife and twist up, the blade flush against the wood. The cautious part of me says to be more gentle so I don't ruin the carving.

Well, too bad. I strike the wood again and again. Each strike is harder than the one before.

I hate getting up early on nonmission days. But today we're all going to SoHo for a briefing on Uncle's latest project, and not showing up isn't an option. So I'm up, dressed and in the kitchen by ten to seven.

Everyone else is here, jockeying for position around the toaster.

My stomach's grumbling from missing supper last night, so I feed it an extra bowl of cereal while I wait for the toaster to free up.

"Caleb, where's the snatch object from Bridgeport?" asks Nassim.

"Oops. Left it in the dorm. Be right back," I say.

I'm two steps out of the kitchen when he says, "Why didn't you turn it in yesterday?"

He's got me there. "Sorry, Nassim," I say, shrugging my shoulders. "It was kind of a rough day."

Nassim nods and says, "I'll be waiting in my office."

"Okay." I hurry to the dorm and check under my bunk where I stowed the pie tin. For a panicky moment I can't feel it. My first thought is, Frank: he must have found it! How stupid could I have been to stash it in such an obvious place? I really should have turned it in yesterday. And then my fingers connect with a cool, rounded edge. Relief washes over me.

I tuck it under my arm and hurry to Nassim's office.

"Here it . . ." The words die on my lips. It's pitch-black and I brace myself.

A blow across my ankles sweeps me off my feet and sends me toppling to the floor. The pie tin goes flying. Lucky for me, flying is what it does best. If it was anything else, I could have been punished for improper care of a snatch object.

Before I can even think of standing, my arms are locked in a vise grip. It's impossible to do anything but sit there and wait for the clue.

"Six letters. Insurrection," a husky voice whispers right in my ear.

"Mutiny," I say without skipping a beat.

The lights come on, and I rub my sore arms. Nassim gives the tin a quick once-over. Then he reaches past me, closes his office door and claps on some classical music. The music thunders and rolls like waves in a stormy sea. It's really loud, but Nassim doesn't look in any hurry to lower the volume.

"What's going on with you, Caleb?" the big man asks. "You don't seem yourself lately."

My mouth goes dry as I make the connection between Nassim's question and the loud music.

I hesitate. I've never talked to Nassim about personal stuff. In fact, I've never even had a conversation longer than two minutes with him, period. Then I remember him showing me his scars from the turtle bites. I'd like to trust him. I really would. But what if he goes straight to Uncle with what I say? It's too risky.

"I'm fine," I lie.

He stares at me, and for a moment, I think he's going to say something. Instead he just nods.

As I make a move to leave, he holds up a hand. "Wait a minute. There's something I want to show you."

Nassim reaches inside the top drawer of his desk and fishes out a small bottle. Shaking a tiny silver pill from the bottle he says, "Do you know what this is?"

"No," I say.

"It's a memory wipe pill," he says. "Take two of these and, within a couple of minutes, you won't remember anything that happened before dinner last night. And I mean *anything*."

I feel my stomach clench. Why is he showing me this?

He pops the pill back in the bottle and returns it to the drawer. Our eyes meet for a moment, and I get a feeling that there's a whole other side to Nassim that I don't know anything about. Glancing at the framed picture on his desk, I wonder how long it's been since Nassim has seen his own father.

"We're done here, Caleb. I'll write up the snatch. Please join the others. We'll be leaving for the Compound in five minutes." His voice is flat, expressionless.

I nod and head for the door. I can feel his eyes on me, but I don't turn around.

XX

June 25, 2061, 7:37 A.M.

The Compound—Timeless Treasures Training Facility

SoHo, New Beijing (formerly New York City)

Although I've heard Uncle mention the Compound, this is my first visit. Following the others up the front steps, my immediate reaction is that this place will never make it into any New Beijing guidebook. The windows have broken panes, the wooden stairs are cracked and there's graffiti on the brickwork. And that's just on the outside.

Like me, Raoul, Lydia and Abbie are staring wide-eyed. Frank, however, doesn't seem affected, which I take as a sign that he's been here before, maybe more than once.

Gazing at the building, I'm guessing that, even with all its faults, the place cost Uncle a pretty penny. After all, this is SoHo, not Queens.

I follow the others inside. According to Nassim, a hundred years ago the building was a shoe factory. But according to my nose, it could easily have been yesterday. There's a big-time smell of leather in a huge room with a gray concrete floor and stout wooden beams crisscrossing a high ceiling. I even see a couple of dusty iron contraptions that I bet were used for making shoes, tucked away in one corner.

We're all tiptoeing around as if we're a tour group visiting a church. Nassim hustles us across the factory floor to a small room. As soon as I enter, I get a strong whiff of "eau de foot." Maybe this is where they stored the returns. Or maybe the smell is coming from Raoul, who's standing next to me with one foot half out of his shoe.

The room is bare except for a couple of benches and a large window looking out over the factory floor.

I try to mindpatch something to Abbie, but my access is denied. I can't believe it. She's blocking me! She's never done that before. Ever.

I'm so focused on Abbie's snub that I jump when Uncle enters the room.

"Good morning, people. I'm so glad that you could all join me," he says.

As if we had a choice.

It's clear that Uncle's been out shopping. His new outfit, a blue and red pinstriped *hanfu* with matching sandals, screams Wall Street meets the Tang dynasty. But if there's anyone who can pull it off, it's Uncle. As always, his sword is tucked into his belt.

"For those of you who have not been here before, this building is the new Timeless Treasures training facility," he says.

I stifle a yawn and sneak a glance at the others. Raoul is looking particularly nervous. Lydia is gazing at her reflection in the glass, and Frank looks bored. I catch Abbie's eye for a second before she glances away.

"All the recruits live and train here," continues Uncle. "This is the Viewing Room. It looks out over the Yard, which is the name I've given to the large factory floor that you can see out this window. That is where the bulk of the training takes place: classes on conventional thievery, pickpocketing, stealth and the like. The recruits also learn about different cultures and periods from history through age-appropriate educational holos. But it's not all about work. We also have an array of sports equipment and games for fun and recreation as well as dress-up days when the recruits can come as their favorite historical figure."

Fun and recreation. Dress-up days. Memories of my own training days bubble to the surface. Those were good times. I remember soccer games where Uncle played goalie. And I also remember some of my costumes, especially the big hat and long blue and red coat I wore when I was Napoleon. Boy, did Uncle clap when he saw me in that one. These kids have no idea what's in store for them when they get to be my age. I suppose that's a good thing, the not knowing. At least they can enjoy what they have now.

"There is a cafeteria/dining hall on the second level," continues Uncle, "and the third and fourth levels house the recruits' sleeping quarters. The uppermost floor, five, is where my office is. Any questions so far?"

Lydia's hand shoots up. No surprise there. In Lydia's world, the next best thing to looking at herself is hearing herself talk.

"Yes, Lydia?" says Uncle.

"Where does that door lead to?" She's pointing to a set of copper-colored double doors on the far side of the factory floor.

"Very perceptive," Uncle answers. "I did not mention those doors, did I? They house an old-fashioned elevator. Back in the days when this was a shoe factory, the elevator was used to transport finished product from the first floor to the top floor where the shoes were boxed and stored until shipping orders were received. The lift only stops on the first and fifth floors. It's not nearly as swift as the newer models, but speed isn't everything is it?"

No matter how slowly it goes, any elevator that goes straight to Uncle's office can't be good news for the recruits.

"If there are no other questions, let us get on with the show," says Uncle.

He sure has that right. This is one big show. And judging by the gleam in his eye, it looks like the curtain is about to rise.

"Behold, people," he announces, "the next generation of time snatchers!"

We all watch through the window as children stream into the Yard, trailed by five men. Adults? Up until now, apart from Uncle and Nassim, there's never been anyone over thirteen years old working at Timeless Treasures. I didn't think Uncle trusted adults enough to hire them as trainers. I guess I was wrong.

The children, about two dozen of them by my count, are dressed in bright T-shirts, shorts and spanking new running shoes. Even through the glass, I can hear laughter and shouting—the same noises you would expect to hear at any gathering of five and six-year-olds. They immediately make a beeline for the hockey sticks and tennis balls that have been laid out for them.

I can't help but stare. Where did they all come from?

Abbie's got a neutral expression on her face, and Raoul is his usual pale self. But Frank has me worried. He's standing closest to Uncle and looking extremely smug.

"The children you see have been invited here from centuries past as part of a new project that I call Project Metamorphosis," says Uncle. "For those of you who are not familiar with the term 'metamorphosis,' let me enlighten you. Metamorphosis is commonly used to describe a process involving a noticeable and sudden change in an animal's body structure. The animal will typically transform into something completely unrecognizable. In the case of the butterfly, the process begins with the egg, then goes on to the larva, pupa and then, finally, the butterfly.

"My friends," he continues, "just as it is with the butterfly, so it is with Timeless Treasures. The time is now for our metamorphosis."

He pauses for a moment and adjusts his *hanfu*. My eyes are drawn to the sword tucked inside his belt. The blade looks as sharp as ever.

"There will be two phases to Project Metamorphosis," Uncle says. "Phase One will be collection. We will be recruiting children from different cultures and centuries to join us. Some but not all of these children will be orphans. After all, why should children from traditional families be denied the same opportunity to enrich their lives?"

Uncle says it like it's a question, but it's not. I grind my teeth. It's bad enough that he's snatching orphans. But ripping children out of families? It's just wrong.

As Uncle speaks, I hear a cry and spot a trainer and new recruit off to one side. The boy is reaching for something on the floor: a gleaming metal object. As he does, the trainer slaps his hand and picks the object up. It's a harmonica. But I don't get to hear it played, because in the next instant the trainer pockets it.

"This facility," continues Uncle, "can comfortably house eighty recruits, although with some creativity we should be able to squeeze in another twenty. Just think of it: a hundred time snatchers! It seems a boggling number doesn't it? That's progress, my friends. Soon enough these new recruits will be trained and ready to join you, skipping across the centuries and liberating precious items from the past for the enjoyment of our clients."

Uncle sure has a way with words. He's the only one I know who can make stealing sound like a public service.

"Phase Two," he says, "will concern what I call 'Guided Snatches.' From time to time, clients have questioned the authenticity of the object that we have procured for them. To address this concern, I will invite certain select customers to accompany our snatch teams on missions so that they can see the snatch firsthand. What greater proof of authenticity can there be?"

I can't believe it. No way. Snatches are tough enough without the added complication of being responsible for a time-traveling tourist.

"To be the best," Uncle continues, adjusting his sash, "we must not be afraid of having big ideas and turning them into reality. We need only to look to history for examples. While I was in the Far East recently, I took a side trip to see the Great Wall of China. What an enormous undertaking! Imagine a wall stretching more than five thousand miles across valleys, mountains and plains. Almost impossible to contemplate, isn't it? And do you know how it came to be?"

He pauses and I pray he doesn't pick me to answer. Chinese history isn't my strong suit.

"I will tell you," he continues, and I breathe a sigh of relief. "The Great Wall of China started out as the dream of one man, the first emperor of China, Qín Shǐ Huáng. That is how great things begin, my friends, with a simple idea. But of course, just as Qín Shǐ Huáng had help to make his dream a reality, I too have selected one from among your ranks to help me realize my dream."

Uncle's eyes flick to Frank. No. Please don't say it.

"That person is . . . Frank," says Uncle.

My legs go all wobbly. I need to sit down.

I glance at Abbie. She's beaming at Frank as if she can't wait to get over there and give him a big hug.

"Frank will coordinate Phase One of Project Metamorphosis: collections from places and times in history where there have been large gatherings of children. Each of you will now report to Frank," says Uncle, "and he will report directly to me. Are there any questions?"

Not from me there aren't. Now that Frank is my boss, I'm doing something I never thought possible—longing for the old days when I took my orders from Uncle.

Silently, I pray that Uncle doesn't have any more news and will call the meeting to an end. But up shoots good ol' Lydia's right hand. A smile spreads slowly across Uncle's face.

"Lydia has a question," he says. "Fire away."

"Thank you, Uncle," she says. "What I'd like to know is how so many children can be collected from across the centuries without affecting the course of history? I mean, isn't there a risk that, by snatching them away from their families and bringing them here, we'll be interfering with how the future of the world is supposed to unfold? And if that happens, aren't we putting all our lives and the very existence of Timeless Treasures at risk?"

Lydia has a smug smile on her face. I bet Uncle mindlinked her the question to ask. There's no way she could have thought that one up on her own.

"An excellent question, Lydia. Permit me to respond by way of example. Frank, can you kindly bring in the boy?"

Frank disappears and a second later he's back, towing a ragged-looking boy by the hand.

My heart skips a beat. But it's not Zach.

Uncle crouches down so that he's eye level with the boy. "*Cómo te llamas?*" he asks gently.

"Eduardo," says the boy, not quite looking in his eyes.

"Eduardo was collected in nineteenth-century Spain," says Uncle, turning to look at us. "Prior to collecting him, Phoebe did a full workup of his family tree extending two hundred years forward from the date of collection. There were no indications that Eduardo or any of his descendants would play roles in any significant historical events.

"Think of history as a river," he continues. "The Eduardos of the world are but pebbles in the stream. They are too small and insignificant to affect the flow of the current. Even a thousand Eduardos dropped into the river would merely sink to the bottom and not affect the course of the rushing water."

Uncle reaches underneath his *hanfu*, pulls out a chocolate bar and holds it toward the boy, whose small hand twitches but doesn't move from his side.

"It's okay," says Uncle. "This is for you . . . *esto es para ti*."

Eduardo reaches out and takes the chocolate bar.

Frank whispers something in Eduardo's ear, and the boy steps forward, gives Uncle a quick kiss on the cheek and says, "*Gracias,* Uncle."

"*De nada,*" says Uncle smiling. He nods and Frank leads Eduardo away.

"Does that answer your question, Lydia?" says Uncle, rising to his full height.

"Yes, it does. Thank you, Uncle," she says.

"Wonderful. Are there any more questions?" he asks.

Blessedly, no other hands go up.

"Very well, then," says Uncle. "You are all dismissed."

People are getting up and heading for the door. I know I should go too, but I can't tear my eyes away from the sight of those children. What if one of them is Zach? No, I tell myself. Zach is safe with his parents.

A meaty hand on my shoulder startles me.

"Stick around, Caleb," says Nassim. "The boss wants a word with you after he finishes speaking with Abbie. I'll let you know when it's your turn." Then he exits the room.

Abbie? What does he want with her? And why hasn't he asked to see us together?

I sit down on the bench in the Viewing Room and wait. After what seems like forever, Nassim returns, and I follow him down a long hallway. Abbie is approaching from the other direction. She looks pale and gives me a thin smile when she sees me.

"Was it bad?" I mindlink her as we pass each other.

"I was lucky," she mindlinks back. "Only a warning. Good luck."

Nassim motions to a door on the right side of the hallway.

I knock and open the door. The room is plainly furnished with a wood desk, a couple of straight-back chairs and a wall screen. As I enter, the screen lights up, and Phoebe's middle-aged woman persona appears, dressed in a jogging suit that's two sizes too small, pedaling a stationary bicycle and flossing her teeth. Uncle, seated behind the desk, gestures for me to take a seat in one of the visitors' chairs. With his crisp pinstriped *hanfu,* he looks out of place in the drab office. On the desk blotter in front of him is a yellowed piece of paper with edges that curl in different directions. It looks like an old newspaper clipping.

He holds it so that I can only see the headline: BOY VANISHES INTO THIN AIR.

"Are you familiar with Rule Number Three, Caleb?" The vein in Uncle's forehead dances wildly.

"I . . . uhh . . . yes, Uncle," I say.

"Recite it for me, please."

I clear my throat. "Rule Number Three: In the course of performing a mission, no field agent shall bring any undue attention upon himself or Timeless Treasures."

"Well done," he says. "A wonderful recitation of Rule Number Three. Wouldn't you agree, Phoebe?"

"Indubitably, Uncle," replies Phoebe with a smirk in her voice.

"Now," continues Uncle, "would you agree with me that a sensational news story could bring unwanted attention upon our organization?"

My throat is dry. But somehow I manage to squeak out, "Yes, Uncle."

He smiles and lifts his hand, revealing a photograph beneath the headline.

I gasp. It's a picture of me at Expo 67, standing in front of the broken display case for the Xuande vase. My body is translucent. Then I remember Sidney Halpern and his Rolleiflex camera. He must have taken the shot just as I was timeleaping. But how did Uncle get ahold of it?

Frank! It had to be.

"You have deeply disappointed me, Caleb," says Uncle. "Did you know that I was within a hairsbreadth of appointing you over Frank as director of the Project Metamorphosis?"

"No, Uncle, I didn't," I say, my legs trembling now.

Uncle doesn't respond immediately. He draws his sword from his belt and lays it on the table between us, pointy end facing me.

"Were you aware," he says, "that even in this modern day and age, there are certain countries in the world that still punish thieves by cutting off their hands?"

"I wasn't aware of that, Uncle," I say, eyes glued to the tip of his sword. My mouth has gone completely dry.

"There is a certain symmetry to that, wouldn't you agree?" says Uncle. "Punishing a thief by cutting off the very limbs he used to commit the theft?"

I nod. The direction of this conversation is scaring me. "But Uncle, I snatched the Xuande vase for you! The mission was a success!" I don't like the sound of my voice. It sounds desperate and frightened.

"You are absolutely correct," he says. "The mission was a smashing success, pardon the pun. And you were duly rewarded for it, don't you remember?"

I say nothing.

"The point is, Caleb, that you broke Rule Number Three. And not in a small way, either."

Then he softens his tone. "Now, I really shouldn't, should I? After all, stealing is your job. If I cut off your hands or even your fingers, I would really only be hurting myself."

My eyes follow Uncle's right index finger as it hovers for a moment over the tip of the sword and then presses down on it, drawing blood.

"Take off your left shoe and sock," he says.

Tears start to gather in my eyes. I have a sudden urge to bolt, but I know it's useless. Nassim is stationed right outside the door.

I bend down and slowly remove my shoe. Then I take my sock off and there it is—my naked left foot. Until this moment I don't think I truly appreciated what a marvel my foot is and how precious it is to me.

"Foot on the top of the desk, please," says Uncle.

I lift it up and onto the desk. My whole body is shaking badly.

"Did you know that nursery rhymes are not only told in the West? The Chinese have them too." As he says this, he raises the sword and slices the air above my naked foot.

"Yes, Uncle," I say, my voice hardly more than a whisper.

He brings the tip of the blade to within an inch of my big toe and says, "But to be honest, I prefer the nursery rhymes of the West. Perhaps we all enjoy the familiarity of things we grew up with. Isn't that true?"

I grit my teeth.

"And the one I'm about to recite is a particular favorite," he continues.

I try to yank my foot off the table, but Uncle grips my ankle roughly and keeps it there.

"This little piggy went to market," he begins.

The blade shifts a smidgeon and hovers over my second toe.

"And this little piggy stayed home." His voice is steady and cold.

Sweat rolls off my forehead. Whimpers come from my throat.

"This little piggy had roast beef," he continues, moving to my third toe. "And this little piggy had none." Uncle lowers the blade until it tickles the skin of my fourth toe.

"Please don't. Please don't. It won't happen again. I promise," I cry.

"And this little piggy cried, 'Wee, wee, wee' . . ."

"No, Uncle!" I plead.

"All the way HOME!"

A beam of bright blue light flashes from the tip of the blade, zapping my smallest toe. Searing white pain explodes in my foot. A burning smell fills the air. My toe. My poor toe.

Just before I pass out, I hear Uncle say, "The number nine, Caleb, is perhaps the most important number to the Chinese. Nine is the dragon. Nine is the number of palace gates at the center of the Forbidden City. Nine is the number of slabs in the circular altar of the Temple of Heaven. And now"—he pauses—"nine is the number of your toes."

XXI

I wake up in my bed at Headquarters. How did I get here? It must have been Nassim. The last thing I remember is Uncle reciting a nursery rhyme. A shooting pain in my foot reminds me of the rest.

I throw off my blankets and sit up. There's a large white bandage where my little toe used to be. A glass of water and pill bottle sit on my bedside table. I wash down two of the pills, then swing my feet over the bed and stand up. Surprisingly, the pain isn't too bad. I take a couple of wobbly steps forward and almost lose my balance before correcting myself.

A million thoughts race through my head. Project Metamorphosis. That Spanish kid, Eduardo. Frank at Expo 67. And Zach. I've got to get out of here and go someplace where I can think about everything and figure out what to do.

I shake another two pills from the bottle and put them in my pocket. Then, on impulse, I take the whole bottle. Next, I grab my carving and knife, shove them in my other pocket, and carefully put on my sock and shoe over the bandage. Ready to go.

The hall is empty. Everyone must be out on missions. I trudge to the elevator.

"Well, if it isn't Caleb the See-Through Time Snatcher. That was quite a photo of you," says Phoebe.

"Yes, it was," I agree.

"Where are you going?" Phoebe asks. Her persona is dressed in a crisp white nurse's uniform, and she's holding a pen and clipboard.

"For a walk," I say.

"That sounds mysterious," she says, jotting something on the clipboard.

"Yes, it does," I say, not taking the bait. The less Phoebe knows the better.

"Okay," says Phoebe, "have it your way. But don't expect to make many friends if all your sentences are less than four words."

"I won't."

The elevator ride is blessedly quiet. I get off at the lobby and head toward the subway.

I feel some pain in my foot, but it's manageable. Balance is a bit of an issue until I realize that if I shift more of my weight onto my right foot, it's easier to walk.

As I board the uptown number one train, Uncle's chilling words come back to me. "Nine is the dragon . . . and now nine is the number of your toes."

Luckily my car isn't crowded, so I have no problem finding a seat. I close my eyes, figuring on a good fifteen minutes before my stop. The pills I took are kicking in now, easing the pain in my foot.

"Want to buy some Girl Scout fortune cookies, mister?" says a voice.

It's "mister" that gets my attention. No one's ever misterred me before, that is, in a serious way. I open my eyes and see a smiling, red-haired girl wearing a green uniform and beret. There's a gap as wide as Fifth Avenue between her two front teeth. I peg her at about nine years old, which accounts for the mister. Her name badge says MOLLY,

211

and she's not alone. Two identically dressed but glum companions stand slightly behind and to each side of her. Each of them has her hands wrapped around four or five red boxes.

For a second, I'm tempted to do what any decent New Yorker would do, and that is ignore her completely. But something, maybe her smile, makes me look up and say, "Girl Scout fortune cookies? When did that happen?"

"It's new this year. On account of the Great Friendship," Molly says.

I should have guessed. "How much for one?"

"Ten dollars a box," she says, without batting an eyelash.

"No, I mean how much for one fortune cookie?" I say.

"We don't sell singles," she says, her smile fading fast. "You gotta buy the whole box. But it's a good deal. And you can share with your friends."

I wonder if I should try for a no-friends discount. But Molly looks like she's getting restless. I dig my fingers into my pocket and fish out the silver half-dollar coin left over from Bridgeport.

"This doesn't look like ten bucks, mister," she says when I hand her the coin.

"Yeah, but look at the date," I say. "1871. Do you know how much that coin is worth now?"

She shakes her head.

"Probably over fifty bucks," I say, although I really have no idea. Molly is smiling again. Even the Sisters Glum look slightly happier.

"Mint or regular?" she asks.

"Mint, please," I say.

"Thanks for supporting the Girl Scouts," she says, handing me a red box.

With that, she spins and bounces off toward her next mark, the Sisters Glum following close on her heels.

I get off at Columbus Circle and cross the line of waiting rickshaw taxis, pausing for a moment at the base of the Maine Monument. Looking up, I see the familiar bronze sculpture of a lady standing in a seashell chariot pulled by three seahorses. I know it sounds silly, but sometimes I imagine her and her chariot breaking free of the top of the monument and flying through the sky over Manhattan.

As I enter Central Park, a jogger and dog duo pass me with their tongues hanging out. The smell of hot dogs and mustard wafts over from a nearby cart.

It's only a short walk to my favorite spot. I like being in the park. It calms me. I can think here.

I'm in luck. My regular bench is free. I sit down, stretch my legs and gaze ahead at what I consider to be the best thing to come out of the Great Friendship: the Xuxu Monastery and Garden. The scoop on the monastery is that the Chinese paid to move it and about a hundred Buddhist monks all the way from a hilltop right outside Shanghai. They even built a Chinese garden, complete with lotus pond, stone bridge, cool-looking rocks and different kinds of flowers and trees.

Deep breath in and then long breath out. I catch a whiff of lilac and can hear the soft clink of wind chimes.

There's a stone wall around the monastery, but it's low enough that I can still see what's going on. Last week I really lucked out—I had a rare glimpse of one of the monks doing his laundry. Today, though, everything is quiet.

"Hi, Cale," says a voice behind me.

I jump.

"Sorry to startle you," Abbie says.

No kidding. How did she know I was here? "It's okay," I say.

"Do you mind if I sit down?"

"Sure, go ahead." I slide over a bit. Abbie is acting all serious, which isn't like her. Something must be up.

"How's your foot?" she asks.

"You heard about it?"

"Yeah. Nassim told me . . . after," she says quietly.

"It's not too bad," I say. "It would have been a lot worse if the Chinese had picked three as their favorite number instead of nine."

"What do you mean?" she asks.

"Never mind," I say. "It's a joke. A not very funny one."

"What's in the box?" she asks, pointing.

"I got it on the subway from some Girl Scouts."

"Shame on you, stealing from Girl Scouts."

"I didn't. If anyone stole, it's them. I gave them my last 1871 half-dollar for this box."

"Well, can I have one?"

"Sure."

I hold the box open in front of her. Her fingers dance in the air for a moment and then pluck up one of the fortune cookies.

Abbie breaks the cookie open and pulls out a small piece of paper. A smile spreads across her face. "Listen to this." She moves closer to me on the bench so that our legs are touching. "*The best ship to have in a storm is friendship.* It's true, isn't it, Cale? Like you and me. Now open yours."

I pick a cookie and break it open. Reading the message silently, a shiver goes through me, and I quickly close my fist over the slim piece of paper.

"Well, what does it say?" she asks.

"Nothing. It's dumb," I answer.

"C'mon, I read you mine." She takes a bite of her cookie.

"All right. But like I said, I don't believe in this stuff. It says, *Dangerous times are ahead for you.*"

Abbie stares at me, mouth open.

"C'mon, Abbie. It's just a cookie."

The back door of the monastery opens. Two monks come out and head for the garden.

"I don't know," she says. "I'm worried about you. You haven't been yourself lately."

She's the second one to say that. First Nassim and now Abbie. The pain in my foot is starting up again, so I pull out the pill bottle, snag one and dry swallow it.

"It's like there's something on your mind," she continues, "weighing you down. It's about that boy, isn't it? The one you saved at Expo 67. That's why you've been acting strange lately."

I turn to look at her. There's real concern in her eyes.

"I have to make sure he's safe," I say. "I can't let anything happen to him."

"But why is that your problem?" she says. "I mean, I know you saved his life and all that, but—"

"It's more than just that," I answer. "It's like he and I are connected in some special way. It may sound crazy, but when I look at him, it feels as if I'm looking at myself—well, maybe not exactly myself—more like someone I might have been . . . if things had been different."

Abbie looks at me for a long moment and doesn't say anything. A gentle breeze starts the wind chimes going. The monks are walking back to the monastery door. Their steps look sure and unhurried.

"Frank asked me to be his special assistant," she says.

My jaw drops open and just kind of hangs there. "And you said no, of course."

She glances away. "Not exactly."

"Not exactly? What does that mean?"

Abbie hesitates for a moment searching for the right words. "I said . . . maybe."

A knot is forming in my stomach. "Maybe? This isn't a *maybe* situation, Abbie! Did you hear what Uncle's got him doing? Snatching innocent children! You want to help with that?"

She continues to look away from me. "Why is that shocking to you?" she says. "We were snatched or adopted or whatever you want to call it too, remember? And some of us turned out okay."

"It's not the same," I say. "We were orphans. We didn't have anybody who'd miss us anyway. But these children have families! And not only that. What happened to us happened in real time, not a hundred years ago!"

"So, why should that matter?" asks Abbie.

"Why?" I say. "Because these kids have had their own children and their children have had children. And so on and so on. By going back and snatching them, Uncle's murdering entire generations!"

Abbie's quiet for a moment. Then she says, "I can't just say no to Frank. We talked about that."

I can't believe what I'm hearing. She doesn't get it, but by saying yes to Frank, she's saying no to me.

I feel my face go hot. But instead of answering, I begin keying in a sequence on my wrist.

She stares at me, eyes wide. "Where are you going?"

"Away," I answer.

"Cale, you shouldn't be using your patch unless it's for a mission," she says.

"This is for a mission," I say. "A personal mission."

"Don't do it," Abbie says. "You're on Uncle's radar. I don't want to think what will happen to you if he finds out."

"So? Why should you care what happens to me?" I blurt out. "You have your precious Frank."

There. I've said it.

"See you later, Caleb," she says quietly. She gets up without looking at me. I watch her walk away.

Did I hear a slight hitch in her voice? For a moment, I'm tempted to stay and analyze it, the big question being: does she really like me? As in boyfriend/girlfriend kind of liking? There are a bunch of other unanswered questions floating around in my brain. Like how am I going to convince Abbie not to be Frank's assistant, how can I get myself off Uncle's radar, and how am I going to keep Zach safe? Yes, if I wanted to, I could easily pass the next several hours, or even days, sitting on this bench, analyzing.

Instead, I tap my wrist again. As I fade from view, I spot a squirrel poised to jump up onto the bench and claim his prize—an almost full box of Girl Scout mint fortune cookies.

XXII

February 7, 1968, 4:02 P.M.
Boston, Massachusetts

Even before I open my eyes, I realize I must have made a sequencing error. My entire body is trembling. I could have sworn that I'd programmed the timeleap for an August arrival. But this feels more like January. Maybe the business with Abbie threw my sequencing off.

Blinking away the falling snow, I realize that I'm standing in the middle of a street with a park on one side and smart-looking Victorian houses on the other. If I didn't know better, I'd say I landed somewhere in the 1880s. The honk of a car horn brings me to my senses. Actually, it does more than that—it sends me sprinting away from a car speeding by without even slowing.

I almost wipe out on an icy patch on the sidewalk. My T-shirt and jeans are a joke in this kind of weather. I have half a mind to timeleap a few months back to summer, but then I see the sign saying Derne Street.

Trudging along the sidewalk with my head down against the howling wind, the only other sound is snow crunching beneath my shoes. Forty-nine, fifty-one, fifty-three. There it is. Number fifty-five.

I pause and study the house. A red brick row house. Not that different from any of the others on this street. So why is my heart beating so fast?

My feet lead me along the snow-covered walkway and then up to the porch.

Rolled-up newspapers lie half buried in the snow. Shards of glass occupy one corner, and the skeleton of an abandoned bird's nest clings to the underside of the porch's small overhang.

The house looks dark. No, it looks more than dark. Abandoned. This has to be a mistake. They can't possibly live here.

But I'm positive this is the address they told me. Fifty-five Derne. There's a bell and a knocker. I knock.

Twenty seconds go by. Then a minute. I hop from foot to foot against the cold.

I try the bell. There's a hollow ring inside the house. Another minute goes by. Nothing.

Just as I begin to turn away, I catch some movement from behind one of the windows. There and then gone.

"Hey! Is anyone home?" To my ears, my voice sounds strained, desperate.

I pound on the door.

A few seconds later, I hear the grinding of a latch being pulled back. Then a click and the door slowly begins to open. The smell of stale pizza wafts out.

"What do you want?"

It's a woman's voice. The words are flat and lifeless.

I study her face, half hidden by the door. It matches the voice. Pale and drawn. Bags under the eyes.

But still. It could be her. I try to speak, but the words die on the way to my mouth. "Di . . . Diane?" I manage finally.

She doesn't answer immediately. I can feel her eyes on me.

"Yes?" she says. Cautious. Fragile. "How do you know me?"

"Diane, it's me, Caleb," I say.

A flicker of recognition. "Caleb? From Expo?" she says. There is something else there too: suspicion.

"Yes," I say. "I've just come to say hello. And to see how . . . how you all are."

She gives me a long look, long enough for me to remember how cold I am. I fold my arms across my chest and rub them with my hands.

"You don't know, do you?" she says finally, wearily.

XXIII

February 7, 1968, 4:14 P.M.
Boston, Massachusetts

Diane takes the chain off. "Come in." She turns away from me even as she says it.

I stamp my feet on the mat and follow her into a dark living room. She clears some empty pizza boxes from a small green sofa and gestures for me to sit down. Then she lowers herself slowly into an armchair.

We sit facing each other. All the words that I thought I would say at this moment don't seem right anymore. So I just wait, looking dumbly at a small chip in the wood frame of the sofa.

"Zach was . . . taken," she says.

My head snaps up, and I stare at her in disbelief. It can't be! She has to be wrong. Kids can wander off sometimes. Yes, that's what Zach's done. He's just wandered off. Any second now, the door-bell will ring and he'll be standing right there asking Diane when supper is.

"When?" I ask, the word sticking in my throat.

"The day we met you," Diane says. Her eyes are filled with sor-row. But it also looks like she's studying my reaction to what she just said.

My stomach clenches into a knot. That means Zach's been miss-ing for months!

"Diane, I . . ."

She gazes past me at the wall beyond the couch. "Jim thinks that maybe you know something about what hap—"

"I swear I had nothing to do with it," I say a bit too loudly, and even as I utter the words, I'm thinking that they're not exactly true.

"You should leave now, Caleb," she says, standing up.

She reaches out but doesn't quite touch my hand. I want to reassure her. Tell her that I'm going to make things right again. Promise her that I'll find Zach and bring him back. But what if I can't?

I leave by the front door and walk around to the side of the house, stepping over a garden hose half buried in the snow. My eyes flick from a rusted hockey net to a broken planter. An enormous sadness comes over me.

Tap, tap, tap on my wrist.

Nothing happens.

I try again. Still nothing.

Shivering now. I don't understand. My patch has never failed before.

Wait. Something's happening in my wrist. It feels like worms are crawling around inside me. Bits of my skin are contracting and expanding as if I have a nervous twitch. But this is no nervous twitch. The patch is programming itself! I can't believe it—this has never happened before . . . I'm the only one who can control my patch. Or am I?

Frantically, I key in the sequence again, pressing down hard with every tap. But still, something blocks me, overriding my commands and replacing them with new ones. Who could be doing this: Uncle? Frank?

In a last-ditch effort, I clamp my hand over my wrist and squeeze as hard as I can. I can't stop it!

Where am I being taken?

I cry out. But the cry is cut short as my vocal cords and the rest of me leave Boston in a hurry.

XXIV

June 25, 2061, 4:40 P.M.
Timeless Treasures Headquarters
Tribeca, New Beijing (formerly New York City)

Total darkness. Then a single, icy light blinds me. I'm lying flat on my back on a cold, hard surface. I try to turn away from the light. But I can't. My arms and legs won't obey me. I'm completely paralyzed. Time freeze? No. This feels different. It's cold here, wherever here is. My whole body is shaking, shivering.

The light moves to my right wrist. A rough hand clamps something over my face. There's a strong medicine smell. Someone wearing green surgeon's scrubs stands over me. The only part of his face not covered by a mask is his eyes.

"What am I doing here? Who are you?" I shout the words, but they only come out as a whisper.

I try to sit up, but I can't. Someone's tied me down.

The masked man leans down, closer to me. His cold blue eyes study me.

Uncle!

"You've been a bad boy, Caleb. A very bad boy," he says.

"Please, Uncle," I say.

"I thought you would have learned your lesson at our last meeting," he says. "But that doesn't appear to be the case."

I've got to get out of here somehow. I struggle hard against the restraints, but nothing gives.

"It's such a shame, really," continues Uncle. "You could have been so much more. I remember taking you out on a mission when you were only six years old. You didn't want to let go of my hand. But I finally managed to pry you loose and pointed you toward the mark. You were magnificent. You moved silently as a shadow and plucked the wallet from his back pocket without the slightest ripple. And how you smiled afterward, running into my arms, proudly displaying your first snatch.

"What happened to that smiling young boy?" he continues. "What happened to make him become so burdened and afraid? What happened, Caleb, to make you stop listening to your uncle?"

"You're not my real uncle!" I scream.

"Tsk. Tsk. You mustn't get overwrought," says Uncle. "The anesthetic I administered is generally slow-acting. And I prefer it that way. It gives us time to talk about things. But if you become agitated, it speeds the effect of the drug. So please stay calm. It would be a shame to have to cut short such a stimulating conversation."

"Let me go," I plead. "I won't be any more trouble. I promise."

"Oh, I'm sure you won't. And, in fact, I am planning to let you go in a little while, although my interpretation of letting you go might not be exactly what you have in mind," he says, chuckling.

"Now, where was I?" he continues. "Ah, yes. Did you know, Caleb, that during China's Ming dynasty one of the consequences of misbehavior was something called *fapei*?"

I shake my head.

"Well, then, let me explain," he continues. "*Fapei* was one of the five punishments contained in the Tang Code and was inflicted by the Ming emperors upon those found to have broken the law. Loosely translated, it means 'exile to the frontier.'"

As he speaks, Uncle's hand strays to the small table beside him, where an assortment of gleaming scalpels, knives and other surgical equipment rest on a white linen cloth. He picks up one of the scalpels and tests the blade with the fleshy part of his thumb.

"At various junctures during history," says Uncle, "some of the world's most important figures have voluntarily gone into exile, only to emerge stronger. One of the great Chinese emperors, Emperor Quianlong, associated exile with the idea of *zixin* or the 'way to self-renewal.'"

I'm cold. So cold. But even so, I'm having trouble staying awake. My thoughts are becoming thick and confusing. Uncle is droning on and on. I hear his words, but they are sounds without any meaning.

"So, my advice to you, Caleb," Uncle says, "is to view your forthcoming exile not so much as a punishment, even though that's what it is, but more as an opportunity to improve yourself as a person."

There's movement behind Uncle. My vision is fuzzy, but I can see others in the shadows. Who are they? What are they doing here?

"I am banishing you to the Barrens," he says. "You will stay there for one year before you may return. But before I send you, you're going to have a little operation. You need to return something that is mine."

What is he saying? So hard to concentrate. I want to sleep.

My mind is floating far away. Fuzzy warmth is enveloping me. Before I pass out completely, I hear Uncle say to one of the others, "Let us begin."

And then the cool edge of the knife is on my skin, prodding, searching and finally, cutting.

The light is going away now. Fading. Or is it me who's fading? No! I've got to fight it. But I can't. I've failed. Failed myself. And failed Zach.

XXV

The Barrens, Day 1

I'm lying on my back. Beads of sweat trace their way along my jaw. Opening my eyes, I'm almost blinded by brightness. I close them and try to go back to sleep, but my brain isn't playing ball. It wants me to wake up and scratch the itch on my arm. I try valiantly to ignore it. After all, waking up leads to getting up; getting up requires effort and effort is best avoided at all costs. But there's that itch again. It looks like I'm going to have to deal with it soon. Not yet, though. I drift away and doze.

The itch is back, and it's worse than ever. My brain tells me it's my right wrist. One good scratch should do it. And then I can get some more slee—YAOWWW!

Burning, excruciating pain. Sitting bolt upright now. There's a jagged line from the base of my palm to midway up my forearm. That's no scratch. Someone cut me.

I turn my head expecting to see my attacker crouching behind me waiting to finish me off.

No one.

But what I do see scares me even more: miles and miles of sand and reddish wind-blasted rocks; as lonely-looking a place as I've ever encountered in my life. This must be what the moon looked like before McDonald's came.

A wind comes up and blows sand into my eyes, stinging them.

Something tickles my leg and, hitching up my pant leg, I see a large spider scuttling up my ankle. I swat if off and stand up.

Endless blue sky and searing heat. Where am I? When am I? I try to remember how I got here but draw a blank. It doesn't matter, though, because I'm not sticking around. I'm leaving right now.

I gingerly tap my wrist, careful to work around the cut.

Nothing.

I wipe my sweaty fingers on my T-shirt and key in the sequence again. It wouldn't be the first time I misdialed.

Still nothing. Then a shard of memory. Uncle's blue eyes and green surgeon's scrubs.

I'm drenched in sweat. The sun is high in the sky, and I need to find shade. Yes, first shade, then try again. But what if it doesn't work?

I start walking. At first, I pick my way slowly through and around the sharp rocks. But after a while there's more sand than rocks and I don't have to be as careful. *Careful.* The word bounces around in my brain until another image (another memory?) breaks free. I'm lying on a table. A man in a mask peers down at me. I want to run away, but I can't move. He's waving a wicked-looking blade over my wrist. *Careful,* he's saying to the others. *Just a quick snatch and run.* They find this funny and begin to laugh. I shout at them to stop, but the shouts are only in my head.

Walking faster now. Sweat is pouring down my forehead. I must not panic. The memories are coming fast and furious. I know now that the one with the blade is Uncle, and I shudder as he makes a long incision. Another peels back the flaps of skin. And a third grabs it with green rubber gloves, pulling it free. He holds it up like it's a trophy. But it's no trophy—it's my time travel implant—they took it!

Running now. Did someone say don't panic? Too late. Calm was yesterday's news. Panic is in fashion, and I'm a supermodel. To prove my point, I'm sprinting through the desert, screaming at the top of my lungs.

Anyone who saw me would probably think that I'm losing it. A vision of Nassim swims into my head. He's got me in a headlock and growls, "Five letters. Time thief gone crazy."

"That's easy," I say. "The answer is Caleb."

My legs feel weak. I stop and bend over, gasping for air, keeping my eyes cast downward on the red and gray rocks. I don't want to look up because I'm afraid that all I'll see is more of the same barren landscape.

Must concentrate on my breathing. Breath in, breathe out. That's better. One step at a time. Only I have no idea what the next step is; Uncle never taught us about wilderness survival. But I do know one thing—there's no way I'm dying here. I've got to get out of this place. Zach needs me.

Maybe things aren't as bad as I'm making them out to be. After all, there's no way Uncle would just leave one of his best time snatchers to rot in the desert, would he? No, he probably just wants to give me a good scare. All I have to do is sit tight and wait for Nassim to come pick me up.

Then a fresh wave of panic washes over me. How is Nassim ever going to find me? I must have already run half a mile from where I landed. I've got to retrace my steps. But how? The ground is hard, and I can't see my footprints.

I turn around and begin walking, praying that I'm heading in the right direction. It's impossible to know—all the rocks look the same.

My shirt is soaking. I remember reading somewhere that it's not good to sweat in a survival situation because sweating uses up precious water that your body needs to preserve. But this isn't a survival situation, I tell myself. It's just a little walk in the desert. Any minute now, Nassim's massive arms will wrap me in a chokehold and he'll demand my help with twenty-four across or thirteen down or some other clue.

But what if he doesn't come?

Best not to think about that one. Because thinking leads to worrying, worrying leads to panicking, and I'm already way over my panic quota for the day.

But it's too late. Panic already has already begun to well up inside me again. No, I won't let it rule me. I've got to think straight. Shelter. Yes, I've got to find shelter. And then food and water. No, water first. A person can survive about two weeks without food, but without any water, you can die of thirst in five days.

I stop and look around. Is this the spot where I landed? It could be, but then again, maybe not. I should have marked it somehow. Now what? Wait around for Nassim to come? Too risky. The heat is relentless, and I'll be fried if I stay here much longer. I can already feel it pouring up through the bottoms of my shoes. But if I carry on, Nassim may never find me. I don't have a choice, though—it's either keep moving or die.

Death. There's that word again. I wonder how Abbie would feel if I died? She'd probably be sad at first, but Frank would be there to console her. He'd wrap one of his big ape arms around her and—

Stop it!

I clear my mind and continue trudging forward. Soon all thoughts go out of my head. I'm on autopilot. One foot in front of the other. If it wasn't for the position of the sun in the sky, it would be impossible to tell how much time has gone by. A minute feels like an hour, and an hour feels like a day. I've lost all sense of time.

Now, that's precious. A time traveler with no sense of time.

A wind comes up and blows sand into my eyes, my nose, my ears and even my mouth. I tear a strip from my shirt and place it over my nose and mouth. But it doesn't seem to help. The air is thick with swirling sand, and I can't see more than a foot in front of me. It's impossible to carry on. I drop to the ground and curl up in a ball with my hands over my head.

The wind rushes all around me. I must be hallucinating, because I swear I can hear laughter. I cover my ears with my hands to block out the sound. But it's no use. The desert is laughing at me.

After what feels like forever, the wind dies down and the sky clears. I raise my head slowly and survey my surroundings. All is calm. I stand up and take a tentative step forward. I'm totally disoriented. Is this the way forward, or will it take me right back to where I was?

There's a shape in the distance. It looks like the rooftop of a long, rectangular building. And even better, right in front of the building is a huge lake, glittering in the late afternoon sun.

Yes! My luck is definitely improving. In a few moments, I'll have scored two out of my top three picks: shelter and water. I start running toward the lake and building. It's really more of an awkward shuffle than a run, but I'm way beyond caring what I look like.

I'm already planning the rest of my day. First I'll have a drink, then check out the building. Maybe it's a lodge for travelers. I can picture the inside: a great big room with cushy armchairs, mahogany side tables, fake palm trees and soft music playing. And whenever you're thirsty, you just say the word and someone hands you a tall glass of cool water with a miniature umbrella sticking out of it and a little coaster to set it down on.

I can almost taste the water on my tongue. Silky and sweet. Maybe I'll go for short swim after my drink just to pique my appetite for dinner . . .

But when I glance again at the building, it's gone. And so is the lake.

Vanished. As if they never existed.

This can't be happening! Maybe I'm looking the wrong way. I spin around, searching frantically in all directions.

A mirage. It was all just a mirage. It feels as if someone has just knocked all the wind out of me. I collapse onto the sand. That's it. I'm done. Whatever energy I had has disappeared just as suddenly as the building and lake. What's the point of even trying to go on? Then, an image of Zach floats into my head. He's the point. He needs me.

Slowly, I get up and start walking. I think about the mirage again and then it occurs to me: I'm thinking clearly. Which means no time fog. But how can that be? I must have been here, wherever here is, for hours already. Maybe it's because I don't have a time patch anymore. Great, one less way to die. That only leaves about a hundred other ways to perish out here.

The weather is cooling. If I wasn't worrying about staying alive, I'd say that the temperature is almost pleasant. There's another shape up ahead, something jutting out of the ground. It's got a kind of a curve on the top.

Another mirage? It could be, but I don't think so. First off, it's not shimmering; it's looking quite solid. Second, it's growing larger as I approach, which is exactly what you'd expect a real object to do. I close and then open my eyes. It's still there.

Closer now. Close enough so that what I see sends a shiver

through me. It's a skeleton of a large animal. At first I think it's a horse, but I look closer and see the remains of two humps. A dead camel.

My spirits plunge again. The desert may be flat, but emotionally I feel like I'm on a roller coaster. If a creature that was practically built for this place can't survive, then how am I supposed to?

On a large rock next to the camel, I see a dozen stones piled into a small pyramid. These stones were placed there by someone. By who? And why?

It will be getting dark soon. I'm beyond tired, but I've got to find shelter for the night. There's nothing here so I walk on.

There are two mountains in the distance: gray and red. Got to get to them.

As I walk, the ground underneath me is changing. Sand and stones are giving way to great slabs of rock. In the gathering darkness, it's difficult to see where I'm stepping. I fall twice and each time pick myself up slowly.

Instinctively, I rub my eyes and switch to night vision. Wait, how can that be? I still have my ocular implant. I guess it was too much trouble for Uncle to remove it.

Oh so tired. My legs feel like jelly. On the next rock slab, they give out entirely, and I crumple to the ground. I crawl on all fours to a place where the giant slab intersects with the next one. There's a small crevasse there, a kind of crawl space between the two ledges. I wedge my body into the tight space. At least I'm somewhat protected from the wind.

I look up and for the first time notice the stars. They're dazzlingly beautiful. For a moment I forget about everything else and gaze at the canopy of twinkling lights. I wonder if Abbie is looking at the same stars right now. I wonder if she's thinking about me.

Have to rest. Just for a couple of hours. Then I'll be on my way again.

My last thought before I fall asleep is of Zach. Hands are reaching for him. "Help me, Caleb!" he shouts, as he tries to fight them off with his five-year-old fists. "Hang on," I want to shout back. But no sound comes out of my parched throat.

XXVI

The Barrens, Day 2

I wake up with a raging thirst. The sun is streaming down on me. As I unfold myself, my brain is flooded with memories of the day before: the endless miles of rocks and sand, the terrible heat, the windstorm and, finally, arriving here.

How long have I slept? Judging from the position of the sun, I'm guessing five or six hours. Longer than I wanted to. I stand up slowly. Every part of my body hurts, especially my right side where I fell yesterday. I have a sudden urge to crawl right back into the crack and stay there . . . until when? Until Nassim comes to save the day? Well, that's not going to happen, is it? The only one who has any chance of saving me is me.

I take a deep breath and start walking toward the mountains. They look closer today, but maybe it's my mind playing tricks again. I'm trudging so slowly that it would be a miracle if I actually reached them before I . . . Don't think. Just walk. What I wouldn't give for one of those dirt bikes. Better yet, a glass of water. With ice. Great. Now I've gone and done it. There's no way I'm going to be able to think about anything else now. Two ice cubes. No, three. I've got to stop this. Think of something else. Like where is this place? Or better yet, what year is it?

Where might be easier than when. Uncle might have his faults, but he's a whiz at geography. I remember him teaching us that the three largest deserts in the world are the Sahara in Africa, the Arabian Desert in Saudi Arabia and the Gobi Desert in Mongolia. This could be any of them. Or, I suppose it could be one of the smaller deserts—there are a whole bunch of those—but I doubt it, since Uncle likes to think big. Personally, I'm leaning toward the Gobi because China is Mongolia's next-door neighbor.

The harder question is when. I haven't seen any sign of humans. Wait, there were those rocks in a pile. Someone had definitely arranged them that way. Except that rock piles look pretty much the same no matter what century it is. My gut tells me I'm stuck way back in the past—sometime in the ninth or tenth century. But it's just a guess. I could easily be in the fourteenth or fifteenth century. Or, for that matter, even in the nineteenth century. A few hundred years means nothing to a place like this.

I've been walking for what feels like hours. My feet are aching, but I don't dare stop. If I do, I'm not sure that I'll have the energy to get up again.

The sun continues to beat down, baking me and sapping all my strength. I fall into a pattern of thinking about absolutely nothing except for putting one foot in front of the other.

A flash of movement from above catches my attention. Two big birds are circling in the sky high above me. Hawks? No, hawks aren't that big. I keep walking and the birds follow me. Soon I'm able to make them out more clearly: they're big ugly things with mottled gray brown wings and black hooked beaks—vultures.

A kick of adrenaline surges through my body, and I pick up my pace. Sorry, guys, you've got the wrong address. I pick up a rock and hurl it at them. They disperse for a second and then form their little hunting group again. After all, that's what they're here for, isn't it? To hunt. These birds are smart too—they don't do any of the killing themselves. No, that's way too messy. They wait for their prey to die first.

"Go away," I yell at the top of my lungs, but it comes out as a pitiful rasp. The brutes continue to hover. I can almost hear them laughing at me.

I take a breath to steady myself and carry on. Time passes. The mountains appear closer now. I might even make it to the foothills by nightfall. My vulture friends are nowhere in sight. Good riddance.

There are other changes too. Where before there were only rocks and sand I now see small shrubs. Something dashes from a shrub right in front of me and disappears into another. Did I imagine it? I stand stock-still, hoping to see it again, but there is nothing. I glance ahead. A new color has been added to the horizon, and my eyes marvel at the sight.

Green.

I want to run to the green, but my body is too weak. Is there water there? Maybe it's another mirage. After all, whoever heard of green in the desert? Well, maybe I'm out of the desert, or on the fringe or in an oasis, or . . . More movement up ahead. Something leaping from the rocks. It's an animal. A big, sturdy-looking animal with huge curved horns. I stare openmouthed as it jumps from rock to rock before it disappears.

I look up and glimpse a great bird soaring in the cloudless sky. Too beautiful to be a vulture. It hovers in the air for a moment, then folds its wings inward and drops like a stone.

I've reached the green now. It's grass. Long, tall strands of grass, some as tall as my head: a forest of grass.

The sun is low in the sky, and I have to find shelter for the night. I also need water and food. I tear off a piece of grass, crush it with my teeth and chew slowly, trying my best to ignore its bitter taste, imagining it giving strength to my body. But it's tough going, and I come close to retching.

Gazing up at the mountains, I notice the peaks are capped in white. Snow. What I wouldn't give for a mouthful of snow right now. But the mountains are farther away than I first thought and there's no way I'll reach them tonight. Even if I did, I'd never have the strength to climb up to the top of even the lowest of the peaks.

With my remaining energy I pull out some of the longer strands of grass and lay them down on the ground. My bed for the night. Exhausted, I collapse onto it and immediately fall asleep.

A tickling sensation wakes me. I open my eyes and see something with two pincers and a barbed tail crawling up my arm. A scorpion. I yell, jump to my feet and shake it off. But the bad news is that my vulture friends from yesterday must have heard all the commotion because they're back, circling in the sky.

I continue my trudge toward the mountains, trying to ignore my terrible thirst.

Ridges up ahead. Great golden-brown cliffs. I doubt I have the strength to climb them.

I slog on. The long grass gives way to slabs of rock, and the slabs to the ridges. The going is slow. So weak now. So hard to keep going.

Movement flickers to my left, and I freeze. A small, furry animal dashes out between two rocks, sees me and hightails it back to the rocks.

If my mouth had any moisture left, I'd be salivating. I shuffle over to where the animal disappeared. Reaching my hand between the rocks, I grab nothing but air. What did I expect? That the little thing would be there waiting for me to snatch it and have it for breakfast?

Sighing, I drag my feet forward a few more steps and stop again. No more energy. All tapped out. The vultures are getting brave. One of them even lights on my shoulder for a moment before hopping off. I wish I had a stick to hit it with or a stone to throw at it or even the strength to swat it away with my hand.

If it wasn't for the horrible image in my head of the vulture's talons ripping into me, I'd be tempted to lie down right here for a little rest.

I close my eyes for a moment, and that's when I hear it. A rushing sound. I'm quite sure it's not the wind. But I'm done with getting my hopes up. It's probably just another mirage, more desert tricks. Still, I have to play this out. I drop down and begin crawling towards the noise. It's getting louder. Is that possible? I mean, can a mirage actually get louder?

It's coming from the next rock ledge over. The same little squirrel-like creature I saw before scoots by me. It looks like it's heading toward the rushing sound. We both can't be imagining it, can we? My heart skips a beat. A sliver of hope is growing inside me. I need to crush it. Destroy it before disappointment destroys me.

I must be close now. It can't be much farther. There's a ledge in front of me. But I don't think I can pull myself up. Images flood my brain. Abbie smiling at me in London. Zach wearing a chocolate ice cream mustache. I wonder if this is what they mean by your life flashing before your eyes right before you die.

At least I won't die alone. Both of the vultures are with me now, hopping on and off various parts of my body. I flail weakly, but it has absolutely no effect on them.

Lifting my feet, my shoe finds a toehold in the rock. Up I go at a tortoise pace. My foot finds another gouge in the rock and then another. Each time I heave myself up, I think it will be the last time. But miraculously, from somewhere deep inside, I find the power to keep going.

And then finally, I'm up and over. I collapse on the flat top of the ledge, breathing heavily.

Something is tapping me on the knee. Sorry, Zach, I can't play with you now. I'm busy. Tap. Tap. Tap. I glance up and the beady black eyes of the larger vulture stare back at me. "No," I scream and kick it off me. It flaps its wings and backs away, but only a few feet. I hear it hissing at me. Hissing? No, it can't be. Birds don't hiss. What am I hearing then?

Slowly I turn my head toward the sound. Water. Falling from rocks. I stare, not believing. It's not true. It can't be. But if it isn't real, then no one's bothered telling the squirrel. She's crouching two feet away, lapping up water from a small pool formed from the waterfall.

On my belly. Pushing forward. Nothing left. But I've got to make it. For Zach. Two more feet. I reach out with my good hand. The squirrel eyes me and scampers away, disappearing into a nearby hole. My fingers form a scoop. Down into the wetness. I bring my finger cup to my lips and drink.

The best drink of my life.

I drink until my belly is bursting. My brain begins working again. I need food. But that will have to wait. The light is fading fast. I must find shelter.

I don't want to leave my water pool. But there's no shelter here. Just open rocks. I climb to the next ledge, my energy renewed. And the next. All the time looking back to make sure I remember where my water pool is.

On the fourth ledge I see them. Strange rock formations just above me. Some with dark spots. As I get closer I see that the dark spots are holes—caves. I clamber up to investigate. The first two

240

holes are no more than shallow recesses in the rock walls. But on the third one, I get lucky. The hole opens into a cavern almost tall enough for me to stand in. It's dark, but with the help of my ocular implant I can see that there are no mountain lions or other nasty surprises in here. Yes, I've found it.

My new home.

XXVII

The Barrens, Day 37

I check my traps first thing, like I've done every day since I arrived at my cave. I've got ten of them now, spread out along three different ledges. Even before I check trap number eight, I know I'm in luck because I can see the end of a tail sticking out from under the rock.

I'm on a roll. This is my second squirrel this week. I bring it back to my cave and pierce its skin with my knife. It's a lucky thing that Uncle never checked my pockets before shipping me off here. If I didn't have my knife with me, I'm certain I wouldn't have lasted more than a week in this place.

There's a crunching sound as the blade connects with the poor thing's backbone. Then I skin it and take out the insides.

I wonder what Abbie would think if she saw me now.

Why am I wasting my time thinking about her? She obviously couldn't care less about what happens to me. She's probably more worried about what outfit to wear to her job as Frank's assistant. And how, exactly, is she assisting him? By telling him how great he is?

I grab some dried grass from my stash and a fist-sized stone.

Maybe I should cut Abbie a break. After all, she was right when she said it's not easy to say no to Frank, knowing what he's like when he's angry. Why should I blame her for looking out for herself? In fact, if I was a bit more like her, then maybe I wouldn't have ended up here.

Now for the tricky part. Holding the stone and the grass in one hand and my knife in the other, I strike a glancing blow against the stone. Nothing.

And another thing about Abbie. Well, maybe it's more about me than her—the way I've been feeling all weird around her. Part of me wants things to go back to the way they were between us: snatch partners and best friends. But another part of me wants something more. I wish sometimes that I could read her thoughts so I could know if she's as confused about all of this as I am.

On the fourth try, there's a spark, but it soon dies out. I try again and again. Finally on my ninth or tenth try, a thin wisp of smoke rises from the grass shreds.

I blow gently on it and am rewarded with a tiny lick of flame.

Crouching down, I lower my hand and join the lit tinder to the pile of grass and branches I gathered yesterday. The little flame flickers, and for a moment, it appears it will die out. But then the grass catches, and soon after that, the branches.

I spear the squirrel with my longest branch, hold it over the highest part of the flames and cook it for a good long time. When I finally remove it from the fire, you would hardly guess what the shriveled brown thing used to be.

The sun is beating down, so I retreat into my cave to eat. As desert squirrels go, this one's not bad—a nice nutty flavor. As I chew, I concentrate on my plan to rescue Zach. He has to be in the Compound with all of Uncle's other new recruits. The boldest way would be to prance right in and snatch him. But that could be chancy. What if I run into Frank? He won't just hand Zach over to me.

Maybe the better way is to go back in time to before Frank snatched Zach and stop the snatch from ever happening. But that's risky too. If Frank has Zach on his radar, it's not going to be easy to stop him from taking Zach.

Whatever plan I decide on, I've got to make sure that once I escape with Zach, we can't be tracked. Abbie said Frank was hypnotizing Phoebe into erasing the record of his timeleaps. And since Abbie has been cozying up to Frank, maybe she has figured out how to hypnotize Phoebe herself. But would Abbie help me, knowing that she could get in big trouble? Would I even want her to? I mean, if something happened to her, because of me . . . I don't want to think about it.

Even if I did get Zach to Boston without being tracked, Phoebe must store files on all the snatched kids, complete with their home addresses. But what if Zach's file mysteriously disappears? That could work. So before I rescue Zach, I've got to somehow have his whole file erased.

A sound interrupts my train of thought. I sit up.

There! A faint whisper. "Caleb."

I'll be the first one to admit that I've had too much sun lately. But I haven't hallucinated since my first day in the desert when I thought I saw a motel on a lake. Which makes this little episode somewhat disturbing.

"Caleb."

The whisper is stronger this time. I peek my head out of the cave, almost expecting to see someone. But there's no one there.

"Caleb, are you there?" the voice says again.

I just figured out why I don't see anyone. That's because the voice is inside my head. If I didn't know better, I'd say it was Abbie talking over my mindpatch. But she's a thousand years and a thousand miles

244

away. No, there's got to be another rational explanation for all of this. I've got it! I must be going crazy. Yes, that's it. A classic case of multiple personality disorder. Which is quite all right with me, actually. I was starting to get a bit lonely out here. At least now I'll have someone to talk to—one of my other selves. I try on an answer.

"Yes, I'm right here," I say. "Taking my little siesta."

The voice comes back stronger this time. "Don't move. I'm coming to get you. Just keep talking."

I haven't done much reading on mental illness, but I saw a movie once where this school teacher had seven different personalities. And, boy, were they different. It must be the same with me. This one sounds like a bossy, female personality. Let's see. I'll call her Agnes.

I really don't have that much to talk about. But to be polite, I dredge up some sayings. "The rain in Spain is mainly in the plain, Agnes," I say. For obvious reasons, rain has been on my mind a lot lately.

"How about this one?" I continue. "What's good for the goose is good for the gander." I immediately regret my choice. Now I'm in for at least an hour of fantasizing about roast goose with gravy.

I'm quickly running out of sayings, so I spout off one of Uncle's creations. "Snatching fine art is a fine art."

"Keep talking," says Agnes's voice. "We're zeroing in on you."

"Who are 'we,' Agnes?" I ask. With any luck, she'll introduce me to my other personalities.

She doesn't answer, so I keep rambling on. "A failed snatch is like half a sneeze. Snatch well and earn your praise; snatch poorly and say your prayers."

"I'm losing the signal. Are you on a mountain?" Agnes's voice is weaker again.

"Yes," I say, playing along. "The one that looks like a crouching lion."

A pause and then she says, "I see it! Sit tight. I'm coming up."

"Whatever you say, Agnes," I say. "Don't forget to bring the others. I want to meet them."

"You will," she says. "Now keep talking!"

"All right, let's see," I say. "Steal from the rich. Give to the richer. A snatch in time saves nine."

And on and on I go. I'm surprised that I can remember so many of Uncle's little ditties. But this is starting to get tiring.

I'm about to nod off when I hear shuffling sounds from somewhere below. Probably one of those mountain sheep with the curly horns. If I could catch one, I'd be set for food for a week.

I poke my head out of my cave, and immediately retreat back inside. It was only a quick glimpse, but I'm sure someone is out there. And judging from the wicked curved blade hanging off of his belt, my guess is that he's not a tourist.

Just then, I hear Agnes's voice inside my head again.

"Hang on. We're almost there!"

"Be careful, Agnes," I say. "There's someone right outside my cave, and he doesn't look too friendly."

I stick my head out once more, and I'm nose to nose with the warrior. He's a short fellow, but from the smug look on his brown, leathery face, he has a high opinion of himself. Despite the heat, he's dressed in a rough-looking sheepskin coat with a leather belt and has a quiver of arrows strapped to his back. The upper half of his coat is covered in armor of closely meshed iron rings and he's wearing an iron helmet shaped like a cone. He looks straight out of a movie set for Genghis Khan.

"*Sain baina uu!*" says the warrior gruffly.

I have no idea what he just said, but it sure didn't sound friendly. My translator doesn't seem to be working, which is odd because my night vision works fine and if Uncle ripped out my translator then why didn't he take my ocular implant too?

Translator or not, ol' Genghis here doesn't look the type that goes in for a lot of small talk. I get the feeling that inflicting bodily harm is more his thing.

"Don't be afraid. He's on our side," says a voice behind him.

"Is that you, Agnes? You mean you're with him?" I say.

Agnes laughs. Except there's a couple of things wrong with the laugh. First, it's not coming from inside my head anymore. It's coming from the person standing behind Genghis. And second, it doesn't sound like Agnes at all. In fact it sounds like . . .

"Nice place you've got here, Cale," says Abbie.

XXVIII

The Barrens, Day 37

I stare at Abbie with my mouth open. She's wearing the same rough clothes as Genghis except without the armor. Her hair is long and wild.

"Miss me?" she says with a flick of her mane.

"A-A . . . Abbie?"

"C-C-C . . . Caleb?" she stutters right back, smiling.

"How did you find me?" I ask.

"My friend here," she nods toward Genghis, "and his chief helped a lot. This place is like their backyard. They know every rock for a hundred miles. The tough part, though, was finding out what year and desert you were in. For that I have Frank to thank."

I can't believe what I'm hearing.

"Frank helped you find me?" I ask.

"Not exactly," she says, laughing, "but I did use some of his little tricks to persuade Phoebe to tell me where and when you were."

"You mean, you hypnotized her?" I ask.

"Yup," she says.

"And then, when you got her into a trance she told you exactly how to find me?" I say.

It feels strange to be using my jaw muscles again after not talking for so long.

"Well, not exactly. Like I said, I knew the desert and the year. But your actual landing spot was a well-kept secret. Even Phoebe didn't know."

Abbie finger-brushes her hair. Part of me still can't believe this is really happening.

"This is actually my fourth visit here, looking for you. The chief's been putting me up in one of his guest tents."

"But won't Uncle or Frank be able to track you?" I ask.

She shakes her head. "Post-hypnotic suggestion. All records of me coming here have been purged and replaced with me on research missions."

"But what if they check up on you and find out that you're not where you're supposed to be? And how are you managing to complete your missions while you've been here looking for me?" I ask.

"My my," says Abbie. "I'm glad to see that the desert heat hasn't scrambled your brain, Cale. You don't need to worry. Uncle and Frank have been too busy with the expansion plans to bother about me. Besides, I have been getting my missions done. All of my searching for you has been on my own time."

I feel dizzy and close my eyes to steady myself. The most complex bit of thinking I've done in the last thirty-seven days is figuring out three different ways to cook a marmot. So I'm finding this a lot to take in at once. But one thing is coming through loud and clear: Abbie is here for me. She's on my side!

"Are you okay?" she asks.

I open my eyes and smile. "Better than okay."

Abbie glances around my little cave and says, "Typical bachelor. Squirrel bones all over the floor."

"Well, I wasn't expecting company," I say.

I look over at Genghis. "Does he . . . speak English?" I ask.

"No. Strictly Mongolian," she says. "But it's a real cool language.

Lots of verbs. At first I thought I was going to have trouble with it, seeing as this is the twelfth century, but Uncle gave us all upgrades recently and now my translator's certified for a thousand years back."

Recent upgrade? That's why my translator's not working. "Did you say we're in the twelfth century?"

"To be exact, 1176," says Abbie. "And, trust me, you lucked out. If this was 1175, I probably would never have found you. Temüjin didn't have anywhere near the resources he's got now."

"Temüjin?"

"He's the tribal leader in these parts. You've got to meet him. He must have something like a hundred thousand warriors working for him. Not bad for someone our age."

I sit down. This is too much for me. "Wait. How long have you been here? I mean in the past, looking for me."

"You mean on this particular trip?"

"Yeah."

"I don't know," Abbie answers. "Maybe three and a half hours or so. It was quite a long ride to get to this ridge."

"Well, then, why aren't you . . ." I begin.

"Time fogged?" she finishes for me.

"Exactly."

"You can thank Frank for that too. He created an app for his time patch to extend the time that he can stay comfortably in the past at one stretch. Of course, he didn't exactly share the app with me. I had to wheedle it out of Phoebe."

Wow. You go away for a month, and the world changes.

"Hey, don't get too comfortable," says Abbie. "We're going. Temüjin's waiting back at the *ger* with food."

"*Ger*?" I ask.

"Yeah, that's what they call their tents," she says. "C'mon. You look like you could use some breakfast."

She squints at my skinny frame and adds, "And lunch and supper."

Abbie nods at Genghis, and he leads the way down the ridge. I'm next, and Abbie brings up the rear. Thankfully, Genghis is taking it slow. I haven't done this much exercise since my second day here, and I'm feeling it.

We go for another couple of minutes before Genghis stops, points to me and mutters something to Abbie.

"He says it'll be faster if he carries you," she says.

"Uhh. Sure," I say. If it means I'll get breakfast sooner, I'd happily have Genghis shoot me out of a cannon, although I suspect that's slightly ahead of his time.

He slings me over his shoulder like a sack of potatoes and navigates nimbly down the rock ledges, pausing twice to put me down and share water from his flask.

When we arrive at the grasslands, I point to a bare spot. "That's where I got my mattress," I say proudly.

Abbie smiles and says, "Very nice."

Nearby, two tawny horses are tied to the branches of a low shrub. Genghis unties them, and while Abbie hops on the back of the smaller one, he hoists me up onto the second horse. I almost fall off the other side, but Genghis steadies me and hops on behind me. The horse gives a whinny and a snort, which makes me wonder if there's a maximum weight capacity for horses like there is for elevators.

I've never ridden a horse before, but since Genghis is steering, I figure all I've got to do is relax and enjoy the ride. And I do, for about five seconds, until the steed goes from a leisurely walk to a full gallop.

I look around desperately for something to hold on to, but the only thing I can see is the horse's mane. She'd better not mind having her hair pulled because I'm already reaching forward to grab a fistful.

Anyone who says the desert is flat is lying. I can barely keep my behind on the horse. On one particularly bad bump, I almost go flying. But, at the last second, Genghis keeps me on with a swipe of his hand.

By the position of the sun, I'd say we've been riding for a couple of hours. I don't want to sound like a whiner, but if we have to go another hour, I don't think I'm going to make it. My arms are so tired that I can barely grip the horse's mane, and my legs feel like spaghetti.

Just when I think my limbs are about to fall off, the horse slows to a trot and then to a walk. I loosen my death grip and glance up. We're on a ridge. Spread out below us is a huge encampment with at least five hundred dome-shaped tents.

We parallel the ridge for a while until we arrive at a path leading down. Soon we're joined by two men on horseback dressed just like Genghis. They say something to him, but all the while they're looking at me.

Genghis leads our little procession through a maze of tents. There are many soldiers around, grooming their horses, wrestling with each other or squatting in front of their tents, sharpening arrowheads on stones. They all wave to Genghis as we pass by.

Finally, we come to a tent that's bigger than the others by half. Genghis dismounts and helps me off. Abbie is already down and handing her horse's reins to a woman in a long red dress, the first woman I've seen since we arrived here. Abbie bows to Genghis and says, "*Bayarlalaa.*"

Then she turns to me. "C'mon . . . I'll introduce you to Temüjin."

Abbie nods to the two soldiers standing by the flap, and ducking our heads, we enter the big tent. As far as twelfth-century desert accommodations go, this place must easily be four stars. A brilliant blue carpet embroidered with stylized flowers and crosses covers the ground. Tapestries hang on the inside tent walls showing warriors in hand-to-hand combat. A fire burns in a pit near the back of the tent. Three figures sit cross-legged in the center, their long shadows reaching clear to me and Abbie.

I sneak a better look at my hosts. They're all dressed like Genghis, with heavy coats and iron mesh armor. Even their faces look tough: brown and leathery from the sun. The man on the right has a heavily wrinkled face and a wispy white beard. I'm guessing he's seventy years old or maybe even eighty. The one on the left I put in his forties. But it's the guy in the middle who's got my attention. He can't be much older than I am. And it doesn't take long to figure out he's the boss around here. When the other guys look at him, you can see the respect in their eyes.

Abbie smiles, gives a little bow and says, *"Sain baina uu."*

The young leader returns her smile and snaps his fingers. The man on his left nods and silently leaves the tent.

"Sain baina uu," says the leader, looking at me.

"Temüjin's saying hello, Cale," says Abbie. "Say *bi zügeer*. It means you're fine. But bow first."

I give a shaky little bow. *"Bi zügeer,"* I say.

Temüjin keeps his eyes on me and says, *"Naash oirt."*

"What did he just say?"

"He wants you to come closer."

I shuffle forward. I'm still aching from my little pony ride, but I thrust my chest out and stand up as straight as I can.

Temüjin squints at me and says, *"Chi tom hamartai yum."*

"Bi zövshöörch baina," Abbie answers.

"What did he say?" I ask.

"That you have a big nose," she says.

"And what did you say?"

"I had to agree with him. But don't worry. I think your nose is cute."

Temüjin stands, clasps his hands behind his back and circles me twice slowly. Then he stops, looks over at Abbie and says, *"Chi burhan shig haragdahgui baina."*

"What did he say?" I ask.

"That you don't look like much like a god," she answers.

"I don't get it," I say.

"Well, I had to build you up a bit," she says. "So that he'd agree to send one of his men to look for you."

"So you told him I was a god?" I say, arching my eyebrows.

"Not exactly. I just said that you and I are equals. He's convinced I'm a god because a few of his men who saw me land the first time told him I came from the clouds. Plus, I think my white skin and auburn hair sealed the deal."

The tent flap opens and the man who had gone is back now, flanked by two women covered head to toe in long, flowing robes. One of them hands me a wooden bowl filled to the brim with some kind of liquid. The other hands me a folded robe. I glance over at Abbie.

"Go ahead, Cale, drink up. They call it *tarag,*" she says. "And don't worry. If you're too shy to change here, you can save that for later."

I lift the bowl to my mouth and take a sip. Yuck. It tastes like sour yogurt. But it's food, and I'm not about to turn it away. I drain it in about ten seconds flat, to the delight of my hosts. I'm instantly rewarded with another bowl.

"You might want to nurse this one a little longer," says Abbie.

I nod and smile at everyone, hoping they'll all stop looking at me.

Suddenly, the old guy sitting next to Temüjin leaps up, kneels in front of Abbie and says, *"Minii zurkh zovkhon cinii l toloo tsokhildog."* Then he turns to me and says, *"Tüünii orond bi hoyor zuun yamaa, tavin shildeg tsereg ögiye."*

Abbie looks at him, smiles, shrugs her shoulders and turns to me.

"What did he say to you?" I ask.

"He said that his heart beats only for me."

"And what did he say to me?"

"He offered you two hundred goats and fifty of his best fighters for me," she says.

"Are you serious?"

"What? You don't you think I'm worth it?"

"Uhh, sure. But what should I say?"

"Tell him you won't settle for less than three hundred goats and eighty fighters," says Abbie with a straight face. "Just kidding," she adds. "Tell him thank you, but I'm not for sale."

"But don't you think that will upset him?" I say, glancing at the sword resting on the ground next to the old guy.

Abbie narrows her eyes at me. "Who would you rather upset . . . him or me?"

"No problem. I just thought we could say something to, you know, let him down gently. But I'll tell him straight out, if that's what you want. Just give me the words."

She whispers in my ear and I turn to the old guy and say, *"Uuch-laarai. ene emegteig hudaldahgui."*

To my great relief, the guy doesn't draw his sword or challenge me to a duel or anything. He just smiles and shrugs his shoulders.

"We'd better start saying our good-byes," says Abbie. "Do you want another refill on your *tarag* before we go?"

I look down at my bowl. It's still half full. "No, I'm fine, thanks."

"Yeah, I don't like it much either," she says. "Let's go. I'll take you for a proper breakfast at Phil's."

"Abbie, I don't think—" I start to say.

"Don't worry," she says. "You might feel full now, but you know how it is with Mongolian food. In a half hour you'll be hungry again."

"No, it's not that," I say.

"Well, spit it out, Cale. If you're worried about running into Frank or Uncle, don't. Phil's is a little hole in the wall on the Lower East Side. There's no way Uncle or Frank's even heard of it."

I wince hearing their names. "It's not that either," I say. "I can't leave here, Abbie. They took away my patch."

"I know," she says. "Nassim told me. But don't worry—you won't need it. We're traveling together."

"Together? How?" I ask.

She grabs my good wrist, holds it against hers, smiles wide at Temüjin and says, "Watch and be amazed."

XXIX

July 10, 2061, 12:43 A.M.
Lower East Side
New Beijing (formerly New York City)

We land behind a Dumpster in an alleyway beside a low-rise building. As soon as we're able to move, we make our way to the front of the building. A red neon sign flashes PHIL'S DINER.

"How did you do that?" I ask, after the time freeze wears off.

"Do what?" says Abbie.

"Take me with you." Up until now, I thought the only way someone not wearing a patch could time travel was if they rode in the Time Pod.

"Pretty cool, don't you think?" says Abbie. "It's a new app that Uncle developed to make it easier to snatch kids from the past . . . no more Time Pod parking hassles. All the person with the patch has to do is grab the hand or wrist of the person without the patch, and— abracadabra—you get two time travelers for the price of one."

I nod. I bet Uncle wouldn't be too pleased to know that his new app was used to rescue me from the Barrens.

We step inside. The décor is early 1950s: black and white checkerboard floor, a long chrome counter, tall stools capped with red vinyl cushions and even one of those old-fashioned jukeboxes. I inhale and am rewarded with a wonderful aroma of bacon frying and fresh-brewed coffee.

Sliding into a booth near the back, I'm salivating even before I open the menu.

"Take your order?" says the waitress. She looks like she stepped right out of the fifties: pink polka-dot dress, bobby socks and saddle shoes. Even her bored expression seems to fit perfectly.

"Go ahead, Cale. Order whatever you want. My treat."

"Really?" I say. "In that case, I'll have an order of pancakes and two eggs over easy. Oh, yes, and a large glass of orange juice."

"And you, miss?" the waitress asks.

"Uhh. Do you have any waffles?"

"Sure do. Best in New Beijing," says the waitress.

"Okay. I'll have the waffles. And an orange juice too."

"Excuse me?" I say, just as the waitress turns to leave. "Can I also have an order of waffles?"

"You bet," she says.

"Pancakes and eggs *and waffles*, Cale?" Abbie says.

I shrug and say, "I'm hungry."

"You smell horrible," she says, sniffing.

"Thanks."

But Abbie's not done yet. "You're not eating a bite until you change into those clothes you got from Temüjin."

"All right." I say, running my fingers over the robe and trying to decide whether I'm supposed to wear underwear underneath. "Back in a minute."

Luckily the men's room is empty. Stripping down to the waist, I wet some paper towels with liquid soap and wash myself.

The sight in the mirror shocks me. I'm not much more than skin and bones. Well, at least I'm alive. I lean forward and take a closer look at my face. It looks different. There are some hard edges that I'd never noticed before.

I slip inside the washroom's only stall and change the rest of the way, throwing my old clothes into the garbage.

The robe feels rough, and I can definitely smell goat on it. For a second I wonder if I'm having an elaborate dream complete with Phil's Diner and a goat-smelling kaftan and that as soon as I try to return to the table, Abbie won't be there. Then I'll wake up back in the desert with a fire that's about to die out.

If this is a dream, I desperately want to hold on to it. But there's only one way to know for sure. I leave the washroom and walk back to the table.

My heart skips a beat. It's empty.

"Did you get lost again?" asks Abbie.

Her voice is coming from the next table over. I look up and see her sitting just where I'd left her. I had stopped at the wrong table, that's all. Relief floods through me. This is all real.

"Again?" I say. "I never got lost in the first place. Unless you count the time when I got turned around in a sandstorm and couldn't find the way back to my cave."

"I'm not counting that time," she says.

It feels good to be joking with Abbie again. Almost at the same time, we both shut up and look at each other.

She's waiting for me to say something. I wish I could read her thoughts right now. To know what she's really thinking and how she really feels about . . . well, about me. I swallow hard. Here's my chance to really talk to her. To tell her how I feel without joking or being sarcastic. Because there she is, right across the table, waiting.

"Abbie?" My voice breaks.

"Yes, Cale?"

Suddenly it's gotten really quiet in the diner. I could use some noise right about now. Clanking pots, clattering dishes. Anything.

"I just want to say, I . . . thanks for rescuing me," I finally manage.

She looks at me and says, "You would have done the same for me. We're a team, remember?"

I nod, but there are a million thoughts swirling around inside of my head, starting with *what about you and Frank?*

As if reading my mind, she says, "While you were away, Frank asked me again to be his special assistant. He said you were never coming back from the Barrens."

"What did you say?" I ask.

"I turned him down," she answers.

My breath catches in my throat. "You did? Why?"

Abbie glances away for a second, and then looks back at me. "I told him I'd never be happy spending my time keeping track of all the other time snatchers' missions when I could be on a mission myself."

"Okay," I say.

"But that wasn't the main reason why I turned him down. I turned him down because he was bragging about a collection he did. He said what made it even more enjoyable was that it was a kid you knew."

A wave of anger is building inside me. I don't want her to see it, so I stare at my water glass.

"It's wrong, Cale," she continues. "What he did. Taking that boy . . . your friend . . . was wrong. He wanted to hurt you."

"I'm not going to let it happen, Abbie," I say.

"It already has," she answers.

"Well, I'm going to undo it."

"No. You're not."

I can feel the heat rising in my cheeks. "What do you mean, I'm not?"

"What I mean, Mr. Smells Like a Goat," says Abbie, "is that you're not going to undo it by yourself. *We're* going to undo it. Together."

Inside my head, the sun is bursting through the clouds and there's a rainbow. Abbie is on my side!

"Are you sure you want to?" I say. "I mean, you could get in a lot of trouble."

"Hey, I'm already in trouble," she says. "Springing you from the Barrens ten months and twenty-four days early wasn't exactly kosher, you know.

"Cale," she continues—and I hear a rare break in her voice—"there's something else I want to say . . . about why I came."

"You don't have to say it, Abbie," I say and then immediately regret my words. Of course she has to say it. I want to hear it. That is, if what she's going to say is what I hope she's going to say.

"Yes, I do have to say it," she says. "I've been doing a lot of thinking about you. And a lot of thinking about us."

Did she just say "us" as in me and her? I've got my elbows on the table now, and I'm leaning forward.

"Caleb, I want you to know that I . . . I care about you," she says.

"I know, Abbie . . . me too," I say, interrupting again. "I mean, I care about you, not about me. You know what I mean." Real smooth.

"More than I care about anyone else," Abbie continues. "Not just because you're my snatch partner. And when you care about someone, sometimes it means taking chances and not thinking about yourself all the time. I just didn't know how much I did care until you . . . went away."

"Thank you, Uncle, for sending me to the Barrens!" I shout. A few of the other diners turn to look at us, and we both laugh.

Abbie cares about me. She said it!

The waitress is back. She sets three plates down in front of me. I pour syrup over my pancakes and waffles. It comes out nice and slow. This is definitely the best day of my life: Abbie cares about me, *and* there's maple syrup!

I dig into my pancakes. Every bite is sheer ecstasy. I don't look up until the plate is empty. After a moment's hesitation, I bend over and lick the rest of the syrup off the plate.

"Here's the plan," I say once I'm done. "First, we erase all Timeless Treasures records and files relating to Zach. But only after we find out exactly where and when he was snatched. Then we go back to 1967 and change a bit of history so that Zach was never snatched. Frank will never try to take him again because he won't know where to find him—Zach won't exist in the Timeless Treasures files."

I take a bite of my eggs. Delicious.

Abbie is quiet for a moment and then says, "I think you're forgetting a couple of things . . . Did you ever go visit Zach . . . I mean at his home?"

"Yes."

"Then Frank and Uncle will be able to find where Zach lives by checking your file for unauthorized timeleaps."

"You're right," I say. "I already thought of that. When we go to purge Zach's file, we'll also have to make sure all records of my timeleaps to Zach's house are erased too."

I spear a piece of waffle slathered in maple syrup. Simply divine.

"All right," she says. "But even if we do that, Frank will still know where to find Zach. All he'd need to do is to go back to Expo 67 where he first saw you with Zach."

I stop chewing. Abbie's right. That's a big hole in the plan.

"Good point," I say, taking a deep breath. "Okay. So here's the fix. We change history so that Zach and his family never went to Expo 67."

It's Abbie's turn to be silent. After a moment, she looks at me solemnly and says, "You know that if we do that, it's like you and Zach never met. He won't know you. I don't think you want that."

She's right. I don't. I feel a special connection with Zach that I don't want to lose. Because, crazy as it seems, I'm afraid that if I lose that connection, I'll be losing a piece of myself. But if it means saving Zach's life, I'm prepared to do it.

"I know, but—" I begin to say.

"There's another way," she says.

"How?"

"Well, instead of changing history so that Zach and his family never go to Expo 67, we erase Frank's memory of Expo 67. If he doesn't remember going there, then he won't remember targeting Zach at all."

I think about it for a moment. It could work. But it's risky. Frank is not your normal unsuspecting person. He's an expert at not trusting anyone. Getting close enough to Frank to erase his memory is going to be next to impossible. And if he suspects trouble, he'll be in Uncle's office in a flash.

"It's too dangerous," I say finally. "There's a big chance that Frank will figure out what we're trying to do and stop us."

"You're right. We won't do it."

"Good."

"I'll do it," she adds.

"Abbie—"

"Listen," she says, cutting me off. "It won't be any more dangerous than some of the things I've done already, like jailbreaking you from the Barrens, for starters."

"But—"

"No buts, mister. You know it's a good plan. And I'm the only one who can pull it off. I'll tell him I changed my mind and that I want to

263

be his new assistant. We'll have a drink to celebrate and our drinks will be the same except that his will have a quarter of a memory wipe pill crushed into it."

"A half a pill," I say.

"No. A quarter," says Abbie. "That should be more than enough to destroy his most recent memories including Expo. Besides, any more and Uncle will definitely wonder how it is that Frank has suddenly forgotten his own name. And if he suspects a memory wipe, then he'll give Frank the antidote and we'll be right back to where we started."

"You mean there's an antidote for a memory wipe?"

"Of course. But it's not something that Uncle keeps lying around. Phoebe knows the formula for it though."

"Okay. A quarter of a pill then. But if anything doesn't seem right, bail, okay?"

"Yessir, Captain, sir," Abbie says, saluting. "I will abandon ship at the first sign of trouble."

"I mean it, Abbie."

"I know you do," she says, softening her tone. "Don't worry, I'll be careful."

I look past her at the elderly couple drinking tea and chatting away at the next table. For a moment I'm jealous of them. Well not *of them,* exactly. More of their conversation. What I mean is, even though I have no idea what they're talking about, it's a pretty safe bet that it's something more normal than plotting how to neutralize your enemy so that you can rescue a kidnapped child.

"Now, if we can't stop him from being snatched at Expo, we activate Plan B," I say.

"Plan B?"

"If we have to, we go straight to the Compound, find Zach and yank him out of there. That will be tougher, but if we have to do it that way, we will."

We spend the next few minutes fine-tuning that plan.

"Sounds good," says Abbie, finally. "So, when do we start?"

"Right after breakfast!"

By the time we leave Phil's it's one forty-five in the morning, but the street vendors are still out in full force. As much as I'm in favor of the Great Friendship, I'm still not crazy about scorpion on a skewer and cricket shish kebab appearing on the same menu as Coney Island hot dogs. But who am I to talk? After all, it wasn't that long ago that I would have killed for some desert squirrel.

As we reach the corner of Lafayette and Franklin, doubts start flooding my brain. I begin to wonder if I'm making a huge mistake coming to Headquarters. I mean, if a spider's chasing you, is it really wise to go visiting its lair? And in my case, I've got two spiders to worry about. But according to Abbie, Uncle and Frank are staying at the Compound tonight so there's no way I'll run into them.

We walk in silence. I'm a jangle of nerves and getting jumpier with each step closer to Headquarters. I feel a wave of panic rising up, threatening to crush me.

Breathe, I tell myself, and I take three deep breaths. On the last exhale, we arrive.

We enter the building, and the elevator is there waiting for us. I press the button for the fifth floor.

Nothing happens.

Abbie and I reach for the button at the same time to press it again. As we do, her hand brushes against mine. It feels warm and soft. I wonder if it was totally an accident or whether she'd meant to touch my hand. She quickly brings her hand up to her head and runs

265

it through her hair as if to say, *My hand was on its way somewhere when your hand got in its way, so don't read anything into it!* But it's too late. I'm already reading whole novels into a second of physical contact.

"All right. All right. I'm coming. You don't have to keep pressing it," grumbles Phoebe. If it was anyone else, I would have guessed that she'd just been torn away from sleep. In fact, the screen shows an empty bed with rumpled sheets and I can hear the sound of a toilet flushing,

"Hello, Phoebe," says Abbie, going for cheery, even though Phoebe still hasn't appeared on the screen.

"It's two in the morning, for God's sake. What do you want?" says Phoebe.

"I'd like to go up to five, please," says Abbie.

A minute passes without a response or any change to the screen. Just as I begin to think Phoebe might actually refuse us, the elevator door slides closed and, with a jerky motion, starts heading up. Phoebe's persona finally appears dressed in a fuzzy pink bathrobe and purple donkey slippers. Her hair is all frizzy, and there are large circles under her eyes.

We arrive at the fifth floor and walk down the main corridor. As we approach Abbie's workstation, her screen comes on.

"Hello, Phoebe," says Abbie.

"You already said that," snaps Phoebe. "Of course, maybe the second time is for your silent partner. Is that right, Caleb, O Prince of the Barrens? What? You didn't think I could see you? Well, peek-a-boo! Or are you just being polite and letting Abbie do all the talking? How egalitarian. How'd you get out so soon, anyway? Presidential pardon?"

"Phoebe, we need your help," I say, settling into the chair opposite the screen. Abbie takes the other chair and does a slow spin.

Phoebe morphs into her business tycoon persona: smart suit, designer eyeglasses, long hair tied up in a bun and expensive Italian loafers. The only thing that she hasn't changed is the sour expression on her face.

Then I hear a noise that sounds like grinding gears and screeching cats. Phoebe's laughing. After a while, she stops and says, "I'd like to help. But I have a hair appointment. And I'm already late." That last remark sends her into another gale of laughter.

I nod to Abbie. She stops her spin and wheels close to the screen.

Her fingers hover for a moment and then attack the keyboard rapid-fire. Arrays of mathematical equations and symbols appear momentarily on the screen, vanish and then are instantaneously replaced by new equations and symbols.

"What are you up to?" asks Phoebe, and I can hear a hint of suspicion in her voice.

"Nothing," Abbie lies. On the way over here, she told me all about how she was going to do it. "It's a piece of cake," she had said. "All I have to do is use the pseudocode algorithm that Frank developed and run a program called P-hyp. P-hyp induces Phoebe to simulate the same ultradium rhythms as humans under hypnosis and also gets her to copy the same neuroelectrical signaling that leads to a dissociative state."

If that's what Abbie calls a piece of cake it must be one really thick slice. She lost me after the first four-syllable word. But I think I understand the basics. What she's doing is fooling Phoebe into thinking that she's hypnotized by using a computer program that mimics how a person acts in a trance.

The only tricky part, Abbie explained, is that Phoebe's own defenses will try to attack P-hyp and destroy it. Luckily, Frank built an override into the program to repel attacks initially. But after two minutes, Phoebe's systems will regroup and find a way to destroy P-hyp. When that happens, she will wake up from her trance and go back to being her usual grouchy self.

In other words, we have two minutes to get all the information we need out of Phoebe.

Abbie's fingers are a blur on the keyboard. I'm impressed. You can't teach that kind of speed.

"Just . . . about . . . ," she says over my mindpatch.

"You'd better not even . . . ," Phoebe begins to say, but her words die mid-sentence.

"Done!" says Abbie, letting out a long breath. "Go ahead now, Cale."

She rolls her chair back, and I roll mine forward.

"Phoebe, I'm going to ask you some questions. I'd like you to answer completely and honestly, do you understand?"

"Yes. I understand," says Phoebe. Her voice is flat, without a trace of emotion.

"And after we finish our conversation and you return to your normal state, you will have no memory of this conversation having occurred. Do you understand?"

"Yes, I understand."

"Good," I say. "Now, there's a boy who was recently snatched. His family name is Rushton. First initial Z, and he was born July 8, 1962. Please tell me when he was snatched."

A moment's silence.

"Nine eighteen P.M. on July 8, 1967," she answers in the same matter-of-fact tone.

Just as I thought. Not long after I left him.

"Where was he snatched from?"

"Rushton, initial *Z*, was fifty-three meters above the ground, on a ride at La Ronde called La Pitoune," Phoebe answers.

I'm beginning to like the new Phoebe: pleasant and no lip. Then I remind myself that this isn't the real her.

"Now, I've got just a couple of more requests," I say. "First, can you kindly purge all records for Rushton, Z. and for any timeleaps I made or Abbie will make to Boston, Massachusetts. And while you're at it, please purge all records you have of any timeleaps that Frank made to Expo 67."

"I cannot purge files or records of timeleaps," she says.

Could it be that the hypnosis isn't deep enough?

I exchange looks with Abbie. Her mouth is set in a thin line.

"What authorizations do you need to carry out the purge requests?" I ask, my eyes back on the screen.

"The chief executive officer of Timeless Treasures alone can authorize purge requests," says Phoebe.

"What is the procedure to be followed when the chief executive officer is not available?" I ask.

"There is no procedure for that contingency," she replies.

I look over at Abbie. There's one other way to do this. But if we get caught . . .

I take a deep breath. "Phoebe, connect me to Uncle's personal system, please."

A moment's silence.

"I can give you access to his screen, but entry to Uncle's system is password protected," she says.

"Do you know the password? And if not, can you access his system another way?" I say.

269

"No and no," Phoebe answers.

Her answer isn't surprising although secretly I was hoping Phoebe could override Uncle's system's security.

Abbie and I glance at each other. Her eyes are saying *you can do it, Cale.*

My heart begins to race.

When I look back at the screen, I see a snake entwined around an hourglass. As I watch, the snake, gatekeeper to Uncle's system, slithers off the hourglass and repositions itself so that it gives the impression of staring right at me.

"User name?" it prompts me.

"Uncle," I say.

"Password?"

Sweat breaks out on my forehead. This is the tricky part. But I spent a lot of my downtime in the Barrens thinking about this, and I've narrowed it down to two possibilities.

"Qín Shǐ Huáng," I say, reciting the name of the first emperor of China.

"Access denied," says the snake pleasantly.

I can't believe it. Uncle idolized that guy.

No reason to panic yet, though. I still have my best shot left: Uncle's favorite emperor of all time and the one whose sword he copied.

"Zhu Yuanzhang," I say and hold my breath.

"Access denied," repeats the snake.

"No!" I shout.

Beads of sweat roll down my face. I was sure that the password had to be one of those two. This is bad. I've only got one try left before I'm locked out.

"Cale," says Abbie, "I hear the elevator. Someone's coming up!"

I hear the whirring noise too. Please don't stop on this floor! I've got to have more time.

The password . . . what is it?

It must have something to do with the Great Friendship. It just has to.

"Abbie," I mindspeak, "ask Phoebe to run a search on two emperors: Zhu Yuanzhang and Qín Shǐ Huáng—I need to know any commonalities."

"There's no time," she says. "And besides, our two minutes are up. She's not hypnotized anymore, and she won't do it for free."

"Offer her two pleasure packs." There's no way Phoebe will be able to resist even one pleasure pack—a program that simulates a wide range of human emotions. Right now Phoebe's repertoire is mostly limited to snarky and rude.

"Cale, the elevator door is opening . . . he's getting off! Get down!"

We drop to the floor. Abbie's screen is on, but there's nothing I can do about that right now. I lie as still as I can. This is hardly a hiding spot. Anyone casually glancing over the divider will see us lying here.

Footsteps approaching. Who is it? Uncle? Frank? But it can't be. They're both supposed to be at the Compound. Is it Nassim then? My heart's pounding big-time.

"And get off Uncle's screen!" Abbie yells over my mindpatch.

Love to. But can't. I'm going down with the ship. Unless of course I luck out and manage to solve it. A second goes by. Two. It's eerily quiet.

"She's run the search," Abbie mindspeaks, "and they're both in the list of the top one hundred generals in history."

"No, that's not it," I say. "There's got to be something else!" The footsteps are getting louder now.

"They were both emperors of China," Abbie continues, "and in the tradition of the Chinese emperors, each called himself the Son of Hea—"

Son of Heaven. That's it!

I'm about to say the words but stop at the last instant. "Abbie, I need it in Mandarin!"

The footsteps are at the next workstation. I hold my breath.

And don't hear anything.

The footsteps have stopped.

Game over. We've been discovered.

"Tiān gúo zhi zi!" she shouts over my mindpatch, relaying it from Phoebe.

I lean up, whisper, *"Tiān gúo zhi zi!"* and then duck back down, praying I've pronounced the words properly.

Just then the footsteps resume again. Continuing by us. The only things in that direction are an empty workstation and then Uncle's office.

I scramble to my knees and glance at the screen.

The snake stares at me, expressionless.

My heart sinks. There's no time for another try.

But then the snake smiles and the screen changes. Purple and orange swirls coalesce into images of misty mountain passes and Chinese temples. And interposed on all of this are the two sweetest words in the world: WELCOME UNCLE.

Yessss! I'm in!

"Cale!"

Only part of my brain registers Abbie's warning. I'm hissing purge commands now. First, Zach's complete file, then my visits to

Boston, then Frank's visits to Expo 67 and finally, any future visits by Abbie to Boston.

"Purges completed," reads the screen.

I can't believe I'm actually doing this. *Don't think. Just do!*

One last thing. I need to find where he's stashed the pleasure packs. If I don't deliver, I have no doubt Phoebe will rat me out to Uncle at the earliest possible opportunity.

A sound catches my attention. The office door is sliding open. If it's Uncle, any second now, he'll be accessing his personal system. And when he does, he'll know immediately that someone else is on it too.

Got to hurry. Files flash on the screen. Scan and close. Scan and close. *Come on! Where are they?*

Scan and close. Scan and . . . wait! There!

"Select!"

Unfiltered data from two pleasure packs streams into Phoebe's interface.

"Shut down!"

The lights from the office stream on.

"Hello, Uncle," Phoebe says.

July 10, 2061, 2:49 A.M.
Timeless Treasures Headquarters
New Beijing (formerly New York City)

No sounds at all. And then Uncle's voice saying, "Phoebe, purge Nassim's file. All of it."

"July 10, 2061. Purge request number five. Purge of file number 5134-89 complete."

There's a lump in my throat. I can't believe it. If he's asking Phoebe to purge Nassim's file, that means Uncle's decided to get rid of him. It might happen tomorrow or even next week—as soon as he can find Nassim's replacement. But it's going to happen.

"And here I was thinking this one would last a bit longer than the others before you'd grow tired of him," Phoebe prattles on. "Silly me. What did he do, Uncle, burn your crème brûlée?"

"Repeat what you just said, Phoebe," orders Uncle. I dare not move a muscle. Uncle's got excellent hearing, and if I can hear what they're saying inside Uncle's office, then I have no doubt he can hear us out here.

Phoebe emits a noise that sounds like a sigh. "I said . . . and here I was thinking this one . . ."

"No. Before that."

"You mean the computer talk?" she says.

"Yes, repeat it," says Uncle.

274

"I said, July 10, 2061. Purge request number five. Purge of file number 5134-89 complete."

"Why did you say 'purge request number five'? I haven't asked you to purge any other files today."

"True," she says. "Nevertheless, yours was the fifth purge request received today. Hence, purge request number five."

Silence.

"Who made the other purge requests, Phoebe?" says Uncle.

I hold my breath. My palms are sweating.

"I don't know," she replies.

I exhale slowly.

Uncle says nothing for a moment. When he finally speaks, his voice is barely controlled. "How is it that you don't know?"

"There appears to be what you might call a gap in my memory of this event," Phoebe answers, her voice wavering.

"That is rather disturbing news, Phoebe," says Uncle. "If there are gaps in your memory of such a simple matter, how can I be certain that more of these gaps won't appear?"

I shift position. My knee clicks loudly.

There's a long silence. Great, he heard that. I picture Uncle exiting his office, walking right up to Abbie's workstation and peeking over the divider. And that large vein dancing across Uncle's forehead is the last thing I see before my life on earth comes to an abrupt and horrible end.

"Purge your pleasure response, Phoebe." I can hear the smile in Uncle's voice.

"No, Uncle. Please don't," she pleads.

Uncle takes a moment before replying, "Purge it. Now!"

There's an awful keening, the kind a small dog would make when cornered by a wolf that hasn't fed in two days. Until that moment, I'd never thought it possible to feel sorry for a computer.

"Pleasure response purged," comes her choked reply.

"Now, thank me," says Uncle.

"Thhhhhank you, Uncle," murmurs Phoebe.

"No need to thank me, Phoebe. It's entirely my pleasure." Uncle's voice is louder. He's leaving the office and coming our way!

As he walks down the hall, he begins to laugh. A bitter, shivering laugh that seems to bounce right off the floor and seep through me, leaving me weak and cold.

I hold my breath as Uncle passes within two feet of where Abbie and I are lying.

As soon as I hear the elevator doors close, I let out a long breath.

"Now what?" asks Abbie.

"We go back to Expo 67 and stop Frank from snatching Zach," I say.

She looks at me for a long moment. "You look tired, Cale. And I know I am. We should both get some sleep before we go back to the past."

"I would, except . . ."

"Except what?"

"Well, I've got nowhere to sleep," I say. "I can't go to the dorm. Not when I'm supposed to be in the Barrens."

"I already thought of that," she says.

I follow her to the stairwell and down the stairs to the fourth floor. She opens the stairwell door, looks around and gives me the all clear. I step out into the hallway after her.

"Meet you at the fire escape," she mindspeaks. "I've just got to grab some things."

I go to Nassim's office first. The door is locked but I have no

276

trouble picking it. I slip inside and pull open his desk drawer. The little pill bottle is still there. I shake out a few silver pills, slip them into my pocket and replace the bottle in the drawer.

Abbie arrives at the fire escape a minute after me. She's carrying a very flowery looking blanket and pillow with matching pillowcase.

"Sorry. I know it's a bit bright for your taste, but it's all I could find," she says.

"Where are we going?" I say.

"To a nice quiet spot." She grabs my wrist.

We land in a forest. For a moment I wonder if we're back in France somewhere near Nicéphore's house. But then I see a familiar bench. This is my thinking place in Central Park.

"In case you're wondering," she says, "we only hopped through space to get here."

Abbie takes the blanket and pillow from me and lays them out on the bench.

"There you go. Sweet dreams. I'll be back at seven to pick you up."

"Thanks . . . did you say seven?"

"Yup. Do you think that's too late?"

"Uhh, no. it's fine," I say.

"Okay, then, good night." She gives me a little wave, touches her wrist and is gone.

I lie on my back on the bench and gaze up at the night sky. Or at least the small patch that's visible through the canopy of branches. There are nowhere near the millions of stars I saw at night in the Barrens. The Barrens. It's hard to believe that it was only yesterday that I was in my little cave, talking to myself and then realizing I was really talking to Abbie, who had come to rescue me. And here I am dragging her into something that could get her into even more trouble.

Turning onto my side, I bring the blanket up to my chin. An ambulance wails from somewhere far off, and I can hear traffic from Central Park South. It must have rained here recently, because when I dangle my hand from the bench, my fingers brush damp grass.

I close my eyes. An image (or is it a memory?) wells up inside of me. A young boy sits on the ground. It has just rained there too (wherever there is), but to the boy, this is a good thing because it means there will be lots of mud for building his castle. He worms his fingers through the gloppy mud and builds the walls first. "Don't look yet," he says and then adds the tower. "Still don't look," he says, and he digs a moat around the castle and pours in the water from his bucket.

"Okay, you can look!" he says but when he glances up to see if she's looking, the beach is gone and so is the mud castle. Instead, he's in a room with walls so white they hurt his eyes. And lying unmoving in a bed in the center of the room is a woman whose skin matches the color of the walls. The boy doesn't want to look. Because if he doesn't actually see her then maybe it isn't true. He closes his eyes tight. So tight that all of the white of the walls and the woman's face are shut out. But he can't stop the scream gathering inside him. And when it comes out it, it isn't a scream anymore. It is a question composed of a single strangled word: "Mommy?"

"Rise and shine, Cale."

I turn my head and squint up at Abbie. It's really bright here, wherever here is. Oh, yeah, my thinking spot.

"What time is it?"

"Ten past seven. I let you sleep in. C'mon. Time to get up."

I swing my legs around and sit up. My back aches, and I rub my stiff neck.

"Here, I found these in the wardrobe closet," she says. "Remember them?"

278

She hands me a brown jacket, stiff shirt and green pants: my outfit from Operation Fling. These are probably the worst-fitting clothes I've ever worn on a mission. I'm not crazy about wearing them again, but as usual Abbie is thinking one step ahead of me. Since I'm about to go back to the same time/place where I gave Zach his birthday present, Jim, Diane and Zach are going to expect to see me in these clothes.

She turns away to give me some privacy.

I take off the goat-smelling kaftan, chuck it into the trash bin by the bench and squirm into my Operation Fling clothes.

"All dressed," I say.

She turns back to face me and tosses me a banana. I peel it and begin gobbling it down.

"The dirty deed is done," she says.

"Which dirty deed?"

"Frank."

I quickly swallow a piece of banana. "How did it go?"

"Well," she says, "which part do you want to hear first—the good news or the bad news?"

"Give me the good news first."

"The good news is that he bought the part about me changing my mind about becoming his new assistant."

Why am I not surprised? Frank's got too much ego to think that anyone can refuse him for very long.

"And the bad news?"

"He didn't finish his orange juice."

"You mean the orange juice that had a quarter of a crushed-up memory wipe pill in it?" I ask.

"Well, about a quarter. It was tough enough chopping that little pill into four pieces, let alone four equal-sized pieces," she says.

"How much of it did he drink?"

"About half a glass. Maybe he just wasn't thirsty. Or maybe the pill affected the taste somehow. I tried to get him to finish it, but I didn't want to push too hard in case he got suspicious."

I nod. Abbie did as well as she could. Half a glass. Assuming the quarter pill was dissolved evenly in the entire glass of juice—that means he only swallowed about one eighth of a memory wipe pill. It's something. I just hope it's enough.

"So what's next?" she says.

"We timeleap to eight thirty-five P.M. on July 8, 1967. Zach and his family should be at La Ronde at the Gyrotron ride. I'll join them there and then go with them to the water coaster ride called La Pitoune. Meanwhile, you go straight to La Pitoune and keep a look out for Frank. If you see him, mindlink me. If we can keep Zach safe until the next morning, then he goes with his family back to Boston, where neither Frank nor Uncle will ever find him because his file's been erased."

"Roger," she says.

"Roger who?" I ask.

"Very funny. Let's get going, mister."

"What should I do with the blanket and pillow?" I say, looking down at my unmade bed.

"Just leave them. I'm sure someone else will put them to good use. And if not, they'll be waiting here for you when you come back tonight."

I'm hoping that was a joke. There's no way my back will survive two nights in a row on that bench.

"All right. Let's do it," Abbie says, reaching for her wrist and mine at the same time.

Right before we leap, I sense movement beyond the stone wall circling the monastery. There, standing near the garden with head bowed in morning prayer, is one of the monks.

I'm not usually superstitious, but right now I'm hoping big-time that seeing the monk is a good omen, a sign that Abbie and I will be able to pull off our rescue and bring Zach home safely.

July 8, 1967, 8:35 P.M.
Expo 67
La Ronde, Montreal, Canada

We land inside an empty stagecoach next to the Cinderella carriage I landed in the last time I came here.

Abbie and I come out of our time freeze at about the same time, but we have to wait another thirty seconds before the carousel finally stops. She hops off first, gives me a little wave and heads off toward La Pitoune. I follow her with my eyes until she's swallowed up by the crowd.

I make my way over to the Gyrotron. Fifty feet from the entrance I stop and scan the area.

There's a line of about a hundred people waiting for the ride. No sign yet of Zach, Jim or Diane . . . or for that matter, my past self.

I take a deep breath and move closer. When I get to within twenty feet, I spot them.

They're standing just beyond the exit ramp. Diane is scribbling something. She finishes and is about to hand the scrap of paper to my past self when he holds up his hands. Then my past self shakes hands with Zach and turns to walk away.

I hunch down. I don't want him to see me. It's not that I'm afraid something terrible will happen if he does. Under the right circumstances, I'd be happy to shoot the breeze with my past self. But now is not the time. We've both got things to do.

I glance up and spot my past self walking toward the washroom.

He doesn't know it yet but the poor guy is going to get a nasty surprise when Frank follows him in.

I wait another minute and jog alongside the fence until I reach the exit ramp area where Jim and Diane are poring over a map of the rides.

"Hi again," I say.

They all look up at once.

"Caylid! Did you find your uncle?" Zach asks. "And did he say it was all right for you to come with me to ride the water coaster?"

"Yes, I found him," I say. Which isn't a total lie. I mean, I actually did see Uncle. Only not in the way he means. "And I can go with you to La Spitoon."

"Yippee!" Zach yells. "Caylid's coming with us, Mom, to La Spi—"

Then his eyes twinkle, and he says to me, "It's not La Spitoon, silly. It's La Pitoune! But it doesn't matter that you got it wrong. We can still go."

I smile, but my stomach is in a knot. Maybe I should try to keep them here longer. Or take them to another part of Expo. Far away from La Pitoune. But I've already been over this in my head at least a dozen times. Zach would never go for it. Not on his birthday. No, there's only one thing I can do, and that's go to La Pitoune with them and somehow keep Zach from being snatched by Frank.

At the entrance to La Pitoune, there's a mural of a canoe with three men inside flying though the air. The men have terrified looks on their faces, but my eyes are drawn to the grinning figure looming behind them: the Devil. I glance around and at first don't see Abbie anywhere. But on my second visual sweep, I see her—seated on a bench about fifteen feet from where the exit ramp ends and leafing through a copy of *What's On at Expo Today*.

I must be the only one in the line without a big smile plastered on his face. Besides having to watch out for a kidnapper who's big on revenge, I'm not a huge fan of roller coasters. It's not that I don't like the thrill of going fast or the feeling that I'm going to die any second. It's just that I always worry about the driver. And from a quick glance, the operator for this ride isn't doing anything to take away my worries. She's working the controls with only one hand, since there's a cigarette dangling from her other one.

The line inches forward. Zach is too small to see beyond the people ahead of us, so it's my job to give him minute-by-minute reports of how much farther we have to go. At the same time, I keep an eye out for Frank.

We finally reach the front of the line. I climb into the seat next to Zach and buckle our seat belts. Maybe this is a bad idea. Maybe I should wait at the side with all the pregnant women, people with heart conditions and short kids. But I've got to be strong, for Zach's sake. According to Phoebe, this is where it happens.

I peek at the time. In just over seven minutes, unless I can change history, Frank is going to snatch Zach.

A father and young daughter are in the car ahead of us. Behind us, an older man is getting into the car with his wife. Normal-looking tourists. In fact, everything around me seems normal, which makes it even harder to believe that Zach could be snatched from here. But as annoying as Phoebe can be sometimes, she's rarely wrong. I take a deep breath and wait for the ride to begin.

The attendant is making her way along the cars checking seat belts. There's a commotion behind me, and the older man helps his wife out of their car and over to a bench near the entrance to the ride. She's looking very pale.

I close my eyes and try to relax by conjuring up the calming image of the monastery and garden in Central Park. But it's no use. The image only holds for a moment before it distorts in my mind into a picture of a mountain-sized mega-coaster.

I glance across at Zach. He's smiling from ear to ear.

Abbie flings a thought my way. "You look *so cute* in that tiny car, Cale."

"Thanks," I shoot back. "But I'd rather look *so cute* far away from this tiny car. Anything happening at your end?"

"Everything's cool," she says. "No sign of Frank."

But I barely register what she's saying. The coaster is on the move. I glance over at Zach. Got to stay alert and keep him safe.

My body presses against the back of the seat as the car rises at an impossible angle. The contents of my stomach threaten to make a break for it, and I swallow hard, willing everything back into place.

We chug up the hill and teeter for a moment at the top.

As we start to go down, everyone around me raises their hands in the air. Ordinarily, I'd consider joining in, but my hands are locked in a death grip with the safety bar.

Abbie blasts a thought at me. "Don't panic. But he's sitting right behind you. Don't look!"

Naturally, I panic and look.

"Boo!" mouths Frank and then gives me one of his stupid grins.

I wouldn't have believed it if I hadn't seen it for myself. Frank managed a precise landing on an extremely fast-moving roller coaster. I try to shift my body to shield Zach from Frank, but my seat belt stops me.

The car rockets down a straightaway and water sprays all around.

Zach's hands are up. Frank leans forward and reaches for Zach's arm.

I grab Zach's wrists and pull him forward.

"Caylid, you're hurting me," Zach yells, struggling to break free.

Frank has undone his seat belt now and is leaning forward even more. The tips of his hands are inches away from Zach's shoulder.

The car screams around a corner. Frantically, I try to swat Frank's hand away.

But he's quick. He feints high and goes down low. I only just manage to get my hand down in time to block him before we go into a tunnel. It's pitch-black, and in the moment before my night vision kicks in, panic stabs me and I windmill my arms frantically against his next attack.

Seconds later, we're out of the tunnel. Water plumes up, making it hard to see. I brace myself, certain that he'll try again.

I glance back. A seat belt dangles lifelessly from Frank's vacant seat. The car is slowing down now. The ride is ending.

"Let's go, Zach," I say. I get up slowly and step shakily onto the platform. The close call with Frank has sapped all of my energy.

"That was a gas!" says Zach. "Did you like it, Caylid? I can't wait to tell Daddy."

I smile and watch him run ahead down the exit ramp, one small fist pounding the top of the wooden railing.

But then, to my horror, I see Frank. He's lying in wait in the doorway of the small ticket booth just beyond the end of the ramp.

"No! You can't have him!" I shout into Frank's head.

"Dreamers dream, Caleb . . . ," he says over my mindpatch.

Zach is within a stride of Frank's position. Before I can say or do anything, Frank's hand lashes out and yanks Zach's wrist, pulling him inside the ticket booth.

"And snatchers snatch!" he finishes.

I sprint down the ramp.

Jim must have also seen it happen because he's racing toward the ticket booth, a look of shock and disbelief on his face.

Out of the corner of my eye, I can see Abbie making a beeline for the booth.

Jim and I arrive first. Adrenaline surges through me as I fling open the door to the ticket booth.

But there's no one inside.

I'm too late.

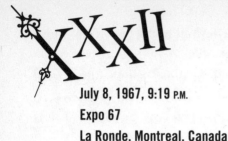

XXXII

July 8, 1967, 9:19 P.M.
Expo 67
La Ronde, Montreal, Canada

Jim is on his knees frantically sweeping his hands over the wood floor of the ticket booth. I know what he's doing—looking for a trapdoor or an escape hatch of some sort. Because that's the only way his rational mind could explain what has happened.

"Where?" he asks. "How?"

Diane is at his side now, screaming, "Zach!"

Hearing Diane's screams, I feel as helpless as a swimmer caught in a strong undertow: no matter how hard I try to break free, the current pulls at me, sucking me down deeper and deeper.

"C'mon, Cale, we've got to get out of here," Abbie says, tugging at my arm. "We can still save him. Plan B, remember?"

I want to listen to her, but how can I leave Jim and Diane like this?

They're both looking at me with questions in their eyes. I can't bear to look at them because I have no answers. Or at least none that they would believe.

Just then, something inside of me shifts. My feeling of helplessness of only a moment ago is changing, morphing into something hard and strong.

"I'm going to find Zach and bring him back," I say. Then I turn to follow Abbie.

"There's nothing else we could have done," she says once we're out of earshot of Jim and Diane. "If somehow we managed to keep him from being snatched from the ticket booth, Frank would have found another way."

"I'm going to undo it," I say. "I'm going to go back again. But this time, I'm not going to let him run ahead of me down that ramp."

"Go ahead," she says. "And as soon as you do that, Frank will go back a third time and snatch Zach before he even gets on the ride. What will you do then?"

"I don't know," I say. Then something occurs to me. "Hey, if you erased Frank's memory, doesn't that mean he won't go back again?"

"I *tried* to erase his memory yesterday. But the Frank who's here, the one who leaped right from the roller coaster to the ticket booth, is probably a Frank from June, when you first saw Zach here. And he didn't get the quarter memory wipe pill."

Only part of my brain is registering what she's saying. "We can't just give up," I say.

"I'm not saying give up. I'm saying we do it another way."

I take a deep breath to calm myself. "I guess you're right. We still have Plan B."

I review Plan B in my mind. It sounds simple enough: prance right into the Compound, locate Zach and escape with him. Once we get him to 1967, he'll be safe because apart from me and Abbie no one else knows where he lives and there will be no record of our escape timeleap or of any other trips I've made to his home. All of that assumes no complications in rescuing him. And, right off the bat, I can think of at least two: their names are Uncle and Frank.

"That's the spirit," says Abbie, entering a sequence in her wrist. "All aboard for the Compound," she holds out her hand, and I take it. Her grip is strong and sure.

We're coming, Zach, I think just as the timeleap kicks in. Coming to bring you home.

XXXIII

July 11, 2061, 8:38 A.M.
The Compound
SoHo, New Beijing (formerly New York City)

I fend off the blow in the nick of time. But just as I do, there's another one heading right for my shoulder. With a battle cry, I step nimbly to the left and the projectile misses me by inches. I spring back to position and ready myself for the next attack.

"Easy does it, Cale," Abbie says. "You've done a good job beating up the sports equipment."

Looking down, I'm still breathing hard. Basketballs lie scattered on the floor. Two hockey sticks swing wildly from hooks on the low ceiling. We're in a storage room.

I open the door a crack and take a peek. This is the Compound, all right. I've got a clear view of the Yard. There must be close to fifty recruits out on the floor, about twice as many as when I was here the last time. They're divided into three groups: the first group is lifting wallets from mannequins, another is practicing elbow thrusts and roundhouse kicks, and the recruits in the final group are seated cross-legged in a corner listening to a lecture from one of the instructors.

I close the door and feel a pang of guilt. My reason for coming here is to rescue Zach. But what about all of the others? Who is going to save them?

"Did you spot him?" Abbie whispers.

"No, but I couldn't see all the faces."

She takes a deep breath, and I do the same.

291

"Abbie, thanks for . . . doing this," I say.

"I wouldn't do it for anyone else," she says, shifting toward me. It's close quarters in the storage room as it is, and we're almost touching. Suddenly, I'm feeling very warm.

"All right," I say trying my best to ignore my quickening pulse. "We split up just like we talked about. I'll check the boys' dorm and the cafeteria on the second floor, and you look for Zach in the Yard."

"I've got a better idea," says Abbie. "Let's trade. I'll do the second floor . . . I always wanted to see how the other half lives."

I'm about to say that we should stick to the original plan and that it's too late to make changes. But there's no use arguing with Abbie.

"Okay," I say. "But the rest is just like we planned: the first one to see him mindlinks the other. And then we meet back here to make our escape. Got it?"

"Got it," she says, leaning even closer to me.

"What are you—" I begin to say, but I'm cut off as her lips connect with mine.

"And . . . got you!" she says, smiling. "Danger makes you even cuter than usual."

She kissed me! On the lips! I'm feeling as light as a feather. If I jump up, I'm sure that I'll be able to fly. And then I'll soar over the Yard until I spot Zach. When I do, I'll swoop down and just in the nick of time—

"Earth to Caleb."

She kissed me!

"Hello. Calling all time snatchers," says Abbie.

"What?" I say.

"We'd better get started," she says.

"Uhh. Right," I say.

Abbie opens the door a crack.

"Wait," I say.

She turns to face me.

"If something happens—" I begin.

Abbie cuts me off. "Don't worry. We talked about that, remember? I know exactly what to do."

"Say it."

"Cale, we're wasting time . . ."

"I need you to say it out loud." My voice cracks but I'm way beyond being embarrassed about it.

I look at her. I mean really look at her. As in memorizing her face. It's crazy, but I've got a feeling in my gut that I may never see Abbie again.

She sighs. "All right. We each have ten minutes to find him. If we don't mindlink each other at the end of the ten minutes or if one of us mindlinks the other and there's no answer, that means something has gone wrong. If that happens then I am not to wait for you. I'm to timeleap straight to the park right across from fifty-five Derne Street, Boston, on July 15, 1967. And you'll meet me there."

"Good."

"Not really," says Abbie. "We both know I'm the only bus around here that's willing to offer you a ride. If something bad happens and I have to bail, I still don't see how you're going to make it to our rendezvous spot."

"I'll be there," I say. This time my voice sounds strong and confident, which is a good thing because I have absolutely no idea how I'm going to get to the past without Abbie. But there's no way I'm backing down on this part of the plan and she knows it. I've already put her in enough danger. I need to know that if I get caught . . . or worse . . . she'll be safe.

We lock eyes. Then she says, "I'm going now. Count to ten and follow me out."

She slips out the door and is gone.

I run a finger across my lips, the lips that Abbie kissed, and start counting.

When I get to ten, I step out from the storage room, keeping my movements relaxed and natural. As if I have every right to be here. I scan the Yard quickly—good, no sign of Frank.

I saunter over to the nearest group of recruits. They're standing near a mannequin. It's rigged with bells that go off if the recruits make too much contact—a standard pickpocketing drill. As I walk down the line, glancing at their faces, a few of the recruits look my way, but no one seems bothered by my presence. When I get to the end of the line, it's clear that Zach isn't in this group.

The next group is listening to an instructor drone on and on about the art of blending in with your surroundings while on a mission. From what I can see, he's already lost most of his audience, who are either fidgeting, staring off into space, whispering among themselves or all of the above. Personally I think lecture-style learning is the wrong approach with five- and six-year-olds. If it was me, I'd use a lot of props or even take them on a field trip to show them my point.

Moving through the back of the crowd, I'm on the lookout for a shock of red hair. There are a couple of redheads near the front who are about the right height, but I can't see their faces. I keep my eyes glued on them, and after a minute, I catch a glimpse of one profile. Definitely not Zach.

That leaves one more. The only thing to do is to get to the front and see his face. That will definitely attract attention. I don't have much of a choice, though.

"Excuse me," I say, squeezing my way forward. I'm almost there when I feel fingers dig into my shoulder like talons. I whirl around.

"Well, well, this is quite a surprise," says Frank, not letting go.

A thousand emotions flood through me: hatred, anger, frustration and a desire to hurt. But the only way I'm going to be able to rescue Zach is if I can stay calm. So I keep my face expressionless and look him straight in the eye.

"Hello, Frank," I say, lifting his hand from my shoulder. "I'm glad you found me. I was looking for you."

For an instant, the glint vanishes from Frank's eye and his smile slackens a bit. But the next moment, he's smiling as broadly as ever.

"You are just about the last person I would expect to see here," he says. "Aren't you supposed to be somewhere else? Somewhere very . . . barren?"

Listening to him, I'm wondering if the quarter memory pill that Abbie slipped into his drink worked. Did he remember on his own that I was in the Barrens? Maybe, but it's still possible that he had forgotten and then someone else, either Nassim or Uncle, reminded him.

"Uncle pulled me out. I'm on special leave," I lie.

"Leave?" echoes Frank. "Is that something like '*leave* my girlfriend alone'? You should know that Abbie and I have gotten quite close while you were away."

He's baiting me. So that I'll do something stupid like try to hit him. Instead, I put all my strength into my eyes and glare back.

"What are you really up to?" he asks. "You have no business here."

"In fact, I do," I say.

The whole Yard has gone suddenly quiet. Everyone has turned to watch the showdown between us, including the redheaded boy in the front row for the blending-in lecture. I glance away from Frank for a split second to try to get a look at the boy's face. It could be Zach. But I'm not sure.

"Well, I'm all ears," says Frank, touching his right earlobe. The bandage is gone, and so is the top half of his ear. It's not a pretty sight, and I think that's why Frank wants me to look.

"In fact, I'm sure that all of us," he says, making a sweeping gesture to the recruits and instructors, "would be very interested in hearing your reason for being here."

Out of the corner of my eye, I see the boy who may be Zach edging closer to us.

Frank's waiting for my answer. I feel the stares of all the trainees.

"Uncle's asked me to escort one of the new recruits to him," I say.

Frank bristles slightly, but it's impossible to tell if he actually believes me.

"Which one?" he asks.

"His name is Zach Rushton."

I can feel my stomach churning. I stare into Frank's eyes, alert to any change at all, any sign of recognition. But there isn't any. So far so good. But that's still not proof that the partial memory wipe worked. It could be that Frank only knows Zach by sight and not by name.

"Do you really expect me to hand a new recruit over to you just like that? That wouldn't be very responsible of me, would it? Putting him in the care of an escaped felon?" he chuckles.

"The boy was not supposed to have been snatched, Frank," I say, keeping my voice even. "Do you remember Uncle telling us about the river of time and how most times a little snatch or two might change a few lives but isn't going to alter the course of history in a major way?"

"Your point?" says Frank, the smile gone from his lips.

"Uncle also said that every once in a while, a person is born who during his or her life plays an important role in the history of the world," I say. "If you take that person out of the picture, by snatching him for example, you risk changing the entire flow of history."

I pause for a second, letting my words sink in.

His fingers are twitching now, which I take as a sign that he's either nervous or losing his patience with me.

"Are you saying that this recruit is going to grow up to be the next president of the United States so I had better return him to the time/place I snatched him from? That's absurd!" He laughs, and this time some of the other instructors join in.

"It's not for me to decide," I say, flatly. "It's Uncle's call. That's why he asked me to bring the boy to him."

I keep my eyes locked on his. I have no idea whether he's buying this. I must have played out this conversation about a hundred times in my cave using my shadow as a stand-in for Frank . . . but you never know how it's going to go in real life.

"Why should Uncle bring you all the way back from the Barrens just to escort the kid to him?" Frank asks. "Why wouldn't he just call me?"

He's made a good point. I've got one card left to play, though.

"I wish I knew," I say, shrugging my shoulders. "Be my guest; go right ahead and ask him. But he might be a bit annoyed if he finds out that you're the one holding things up with all of your questions. I've got strict orders to deliver the boy to Headquarters as soon as possible."

I know that Frank can easily call my bluff. But I'm counting on him being as afraid of Uncle as I am. There's no way he'd bother Uncle unless he was sure that I wasn't telling the truth. And if I'm reading his foot tapping correctly, Frank's nowhere near sure.

Just then, his eyes light up and his lips start to curve upward in a smile. Panic stabs me. I wasn't expecting this reaction. Was it something I said? I quickly replay our conversation in my head but can think of nothing in our chat that should make him happy.

He calls out in a loud voice. "Recruit Zach Rushton, step forward, please."

I see some rustling in the crowd. Someone is making his way to the front. The ring of children parts to let him through.

I glance quickly at Frank as he watches the boy step forward. There's not a trace of recognition in Frank's eyes. Relief floods through me.

"Well, Caleb. Here he is." Frank's tone is casual, almost sleepy. But I know better. He's watching me intently, studying my reaction.

I don't want to look at the boy because if he really is Zach, I'm afraid my emotions will give me away. But looking is the normal and expected thing to do and if I don't, then Frank will suspect that something is up.

So I steel myself and glance across at him.

It's him! It's Zach!

There's the tiniest flicker in Zach's eyes, but it's quickly gone. Seeing his reaction makes me both happy and sad. Happy because I know he has recognized me, and sad because he has already mastered the first lesson of being a time snatcher: how to mask your emotions.

"What is your name, recruit?" Frank says.

"Zach Rushton, sir," he answers, his tone as devoid of expression as his face.

Why is Frank asking him who he is when he already knows? Then I get it. He's putting on a little show for the benefit of the other recruits who are watching.

"And how is your training going? Do you find your lessons interesting?" asks Frank. His tone is gentle, even friendly.

"Yes, sir," says Zach.

"Excellent. Do you see this person?" Frank says, pointing to me. Zach's bottom lip trembles slightly as he answers. "Yes, sir."

"He is saying that you are more important than any of the other people in this room. Do you believe that?"

"It doesn't matter what he believes, Frank," I say before Zach has a chance to answer. "What matters is that Uncle won't be pleased when he finds out that you were the cause of the delay in my bringing the boy to him."

Frank glares at me for a moment but then his eyes soften and he actually smiles. "Not to worry, Caleb. I have no more questions right now."

I don't like that smile.

"Come on, then," Frank continues. "I'll walk you both to the elevator."

"No," I say, a bit too quickly. "Like I said, I have strict orders to bring him to Uncle at Headquarters."

"But Uncle isn't at Headquarters," says Frank. "He's here."

I feel the blood drain from my face. I'm stuck. There's nothing I can do now but follow him. I try to mindlink Abbie to warn her. But I can't get a connection.

The crowd parts, and Frank leads me and Zach toward the twin copper-colored doors.

I've got to do something. "I told you, Frank," I say, "Uncle wants me to bring him to Headquarters. If he wanted to see the boy here, he would have said that."

Then I turn to Zach, take his arm and say, "Come on."

I start leading Zach away but don't get more than two feet before rough hands grab me.

"Nice try," says Frank. "Why don't we leave it for Uncle to decide where he wants to see you?"

The two instructors gripping my arms turn me around and march me forward.

We arrive at the entrance to the elevator. The doors slide open.

I hesitate at the threshold. Frank pushes me forward. There are scuffling sounds and then someone crashes into me. Zach.

The elevator doors close. I wonder for a moment why Frank didn't get on with us. Maybe the partial memory wipe worked after all. If Frank remembered about me and Zach, then for sure he wouldn't want to let Zach out of his sight. Then it comes to me. He doesn't have to worry about that. Because in twenty seconds, the elevator will arrive at its one and only stop: Uncle's office.

The elevator is completely bare except for a speaker in the ceiling from which music begins to play. Somber classical music. Funeral music.

The next moment, I hear a whirring above the music.

We're going up.

My heart's racing. Zach's trembling on the floor in the corner, knees curled up to his chest.

"Caylid? I want to go home!" he cries.

"That's where I'm taking you, Zach," I say. But my words come out hollow. The truth is, I'm all out of ideas for how to save him. And all out of courage. My legs feel weak, and I hold a hand against the wall to steady myself.

The elevator stops, and the doors begin to open. Zach doesn't move from his corner. I take a deep breath.

The attack comes swift and silent as always.

"Seven letters. A towering fear!" says a voice.

So Uncle hasn't gotten rid of Nassim yet. I try to maneuver, but it's impossible. Before I know it, I'm facedown on the floor next to Zach with one arm pinned behind my back.

"Vertigo," I say through clenched teeth.

Instantly I'm released. Nassim takes half a step back, one foot inside the elevator and one outside.

"How did you escape from the Barrens?" he asks.

"Lucky, I guess," I grunt, standing up and massaging my arm.

"And who's this?" Nassim's eyes flick to Zach.

"His name is Zach Rushton," I say. "He doesn't belong here, Nassim. I'm taking him home."

At this Nassim laughs. "This is home for him, Caleb. Just as it's home for you. And for me."

"Well, maybe for me. But not for him. And certainly not for you . . . much longer," I blurt out.

Nassim leans in close. So close that I can see a small chip in one of his front teeth. "What do you mean, 'not for me'?" he asks.

I take a deep breath to steady myself before answering. "Uncle purged your file."

He narrows his eyes to slits. "Are you certain? How do you know?"

I keep my eyes locked on his. "I was there when he did it."

Nassim's face is a mask. I can't imagine what he's feeling right now. But I know what he's thinking. No more file means his debt is wiped clean. And since he doesn't owe anything to Uncle anymore, technically he's free to leave.

"Uncle's about to get rid of you, Nassim . . . forever," I say.

Was that a flicker of emotion in his eyes?

I hear Zach whimpering quietly behind me and take his hand.

I try mindlinking Abbie again. Still no connection. My eyes flash to my fingernail. Twelve minutes since I left her. Surely she's not answering because she stuck to our plan and went to 1967. My mind refuses to accept any other explanation.

"Nassim, I've got to go now," I say. "I'm taking Zach with me. If you'd like, you can come with us. But please . . . don't try to stop us."

Truthfully, I have absolutely nowhere to go. Unless you count going back down the elevator to face Frank.

Just then, a shadow appears across the threshold.

I follow the shadow to a figure robed in a yellow *hanfu*, holding a gleaming sword.

"*Zǎo Sháng hǎo*, Caleb!"

July 11, 2061, 9:13 A.M.
The Compound
SoHo, New Beijing (formerly New York City)

"**D**id you two enjoy your ride on my elevator?" asks Uncle.

I hear his words, and amazingly, my brain is telling me that they are only words and words can't hurt me unless I let them. And at the same time, something else is happening inside of me. The familiar fear, the cold, white, paralyzing fear of Uncle is changing somehow. Transforming into something hard and strong.

"Why don't you stay awhile," he continues, "and tell us all about how you managed to escape from the Barrens. I am certain that we will all find it most entertaining. In fact, I will make you a bargain, Caleb. If I find your story amusing, I will spare the boy and send him home. If I don't, he will stay here and resume his . . . training."

"No." My voice is even and strong. I tighten my grip on Zach's hand.

For a split second, Uncle's perfect control breaks and there's a glint of anger in his eyes. But then his face returns to an expression of calm. "Nassim, will you kindly escort them from the elevator," he orders.

"He has no power over you anymore, Nassim," I say, glaring at Uncle. "You don't have to listen to him."

For a moment all is silent. Nassim doesn't budge.

"Nassim," Uncle repeats, holding my gaze, "I said bring them to me!"

But Nassim makes no move. He just continues to stand there.

My eyes stay locked on Uncle's. I feel my lower lip begin to quiver. But I dare not look away.

"Do you realize what you are doing, Caleb?" he asks.

"Yes, I do," I say. "I'm doing what's right."

"You owe everything to me," he thunders. "If not for me, you would have died a child in the streets. I took you in and raised you as my very own, fed you and clothed you and taught you about the world. Do you remember our trips to the zoo and to the world's great museums and art galleries?"

No. He's trying to trick me. I have to stay strong.

"And do you remember," continues Uncle, "the toy soldier that you wanted more than anything else in the world and that I, your Uncle, acquired for you?"

"I don't owe you anything anymore," I say.

He flashes his eyes at me and then turns his glance to Nassim. "Nassim, I am your master. The penalty for disobedience is death."

Out of the corner of my eye, I see Nassim reaching for the elevator buttons.

"You will bring them to me now!" Uncle's voice is shrill. He raises his sword.

I dive for the floor, pulling Zach down with me, and shut my eyes tight just as blue light explodes from the tip of the sword. There's a burning smell. Someone cries out and the doors close.

Opening my eyes, I spy Nassim crumpled next to Zach. The elevator is going down. In twenty seconds we'll arrive at the Yard . . . and Frank.

Nassim is holding his shoulder. Blood seeps between his fingers and drips down onto the steel floor. Viennese waltz music plays in the background.

"Give me your hand, Nassim!" I shout over the music.

Either he doesn't hear me or is in too much pain to do anything about it. I grab his massive right hand and turn it palm up. I've never programmed someone else's patch before, but I hear Abbie's voice inside me. *Don't think, Caleb. Just do.* Is she mindspeaking, or am I just remembering?

I rest his arm on my knees and go to work. Then the music changes to marching music. Blaring loud.

Eight seconds left.

Must continue keying in the sequence. Nassim's wrist is cold to the touch. His breathing is ragged.

From a tiny heap in the corner comes the sound of whimpers. I reach out, grab Zach's arm and pull him towards me.

Three seconds until we reach the ground floor.

I close my eyes. Come on. Come on. Why isn't it working?

The music is reaching a crescendo. I want to cover my ears, but I've got to keep my grip on Nassim and Zach.

The elevator jerks to a stop. My heart is beating wildly. What's going on? We haven't reached the bottom yet.

A second later I have my answer. We begin to move again.

No! It's going up!

Holding Nassim's wrist up to eye level, with shaking hands I re-enter the sequence.

Nothing happens.

Blocked! Something's blocking it. Then I remember—the cast-iron walls. Just like at Headquarters. They must be interfering with the sequencing!

Got to keep trying. I enter the sequence for the third time.

Still nothing.

A bead of sweat rolls off my forehead. I glance at the speaker on the ceiling. There's another burst of music. Anywhere else it would be beautiful. But here it feels like a noose drawn around my neck. Squeezing me tighter with every note. I want to smash it.

Ten seconds to go before we reach Uncle's office.

Ten seconds to save Zach's life and mine.

Time enough for one more try. But what if it still doesn't work? *Don't think, just do!*

I take Zach's small wrist in my hand.

Quickly. Tap, tap, tap on Nassim's wrist. Now grip it tightly with my other hand. Wrist to wrist to wrist. Don't let go!

Eyes closed and praying.

Three seconds later, the elevator arrives at Uncle's office. The doors slide open.

But no one is inside.

I take a deep breath and open one eye. It's dark, and I can't see much of anything. I sniff the air and inhale the smell of plastic. I open the other eye. Light is filtering into the tunnel. Because that's where I am . . . some sort of plastic tunnel.

"Zach?" I call out.

No answer.

"Nassim?" I shout.

Still nothing.

I tip forward on my hands and knees, and the tunnel takes a sudden dip. I lose my grip and begin to slide. Downward I go, headfirst, picking up speed with every second.

I try to reach for the walls to break my speed, but my arms won't obey me. I'm about to try the same move with my legs, but just then my body shoots out of the tunnel.

I land in a heap.

Raindrops on my forehead. And then a hand on mine, gently placing a piece of paper against my palm and curling my fingers around it. I squint through the blackness but the person is gone.

My eyes begin to adjust to the night. To my left I can make out a seesaw and a set of monkey bars. To my right, a sandbox. And straight across from me, a set of swings.

Zach lies on the ground two feet away. I want to reach out to him, but I can't—I'm still time frozen.

There's no sign of Nassim.

A second later, I come out of my time freeze and crawl over to Zach.

He's not moving.

"Zach!" I shout.

Panic seizes me. What if the timeleap killed him? I've never heard of that happening before, but if it had, Uncle wouldn't have advertised it.

I try to remember my first aid training from the early days but draw a big blank. And then, just as I'm about to really lose it, I see Zach's left foot twitch.

Come on.

His right foot follows suit. Then his legs move slightly and his hands unclench.

I breathe a sigh of relief.

"Caylid?" says Zach, opening his eyes, and I've never been more happy in my life to hear my name mispronounced.

"I'm right here, Zach."

Zach sits up slowly and looks around, wide-eyed. "We're here! This is the park! My house is there." He points past a grassy area toward a row of porch lights and starts pulling my arm.

"Just a second," I say, remembering the piece of paper.

I unfold it and strain to read in the dark:

Hi Cale—

Had a close call (I'll explain later) but made it here okay.
Have to take care of something ASAP.

Be back soon. Don't wait.

XOXO

Abbie.

PS Nassim said to tell you he's off to the races.

As I refold the note, I get a whiff of mango. Then I think about the PS and laugh.

"What's so funny?" Zach asks.

"Do you remember Nassim, the big man who came with us?"

"Yes."

"He wanted us to know he's 'off to the races.'"

"What's so funny about that?" asks Zach.

"Well, it's one of those expressions that can mean more than one thing," I say. "It could mean that Nassim is going off to start a new life for himself. Or it could mean that he's going to the racetrack to do some betting on the horses. Either way, it's his way of saying good-bye."

And he's free. Uncle can't trace him because his records have been purged from the system.

Zach looks up at me. The expression on his face reminds me of a passing storm. Cloudy one moment and clear the next. He grabs my arm and almost yanks it out of the socket.

"C'mon. We gotta go," he says.

"All right, where to?" I ask. I already know the answer, but I want to hear him say it.

"Home! To my house!" Zach shouts.

Moments later, we're standing on Zach's doorstep. It's cold and dark, and I'm exhausted. I've had very little sleep in the last two days. I have no idea what time it is, but judging from the darkness and the fact that we've seen no cars on the street since we arrived, I'm guessing it must be close to midnight or even past.

The rain continues to pelt down, but the small overhang of the front porch shields us from the worst of it. Zach stands next to me, shivering in a T-shirt and shorts.

I ring the doorbell and it chimes inside the house.

No one comes to the door.

I press it again.

For a moment, I wonder if this is the right house. But then I dismiss the thought. I've been here before. Plus Zach knows his own house.

But what if I really botched things and this is 1969 or 1970 or some other year in Zach's future? Maybe Jim and Diane have long since moved away and somebody else is living here. I try to reassure myself that, even programming Nassim's time patch, I couldn't have messed up that badly. Maybe a few hours off. Or a few days at worst. But years? Never. Besides, doesn't Abbie finding me in the park mean I didn't mess up?

Just then, the porch light comes on.

Instinctively, I take a half step back.

The squeal of a lock being pulled back. The door opens a crack.

"Who's there?" says a man's voice.

"Daddy, it's me!" cries Zach.

I look over at Zach. He's soaking, and his wet hair is matted to his head. But his eyes are shining.

The door opens as far as the chain will allow. I almost don't recognize Jim. His face is pale and drawn, and his hair, mussed by an interrupted sleep, is gray at the fringes.

"Zach?" Jim says.

"It's me, Daddy . . . and Caylid too." Zach pushes me forward as if to make his point.

Jim stares at the two of us. I can't imagine what's going through his mind. I take that back, I can actually imagine very well. I'll bet he's wondering what I, Caleb of no fixed last name (and now of no fixed address), had to do with the disappearance of his son. He's probably asking himself if it was me who kidnapped him.

We're in a standoff. Jim continues to stare at us and we at him. Then, without taking his eyes off Zach, he shouts, "Di!"

I hear feet on the stairs, and Diane appears. She has the same drawn and tired look as Jim. But when she sees Zach standing there, something changes in her face. It's like she was in a prison cell with

311

no windows and has just come out into the light. She gazes at Zach with an expression of total disbelief.

"Mom!" Zach shouts.

"Z . . . Zach?" says Diane.

She flings the door open, and for a moment, we all stand there looking at each other. Then Diane reaches out toward Zach, slowly, tentatively. Her fingers are on his face now, gently exploring his forehead, then cheeks, then mouth as if to make sure that he's real.

"Zach!" she says again. But this time there's no hesitation. She wraps her arms around her son and hugs him fiercely. Jim reaches out and embraces both of them.

A feeling of great contentment washes over me. Zach is home with his family!

I want to cheer, to dance in the street, to wake up everyone in the neighborhood—heck, everyone in the year 1967—and tell them the good news.

But I can't for one simple reason.

I'm being invited to join the hug.

Hours later, I'm lying in a bed in the Rushtons' spare bedroom with a light sheet pulled all the way up to my nose.

I'm having trouble falling asleep.

Will they believe me if I tell them the whole story? Or will they think I'm one proton short of a full atom and put me in a place with white walls where they feed you Jell-O and take away your shoelaces? Or maybe they'll call the police, who will come and lead me away in handcuffs.

Even though it wasn't part of my and Abbie's original plan, I wanted to tell Jim and Diane everything as soon as Zach and I walked in the door. Just lay it all out. *True Confessions of a Time Snatcher.*

And I could tell from Jim's face that he had plenty of questions to ask me and not just for the sake of pleasant conversation, either. But after a little huddle with Zach and Diane in the kitchen, they came back out.

"Tell us all about it in the morning, Caleb," Diane had said. "We could all use some sleep."

So here I am, waiting for the morning to come. And believe me, I've seen whole centuries pass a lot quicker than this.

I snuggle deeper into the bed. Maybe if I tell them, it'll be all right. Why shouldn't they believe me? After all, in a couple of years they're going to put a man on the moon. Surely, the idea of someone traveling through time shouldn't be that tough to swallow. But if I told them the whole story, the real true whole story, would they ever believe that Zach is safe?

An itch near my wrist triggers a whole bunch of new thoughts. One of which is: without time travel, the only way I'm ever going to leave 1967 is the same way as everyone else—by growing older.

I reach across to the bedside table, turn on the lamp and take my driftwood carving into my hands, running my fingers along its surface. For a long time I didn't know whose face I was carving. But now I know.

It's my face. The face of my new beginning.

I run my fingers over it; first the chin, next the cheekbones, then the nose. I stop at the eyes. They're still there. Exactly where I placed them. One in each eye socket. I pluck them out and hold them in my hand. Two small silver pills. Nassim's words come back to me: "Take two of these and, within a couple of minutes, you won't remember anything that happened before dinner last night."

I glance at the clock on the table. 4:03 A.M. There's really no reason to put this off any longer. Abbie is safe.

I gaze at the pills in my hand. They're so small. It's hard to believe that something that tiny can have such a devastating effect.

"You'll need to take both of them," Abbie had said. "One isn't going to be enough. And don't wait for me to take them."

She had made me promise. And so far I've really only broken one part: the bit about not waiting. But since I'm on a roll maybe I should break the rest of my promise and not take the pills at all.

"I don't want to forget you," I had told her.

"You won't have to. I'm coming with you, remember?"

"No, I mean once I take them you'll be a complete stranger to me. We won't know each other."

"We won't be strangers for long. We'll get to know each other just like new friends do. Besides, if something goes really wrong . . . I'll get the antidote."

I place one of the pills on my tongue.

"You have a chance that most people never get, Cale," she had said.

Abbie's right. I have a chance to do what I've always dreamed of. To start over. To live a normal life, with a real family. This is exactly what I want.

I close my mouth and swallow.

I don't feel a thing.

Then I pop the other one in my mouth. Down the hatch with that one too.

I'm starting to feel sleepy. One pleasant thought should do it. Well, how's this one, then:

Zach is safe.

It's not even noon, and already it's been a full day. I spent most of the morning at the Child Welfare Office. The people there were nice enough, but it was clear that they had no idea what to do with a kid who had no ID and didn't know his own last name. As soon as Diane mentioned that she thought I might be Canadian on account of the fact that once she heard me say "ay" instead of "huh," the Child Welfare people were all over it, which meant I got to spend two hours in a waiting room playing Etch A Sketch while they called around to a dozen different Canadian Government offices to see if there had been any recent reports of runaways.

After Child Welfare, Diane took me to the police station to meet with the policeman assigned to Zach's case, Detective Portelli, a roly-poly kind of guy with a crew cut. At first, he did all the talking, confiding that he was trying to lose weight but couldn't stand eating the carrot sticks his wife packed in his lunch, so he'd sneak out to Hamburger Haven for a burger and fries, which in his opinion was still a diet lunch on account of the fact that he said hold the ketchup. But when it came to my turn to talk and I couldn't tell him a single thing about what had happened to Zach or even what I was doing with him at the park late at night, he frowned and reached for his desk drawer, where he kept his stash of Oreos.

Now I'm at the doctor's office, sitting on a bed in the examining room, waiting for the doctor to barge through the door. This is my fourth medical visit this week. All of these doctors must use the same interior designer because the décor hasn't changed from one examining room to the next: narrow bed, scale, eye chart and a poster of the inside of an ear. By now I'm an expert on cochlear fluid and earwax. I've also memorized the tiny letters on the bottom line of the eye chart—which, when I think about it, won't do me any good. I mean, what's the point of cheating on your own eye exam?

I cross my legs, and the paper underneath me crunches. It's hard to get comfortable wearing nothing but underwear, white socks and a sky blue hospital gown that no matter how much I tug doesn't come down far enough.

A short, middle-aged man strides in flanked by two young men and a woman. Everyone except me is wearing a white lab coat and carrying a clipboard. His name tag says DR. WINTON, and the tagalongs I figure to be his medical students. The doctor's stethoscope swings as he turns toward me. Which is another thing that I don't get. Even though I have absolutely no recollection of a big chunk of my life, somehow I still know a bunch of stuff, like what a stethoscope is.

"Good morning, Caleb. How are we today?" he asks. When he says this, a vein in his neck does the tango, and for a moment, I feel the edge of a memory poking through. But when I try to grab it, I can't.

"Good morning, doctor. I'm fine," I say, which, except for the empty parking lot in my brain, is the truth.

"Are we getting any of our memories back yet?" he asks. That *we* is starting to grate on me. Almost as irritating is the fact that the medical students are eyeing me like a piece of gum they just discovered under their shoes.

"I get flashes of parts of things," I say, "but they don't make any sense."

Dr. Winton smiles. The medical students follow suit. I get the feeling they want me to keep talking, so I do.

"They're all jumbled together," I say. "Snapping turtles and a pie tin spinning through the air and a cave and a yellow kimono."

The students are jotting notes like crazy. I'm tempted to say rhinoceros droppings and see if they write that down too.

Dr. Winton leans in and shines a light in my eyes. I smell onions on his breath. The students edge closer, taking up positions on either side of me.

"Look to the left," he says, and I comply dutifully.

"Look to the right," he continues. "And now, straight ahead."

I do as I'm told.

The doctor pauses for a moment and turns to face the students. "The patient is suffering from profound amnesia. Etiology?"

"Physical trauma to the brain?" asks the female student.

"His X-rays aren't consistent with trauma," answers Dr. Winton.

"Ingestion of a toxin?" volunteers one of the guys.

"Not indicated."

I'm not sure what bothers me more: the fact that I can't understand a word they're saying or that they're talking about me as if I'm not even in the room.

"Doctor," I say, "have you ever seen any cases like mine before?"

He smiles. "Not every day. But yes, I've seen a couple of cases like yours over the years. The brain is a complicated organ. We still don't understand it completely. Sometimes it does things to protect itself."

"Do you think that's what my brain is doing?" I ask.

"Perhaps," says Dr. Winton, and out of the corner of my eye I can see the students scribbling "perhaps" on their clipboards.

"I'm going to order some tests for you, Caleb," he says, and I groan. More tests. "And in the meantime, I'm going to give you something."

He pulls open the desk drawer and hands me a pen and a spiral notebook. I open the book and flip through the lined pages. They're completely blank.

"This is your memory book," he says. "I want you to bring it with you wherever you go. When you remember something, jot it down. Don't worry about it making any sense. Just write it down as it comes to you."

I nod. I like the feel of the notebook. My own book, for my own memories.

"And when you're back next week," he continues, "we'll talk about what you've written down. All right?"

"All right," I say.

The doctor smiles and then exits the room, the students trailing him.

As I get dressed, an image flashes in my head. Boy, that was quick!

I whip open the book and scrawl July 29, 1967 at the top of the first page. And before the image fades away entirely I scribble, *girl dressed like warrior.*

It makes no sense at all. But for some reason it feels good writing it down. Maybe one day all the memory fragments will come together like the pieces of some giant puzzle.

I close the book and finish dressing. Jim, Diane and Zach are all there in the waiting room when I get out.

Zach leaps up from his seat, and grabs my hand. "Caylid. Mom said when you're done your 'pointment we're going on a picnic, and you're done, so let's go!"

I let myself be dragged along. Zach doesn't let go until we're outside in the sunlight. It's so bright I have to squint. It feels good to be breathing in fresh air.

"C'mon. Let's race there!" shouts Zach.

The next second, Zach takes off, sprinting along a footpath.

As I run to catch up, I can hear Jim's footsteps right behind me. Ever since I showed up at their doorstep that night, Jim has made sure that I haven't been left alone with Zach for even a minute. I think there's still a part of him that suspects I had something to do with Zach's kidnapping. But it doesn't make me angry. If I was in his shoes, I'd be suspicious, too. In fact, even without being in his shoes, I'm suspicious—that is, sometimes I wonder if my brain purposely blocked out my memories because I've done something horrible.

We follow Zach over a pedestrian bridge that crosses high above a bunch of lanes of traffic. It's obvious he knows where he's going.

We come bounding off the bridge onto a grassy area with a bunch of picnic tables and a concession stand. But Zach doesn't stop there. Jim and I chase after him along another path until he finally comes to a stop in the middle of a small footbridge crossing a pond.

"Look. Ducks!" he cries.

Much quacking follows from both the duck and us. Zach starts waddling, which is a good thing because waddling is slower than running, and by now I'm tuckered out.

As soon as we step off the bridge, Zach announces, "We made it. This is the 'splanade, Caylid. You can walk forever, but we're not gonna. Look, there's the river!"

I glance through the trees and sure enough I can see the blue gray water of the Charles River only a stone's throw away. But it's only a quick look because Zach's tugging at me again.

"C'mon, there's a better view from up there," he says, pointing to a grassy knoll.

We race up the small hill, and as soon as we get to the top, we flop down on the grass. When I look up, I'm surprised to see that Jim hasn't raced up with us. He's still at the bottom of the hill, waiting for Diane.

Zach plucks a tiny flower from the ground and holds it under my chin.

"Caylid, you like butter!" says Zach.

He hands me the flower and guides my hand so I'm holding it just under his chin.

"Now do me!" he says.

I scrunch my eyebrows and study the color of Zach's chin. It's hard to tell from my angle, but I give him the benefit of the doubt.

"You too," I say. "You are definitely a big butter lover. In fact, I'd say you'd like butter on everything. Even your Cheerios!"

That sends him into gales of laughter. I open my hand and let the wind take the flower. I watch it as the breeze blows it down the hill and clear of the walking path. Another gust comes along, and for a moment, it looks like the small flower will be home free. But the next second, it gets lodged in between some rocks.

Jim and Diane arrive, and she lays out a big blanket for us to all sit on.

The last two weeks have been a whirlwind—appointments with doctors, Child Welfare people and the police. Hours spent in Jim's old station wagon driving around Boston. All of this to help me try to remember who I am. Where I'm from. How I found Zach. But so far everything's come up a big fat zero.

It's not just me who everyone's interested in. The doctors and police are also talking to Zach and asking him lots of questions. But when it comes to me, his answer is always the same: that I saved him from the bad place and the bad man. It's a lucky thing for me that Jim and Diane have stuck by my side through everything. Not knowing the whole story has been hard for them, especially Jim, but as Diane said to me after my first visit to the police station, "Zach believes in you, Caleb, and that's good enough for us."

Diane hands out paper cups and pours lemonade for everyone from a big thermos.

"Zach, give this one to Caleb, please."

He does, but not without spilling a bit on my thumb. I lick it up, which starts Zach laughing again.

I gaze out at the Charles River and see a sleek-looking rowboat with eight rowers aboard. The boat is moving at a good clip. It amazes me how well the rowers work as a team, dipping their oars in the river, pulling them through the water and then taking them out, all at exactly the same time.

"Caleb," begins Jim, "Diane and I have been thinking that maybe, if you agree . . . we'll take a break from things. You know, and just enjoy all of us being together. I mean, not worry so much about who you are or that you're not where you're supposed to be."

"But, Daddy, we know who Caylid is. He's Caylid. And he's just where he's s'posed to be," chimes Zach, "with us!"

I smile at Zach and catch Jim's eye. He doesn't say anything. Just nods at the wisdom of his five-year-old son. I nod too and close my eyes. For the first time in two weeks, I feel light. As if a great weight has been lifted from me.

After a moment, I open my eyes and look out over the river. The boat is nowhere in sight.

CREDITS

ACKNOWLEDGMENTS

Sincere thanks go to Peter Carver and everyone in his George Brown College writing critique group in Toronto over the years for encouragement and support; the staff at the embassies of Mongolia in Canada and the United States for help with certain Mongolian words and phrases; Jennifer Mook-Sang, Alvin Yang and Terry Huang for help with Mandarin words and phrases; Maya Ungar and Marg Gilks for encouragement; my agents Josh Adams and Quinlan Lee for taking a chance on me and finding a great home for my manuscript; John Rudolph for believing in my writing and, along with Shauna Fay, for tackling the first round of edits; Ana Deboo, Rob Farren, and Cindy Howle for their excellent copyediting; my editor Susan Kochan for inspiring me to produce the best book possible; and my family Dayna, Rafi and Simon for continued love and support.

AUTHOR'S NOTE

Time Snatchers is a work of fiction, but there is a historical basis for many of the events mentioned in this book (e.g., the developing of the first photograph, the invention of the Frisbee). I have been as accurate as possible with information about events and historical figures, though some details have been imagined to suit the storytelling.